With Eyes Turned Skyward

Gregory Stravinski

ISBN-13: 978-1530804238

ISBN-10: 153080423X

DEDICATION

To all the folks out there who have a story to tell, this book is for you. Do yourself a favor and write it down. Believe me, the rest of us want to hear it too.

ACKNOWLEDGMENTS

Thank you **so** much to:

Terri Mertz of Ossiwary Comissary – For editing my book. Thank you so much for helping smooth out all of this rookie's mistakes. For those looking to have their own works edited, send her a message at rrats123@gmail.com

James Mayfield – For the gorgeous cover art. One of the best surprises I've ever had is you sending me that imagery after remembering a conversation we had about it four months prior. Thank you for giving the cover the punch it deserves.

Bob Marshall – For helping me concept the cover art. You put in a ton of time and effort to assemble a design to match the story, and all of it was appreciated. Check him out at marshalldesign-portfolio.blogspot.com.

Dan and Elizabeth Stravinski - You raised me right! Thank you so much for putting in all that patience and resources. You taught me from a very young age that if I had the right idea, and a little elbow grease, there's really no obstacle that could stand in my way. Looks like you were right.

Alexander Stravinski – For lending his voice (once described by a critic as "chocolate ribbons") to my audiobook. I'm extremely proud to be your brother, and you're amazingly talented. For professional voice or stage acting, contact him at astrav1@verizon.net.

Ramsey Khudairi – For pulling me up off my ass after a tough loss in my high school wrestling career. It might not seem like much, but that moment reset how I looked at goals and the failures that are bound try to keep me from them.

Annie Drabant – You've been amazingly supportive of this book and my passion for writing. Sorry for all of the late night, glaring bed side lamps when I should have been asleep hours ago. Hopefully you think the finished product is worth it!

Sun Tzu – Um, I guess he doesn't actually have too much relevance to this book, but he was a really amazing military strategist during the Warring States period in 500 B.C. China. Still feel like I should thank him though.

Jess from Indie Coffee – For letting me stay to finish a few more pages all those nights, even after the cafe closed. Your feedback helped shape what the story looks like today. Congratulations on getting into your Computer Science PhD!

The Midwest Crew, especially RJ, Eric, Katelyn, Jessica and Ilana – Yeah, we should have probably been selling radio, but you guys helped lay the foundation for this book. Without your constant feedback, week after week, this story would have never gotten off the ground. (pun semi intended)

To everyone who read my drafts – There were many, but to James, Helen, Megan, Jane and Andy in particular, thank you so much for all of your feedback and the time that you put into reviewing it.

Amazon.com – Without the network you guys created, this book probably would have never made it past a publisher (let's be honest). Thank you so much for creating a space where both you and fledging authors like myself can flourish.

Lastly, to everyone about to read this book – Every author loves an audience. Thank you so much for taking the time to sit down to check out this story, even if it's a small sci-fi adventure piece. You guys and ladies are the real heroes.

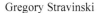

"Once you have tasted flight, you will forever walk the earth with your eyes turned skywards, for there you have been and there you will always long to return."

-Leonardo da Vinci

1

The crackle of gunfire ruins what would have been the perfect morning. A slight crosswind blows out of the east, but it's the kind you appreciate with the southern summer sun beating down as hard as it is. Our eyes trace the planes as they dance. Black and gold flits by, as white and black does its best to keep time with the steps. The Admiral didn't consider piracy when he chose our colors.

Every crack tightens my grip a bit more on the rusted banister. You can tell which spot's mine: I've twisted away all the black paint, leaving trails of previous anxieties. It's really not my fault that the Admiral won't spring for some quality coating. I flinch as belt feeders send several more rounds exploding from their barrels at 1,700 miles per hour.

It's a simple job, really; one that's necessary to our survival. That's how I need to frame it. I let the oxygen flow deep into my lungs. I've done this before, and I can do it again. Closing my eyes, I imagine the pressure of the seat folding against my back, and visualize the gunstocks pressing into the palm of each hand. I release another breath into the wind.

The breath barely blows away before I hear another crack. It's not a hollow one this time, unlike the others we've heard this morning: this one has some weight to it.

My eyes snap open, but I'm already two steps behind the others. Sasha grabs her helmet, barking orders. I already know them by heart. Taking advantage of this small opportunity, I lean out over the railing to see what's summoned us. One of our Goldies is already on its descent, a plume of fire cascading from its wing. It's a pretty sharp plummet. I'm not even sure our services are going to be needed, but that doesn't stop Sasha.

"Baz, get your ass moving!"

Warmth rises up my shoulders into my neck. I hate being called out in front of the entire squadron, but it's what I deserve for being the last to react. Every second counts. My training kicks in and I leave my rust trails behind. There'll be more than enough time to etch new paths tomorrow.

"Cry Havoc," I mutter.

I drop into a sprint, struggling to get my hand through the arm of my flight jacket. The embroidered letters *"Semper Parati,"* Latin for "Always Ready," press against my back. The Admiral has a penchant for Old World theatrics. Once again, we're putting that pledge to the test. Luckily for me, there's one strength I have over my squad mates: speed. I surge up past Katz, but can't get to the craft before my lieutenant.

The Helios sits there, waiting patiently for us, as it always does. It's an odd craft, really, painted red and black, with a large cockpit and two stubby wings over its top. Both wings sport a golden bow with three splayed arrows against a black background, with a large propeller fastened to the tip of each. A short, upright tail reinforces the feeling that the Helios' growth was stunted at some point.

Its two side doors house the Helios's hidden power. Pulling hard on the latch of the dented metal, I reveal an object of beauty; at least, to me. Her name's *Talia*. She's a long barreled, mounted machine gun that's capable of punching through pretty much anything I point her at.

We had to make it a fair fight somehow.

As the rest of the crew closes in, I throw myself into the gunner's seat. A strong hand clamps on my shoulder. Recoiling, I discover our flight doctor Chet has already made it to the Helios before any of the rest of us.

"You feelin' steady Sage?" he asks from the side of his mouth.

"Ready as always," I lie. Uncertainty slithers through my gut.

Chet's one of the few people who still calls me by my first name. I don't know why, but he's never been much for monikers. Glancing back at the seats, I see Chet's already laid out his supplies for quick access. Now that I think about it, it's not uncommon for him to just sit in the cabin and wait once a fire-fight begins. Just in case.

Micolo throws himself into the other gunner's seat, wiping the rest of the shaving cream off his face. It appears the Italian will be plunging into the depths, not only without a shower, but also with half a beard.

Sasha doesn't bother opening her door, opting instead to grab both sides of the window and throw herself through. Seemingly unaware she's the last one to the ship, Katz saunters up to the side hatch of the cockpit and lets herself in. With her co-pilot onboard, Sasha begins her preflight checks. The appropriate clicks echo from the cockpit.

They've been tailing us for three days now, but this is the first time they've launched a full-on assault. They want what we have: supplies, passengers, fuel; and from what I've seen, they've got the means to take it, too. An assault's never a good sign in this business; it usually means they're certain they have the upper hand.

All previous thoughts of the day's beauty, my sad little fantasies, what I ate for breakfast – everything - is forgotten. It's all excess; all of them luxuries I can't afford right now. Fresh air slowly enters my lungs against the rising hum of the engines above. I don't care much for religion, but I say some half-remembered prayer anyway. What can it hurt?

"Anyone see whose plane it was?" I shout over the engines.

Ah shit. I haven't turned on my comm yet. I press hard against the thin layer of plastic nestled just under my cheek until the greeting signal pings against my ear. Two deckhands remove the blocks underneath the Helios' landing gear while I fiddle with the volume of the earpiece.

"I think I saw Carter's emblem on the tail," Micolo's voice clips through. Still too loud.

He's got keen eyes, but I've always disliked the Italian's tendency to fish for recognition. Even so, I indulge him. "What emblem was it?" I ask.

Micolo throws his arm over the seatback, smiling. "I believe it was a hornet," he offers, appreciating that someone's taken an interest in one of his unique skills. His slight accent's always been popular with the opposite sex, but it's never done anything for our friendship.

"Fantastic . . . Never met him," I respond with a little bit more gall than I intended.

A hornet, huh? Now that Micolo mentions it, I do remember

seeing a new call-sign towards the bottom of the kill board. "Stinger," I think it was. I don't remember any kills being listed. I guess with some of our new pilots, that's to be expected. Gotta start somewhere, right?

Great . . . We're going in for a rookie. Knowing my luck, he'll probably panic, maybe even set off his sidearm inside the cabin. I wonder if I could get a Purple Heart for catching a ricochet, even if it was from one of our own guns? Might be worth looking into. Maybe it would net me some extra rack time.

"Get your fucking head out of the clouds Baz!"

My commlink crackles to life with my lieutenant's ironic comment. Her turn of phrase is showing its age: we do, in fact, live up here now, at least, the people who can afford it.

As the wind funnels down from the open hangar bay, I realize this could be the last time I see the skeletal structure spanning the roof of the *Artemis*. She's a good airship, really, although, I suppose I'm a bit partial since I was born on her . . . and never really left.

The Helios lurches under us as it leaves the hangar floor. Sasha's encouragement has the desired effect. Strapping myself into my harness forces me to narrow my focus to a needle-fine point. I tuck in any loose strands of my uniform as the other large craft flow beneath us. We're going a little faster than regulations allow, but no one's ever going stop a Helios on a mission.

As I tuck my feet in, one of the deck crew throws me a quick salute. Surprised, I barely manage to return a rushed wave; she must be new. The tension between the deck crew and pilots would be a much larger worry among the general population if more of them realized just how extreme it is.

Fresh light pours through the hangar doors as we close in.

A smile vibrates in Sasha's voice. "Everyone hang tight! Especially you Baz."

Oh God. She'd better not try it.

My fingers fumble to tighten my harness, but it's too late. A cold gust whips across my face as we stick our nose out of the stern's hangar bay. If there's one thing I hate about flight, it's the rapid weather changes; then again, I don't really have much time to contemplate meteorology before Sasha drops us into a freefall.

My feet jerk over my head and I let go of Talia entirely.

Clutching at my harness, I choke down the sheer amount of G-force rushing up through my stomach. The only thoughts keeping me together is imagining all of the ways I can make Sasha's life miserable once we get top-side again: horrible things can be done to an unguarded toothbrush if the opportunity presents itself. Although I suppose her reprimand is my punishment for not being on task all morning. Either way, my sentence is being executed with Sasha's trademark precision.

Plummeting earthward, Sasha tilts the Helios just enough for me to have the pleasure of experiencing the full momentum of our free fall. Taking a respite from my panic, I glance over, gauging Chet's reaction to our little drop. His dark skin blends in with the shadow of the cabin, but his straight white teeth cut through the darkness, creating his big signature grin. He's planned for this too, with his supplies all doubly strapped down. Just in case.

If there's one positive to be gleaned from my gut-wrenching position, it's my excellent view of the *Artemis*. Not only is she a solidly built ship, she's beautiful for her class. A slew of large propellers line each side of her white, compartmentalized balloon, under which sits our workspace, affectionately known as "The Roost." All large craft dock there, from transports, to zep hunters to our comparatively tiny Helios.

Under The Roost sits the multitude of the Living Quarters. My little corner of the world is nestled in there somewhere, but I never like to think about it while I'm working: it makes me wish I were still asleep. Below that sit the gun ports and the small craft hangar, also known as "The Cellar". The hangar's doors gape open as one of our cranes positions another wing of fighters for launch.

We hit our desired altitude.

The Helios shudders under its own weight, then rights itself. My stomach detaches from my throat. My left foot also releases from the free fall, and obeying the law of physics, slams into one of the struts. Pain shoots up my side as I try my best not to swear over the com.

"Goddammit Sasha, that was my leg!" I growl.

So much for self-discipline.

"Aw . . . sweetie - If I weren't so busy leading this mission, I'd come back and make it all better," she retorts.

That thought's an oddly comforting one, but then that

breaches the whole chain-of-command business, and that tends to get messy very quickly. It's probably best that age discourages me from trying anything stupid, although I do have to admit her daughter Rosie is one of my favorite kids on the Artemis. Rosie shares her mother's playfulness and her late father's sense of adventure.

I never knew Sasha's husband, but apparently he was one hell of a pilot. The day he was shot down was the day that Sasha joined the Support Squadron. She swore no one would ever touch her daughter, because that would require going through her first. After getting to know my lieutenant, it was hard for me to argue otherwise. Still, it was probably best that Sasha left Rosie with her sister back in the Charleston Flats. Today's proof that we're traversing one of the roughest stretches of the Appalachian Spine.

As I scan for possible threats, my mind wanders to our other crew mate, Katz. I once heard one of the other pilots joke that Katz and I would have made a good couple if we hadn't ended up in the same crew. I'm gonna guess they said because Katz and I share almost all of the same physical attributes: brown hair, green eyes, tanned skin. We're even close on height, but I've still got her by an inch. I'm also a little stockier, but I guess that's to be expected, even if she does serve the fleet.

There's something about Katz that's always caught my attention. She spends so much time locked in her own world that I want to be the one who breaks through to her; I guess for the sake of the challenge. Or maybe I just like the idea of having the odds stacked against me.

The gun fire gets louder, serving as a reminder that we still have a job to do. Both Micolo and I scan for any signs of the crash. Spotting a large fire emanating from wreckage is a double-edged sword: on one hand, it helps pinpoint the location of the downed pilot faster, but on the other hand, a fire that big means the pilot's probably already dead.

My eyes flit from tree to tree, searching for anything out of the ordinary. To call them "trees" is generous. In reality, they're large thickets of amphibious seaweed—a holdover from a time that's not quite ancient enough to call history. A shudder runs through me as I try to think about something other than the creatures dwelling in that swampy mire.

As I continue my vigil, I can't help but think about what was probably here before. The books from my childhood always had these pictures of glass cities covering most of the earth: sprawling towers standing hundreds of feet high. Our ancestors had such magnificent power; how is it possible that could they have lost it all?

What the sea did leave behind were coarse forests of gigantic seaweed that still continue to thrive despite the absence of standing water. That repulsive seaweed persisted, along with the austere creatures that were able to adapt after the Drowning had come and gone. If Mother Nature couldn't kill these nightmares, then we stand a pretty slim chance.

A pop interrupts my thoughts.

A red flare bursts into the sky.

"You see it?! Port side, ten o'clock center!" I yell.

"Good eyes Baz," Katz chirps.

I'm somewhat surprised she said anything at all. She usually keeps pretty quiet for the whole flight, assuming things don't get too hairy. Katz is a technician at heart; she hardly ever makes eye-contact with anyone on the crew, seeming most at home in her own head. However, having said that, I know that if you put her in front of a console, you would swear the machine actually talks to her. Despite the apparent disconnect, I wouldn't want anyone else monitoring our systems.

The Helios veers to the left, dipping towards the crash site. The clicking sounds of Micolo and I readying our guns echo through the cabin. Red flares are bad. Well, I suppose they're a net positive, since the pilot's alive enough to fire it, but their color indicates severe injuries or immediate peril.

Or both.

I track the flare, following it to the ground as it marks our makeshift LZ. Another reason why I'm glad I'm not a pilot: you have to be a hell of a shot if you're ever blown out of the sky. Wherever your flare lands is where you get picked up, otherwise, it's almost impossible for us to find you in the dense foliage. Just pray there's no wind that day.

We've almost arrived to the fire fight. Sasha moves to keep us out of it, skimming along the tops of the trees. I can feel Micolo tense as both friend and foe swoop around us, continuing their dance.

"I want guns silent unless necessary," Sasha barks, sensing our anxiety.

We don't want to provide any more incentive for a bandit to take notice and fill us full of holes. Taking my eyes off the red pillar of smoke, I glance back at Chet. His eyes keep straight forward and he's not smiling anymore. I bet if I were to say something, he wouldn't even hear me.

A shockwave hits the Helios. Rocking back to center, I see a fighter split in half and engulfed in flames. I sigh in spite of myself: now that's two pilots we need to save.

Chet senses my disappointment and grabs my shoulder again. "It's alright Sage, that one had pirate markings," he reassures me. I try discerning his pupils from his dark irises. "He can burn as far as I'm concerned," Chet says with uncharacteristic curtness.

The explosion may not have been from one of ours, but it sparks the attention of one of the other enemy fighters. It breaks from the melee, making a run at us.

Micolo's been waiting for this. "Guns hot, marking craft at 4 o'clock high!" he shouts.

Before he can get a good bead on the target, tracers start whizzing past the Helios. Looking back at the bogey, I see small bursts of fire spout from its nose. Two rounds slam against the Helios's hull, prompting Micolo to fire back even though he doesn't have a clear shot.

Thump, thump, thump, thump!

The high caliber rounds do their job, but only succeed in fending off the fighter. Tracers lead the enemy plane close enough that the pilot decides there are more vulnerable targets than the heavily armed Helios.

"Gold Squadron, this is Reaper. Running retrieval along the treeline. Picked up a bogey. Assistance requested," Sasha relays over the comm.

"I see you Reaper! Keep your current vector. Mantis engaging."

A black and gold fighter dives out of the sky, gun barrels white hot and hissing. Despite the amount of lead our pilot puts in the air, she doesn't score any significant hits on our assailant. The two planes swerve off, chasing one another as a second pirate dives to join the fray. Mantis buys us some time, and we spend it throttling the rest of the way to the LZ.

As I suspected, we're confronted with a mission critical issue. The foliage where the flare burns is so thick we can't land. Sasha pulls Helios in as close as she can, flipping the propellers upward into a hover.

"Poor bastard's gonna have to climb," Chet says, hunching back into the cabin to get the double knotted rope.

Chet's about to tie a second knot to secure the rope to the strut when I notice something that catches my breath. The trees about 300 feet in front of us are parting in a rapid fashion. It's a bigger disturbance than anything human would make. Before my imagination conjures what kind of creature's taken interest in us, an explosion lights up the sky.

"It seems our angel's luck has run out," Micolo says grimly. Holding a pair of binoculars to his eyes, he watches the fireball plummet towards earth. "No parachute . . . "

Micolo turns off his comm, whispering a short Italian prayer to himself.

The disturbance in the trees can no longer be ignored.

"You guys, movement left flank!" I caution.

My grip tightens on my gun, readying to face whatever's so eager to greet us. Above the gunfire of the planes swirling around us, I hear smaller pops.

Our pilot bursts out of the brush. Sprinting, he indiscriminately fires his pistol behind him as he runs. A pack of mire wolves explodes out of the brush behind him, eager to catch up to their meal.

Such disgusting animals. About the size of a large dog, these otter... rat things have adapted to the hostile terrain over time. With their thick, oily coats, they thrive in the swampy forests. Whoever had the gall to call them "wolves" when they were first discovered must've been quite the romantic. Our stricken friend probably interrupted one of their dens. Worst of all, their dense, matted fur presents another danger to our pilot: it makes the pack creatures largely resistant to conventional bullets.

Similarly disgusted, Chet drops the rope. "Let's go! Get as much distance between them and yourself as you can!" he yells.

If we can get enough room, I can mow the animals down and make this a much easier job. It doesn't seem that we'll get this chance though. The mire wolves seem to sense their quarry is closing in on freedom, and redouble their efforts.

Out of ammunition and out of options, the pilot rips off his helmet, hurling it at the pack in a last ditch effort to create some space. The helmet catches the lead wolf in the snout, causing it to stagger, but only momentarily, just long enough for it to shake off the impact. The pilot jumps as high onto the rope as he can, doing his best to climb despite his exhaustion. He's not going to make it if we don't do something fast.

"Take this thing up Sasha!" I cry.

"What? He's not even in the cabin," she bristles.

"And he's never going to get there if we don't put some altitude between us and those things!" I shout back.

The wolves are close enough to almost hear them trying to pull in air through the slits they have for nostrils. If it weren't for the engines, we'd be treated to the horrible sucking sound.

Sasha starts pulling the Helios away while I abandon my gun to help Chet drag the pilot up. Not to be denied, the mire wolves lunge at the rope. Chet shouts as one particularly spirited canine throws itself towards its meal. Tapping the last of his energy, the pilot kicks his foot around, connecting with the wolf's jaw.

Stunned, it falls back to earth.

The pilot gets close enough for me to grab one of his shoulder straps. Between the two of us, Chet and I manage to pull the drained pilot into the cabin.

I twist around in my seat. "We got him! Let's go Sasha!"

Wasting no time, Chet begins his preliminary scan for injuries. "What's your name sir?", he asks the dazed man.

"Airman First Class Carter . . . Jake Carter," the pilot replies in between shaky breaths.

Micolo throws up his hands victoriously. "I am good!"

Chet grins, looking back to Carter. "Well Mr. Carter, we haven't saved your ass yet. So look sharp."

Our window of time is closing. We've begun attracting more flies. The reason why I get hazard pay begins now. Time to earn it.

"Left gun up!" I warn, flicking the switch on my console. "See you topside!" I quip to Micolo.

The hydraulics kick in, lifting my gun and me up over the cabin and onto the top of the Helios. I have 360 degrees of coverage from up here, but also a much better chance of getting shot outright. There's no protection whatsoever - unless you count the gun in front of me.

Our game of stealth is over. Everyone in the sky's fully aware of our presence and now we're as much a target as anyone else. Weapons free. Pulling both triggers on Talia, I let the recoil course through my body. The sound's deafening, but reassuring. A wall of lead is just as good as armor plating.

The same plane that came after us before wants another go at bringing us down. He comes in low, but takes his time aligning his sights. The image of the pilot he killed flashes through my mind. He won't have that pleasure again. The vibrations alone threaten to tear my arms out of their sockets, but I pump as many rounds in his direction as Talia will allow. The lead and angle connect. His propeller flies up and over his fuselage. The nose of the craft rips apart, exposing a convulsing engine blowing out bursts of flame. The plane twists, exploding in an oblong shower of metal. Satisfaction pulses through me.

"Good shot kid."

The pleasure is short-lived. Who said that? It didn't come from the radio.

Before I can detect the source, a second pirate takes the first bandit's place and bears down on us. Rounds ricochet off the top of the Helios, curling me up into a ball. A pop and a hiss flare out from the tail. Something squirts free of its piping.

The pirate streaks by, turning its nose to line up for another run.

I pull up my com. "Everyone ok?" I shout.

Sasha answers, "We're more worried about you Baz!"

"No holes yet!" I assure her.

The roof of the plane is no longer a good place to be. I hit the console button repeatedly, trying to return to the safety of the doorway, but my chair makes no effort to move.

Something's wrong.

Scanning the ship, I see honey-colored fluid squirting from of the side paneling. They hit the hydraulics. I guess I'll have to do this manually. I kick out the safety pin holding me up. My stomach flips as my seat gives way, crashing back down to its original position inside the cabin.

"Our time's up. We need to get out of here!" I yell.

"Working on it; the controls are fighting me. I can't bring the nose up!" Sasha growls back, struggling with the joystick.

The pirate comes straight for us, head on. Neither I nor Micolo can push up to the roof to cover the front or back of the Helios. We're defenseless against the coming attack, and to make matters worse, I've slid into the path of the spurting hydraulic fluid. It's hot and obviously something that shouldn't be coming into contact with bare skin, but at this point, I have more pressing things to worry about.

Deciding whether or not to try angling away from the rupture or just abandon my chair all together, I instinctively duck as another wave of bullets rips through the cabin. A second spurt of hydraulic fluid shoots out, catching me in the face and neck.

Spitting, I try to wipe it off when I suddenly notice the taste iron. That isn't right. I look down at my hands. They're slick with red. Panicking, I check myself for entry wounds. I don't think I've been hit, but adrenaline has a tendency to lie.

Then the pilot's seat catches my eye.

The large red hole torn through its middle stops every other thought process. No . . . this isn't how it's supposed to work . . . Jumping out of my seat, I run to the cock pit. It's red. All of it.

The left side Katz's face is covered in blood.

2

Katz trembles silently.

Swallowing my panic, I look to the left. Sasha stares back at me, unblinking. A hole leaks from the center of her chest.

Blood pumps past my ears. It's so loud it blocks out the rest of the battle and everything else that's happening. I glance back into the cabin. Airman Carter writhes on the floor. Chet tries holding him down as blood spurts from Carter's left thigh. Micolo's dinner-plate eyes dart frantically, the gun in his hands firing burst after soundless burst into the maelstrom engulfing us.

Chet locks eyes with me, shouting something I can't hear. Shaking my head, I look at him helplessly.

"Get in the damn cockpit!"

Chet's voice breaks through, forcing me to find my senses again. I look down at Sasha.

"I'm sorry Lieutenant," I whisper.

I pull her out of her seat by her flight straps, doing my best to push her back towards the cabin. My hand slips. The exit wound on her back sucks around my arm. Slick, torn innards clasp my fingers.

Choking back bile, I stop. Taking a deep breath, I wipe the gore off on the seat back and continuing trying to position her through the separation and back into the cabin. Chet grasps her by the straps and places her next to Carter.

Settling into the slippery pilot's chair, I look down at the instruments below me. I have no idea how to fly a Helios. First things first - I need to clear the windshield. I grab the cuff of my flight suit with my fingers and spit on it. Pressing the damp cuff up to the windshield, I scrub away the blood. It doesn't come off easily. It's already starting to congeal, but I'm able to create a big enough window to see where I'm going. Glancing at Katz, I notice she's still trembling. She's locked herself back into her own world. She's been trained for combat, but seeing her friend get shot through the middle was one stressor too many.

I take a hold of her hand. "Katz! Katz, look at me," I plead.

My voice seems to pierce the barrier. She slowly turns her head in my direction.

"Katz, I'm going to need your help with this. I don't know how to fly this thing, and you're our only hope for getting back home."

She says nothing.

I tighten my grip on her hand. "Katz, will you help me?"

She shuts her eyes, squeezing out a tear. It rolls silently down the side of her face, inscribing a white path through the spattered red. She nods, but still says nothing. Then, instructions start trickling out. Haltingly at first, but as she drags herself back to reality, they become a steady stream. With Katz's guidance, I pull the Helios out of its downward spiral.

It takes a few tries, but with great difficulty, I'm able to fill the windshield with a view of the *Artemis* again. Katz takes over the throttle. We're flying towards the *Artemis* as fast as the Helios can carry us, but I'm worried the ship can't take the speed.

A loud pop and a rush of air from behind my head signals that something I can only assume is vital has broken its seams. Despite the ebbing flow of hydraulic fluid and the new trail of smoke erupting from the tail, we're still on course to *The Artemis* and maintaining speed.

Taking notice that the Helios' doomed spiral has been averted, several pirates renew their attacks on us. Tracers flit by the cockpit. I grit my teeth, tightening my grip on the joystick. Pressing my back against the damaged upholstery; I can't help envisioning the large hole ripping through my chest.

If I can't keep calm, none of us are getting home.

I keep repeating this is in my mind, over and over again, clumsily ducking and maneuvering the Helios through pirate fire. We're not alone in our escape. The Goldies form a "V,", streaking in force after the bandits. Planes from both sides begin breaking off, initiating their own duels.

That's when I see a small cloud descend from the underside of the *Artemis*. A buzzing, red, amorphous form.

"Perimeter breached. We're dropping now."

The voice belongs to Captain Adrian Baltier, leader of the Southeastern Seaboard Chapter of the Red Swans.

The high rolling mercenaries have committed their craft to the fray. I pound the dashboard, laughing as relief washes over me, but it's quickly replaced by frustration. The Merchant Class of the *Artemis* couldn't be bothered to join us earlier? Maybe then Sasha wouldn't have had to die.

"Where the hell have you been?" I shout.

"We followed our orders," Baltier quips back. "A perimeter was established. The perimeter was broken. We're dropping now. Simple as that."

"Well thanks to your 'orders', we have one wounded, and Reaper is KIA."

"In that case, advise Admiral Khan to pay for a larger perimeter next time. Otherwise, it's not my problem. Engaging," Baltier states, diving into the battle.

The Red Swans surge, allowing our Goldies to peel off and set a course for *The Artemis*. Their power is terrifying. The sons and daughters of the Merchants often opt to purchase their own top-notch equipment, rather than use the stock of the *Artemis*. Their fighters are varied and effective, but leave it to them to wait until the fight's almost over to come to our rescue.

The pirate in front of me explodes in an onslaught of flame as a Red Swan bursts through the wreckage. I don't recognize the pilot's emblem, but I can see her pump her fist, hollering. More pirates peel off, the numbers turning against them. Some bug out entirely. Self-preservation's a powerful incentive. The Swans eagerly begin their pursuit. That's when I notice the voice whispering in my ear.

"I'm . . . ry. I . . . so sorry."

I look back into the cabin. Carter cradles Sasha's head in his lap, rocking her back and forth. His voice is being picked up by her comm. I feel bad for the kid. He can't be more than twenty. He's going to take this with him for the rest of his life.

He and I both.

Fighting the joystick, I listen to pieces of the Helios tear away. The Red Swans split up, criss-crossing past my windshield. The sound of high caliber cannons fills the cockpit. One by one, the pirates who've stayed to fight either explode or plummet to earth. To my surprise, one of the pirates actually scores a critical hit on a Swan. The tail of the aircraft blows off, tumbling the fighter end over end. As it falls, a small figure places their feet on one of the arched wings before throwing their body as far away from the doomed aircraft as possible. Once they clear it, a chute opens. A piece of my mistrust for the Red Swans chips away. Just a small one.

Another Helios drops from the Roost. Our other team realizes we're in no position for further rescues.

We're almost to the hangar bay when I smell something burning. We're starting to turn sideways. Looking back the port side of the Helios, I notice our left rotor's spinning much slower than our right one.

"What do we do?" I yell over at Katz.

She runs over the diagnostics, rapidly tapping her finger on the console. "I'm going to put the remaining power into getting us enough altitude to coast into the Roost," she says, nervously biting her lip, checking all of her controls again. "We only get one shot at this. Do you think you can do it?"

My heart pounds in my throat. There are so many things in this life I haven't done yet. I regain my composure. If I hit the side of the *Artemis*, it's not going to be as a coward.

"It doesn't really look like we have a choice," I say, rolling my neck and focusing straight ahead.

"Do it!"

Katz throws all of the residual power into our thrusters, blasting us straight up. It isn't an even surge. The Helios pitches forward violently, swinging the Roost's bay out of view. The only thing visible is the vast expanse of green stretching out below us.

I pull up hard, fighting to get us balanced again.

The landing bay starts getting bigger and bigger until I realize we're going way too fast to touch down.

I look back at Micolo. He clutches at his harness, head towards the sky, whispering prayers to himself.

"Micolo get both doors closed! We've got too much heat on us," I shout. "Everyone grab onto something!"

Micolo jumps to his feet, throwing his side of the craft closed before rushing to the other panel. The frame of the forward hangar blasts past us. As Micolo grabs hold of the second door, our landing gear hits the hangar bay, ripping apart. A wake of sparks shoots out from under our hull, scraping against the deck. I pull my feet up off the floor as the heat builds, sending us on a crash course with the zeppelin hunters. The large bird-like contraptions line the opposite wall.

We're still going too fast.

"Everyone brace yourselves!" I yell, slamming my foot against the floorboards as if it were a break.

The piercing sound of screeching fills the hangar as the deck crew sprints towards the targeted crash site. One zeppelin hunter obstructs our view. I throw myself over Katz as she curls herself up into me.

The last thing I hear is the shattering of glass and the cold clang of steel on steel.

The sky is orange, changing colors faster than I've ever seen before, switching from red, to orange, to white and back to red again. The effect is calming. The clouds maintain the same shape with sharp blades of the night sky punching in between them.

How are they all the same shape?

I suck in a deep breath, choking on the acrid taste of smoke. I keep pulling in more oxygen until I've made up for the deficit. As my eyes focus, I realize the night sky is actually just the roof of the *Artemis*, and my morphing colors, just the projected lights of the dancing flames from the hangar bay.

I try propping myself up to see if I still have legs, but a hand forces me back down.

"Don't move son. Wouldn't want to break your spine, now would we?"

An elderly deck-hand kneels beside me, watching the others fight the flames. Thick unwieldy hoses snake their way through the hangar. The deck crew sprints back and forth, helping douse the fire. An enterprising young crew member climbs a support beam, putting out a flame sprouting from the roof.

Panic rises to the surface. "Where is the rest of my crew?" I croak.

I struggle to roll to my side, but the old man's gentle push overpowers me.

"Save your strength son, you've done enough already. The medics are on their way," he says.

That's when I notice the blood. A sizeable pool of it surrounds me. Shaking, I lie back down. Someone lights hot coals beneath my back. Even as the pain takes over, darkness pulls me back under again.

I awaken to a sea of white. I'm face-down on a cot. It's dark, but enough light leaks in from the next room for me to make out silhouettes. The bed to my left accommodates a woman with a heavily bandaged head. The occupant to my right sports sharp Mediterranean features.

Micolo. He's alive. His right arm's lassoed up over the bed, and he has several cuts lashed across his face. Upon further inspection, I realize the heavily bandaged woman is Katz.

We're still missing too many people.

"You awake Sage?"

The voice startles me. "Chet?" I ask.

Chet materializes out of the shadows. "The one and only." His telltale smile takes over again. "Someone had to watch over you to make sure you didn't die."

I try turning towards him, but my back ignites once again. Crying out, I lie back down. "Chet, what's wrong with my back. What happened?" I ask.

He looks me over. "You're lucky you're alive Sage. You popped right through that windshield. Took a couple of shards with you. The rest of 'em cut you up pretty good."

Just lie still. Find out more. "What happened to Carter? Please tell me he survived." I pause, pulling in a ragged breath. "There's no way we went through all that for nothing."

Chet's smile appears again. "Don't worry Sage, he's in the bed across from you. You never were any good with blind spots," he assures me.

His eyes lose their warmth. "Sasha proved even in death she could still save lives. She took the brunt of the hit when we collided with that hunter . . . for the both of us."

I let my head roll back. It's a gruesome thought.

"So she's gone then?" I ask.

Chet looks back down, nodding. "Yeah, she's gone . . . "

Closing my eyes, I picture Rosie running through the streets like I did. I shake my head. An orphan at the age of seven. I should be one to write the letter to Sasha's sister, her next of kin. What do I even say? How do I even find her address?

I chance a look at the other beds. "Micolo and Katz?" I ask.

Chet moves over to Katz's bed. "Micolo nearly got his arm torn off closing that second door. He's lucky he got away with just a nasty break and some scrapes," Chet replies. "Katz smashed her head pretty good. We think it's just a concussion, but she hasn't woken up yet. If you hadn't braced her, she'd have ended up through that windshield too."

I take a deep breath, studying the bland whiteness of the wall. Why is it that infirmaries never give you anything else to focus on?

"She saved us you know," I say.

Chet sits back down in his seat. "Yeah, but she wasn't the only one, if I remember correctly," he offers.

I sit up a little bit farther than I should. "Chet, I trashed the Helios, destroyed a zep hunter, and put us all in the hospital."

His dark eyes scan the room quietly. "Better than the morgue,", he quips. "Go back to sleep, Sage. It's late."

I take his advice.

The morning light pierces my half-remembered dreams, prying my eyes open. A face that doesn't belong to Chet glances down at me.

"Cass?" I manage.

"You made it back," she smiles.

Sitting back, I take her in. "I'm as surprised as you are," I say.

She puts a hand up to my forehead, searching for a fever. "They're letting you go home today."

I frown at her, confused. "They're letting me go already?" I ask.

Her fair features contort. "What do you mean 'already?' The crash happened two days ago."

Two days? I've been asleep for two days? "Cass, why didn't you wake me up?" I ask.

She pulls back. "I would have, but your unconscious kicking and punching persuaded me that rest was the best option. Oh, and by the way, it's nice to see you alive too."

Whatever drugs they've pumped into me are muddling my thoughts. The first thing I should've done was let her know how happy her visit makes me.

Cassandra Dawson. A short-contract nurse on the *Artemis*. Well, more than that. To me anyways. She came to our ship from one of our ports-of-call and just never left. She found too much work to do, too many people to take care of. For whatever reason, she just keeps re-upping her terms. I think she's stayed on with us just to get away from the squalor of the rest of the world. Even so, she commands the natural ability to calm anyone she lays eyes on. Her kind is in short supply these days.

Her talent, along with her beauty, led me to try very hard to be her favorite, and then some. For a very short time, it worked. Too bad things had to turn out the way they did. Some loves just aren't meant to be.

She brushes a dark lock of hair past her sea foam eyes. "Do I at least get a hug?" she asks.

It's a bittersweet request, but I nod anyways. "Of course . . . Gently! Gently.'"

I can't help it. Even with my back in shreds, I'll use pretty much any excuse to hold her again just for a little while.

She gently folds herself into me, lying her head on my chest. Her hands lightly caress my side, careful not to reinjure me. She doesn't seem to care that the bandages aren't enough to keep her hand from slowly taking on a red tinge. I let out a sigh, wondering if crash landing another ship would be so bad if this were the reward.

"Excuse me my dears, am I interrupting something?"

The one voice from the entire crew I don't want to hear: Sanjar Khan.

Cass shoots upright immediately. She wipes her hands together, trying to clean off the blood. I also attempt to prop myself up into a more respectable pose before managing a very crimped salute.

I stumble over my words. "Uhh . . . Admiral Khan, I wasn't expecting your presence. Please excuse my appearance."

Cass doesn't say anything; she keeps her eyes lowered instead.

Wracking my brain, I try finding a reason why the owner and commander of the *Artemis* is paying me a visit.

Sanjar's pale eyes sweep the room. They match the shock of grey that highlights his well-trimmed beard and mustache. Flecks of it can also be seen in his precisely combed hair.

"Please, please, you are embarrassing me with your formalities. Be at ease my friends," he gestures.

In no way does he actually mean this.

His diplomatic smile renews. "I came to congratulate you on your being alive, not to discipline you," he assures.

The Admiral is well-dressed as usual. His gold-rimmed collar buttons all the way up to his throat. Next to his covered Adam's apple is a pin of a golden bow. Since its inception, the Artemis has flown the standard of a golden bow accompanied by three equally-angled arrows, all over a black background. With the exception of the Red Swans, the same bow is printed on the wings of every aircraft launched from this ship, and every shoulder of its pilots and marines.

I fight the urge to look down at my dressings. "Admiral, I appreciate that, but I crashed two of your aircraft and lit half the Roost on fire."

The Admiral steps to the side of my bed. "Yes, and it was a crash that took staunch bravery. The kind that is not commonly seen these days," he muses.

I bite my cracked lips. I'm no state to be in front of anyone. "Regardless, my apologies Admiral. It must have been very expensive for you," I say.

Flinching, I mentally calculate the projected costs.

"Corporal Basmon, in my time commanding this vessel, I've found that the most expensive pieces of the puzzle are often the ones dealing in human capital. You have saved me four of these pieces. Five, including yourself."

Sasha's bullet-riddled body flashes through my mind. "My apologies it wasn't six, sir."

The Admiral betrays a glimpse of frustration. "Corporal Basmon, if you continue to apologize for your gallantry, I may change my mind about disciplining you," he grumbles.

"Understood sir," I respond, sitting up a little straighter.

Sanjar pauses. "Miss Dawson, if you would please excuse us for a moment, I would like to address Corporal Basmon alone."

Cass recomposes herself, giving a curt nod. "Of course, Admiral."

Sanjar's eyes follow Cass as she takes her leave. Once she's gone, their iron gaze returns to me. "Congratulations, Corporal," he says.

I'm confused. We've already gone over this. "On what, sir?" I ask.

The Admiral grins. "On your promotion. You are an Airman now."

I forget I'm speaking with a superior officer. "What? I don't even know how to fly!" I blurt out.

The Admiral sweeps his large arm, stretching toward the one window in the infirmary. "Did you not pilot a Helios into our hangar with little to no training?" he asks.

"Admiral, I played a small part in that rescue. Comms Officer Cheryl Katz was the main operator once Lieutenant Sasha Urbansova was confirmed KIA."

The Admiral lowers his arm, pacing across the room. "I understand Miss Katz's involvement in the event, and she too will be commended. The fact of the matter remains that you were in the pilot's seat of that ship. For that, you are not only an Airman, but a man of initiative," he asserts.

I realize I should thank him, but no words come. The prospect of individual flight is a horrifying one.

But the Admiral knows he has me. He makes one more move before achieving his checkmate. "Airman Basmon, how long have you lived aboard this ship?"

The Admiral already knows how long. "My whole life, sir," I answer anyway.

Sanjar steps to my side, folding his hands behind his back. "And in that time, when have you felt that the population aboard this vessel has been particularly stable?"

I reflect on all of the different people on board; the personalities are constantly shifting and transitioning. Some stay, while others are born into loyalty. Most are just passengers trying to get to their next destination.

"Never," I answer.

Sanjar nods, turning away. "Ah, then would you not agree that we must take advantage of every opportunity available to unite our transient community?, he asks.

I'm not following.

"Mr. Basmon, stories of the crash are making their rounds throughout the ship. It can either be painted as a terrible failure on our part, or a heroic action by our crew." The Admiral pauses. "Which do you think I would prefer it to be?" he asks, fixing me with his grin.

I sink back into the covers in spite of myself. "So you're gonna to make me a poster child?" I ask uneasily.

The Admiral raises his voice. "I am going to make you a hero! It's not as though you do not deserve it."

He makes his way to the exit. "Corporal Basmon, one day you must understand that there is much more to this world than just yourself. There are people depending on us who you don't even realize. If we can't put on a strong face, we will sink back into tribal warfare." The Admiral pauses at the door. "I've owned the Artemis for thirty-two years. It is because of men like you that we have kept control of this ship. Men like your father."

My jaw tightens at the mention of him. Of course the Admiral would play that last card right before he leaves.

"Understood sir," I manage.

Taking my response as acceptance, the Admiral nods his head my way. "Congratulations again on your promotion. You will report to Gold Squadron as soon as you are fit. Keep your nails clean, your hair trimmed, and your beard off." He fixes his grey gaze on me one last time. "Look like a hero."

The door slams, his footsteps echoing outside the doorway.

Sinking back into my cot, I wonder how many 'men like me' have been used to bolster the populace since this ship first left ground.

If they were anything like my father, how many of them are still alive?

3

The wind howls like an anguished, unseen animal. Orange signs posted by the bulkheads state that one should traverse the Outer Rim 'at their own risk'.

With all that's happened, I feel like taking a risk today.

"You survive one plane crash, and now you think you're invincible?" The Voice says.

"Shut up," I say to the wind. "Let's test it out."

I step out of the doorway and into the rain and darkness. It's a needless gamble on my life, but it's felt so numb since the accident; since Sasha's death. Maybe this can jumpstart something inside me.

I let the wind blow me through puddles and rain-slicked steel. When I feel I've lost control, I grab onto the prominent railing that dominates the outer-most area of the Rim. The rain lashes at my face as I cling there until the winds die down for a moment. Of the many ways to reach the Cellar, I doubt any of them provide as much of a challenge as this. The numerous stitches pull on my back, threatening to rip if I stress them any further.

This whole training process should be interesting. I may have served as a gunner on a Helios, but that's an entirely different responsibility compared to singular flight. Running retrieval, you're part of a team. If something goes wrong, you can work together to find a solution.

As a pilot, if you start leaking coolant, you better find yourself a friendly zeppelin or a rare patch of grass because nothing else is going to help save you. Your best bet is just to hold your rig together long enough, because you sure as hell aren't getting out of your seat to make repairs. Let's hope I can remember all of the little tricks and basics I learned in Foundational Training.

Sliding by a drenched crewman checking the integrity of the balloon's steel cables, I spot the Cellar's bulkhead door at the center of the starboard side. Opening it gives life to small rivers that pour down the steps and around the corner. Shuffling down the stairwell, I realize I've never actually been inside before. We had always tried as kids, but we were constantly shooed away by the guards. What little boy wouldn't want to see their favorite fighters and heroes close up? Especially if one was your father?

The stairwell opens up to a massive hangar bay lined with aircraft. The blocks of colors are readily apparent, coupled with some of the decals applied by veterans who have lived long enough to customize their fighters. Some planes sit idle, and emblemless, waiting either to be claimed or used as replacements. Others bear tangible scars the Cellar's deck crews were unable to refinish: aesthetics aren't their specialty.

A tight formation of pilots stands at the apex of intersecting shadows in the middle of the bay.

I let out a groan.

The Cellar must be a place where an 0630 meeting actually means 6:15, or suffer the consequences. I can't decide whether to run to make up time, or try sneaking to the back. Naïvely, I choose stealth.

Using the docked planes as cover, I slip through the hangar to the edge of the group, unnoticed. Edging close enough to hear the Flight Captain giving orders, I take advantage of the eyes facing forward and join the back row.

"Airman Basmon!"

I shut my eyes, trying my hand at invisibility. Opening them again, it appears my attempt was ineffective. So much for stealth.

"Yes ma'am !" I pipe up.

My attacker's voice carries an edge that sends my hair standing on end. "I am a Sir, not a fucking ma'am," she bristles. "Rank over gender. If I hear that from you again, you'll be scrubbing every single aircraft in this goddamn hangar until I can see my reflection. Understood?"

I swallow, careful to put my latest lesson into practice. "Yes, sir!" I shout.

Appeased, the Flight Captain takes her attention off of me. "That's more like it! Maybe you'll have the chops to fly after all. That is, if you make it on time to your training," she quips.

I haven't been in my squadron for five minutes and already I'm getting myself singled out. I make a vow to top the kill board. It could serve as armor against any condescending veterans.

As the Flight Captain outlines specific orders for each pilot, I take the opportunity to inspect her face. The first thing I discover is that she has one eye. A plain black eyepatch adorns the left side of her head. Behind it, some of the flesh is also missing. A pointed flight cap sits at a jaunty angle directly over the patch, her hair tied underneath, clasped with a golden bow barrette. She's tall, most likely in her forties. Her presence is severe, and communicates a distinct distaste for bullshit. Above all, she commands absolute respect. I can't shake the feeling that if my irises so much as twitch, she'll notice.

Regardless, I steal quick glances at the pilots around me. They come from all corners of the earth. I guess at a few: Japanese, Italian, Russian, Indian . . . one ghostly white woman I assume is a descendant of what used to be Finland.

The squadron begins sub-dividing. I decide to stick with the group of people who are closest.

Deeming that it's now appropriate to speak, I turn to the pilot next to me. "So where are the newbies?" I ask.

He glances to either side, unsure of whether he's breaking some sort of code. "You're looking at them," he replies cautiously.

For once, my intuition pays off.

I extend my hand. "The name's Baz."

He begins loosening up a bit, extending his own. "Yeti."

He's got a strong handshake. I jot down a mental note that making him an ally is a good choice.

"Your name's Yeti?" I ask.

"Your name's Baz?, he questions back.

"Fair enough."

The other pilots migrate to their own planes to help perform basic maintenance. Some grab spray cans and begin touching up their plane's decals, or create new tattoos signifying their call signs.

Our gaggle of rookies stands awkwardly, unsure of what to do. The click-clack of well-polished boots pierces the air. We turn to see the Flight Captain striding toward us. Stiffening, I do my best to keep at attention. I've already started off on the wrong foot, so I'm eager to wipe that slate clean. My efforts are ignored. The Flight Captain stops in front of us, her eye glossing over me as if I don't exist.

She adjusts her flight jacket from side to side before addressing us. "Alright rooks, my name is Captain Janna Dixon. As you may have guessed, it's my job to make sure you sorry pieces of shit don't cost us money by losing Admiral Khan's planes. Keep your mouths shut, do what you're told, and you'll make it a long way with me."

"Any questions?" she asks.

No one says a word.

The Captain allows herself to crack a tiny smile for the first time. "Looks like we've got a good batch here; you're learning fast."

Still in tight formation, all of the student pilots file into the makeshift classroom that has been hastily set up in the corner of the hangar. Comically small desks sit in rows in front of a patchy, over-chalked blackboard. This is where I'll learn the basics of flight. Captain Dixon strides out from the group, reaching the small podium in front of the class. All of the pilots freeze, cautiously waiting for her instruction.

Enjoying her high degree of control, Captain Dixon finally opens her mouth. "Well, I'm not much for the classroom, but considering your teacher, Lieutenant Bohrakati, didn't make it back from our last scuffle with the Legion, I'm going to have to fill in for now. Everyone take a seat," she says.

I find a chair whose seat back doesn't fold over, and settle in. There is no paper; trees are scarce these days. There aren't any pens either; ink isn't exactly a routine commodity. It's assumed that anyone chosen to be a pilot is fast enough to learn concepts as quickly as they're presented.

They've grossly overestimated my abilities.

But as the lesson begins, the smell of oil and the clank of wrenches lull me into a sense of security. This is where I belong. This is my world. I dare to I take my eyes off Dixon, and look at the planes around me. They're just as I imagined as a kid. Our classroom's snugly placed in a corner of the Gold Squadron section. All of these planes are purchased and provided by Sanjar Khan himself; thus painted with his trademark black and gold. These aircraft are hardly top-of-the-line. Hell, they're not even near it. But most of them can take a punch in the mouth and keep bolted together long enough to return fire. That's a lot more than most crews can ask for these days.

Gold bows adorn every wing, while the tails of claimed aircraft sport the different pilots' personal emblems. Out of everything in this hangar, that's what I want the most. As kids, we picked our favorites. Each veteran having their own emblem, their own brand, made it easy.

It also made it that much harder when they didn't come back. If a fallen pilot had been especially valued, their emblem would be "retired" and placed on a shield to be hung on the Wall of Service. The Wall resides on the port side of the hangar. A lot of shields hang there. One shield in particular fights for my attention, daring me to keep my gaze there. I maneuver past it, swinging my focus back to the classroom. There's no need to let him creep into my psyche now.

As excited as I am about the prospect of my own emblem, I can't stop the nerves. Traditionally, your own emblem's bestowed after your first firefight; chosen by surviving veterans. Assuming, of course, that you survive as well.

After going over the details of landing in midair, the lesson ends. We're free to go about the rest of our day as we please. As the rest of the student pilots file towards the stairs to the Outer Rim, I catch up with Yeti.

"It's Sage, by the way."

"That's not any better than Baz," Yeti muses.

"Oh, fuck off. What's yours?" I ask.

Yeti squares his shoulders, thrusting his hand at me. "First Airman Ettero Gomez, at your service."

"Ettero's not a real name either," I quip, shaking his hand.

For once, meteorology favors us. The storm has passed, and a balmy wind greets our faces when we step out into the Outer Rim. The sun's just broken over the cloud bank and it's gorgeous, despite being a little blinding. The rest of the *Artemis'* inhabitants also rise. Small stalls cling to the Outer Rim like mushrooms to a tree, vending everything from snacks to ceremonial weapons.

The passengers of the *Artemis* tend to use the merchants as a barometer of safety. If no merchants are vending that day, it's probably best not to go outside at all. Well-connected merchants have ears on the Bridge to find out what other groups are nearby. There's still a certain tension in the air though. Most of the talk I overhear concerns the Legion.

No one's seen a zeppelin yet, but scouts are reporting more and more bogeys in our airspace each day. With their attacks becoming bolder, many of the passengers are preparing to repel a full on assault. I shudder at the prospect of being the first line of defense.

We make our way through the crowd. The PA's been converted to pick up the local radio broadcast relay from the settlement below us. The price of grain and soybeans fails to catch my interest.

"Reports are pouring in that Promontory has fallen to outlaw attack."

This piece of information does.

"Intercepted distress calls indicate high casualties, but no occupying force. Initial impressions point to the attack stemming from a brutal supply raid. Most of the casualties confirmed are civilian; among them is prominent businessman and manufacturer Amani Ibrahim," the PA states.

"Amani Ibrahim?" I say, stopping.

"He owns Kafi Exports, right?" Yeti asks.

"Well, owned, anyways. He's one of our major trade partners. At least a quarter of our hold's made up of his products," I say.

My mind races with the implications. I strain to hear more details, but the PA is suddenly silent. That's odd . . .

"I wonder what Sanjar's gonna say about that," Yeti muses, moving once again.

I frown at the silent system once more before following his footsteps. If our supplier's in flux, that could be very bad for business.

These thoughts are banished when we reach the Veranda, arguably the most eye-catching place in all of the *Artemis*. Located at the very middle of the ship, the Veranda's composed of two intersecting circles on both the port and starboard sides of the zeppelin. The deckhands responsible for the maintenance of our balloon remark that the Veranda looks like a thick hourglass from above.

In addition to the rare open space, the Veranda draws

passengers because of its patchwork of designs. Being the most outwardly aesthetic place in the zeppelin also means that it's the most vulnerable. Its collection of designs stems from the constant need to repair the large holes blasted through its middle during combat.

It's not uncommon to witness groups of artisans eagerly awaiting the end of a fight so they can rush to claim new holes. It's a special honor to have your designs featured on the Veranda, even if their appearance may be brief. The walkway's continual evolution draws crowds who savor the opportunity to view some semblance of art.

Diversions are scarce these days.

Admittedly, the swirling patterns and colors draw me in as well when I walk over them. Copper tiles, steel circles, spiraling glass, all meld together to create a makeshift mosaic. At the very center, a small red-haired girl chases bubbles in the wind. Squinting through the sun, I try discerning who it is. Once I see the mountain of a man beside her blowing soap bubbles, there's no question.

I turned to Yeti, "Excuse me for a second . . . "

Yeti looks on in surprise as I start running, pushing past the crowd to get to the inner circle.

"Aoife!"

The ginger girl snaps her head up. "Uncle Sage!"

She runs over in stunted little steps, throwing herself at my chest. Her aim isn't that good.

She almost knocks me over as I crouch down to give her a hug. "Hey little lady," I say.

I'm not actually her uncle, just her father's roommate. When I was younger, Olan looked out for me, doing whatever he could when he had the extra time and cash. With a family to feed, it wasn't much, but it meant everything. Ever since Aoife's mother died, I just kind of slipped into the role of caretaker. I didn't have anyone else to take care of, so I never saw anything wrong with the arrangement.

Looking up, I see her father has screwed the cap back on the soap and begun lumbering toward us.

His bushy red beard separates from his equally shaggy mustache. "Well look who's alive," he rumbles, his thick Scottish brogue parting the crowd.

"C'mon, Olan. Did you doubt me?" I reply.

Olan catches up to his daughter, placing a giant hand on her head and ruffling her hair. He lowers his voice, "Well you know, you did soak through the stretcher when we carried you out of there."

It's my turn to snap my head up.

I lower my voice. "You were there?"

Olan looks down at his daughter, continuing to caress her hair. "You're not the only one looking for downed pilots you know. Especially if they down themselves right in their own damned hangar."

I eye Yeti as he makes his way through the crowd to meet us. "How bad was it in there?"

Olan rubs his furry chin. "Oh there was quite a bit of fire and brimstone to be had. At least it got those old bastards some exercise."

As a member of the boarding crew, Olan holds a similar view of the deckhands as the pilots do: if you don't hold a weapon, you're not worth knowing.

Yeti weaves his way to our triangle, making it a square.

Olan looks up. "Who's the lad?"

Yeti extends his hand, leaning forward. "First Airman Ettero Gomez, at your service sir."

Olan takes his hand, raising an eye brow at me expectantly.

I wave him off. "We're part of the same flight class."

Olan's laugh booms through the throng. "So it's true! They're putting you in a wee jumpsuit, are they?"

I almost make a sharp comment before noticing little Aoife's giggling too. She adores her father. Anything he finds funny must be hilarious.

Disarmed, I just nod, listening to the artisans' hammering. "I'm a bit surprised there are this many people out today," I admit.

Olan leans in, lowering his voice again. "They say that people are trying to get in their last lungful before everything gets all shut up. Word's about that there might be a siege coming."

Yeti leans in as well. "Where'd you hear that?" he asks.

Olan looks wistfully at his daughter before adding more quietly, "Word on the Bridge is that the Legion zep's right on our tail . . . Just hiding in cloud cover, waiting for a good chance."

I bite the side of my index finger, an odd stress habit I've never quite kicked. "Olan, you know what they say about rumors," I offer.

Olan walks Aoife out of the center of the Veranda. "Ay, they're just like clouds:. . . big and ominous until you realize they're not made from much," he says.

Yeti follows us back to the doors, taking one last look over the railing. "Unless they're thunderheads."

4

The first rays of sunshine pierce through tattered shades. My alarm clock reads 5:58am. Two more minutes of sleep. How useless. My body's taunting me. What can I possibly accomplish lying here for two extra minutes?

I jump down from my cot, careful not to wake Olan. Aoife is curled up in her father's arms, fast asleep.

Before slipping on my flight jacket, I glance at my back in our cracked mirror. At least it's a full length. A checkerboard of lacerations and stitches greets me. I hope the next woman I meet really likes scars, because my back's gonna be a mess once it heals. That reminds me, I haven't seen the rest of my former crew since the crash. I make a mental note to visit the Roost after training today to see if they're back on duty.

Fully dressed, I shut the door as quietly as possible, and make my way down the corridor. The gaudy red carpet curls up to meet my feet as I try not to stumble over it. Bits of mold grow here and there. I add "Cut out affected pieces of the carpet" to my checklist. A cold wind greets me upon opening the hatch of the Living Quarters. Like yesterday, the squalls are too strong for practice. Most planes will be grounded, unless absolutely necessary. Works for me, considering our next lesson consists of sitting in our cockpits, learning the different instruments. Hopefully it'll also give us time to lick our wounds before the next Legion attack.

My heart leaps as I enter the Cellar. A line of Jackals, numbered one through sixteen, sits separately from the rest of the hangar. In front of a small table, a rank of cadets forms. By my count, I'm not the last one. Enjoying my personal victory, I join them without incident.

I'm not in the back this time, and I'm feeling a lot more comfortable than yesterday. As the rest of the students file in, Captain Dixon leans against the table. She's obviously bored, counting down the seconds until 6:15. Her tapping hand indicates she's looking for something or someone to rip into. This desire is denied though, since every pilot arrives before the clock reaches her deadline. It's become quite clear, even to the more obtuse pilots, that the Captain is not to be tested.

The clock's minute hand hits the large three.

Everyone straightens as Captain Dixon barks, "As you walk by this table, you will be assigned a number. That number corresponds to the one in front of your designated aircraft. Consider this your wedding. For better or worse, that plane sticks with you. Some of them are some ugly fuckers, but don't worry, they've got more than enough personality to last you." I look over at the Jackals. Standing over the bold numbers of each plane is a deck technician or 'Deck Tech' for short.

The Captain snarls again, "At each station, you will find your assistant. They'll teach you the ins and outs of your Jackal."

She pauses, looking us in the eyes. "For those of you who have an attitude concerning deck hands, I suggest that you cram it up your ass," she says, motioning her hand to one of the Jackals. "I would even suggest making friends with your technician, since they'll be the ones arming your fighter before battle. I'd hate to have you drop without any ammunition."

A tall cadet in front sniggers in spite of himself.

The Captain snaps her head in his direction, taking slow, deliberate steps his way.

Realizing his peril, the cadet shuts his mouth.

Captain Dixon walks up to him until they're nose to nose. Cocking her head to the side, she leans in. "It's fucking happened before," she says, glaring into his eyes for emphasis before turning to the rest of us.

"All of you who think you're hot stuff and better than the deck crew supporting you, it'd be in your best interest to cut that shit immediately. You may be able to pull a joystick faster than them, but they built that fuckin' joystick. So you best listen up," she says.

We all nod in silence.

"Everyone grab your number!" she yells.

Filing past the table, I'm handed a card with the number six on it. Careful not to break any sort of code, I stand in the winding line to the properly marked Jackal.

A smile breaks across my face, despite my best attempts to keep it in check. My very own Jackal. Who would've thought?

The Captain's not wrong. The Jackal is an ugly craft. It's most prominent features are its overlarge engine with matching propeller, upturned wing tips, and tail fins that make a perfect T. The model's not only easy to build, it packs enough speed and firepower to hang with most aircraft out there. That being said, they're really no match for Wraiths, the planes heavily favored by the Red Swans.

That fact makes me uneasy. I've always wondered what would happen if the Merchant class of the ship all of a sudden felt like wresting control. I shake my head, banishing the thought.

My technician keeps his eyes forward without saying a word. His thick black eyebrows and matching black beard place his ancestry somewhere in the remainder of the Middle Eastern subcontinent. His finger nails are soiled, the rest of his hands bathed in old grease. The tan of his skin camouflages his appearance a bit, but not enough to obscure it.

Not knowing what else to do, I extend my hand out to him. "Corporal Sage Basmon, a pleasure to meet you," I offer.

The technician looks shocked, tentatively taking my hand. "Specialist Ja'el Hackim, at your service."

Still lost for words, I try making light of the situation. "So what are the chances you'll be able to keep me alive?" I ask.

A small smile breaks under Ja'el's beard. "Well sir, most of that will depend on you. But for your kindness, I will do the best that I can," he says.

That should be sufficient to break the ice. We both turn, clasping our hands behind our backs, waiting for the Captain's orders.

Seeing that almost all of the pilots have introduced themselves, Captain Dixon's voice echoes across the hangar. "Listen carefully now! Knowing which switch does what will be the difference between life and death. I will be making my rounds if you have any questions. Begin!"

I don't need any encouragement. Bounding up the ladder, I

settle into the cockpit. There's plenty of dust and a few wads of old gum, but everything else seems to be in working order. Ja'el's face appears at my side, calmly guiding me through all of the different systems. The hangar air fills with the clamor of thirty-two voices as we all learn how to fly our Jackals. At one point in the training, I realize that come tomorrow, I'll be dropped out that hangar bay all alone. It'll be up to me to know how to turn the nose up, otherwise there won't be a need for landing gear. That's enough of an incentive for me to create the mental games needed to remember all of the cockpit's functions.

Night becomes day again. I almost pass out during our first drop. The sheer amount of G force pressing me into the back of the cockpit, coupled with pure stress, is a potent cocktail. Only Ja'el's voice crackling through the comm gives me something to hold onto.

More days pass. Drilling drops, weapons functions, anything to get us ready. I rebel against the rote learning. Practicing mundane, simple tasks hundreds of times seems useless at first. It's not until my fifty-seventh hand switch from the monitoring instruments to my joy stick that I realize I no longer need to search for it; it's part of me now. I don't need to take precious seconds to look through my cockpit to find anything within it.

The drops never become normal though. The idea of a plane hanging by its wings, hoping the mechanism will release it evenly through a hole cut in the bottom of the ship never loses its terror. I envy the other pilots' ability to laugh through the adrenaline of being released, their voices crackling through the radio. I realize I'll never join those ranks.

Hunger rumbles from the pit inside my stomach as Officer Dixon finally grants us the mercy of a reprieve. An afternoon lunch break gives us all time to catch our breath and clear out some of the mental build up. Some perspective pilots break out sandwiches on the spot. Although the open hangar provides substantial ventilation, I need more fresh air than that.

I decide to tag along to the galley with some of the other recruits. I contribute to their conversations where it's easy. Otherwise, my attention's fixated on the large bank of clouds sailing to either side of us: giant vapor chasms most could only dream of exploring. Forget some of the rougher points, and the life of an air mariner isn't so bad.

The door of the galley opens with a whoosh; with it, the smells of meat and rebaked bread waft through. I can detect corn, ham, and some sort of pea mixture. The haul from the Charleston Flats was two weeks ago, so our store of agricultural delicacies is dwindling. The scent of processed seaweed is becoming ever-more present.

Chatter dominates the hall. Favoring beauty over protection, the galley features portholes big enough to lie down on, adorned with a sturdy wooden grain. I wouldn't want to be here during an assault, but there's no better place to barter with your newly procured information while pretending you're eating something other than reprocessed shit.

The line is stagnant, as usual. It's an incredible phenomenon to me. It's not like we have much choice in what we're being served: a protein - how wonderful. A source of carbs – oh, excellent. A vegetable - if we're lucky. I'm not ungrateful, it's just the monotonous repetition that wears on me. There are people far less fortunate than us: folks who have no food at all.

The relatively constant flow of foodstuffs has made me complacent. I've almost forgotten the hunger I felt as a child. It kept me sharp, because I had to be. Somehow, we always found enough right before we started trying to catch rats, though. This rationed bread may be tooth-chippingly tough and taste like cardboard, but it keeps your stomach from growling for a little while.

Slowly but surely, the line winds around to the unforgiving face of the sous chef. I take the usual: a disk of canned meat splats on the largest partition of my tray. I truly believe in my heart-of-hearts that this once came from an animal, despite all evidence to the contrary. Shaved corn fills in the rest of the holes. What comes next isn't a vegetable, at least not by my estimation. A cube of condensed seaweed crackles onto the last bit of plastic territory.

The smell assaults my nostrils: it's the stuff that came with the waves that killed us. It's also the same stuff that gave us a second chance. Packed full of calcium, iodine, and more protein than most land grown vegetables, it's what grew under the waves that pushed us up into the mountains. What saved us when we figured out how to harvest it, after we realized we couldn't eat our guns.

Still tastes like shit though.

A fog of steam covers the line as another set of cubes is

dropped into the kitchen pots. Through the haze, I see a face that dissipates all my frustration. Cass's sea green eyes float through the crowd.

"Hey Cass!" I shout.

Her head pops up, searching for the sound.

"You get a chance to eat yet?" I ask, coming up to her side.

Her lips pinch into a tired smile. "Hi Sage. They let you off from training that easy?"

I laugh. "No, just lunch. Don't worry, we're not slacking on the defensive measures."

She finds a table. "Well that's a little more comforting. Actually, you're just the person I was looking for," she mentions.

My heart double pumps. "Oh yeah?" I venture.

"Yeah, take a seat," she says, pushing the opposite chair out with her foot.

It's nice to catch up. With her shifts and my training hours, we don't get much time to talk anymore. The outside world might ponder why ex-sweethearts would make time to see each other at all, but anyone who's loved and lost could answer that. Bit by bit, the flakes of seaweed all get sopped up by increasingly pliable bread.

"What time is it?" I ask.

Cass turns her wrist over. "Quarter to noon, give or take."

Still some time before our next exercise. "Care to take a stroll?" I ask.

"I'll have to take you up on that," she responds, clearing her tray. "It's too gorgeous not to say yes."

We step out into the Outer Rim. It appears the wind's died down quite a bit. Families stroll about in short sleeves. Their children run in front, jumping around, ecstatic at the chance to be outside. Deciding not to infringe on any of the children's territory, Cass and I stick to the railing as we move through the crowd.

The PA system has now been converted into a music broadcast in place of the news, showcasing an ancient vinyl record playing on an equally antique Victrola. Admiral Khan always did have a penchant for Old World artifacts.

"I've got something to tell you, you know," Cass says. Her eyes lose their playfulness, but gain a smile. "And I don't think you're going to like it."

I furrow my brow, thinking of all of the possibilities. Nothing comes to mind that would make me as angry as the thought of it makes her happy.

"You got me, what is it?" I ask.

The lyrics from the Victrola break through. "*I don't want to set the world on fire.*"

Cass brings her sea foam eyes up to meet my blue ones. "I'm applying for transfer."

She's right; I don't like this at all. "You're what?" I ask.

She repeats herself with more emphasis this time. "I'm getting off this ship."

My shoulders sink, my chin following, as I glance off to the side.

Her voice rises up from behind. "Hey, I thought you'd be proud of me."

The lyrics croon back into focus. "*I just want to start . . .* "

I turn back, taking in her entire person, face, hair, eyes, body and all. "Cass . . . I am proud of you, but you can't go. We really need you here."

"*A flame in your heart.*" the Victrola punctuates.

Her jaw tightens as her eyes flicker out to the cloud basin. "I know you do," she says.

She knows *I* do.

"Cass, there are very few ships along the Appalachian Spine that can match the militia and trade potential of the *Artemis*. We have it really good here," I offer.

She wraps her arms around herself, turning away from the wind. "Baz, I know you want to protect me, but honestly, I'm so sick of the never ending stream of bodies coming through our doors." She tucks in her chin. "I'm so tired of watching people die because some prick wants more than his fair share, and figures that we have it."

She moves a little closer. "I figure if I transfer to another vessel, I might be able to find a little peace. I love healing people, but there's no relief here. I wasn't trained for this kind of trauma care. I really don't know how many more times I can wrap someone's intestines back up into their chest."

I'm speechless; this isn't the Cass I know. The stress is finally starting to bury her.

"Cass, you could find peace here," I protest. "I bet with my pilot's salary, I could prop us both up until you get a chance to set up a smaller private practice. You don't have to serve in the main infirmary."

"I wish it was that simple Sage," she says, her eyes looking up into mine. "Thank you for the offer – but as long as I'm stationed on this ship, I'm going to run to that infirmary after every firefight. The thought of it makes me sick every time, but it's even worse to think of being a few cabins down and not lifting a finger to help. "

The lyrics strike back up: "*In my heart I have but one desire* . . . "

"I . . . I was hoping you would come with me Sage."

Again, no words come, but the shock has a different origin. I've never considered leaving the *Artemis* before. Sure, thoughts have approached that territory, but they've always been shooed away by a subconscious loyalty. The possibility's terrifying.

And intoxicating.

The PA system echoes. "*And that one is you,*"

I want to give her an answer, but my mouth's still dry. She deflects the silence, wrapping her hand around my waist, pulling me to her.

A gust of wind nearly overpowers the tinny speakers. "*No other will do.*"

She looks up. "Either way, I need to leave soon," she says.

She's searching for a sign. Do I leave everything behind, choosing her? Or do I stay with the world I know? Surely, there will be other women? Then again, I know for a fact there are other ships.

"Cass, I've lived here my entire life," I say, "This crew's more than just a group that makes the ship go . . . They're everyone I care about. You're part of that."

She leans into me. "I know, I know. It's just that . . . you've felt what it's like to be shut in this deathtrap in the middle of a bombardment. We control nothing. At least you get to point a gun and be part of what happens to us."

My eyes close. *The Living Quarters rise around me, smoke billowing from where the portside wall used to be. Rain hisses into the heat of the fire from a shell that's just pierced our tiny cabin. Pieces of the flesh that once was my little sister cling to the wall. My mother's eyes stare upwards, her body riddled with shrapnel. She's not moving. My father's not there. If he had been, this wouldn't have happened.*

I'm lucky; I'm hiding under the bed. The angle of impact grants me only minor abrasions and burns. Pela was only six years old. She was only six . . .

I blink back the memory - my physical surroundings seeping back into view.

"Alright . . . I understand," I relent. "If it means that much to you, we'll look into booking passage on a different vessel once we reach Shipwreck."

I feel sick: the kind of remorse that comes only after making a spontaneous decision. I need to look at my pilot's contract to see if a transfer off the *Artemis* is even legally possible at this point. They certainly won't let me take my Jackal with. Who says the ship we book would even have a hangar to store one?

Unaware of my struggle, Cass's eyes light up, nearly banishing all practical worries from my mind. It's the kind of reaction I always wanted but never got, even when we were together.

"Cass I . . . "

A white light blips around the Outer Rim.

The crowd freezes.

The white light goes off a second time.

Silence hangs in the air.

The Victrola scratches, silencing the music. The PA system shuts off.

My jaw tightens.

The white blips flash into glowing red alarms. A siren screams: it's an air raid. A zeppelin's been spotted.

Cass's hands turn white against the railing.

"But, we're not leaving just yet!" I yell.

The crowd explodes into chaos, pushing, shoving and shouting.

I take her hands, yelling over the sirens, "You know what to do!"

She looks up at me, yelling back, "Don't do anything stupid! Come back to me in one piece, ok?"

Without thinking, I pull her in, planting a kiss on her lips. The wet warmth sparks a surge of adrenaline.

She's surprised. I don't know, I figured I might as well. Maybe she doesn't want to stray back into that mess, but I'd kick myself in the grave if I'd never given it one more shot. Consuming all the time we can afford, we push away.

Our lips break apart. "We'll be ok!" I yell.

Recollecting herself, Cass gives a curt nod before sprinting off to the nearest bulkhead.

5

I pause, realizing my post isn't in the Roost anymore. Pushing through the crowd, I try making my way to the Cellar's bulkhead. It's absolute pandemonium. People yell out names of separated loved ones, while others dive head long into doorways, getting away from the Outer Rim. I feel guilty running through civilians, but I have priority. The Albanian man I just knocked over may be mad at me now, but I'm sure he'd much rather trade the collision for an extra plane in the air.

But that's just it! I'm no pilot. I've never flown a Jackal in combat. They can't really expect us to fly without full training, right?

As I catch sight of the Cellar's bulkhead, the gun port doors begin flying up along the wall. They're three-foot thick steel, engineered to envelope the Living Quarters and cargo hold of the Artemis when it exposes its guns. Although they serve as excellent protection for both human and inanimate cargo, the gun port doors are known to cause grisly accidents: they have a tendency to slam up into the Outer Rim without warning.

Civilians pour through open doorways as uniformed officers of the *Artemis'* boarding crew dodge out to direct traffic. Many of the marines stand at the doorways with one foot on the port door below them, ready to block any incoming civilians if the door launches upwards.

Two doors down from the Cellar's bulkhead, a gun port door slams up, launching a boarding crew member ten feet in the air. He flips over before crashing back down on his shoulder. I hear an audible snap as he cries out. Communication between the boarding and gun crews has never been perfect. Two fellow crewmen pull him into the next bulkhead before it too, slams up into the ceiling's frame.

I sprint past the armored door, finding the entryway of the Cellar. As I cross the threshold, our flak cannons start drumming. Those enemy fighters are right on top of us. That zeppelin can't be far behind either.

I'm not the only pilot clattering down the steps. We all make our way to the central meeting area. I stop, looking up at the mission platform. Janna Dixon stands there with the same poise I saw this morning. The woman is incredible; I don't believe she ever changes out of uniform.

Veteran pilots sprint around me, leaping into their planes, making final take-off checks. A small, confused group of rookies stands to the left of the platform.

Captain Dixon looks down at us. "You're probably asking yourselves if you're going to be flying today," she says, folding into her flight jacket. "Truth be told, I'm not going to tell you to drop today if you don't think you can handle it."

She strides across the platform, cocking her head to the side. "Frankly, we don't have the resources to drop you out of the ship and waste a perfectly good aircraft." She turns, facing all of us. "However, if you do think you have the chops, you better fucking be out there, because I don't have the numbers to be able to spare pilots." Her eye fixes on me. "Otherwise, it won't be my fault if you're sitting in here getting cooked alive while this metal prison falls to earth because you didn't have the balls to fly out and defend it."

She pauses. "So, if any of you don't feel like flying today, you may step away."

Silence. No one moves a muscle.

Dixon nods her approval. "Damn right," she says, spinning on her heel. "Volleys One through Seven, you'll form the First Wing. You're dropping in five minutes. Volleys Eight through Fourteen, you'll drop in ten as Wing Two. Volleys Fifteen and Sixteen, you sit here and wait in reserve. You're only to leave this hangar if I give the order, or if I'm dead and the walls suddenly catch fire. Either way, you better be in your cockpits with a spit shine coat, you fucking understand?"

"Cry Havoc!" we answer.

Dixon almost smiles. "Good. Now get to your planes!"

Our tight circle breaks. Heavy footfalls are the only things I hear as pilots race to their aircraft. Five minutes? That's all we have?

Technicians scramble from plane to plane, loading enough ammo to last a dogfight. I find myself running behind an Austrian who's frantically searching for his fighter. I vaguely remember him being assigned to Volley Three.

Spotting his craft, I point it out to him. Gasping his thanks, he sprints his way down the hangar. I move from Jackal to Jackal, searching for mine. A stenciled "6" catches my eye. Bounding over a collection of electrical wires, I duck under the wing and grab the boarding stairs.

Ja'el's there to greet me, feeding a fresh belt of rounds into my left wing guns. Slowing down, I survey my plane, freshly buffed and shining in the overhead lights. Ja'el comes out from under the wing.

"Did you do this?" I ask, pointing at the sparkling fuselage.

A smile breaks across his face. "It is your first combat flight, it seemed only fitting. What I think you'll find to be more useful is my calibration of your front and wing cannons. I have programmed them to overlap, so that if the 50 caliber cannons jam, you will still have the two 30's in reserve as you work out the belts."

I take a moment, standing back before nodding my approval. "Thank you, Ja'el. Please let me know how I can return the favor," I offer.

Ja'el gives a curt half bow before rubbing his hands together. "Sir, it would be best if you got into the cockpit now. The cranes will be activated soon." Snapping back to my surroundings, I bound up the ladder. Jumping into the hard plastic cockpit, I feel around for my helmet. As I pull it out from my seat, I glimpse a crudely drawn minuteman with a "6"on his tricorn hat. I suppose I'm Call Sign Volley-Six until I earn one for myself.

"You have 20 seconds before pull up. Ensure you have everything you need before that happens," Ja'el urges.

In addition to my pre-flight checks, I take inventory of the cockpit: a small med-kit, a grappling hook, a flare gun . . . Essentially, everything I'll need if I'm downed. Everything except for a real gun . . . I guess I just won't get shot down today. Shaking away the thought, I strap on my helmet and switch on the comm.

Everything looks clear. My mental checklist zips by. I sing myself all the necessary little rhymes I've created to remember everything. The hangar bay whooshes, its massive doors giving way to a gaping hole. This better work.

"You may want to remember this sir!", Ja'el says, slinging up a compact bag.

"Jesus," I breathe out. "Would've been a sad story if I took off without that, wouldn't it? Hope I don't have to use it."

Ja'el nods, removing the ladder. "Yes it would sir."

Buckling into my parachute, I slam my cockpit shut. The glass of the canopy traps my breaths as I flash Ja'el the thumbs up.

Ja'el acknowledges me, gesturing towards the main tower in the middle of the hangar. One by one, the other technicians telegraph their readiness to the main tower.

As the last hand goes up, a green light illuminates the hangar. I cringe against the squeal of hydraulics straining to pull the necessary machines into place. Small cranes maneuver over our fleet, hovering above each plane before clamping onto its fuselage. Ja'el climbs up on my left wing, ensuring the clamp is properly locked. Appeased, he jumps over the cockpit to check the other wing, then, confident everything's in place, he hits a small green button on the clamp.

His feet hit the hangar deck. As the coils whir on either clamp, Ja'el turns back, pressing his index finger to his temple and extending his hand. Assuming this is a gesture of good luck, I return it. Here's hoping it's not Urdu for the middle finger.

The crane shudders to life. Ja'el's grim face disappears out of view as my plane lurches into the air. Grasping onto the controls, I struggle to find my center of balance.

The other pilots turn their engines on, waggling their tail flaps. Frantically, I search for my own ignition and follow suit. The engine roars to life. The force of 1200 horses sends goosebumps prickling over my arms as the Jackal's power courses from nose to tail. The fighter strains against the clamps of the crane, its engine beginning to pull in earnest.

Despite my lack of belief, I still offer up a little prayer; it's not going to hurt anybody. With the wing pulling into the center of the hangar bay, I focus on my breathing. It's the only thing keeping me from panicking. I sift for happy thoughts. Cass's body presses up against my hands.

I smile to myself. "Now that's something worth looking forward to."

"What was that Volley-Six?"

Shit.

The comms are live. "I, um, now this is worth looking forward to!" I stutter.

Despite my horrible delivery, my wing leader Petrowski leaves it.

"You day dreaming right now Baz?" Yeti's voice pops in.

I see he's communicating on a different frequency than the one the wing's using. "I don't know, man. I'm freaking out."

"Hey, it's just your run of the mill 2,000 foot drop . . . or more, if you don't do it right," Yeti muses.

"Oh, fuck off man! That's not useful right now. Where are you?" I ask, gulping in air.

"Hey! Hey. I'm at your 10 o'clock. Big ol' four painted on my tail, remember?" he says.

"Yeah . . . yeah. I see you."

One by one, our Jackals line up on either side of the bay. Without warning, my plane tilts forward 180 degrees, locking into position. I almost have a heart attack. I thought the clamps failed. Regaining my composure, I feel for the platforms along the floorboard and brace my feet against them. There's got to be a better way to do this.

Trying to take my mind off the chasm below, I chance looking at the other pilots. Their cockpits all point downwards as well, appearing almost as if they're all being dropped in glass tubes. Yeti's lined up right in front of me.

He smiles. "Hey, if we do our jobs as wingmen, we're gonna get through it just fine. Plus, have you seen the colonial propaganda they put on our shit? Terrible. We've to get us some proper call signs man!"

I laugh before fixating on the abyss below.

Small dots swirl in the ether. Tongues of fire branch out as the first echelon engages. A stalemate looms.

"Yeah . . . It'll be ok," I say breathlessly.

"Get a hold of yourself." The Voice laughs.

"I don't need your help." I growl.

Volley-One crackles through the radio. "And . . . We are go!"

To my left, the clamps clang open. Like dominos, the line falls into the sky in a perfect wave. The fighter directly to my left plummets. I have less than a second to grab my joystick and readjust my feet before the lights in my cockpit flash green.

My gut pulls back into my spine, releasing into the free fall. My harness pulls my chest back while I search for Yeti's tailfin. Keeping a tight formation, we hurtle down in a straight drop. Small clouds flit past as the force of the wind shakes my entire cockpit. The haze breaks, and I finally see the airspace clearly for the first time.

It's not what I was expecting. Our first-response team's scattered and overmatched. Black and white blankets the area. The bandits have begun reforming their wings. One group advances to take us head on.

"Break! Break! Break!" Volley-One shouts.

Our formation peels off in all directions, narrowly avoiding the tracers swooping in our direction. One line of fire catches the tail of Volley-Five. His tailfin and flaps separate from the rest of the fuselage, flipping the plane end over end.

Our wing breaks off to avoid the onslaught, but for some reason I can't move. At this point it feels too late to pull up. Facing them head on is the safest route. They won't be expecting it.

"Baz! Pull up!" Yeti shouts.

I test my hunch.

Flipping open the safety, I pull both triggers. My legs jolt forward from the change in momentum generated by the sheer recoil of the cannons. I've fired a machine gun before, but never four at once.

It's beautiful.

Tracers fill the air as the enemy squadron bears down. At the point of intersection, one of the enemy's wings buckles, triggering a violent spiral. Shards of debris spark off my propeller, scratching my canopy. The space created by the fallen fighter should be just enough.

Making like a cockroach, I squeeze through the small hole in the enemy line. Wind blasts from the passing planes rock my canopy. The second blast knocks the side of the windscreen into my helmet, ricocheting my head between the panes of glass. Readjusting my goggles, I quickly take inventory to ensure I'm still conscious and flying.

Finding only the scratches on my windshield, I catch my breath.

Volley-One crackles through. "Volley-Six, that was a direct order. You're gonna get yourself killed!"

A second voice drops in. A slight British accent, associated with a pilot I know only as "The Lionheart".

"Bullocks - never turn down a clean kill. Good on you, lad!" he shouts.

Lionheart just congratulated my flying. This is an awful place to get star-struck. Known to pilots and citizens alike for having his landing gear up first, and pulling in hangar last, The Lionheart's a ship favorite.

My comm scratches back to life. "You seem like you've got proper rocks kidda!" Lionheart laughs, "What'd you say to routing these bastards and having a brew on me once this shite's over?"

And that's when I see it.

A huge mass punches through the cloud bank to the west, the white replaced by a dark shroud. Flashes erupt from its heart, sending black, choking smog tearing through the sky.

A flak burst explodes in front of one of our lead fighters. Only shreds remain.

"Flak! Flak! Flak!" Volley-Seven shouts. "Volley-Two is down! I repeat, Volley-Two is down!"

I shudder.

If I'm going to bite it up here, I don't want it to be like that. My worries are ignored as the number of black explosions doubles. The *Artemis* cuts through the eastern cloud bank, adding our own flak cannons to the fray. The rising sun lights up our rearing bow as the *Artemis* turns to fire a broadside.

Satisfied with our apparent confusion, the pirate fighters turn their attention toward the *Artemis*.

I follow the roaring feline on the tail of Lionheart's Jackal as he veers after the attacking planes. Shaking out a hand, I wipe off the sweat pooling in the lens of my goggles. My body's never felt this kind of G force before; it'll take some time to get used to.

Time I don't have.

The Legion's ship pre-empts the *Artemis'* turn, bringing its own guns to bear. With the sun glinting off the Legion balloon, I can make out a Jolly Roger painted over the winged emblem of the zeppelin's previous owner. Squinting, I realize it isn't the classic skull and cross bones. Instead of a smile, the skull sports a grotesque set of pointed teeth, coupled with an equally disturbing sneer. I don't think these people are in the prisoner-taking business.

A volley rips from the side of the Legion zeppelin. Most shells miss their mark, continuing their hurtle toward earth, but several score hits along the Artemis' hull. One explosion tears a twenty-foot hole into the Living Quarters.

Bile collects at the bottom of my throat.

I rip the splintered wood out of the way. Part of our wall butts up against the bed. I fight, trying push it off my chest, but the heat of the metal bites into my hands. It's still too hot from the impact. Hyperventilating, I search for another way. I'm trapped, unable to help anyone.

I shake it away. This isn't the time to lose focus. I'm not in that room anymore. It's not real.

Despite a direct hit deflating one of its balloon compartments, the *Artemis* fills the sky with smoke and sulfur. Our volley blasts away more of the enemy hull. Our crew's experience shows. We've been at this a long time. A support cable fastening the Legion's balloon to its hull snaps; the wind whipping the one-ton line like a piece of string. I tell myself not to fly anywhere near that side of the ship; a hazard like that will cut a man in half faster than you can blink.

Pushing away the smell of smoke and blood, I bring my focus back to where it needs to be. A fighter flits past with pirate markings. He's close enough that I can match his speed.

The *Artemis* and Legion zeppelins draw close, trading volleys.

My target notices me. Trying to lose my crosshair, he ducks under the hulls of both zeppelins. We weave through the falling plate metal as it's blown off from above. I lose my concentration for a moment as a body falls past. It's too far away to see who, but my stomach twists at the thought of having fewer familiar faces aboard the Artemis when this is over.

Rounding the corner of the Legion's hull, my engine whines as I follow the enemy fighter up the side of the ship. Grappling hooks fire from both zeppelins; both are sure they have the upper hand if they're initiating boarding actions. Olan's no doubt suiting up, checking his weapons, his face turned to slate. I need to make sure none of these fighters ruin his party.

The zeppelins engage one another, closing their gun ports. Every crew member is critical. Any volley fired at this distance will destroy both ships anyways.

Tracking my target up the side of the Legion ship, I catch sight of our marines jumping onto the pirates' deck. Small arms fire trades back and forth. The glint of swords catch the sun as the two factions clash.

I pull hard on the joystick, staying with the bogey as he spins out of our climb. The nose of my plane swings up, wings rattling against the G force. The edges of my vision press in. I'm blacking out. Taking a deep breath, I let my crosshairs follow the target on their own. My hearing goes too. Everything muffles. My shallow breaths are the only thing that remains.

The cabin of the Helios looms back around me. I take my hand out of Sasha's back. Strings of red ooze onto the floor. Something ignites inside, burning my field of vision back into focus. All sound thunders back at once. I realize I'm yelling.

The plane crosses over for just a heartbeat.

I pull both triggers, blowing the dark form apart.

I must've hit the magazine. My cry of triumph turns into one of alarm as the victim's wing hurtles at me. Throwing down the joystick, I realize there's not enough time: I'm too close.

I duck as the wing fills the view of my cockpit.

The impact jars the entire fuselage. I can't breathe. Searing pain tears down my back ripping out most of my stitches. I gag against the shock. But pain means I'm still alive. For now.

Arching my neck, I try to gauge the damage.

A pillar of wind throws me up against my seat. There's no canopy. It's been completely shorn off, taking a part of me with it. I can't fly like this. The metal of my harness snaps up, smashing my googles and knocking them sideways. The gust takes advantage of the separation, ripping them from my head entirely. Holding onto the one strap keeping me in my seat, I struggle to protect my face from the other belt as it slashes wildly.

Grabbing the joystick, I fight to regain control of the plane. My Jackal doesn't respond. I try my flaps as the plane pitches forward. Again, no response. Looking back at my tail, I see there are no flaps.

There is no tail.

Panic shoots through me as weightlessness pulls me from my chair. Fabric cuts through my hand as I scrape down the length of the strap. My feet fly out of the cockpit into the open sky. Instinctively, I snatch the grappling hook that falls out after me. The med-kit dislodges too, plummeting into oblivion. I don't have time to grab the flare gun as my grip fails.

I hurtle towards nothingness.

6

Wind roars past me, forcing water from my eyes. My adrenaline spikes as I try to focus. Think of a plan. It's hard to chain together thoughts while falling at 150 miles per hour. Clipping the grappling hook onto my belt, I survey the sky below. The *Artemis* and Legion zeppelins lock together directly underneath me. It's the only choice I've got. Missing them and falling into the hell below is not an option. I'm not gonna die at the claws of those nightmares.

Using the wind to my advantage, I maneuver toward the head of the lengthwise balloons, bracing myself.

I pull the cord.

My head snaps forward as the world pulls away. I grasp frantically at the cords,   fighting to regain my position above the balloons. Twisting, I aim for small corridor of space between the two rows of propellers. I'm falling way too fast.

The white of the balloon races underneath me.

I have one shot.

I start sprinting the second my feet hit the canvas. I make it for a few steps, but I can't keep up with the pull of my chute. A wind gust forces my face on to the balloon, dragging me along its canvas surface. I cry out as my harness begins smoking from the heat. The rushing canvas bites against my bare skin, burning my hands and face.

As I struggle to grab hold of my harness, the wind pulls my chute towards the side of the balloon. Spinning blades whir up at me. In a last-ditch effort, I find the emergency release. I smash it with everything I can muster. The cords tear up over my head, pursuing the chute as it drops over the side of the balloon.

I barely slide to a stop.

Almost over the side, gravity pulls me towards the curvature of the balloon. I lift up my head, my nose scrawling red splotches on the bleached white canvas. I shiver, trying to get a grip on the taut material, but there's nothing to hold onto. Every movement I make drags me a bit further towards the edge. Propping myself up on my elbow, I blow on my burnt hands. I can feel the heat rising off them. I try making a fist. With a great deal of effort and searing pain, I discover it can be done.

An engine drones behind me. I barely get a chance to glimpse its signature before the aircraft opens fire. Pressing myself to the canvas, I brace for the holes I know will explode into my back. Instead, the fighter screams past. A large explosion ignites from behind, bathing me in heat. A giant blade flips over the side of the balloon to my right. They've hit a propeller. Chancing a look back, I see the remains of the strut that once held the blades aloft. It looks more like a torch now.

Terror spikes as the balloon compensates without the propeller to hold it up. I pick up speed, sliding towards the edge. Spiking my elbow down, momentum flips me around, away from the edge. In a final desperate effort, I fire my grappling hook. The hook arcs over the burning strut, disappearing past the curvature of the balloon.

I overshot.

I had one chance to make it. I'm dead because I couldn't hit a target. A sickening mixture of sorrow and fury grip me. I claw and scrape for some way to slow myself down, but its no use. I begin hyperventilating as the edge charges towards me. No parachute, a grappling gun with no hook, no hand holds.

No hope.

I soar over the edge. The sky opens up underneath me, knocking the wind out of my lungs. I couldn't protect Cass. I couldn't come back to her. I should never have kissed her. It would've been much less painful if I were just a crewmate who didn't make it back. I just had to try one more time to make myself something more.

All previous promises to myself to die with honor, grace and all that bullshit disappear in the cloudy vapor. I flail, punching at the air, trying to find some way to save myself. There's nothing. An anguished scream escapes in the face of the final drop.

Then the hook catches.

My arm strains, fighting to pull from its socket. Shock snaps my feet together. Recoiling, I swing back towards the balloon. I don't have time to ponder what act of providence swept down to intervene before I seize the gun with both hands. As the balloon swings back up, I pray it's lost enough air to cushion my impact.

It hasn't. I slam into a wall of cement. My vision muddies. I open my eyes to a cluster of rotating stars. I cry out as I realize they're the least of my problem. Shaking off the impact, I can feel my left arm is dislocated clear out of my shoulder.

I grit my teeth as I tuck the grappling gun under my armpit. Shifting my weight, I use my one good arm to pull myself up with the cord. Once I'm high enough, I clamp the wire between my legs and clip the grappling gun back onto my belt. My strength's failing. I just have to trust the clip's going to hold me.

I let go.

My freefall ends in a merciful jolt and a taut line. Wind begins swinging me alongside the balloon. I let myself breathe. One crisis at a time. My mangled arm swings uselessly next to my side. Wracking my brain for solutions, I remember watching Cass reset a dislocation once. What was it she did? I think she circled the arm up over the patient's head before proceeding to pop it back in. Well . . . it's not like I have much of a choice.

Pressing my back flush against the wall of the balloon, I take a deep breath, then, taking hold of my limp wrist, I swing it in an arc over my head. Intense shooting pain immediately indicates that my technique's incorrect. It feels like I've knotted the tendons. Pain explodes through my left side. My involuntary yell echoes out across the zeppelin, reverberating back to me. With my shaky good hand, I wipe the saliva and sweat stringing off of my lips. One more time.

Grasping my wrist again, I let the sweat pour over my closed eyes, visualizing exactly how Cass did it. More cautious this time. Slowly, I lift my arm towards my head. Pulling it in the widest arc I can, I feel the knob of the bone scraping around the recessed opening. I give it a little more encouragement.

A pop echoes out into the sky.

It's in. Shock threatens my consciousness, but it's in.

My body exhausts the last of its adrenaline. The stress and

pain from my other wounds hit me harder than the balloon did. I try suppressing the retching, but fail. I vomit over the side of my grappling clip. Spitting, I watch with morbid curiosity as the wind sweeps my old lunch away into the abyss. The gusts swing me back and forth as I lie my head back, collecting myself.

Well . . . at least I'm alive.

Tenderly, I take my back off the wall. Planting my feet on the side, I look at the balloon for the first time. A giant-fanged skull stares back at me. You got to be fucking joking.

I landed on the wrong ship.

I shut my eyes and open them again, expecting a different outcome. The skull continues sneering at me. I slam my fist against the canvas. That was a mistake. My burns crack open, oozing blood.

Swearing, I suck on the open wounds, trying to formulate a plan. Ears pricked, I listen for any sign of life. The intermittent chatter of gunfire pulsates from below. The only way to go from here is down.

Slowly, I shift the base of my feet, placing them on the canvas until my torso is sitting in the air. Carefully, I release my grappling clip length by length, rappelling my way down the face of the balloon.

How could I have made such a stupid mistake, following that fighter so closely? All of this could've been avoided if I'd just kept my distance. I try comforting myself by imagining an alternate scenario wherein keeping my distance would have led to me becoming a fireball later on. Yeah, this is the best case scenario. I'll make myself believe it.

The shots get louder as I crest the underside of the balloon. Figures move beneath me, flashes of light punctuating their gunfire. Dark objects scatter across the deck. Bodies: a lot of them. Unable to decipher who the figures are, I decide it's best not to hail them. I'll stay quiet for now.

One last click echoes before my harness jolts. My heart hits the bottom of my stomach. Looking down, I see the bare reel glint back at me as the sun shines through a blanket of clouds.

I'm stuck.

I bite the knuckle of the index finger on my newly reset arm. Hard. Old habits are tough to kick. I become acutely aware of how tired I am. All the bleeding and fighting for my life is wearing me out.

A glimmer catches my eye. I spy one of the cables fastened

the balloon to the hull. It's about twenty feet away, but it's all I've got. Turning to my side, I press my hip up against the canvas. I let my childhood instincts kick in as I begin running along the side of the balloon. Gravity grabs hold toward the edge, dragging me back. Bit by bit, I gain momentum, swinging back and forth.

At the apex of a swing, I almost touch the cable with my foot. Swinging once more, I push my foot off the cable for extra propulsion. With this extra thrust, I swing my legs over the cable, hooking it with all of my strength.

My muscles tense against the strain. Sweat flows into my eyes, threatening to blind me. Throwing a hand up onto the cable, I inch the rest of my body onto the line. The grappling rope fights to rake me back over the side. Balancing, I unclip my grappling gun, letting it swing away. Perching on top of the cable, I take a few breaths, preparing myself.

My new view allows me to gaze into the expanse below. The clouds have moved in, covering the ground. There's no green to be found, but the angle of the sun throws a purple shade across the tops of the clouds. They would be beautiful if they didn't remind me of impending death. Wiping my hands on my jumpsuit, I begin climbing down the cable.

Luckily, the cable's thick enough to allow me to get a good grip as I maneuver myself down. The wind laps lightly against my face, providing another blessing against the heat. In between my efforts to lower myself, I take tentative glimpses down, tracking the dark figures below. They don't look friendly.

My hands could care less about all of my good fortune. They crack and bleed as I grip the cable. The blood makes the twisted steel rope slick, forcing me to take momentary breaks to wipe off my palms on my flight suit. It's not very effective, but every little bit helps. I make it half way down the cable when I notice the guns cradled in the figures' arms. They're still too far away to make out their uniforms. For once, I wish the Admiral had made our uniforms bright pink: anything to help distinguish friend from foe.

I have to play it safe. The plan is to touch down on the hull as fast as I can and sprint to a door. I can't stay out in the open. With this requirement in mind, I dash down last length of cable before stretching a boot onto the deck of the zeppelin.

I stop.

Mangled bodies lie everywhere. Flecks of gold peek out from the mess, but black and white uniforms dominate the carnage. My stealth plan falters as I catch sight of the nearest dead pirate.

I creep over to him. His eyes gaze out into the cloud bank. War paint covers his face. A grotesque, oversized, black-and-white mouth is super-imposed over his own. Sharp, pointed teeth extend past his lips, reaching almost to his ears. The ghoulish effect is unnerving.

Footsteps clack from behind the nearest through-way.

Flinching, I dive towards the nearest pile of bodies.

I gamble that my black flight suit will blend sufficiently into the pile of my own fallen marines. There's enough blood on my back to make it appear as though I've been stabbed. For once, I breathe a prayer of thanks for my many injuries. I take a deep, quiet breath and lie motionless. The footsteps on the other side of the pile march closer. I splay my arms and legs out in an unnatural position for added effect.

The wind carries the sound of occasional pops of gunfire. Shutting my eyes, I listen to the soldiers' conversation.

"Well, the Sergeant said we drove their line all the way back to the bow. I don't know what we're still doing here," one says.

Another heavily accented voice answers, "We're here because the boss thinks there's gonna be a counter attack. We don't know what their full strength is."

Damn it, they need to mention something specific. I still can't tell if they're friend or foe.

"Hey Cliff! I coulda sworn this guy wasn't here the last time we came through," the first voice mentions.

I freeze.

Exhaling, the accented voice replies, "Well, maybe somebody killed him in between then and now."

The first voice draws closer. It says more slowly this time, "Fuck off, the fighting's down on the bow. Nobody's been shot here for a while."

His weapon snaps up.

I can't help tensing. Did I give myself away?

"Hey! We know you weren't here before. You best get up nice and slow if you don't feel like getting shot in the back of the head," the first voice commands.

I place my wager on feigning death.

The deck presses down underneath me as his boots draw up to my side. Phantom bullets drill into my skull. All I can do is hope.

The barrel of his rifle jams into my back.

A cry of pain betrays me as I reach back instinctively, putting pressure on my wound.

The second gun snaps up.

The soldier closest to me jumps back. "I fucking told you he was alive!" he yells.

The accented voice stops joking. "Alright Rex, I got your back. If he tries anything, I'll paint the deck with 'im."

Time to make my move.

"That won't be necessary," I grunt through clenched teeth.

Slowly, I press my front up against the pile, raising my hands to the sky. Failure seeps into my chest. It's not even the prospect of torture, I just never thought I'd surrender.

The soldier behind me pipes up, "Turn around, now! Slowly."

Swallowing, I carefully turn to face them.

Their guns aren't the first thing I notice. Both men sport gold bows over their hearts. Exhaling, I let myself relax for the first time, and hooking my index finger into my collar, I reveal my own brooch.

"Well, fancy that," I breathe.

Their tension eases, and they drop the barrels of their guns.

"Are you trying to scare the shit out of us?" the marine closest to me shouts.

"Me? Scare you guys? Who's the one with the gun?" I answer back.

The one with the heavy Southern U.S. accent moves his gun to the side. "Well hell, we didn't know what you were packing. You're lucky we didn't drill you a new one," he offers.

As the latest surge of adrenaline ebbs, exhaustion threatens to take my consciousness.

The marine called Cliff must've noticed I've gone pale. "Damn son, you need a medic bad," he says.

I nod, trying to stop the shaking in my hands. "I think you're right. What's the quickest route to the *Artemis*?" I ask.

The southern man points at the passageway they just strolled through. "That pass, right there."

I begin stumbling toward it, but the man blocks my way.

"Now, I wouldn't try that just yet. We ain't shot the green

flare yet, far as I've seen, and our deck guards tend to have itchy trigger fingers."

Right. Green flares also signal a successful boarding action. "Alright, what's our next best option?" I ask.

Cliff breaks into a grin. "The frontlines, baby. We need every hand we can get. The faster we clear 'em, the faster you can get out of here."

A lump forms in my throat. I've never been in a boarding action before. "Ok . . . Take me where I can get patched up," I say.

Cliff's grin widens. "You got it Corporal." He turns to his companion. "You got it from here Rex?"

Wondering how Cliff knows my rank, I remember the two chevrons pressing against my throat. Rex nods, turning over a body as he searches for loot.

I grimace. It's a disgusting habit.

Cliff notices my unease. "You're gonna to have to do it too. You better grab yourself a gun," he says.

He's right. Shaking out the tension in my hands, I kneel down to remove a rifle from one of our soldiers. She fights for it. I recoil before realizing it's just rigor mortis setting in. I peel her white fingers away, one by one. She doesn't need this gun any more. Her sidearm also makes a nice home in my empty clip.

Cliff appears disinterested, turning away to protect his newly lit cigarette from the wind.

Moving down the hull, I cock my new rifle, letting the barrel fall to my leg. Cliff keeps his eyes ahead, looking for any signs of trouble. As we make our way down the concourse, our soldiers' ranks become thicker and the shots grow louder. One group of marines clusters around one of the ship's bulkheads. It's a dangerous ambush point for us, and a possible exit for the pirates. One marine holds a large shotgun up to her shoulder, covering the demo team placing charges along the outside of the door. I quicken my pace a bit to catch up with Cliff. I don't want to be anywhere near that door when they decide to blow it.

I fall back in step with my southern guide as he gestures over with the cherry of his cigarette. "So Corporal, you're one of the Admiral's pilots, right?" he asks.

I keep scanning the upper levels of the ship. "That's right," I reply

Gregory Stravinski

Cliff pulls the sides of his lips down before taking another puff of his cigarette. "There were two flight officers attached to our battalion before we boarded this ship. One got dinged before he even made it off the *Artemis*. The other was some tough son-of-a-bitch who was the first one into the fray" he recalls.

I take a second to smile before asking, "Was this son-of-a-bitch a man or a woman?"

Cliff kicks aside a fallen pirate's leg. "I reckon she was a woman, but you'd never know, the way she was barkin' orders. She seemed a little higher ranked than what we're used to gettin'", he says. "Didn't seem to care much for us grunt types."

My smile broadens. "Did she happen to have only one eye?" I ask.

Cliff raises his eyebrows, nodding. "You know . . . she did. She was a damn good shot too, although I suppose she doesn't have to shut the other eye for every target she lines up. Could be real a time saver," he laughs.

He lets his cigarette drop to his side. "What I'm saying Corporal, is where the hell'd you come from? 'Cause you sure ain't made it over since the blockade went up, and you didn't jump with us."

I carefully step over another one of our fallen marines. "I fell," I say.

Cliff furrows his brow. "Whaddya mean 'you fell'?"

I let out a sigh. "Well, I dropped with the rest of Gold Squadron and got tangled up. Long story short, I got my tail blown off and had to bail out onto this zeppelin," I say.

He stops walking. "You landed on this ship?" he asks.

I gesture to my mangled face. "It didn't exactly work out how I wanted it to."

Cliff keeps his eyes on me. "Well, how in the world did you get down from there?"

I look up at the balloon. "I climbed, I guess."

Cliff squints at me, pointing. "With those hands?"

After looking down at my cracked palms, I look back up at Cliff. "Yup."

Cliff lets out a low whistle, flicking away the remnants of his cigarette. "And I thought that Flight Captain was a tough son-of-a-bitch."

I start walking again. "She is. She taught me everything I know about flying," I add.

Cliff stays rooted to his position. "Wait a minute, what'd you say your name was again?" he asks.

"I didn't," I answer, flexing the back of my jaw.

Cliff holds both his palms out in exasperation. "Well, what is it?"

I turn towards him, unable to stop myself from drawing up to my full height. "Corporal Sage Basmon," I say.

Recognition flickers in Cliff's eyes. "You wouldn't happen to have anything to do with that Helios crash a little while back, now would you?" he asks.

Sighing, I roll my eyes. For once, I'd like to be known for something not tinged in controversy.

Cliff snaps his fingers, pointing at me. "That's right, I heard your name on the PA. Damn, you seem to have some trouble keepin' your planes in the air, don't ya?"

I shake my head and keep walking. What can I say to that?

Cliff pads up behind me. "Oh come on now, I was just making light of a dire situation. I didn't mean nothin' by it," he says.

Cliff stops me. He lowers his voice, finding my eyes. "But in all seriousness, I heard you saved a lot of lives on that flight. It was pretty impressive." He carefully takes my hand in his and shakes it.

I let myself relax a bit, thanking him.

We start walking again. He whispers to himself, lighting up another cigarette. "Man, escorting a real live celebrity. Not too bad."

Smiling, I allow myself a few illusions of grandeur. I wish I hadn't been unconscious for my fanfare after I crash landed the Helios.

The shots echoes get louder. A triage center pops out of the side of the concourse. Blood spattered rags and soldiers lie everywhere. There are a lot of wounded. Looking down at my hands, I realize my injuries are laughable compared to theirs.

Cliff rubs his latest cigarette out on the railing. "Well Corporal, this is where I leave you," he says, the fatigue in his voice no longer veiled. "I need to get back to my post to make sure my partner hasn't been captured or killed in the time I've been toting your ass around. It was a pleasure meeting you." He snaps a quick salute.

I return it. "Keep your head down, huh?"

Nodding, he starts heading back to the stern of the ship.

I realize that's the first time I've been saluted. I could get used to that.

I make my way to the triage tent. It looks like little more than an equipment tarp rolled out over an expandable set of 2 by ten planks. At the entry way, a medic holds a bag of saline solution over a soldier.

He looks up at me. "We've got walking wounded!" he yells to the back of the tent.

I protest, both against diverting precious resources for my unnecessary treatment, and my legs wobbling beneath me. They're losing strength fast.

One of the medics rushes out from the back. She looks me over, opening both my eyes and peeling back my cracked lips.

"When's the last time you had water?" she asks.

I shake my head. "I, uh, I really couldn't tell you."

She bites her lip, motioning me over. "Come with me. We'll get your hands and back patched up as well. Not much we can do about the face."

I stop, staring at her.

"Gallows humor, kid," she says. "I have some ointment that might be able to help."

I follow her outside. The tent runs along the wall of the ship. Row after row of wounded men and women groan in pain as far as I care to look. Marines cry out for water as we walk past. Some just drool, lying still. I feel guilty being here.

The medic leads me over to the one open spot along the wall before asking me to sit down.

As I oblige, she leans over, checking my eyes again. "You're so dehydrated we're going to need to you fill you back up with an intravenous bag. While you're refueling, we'll work on your hands, ok?" she asks.

I nod, pressing my back against the cool steel wall.

Her footsteps fade away, and I am left to take in my surroundings. A flood of black and gold uniforms assaults my senses: not exactly something you'd find on a recruitment poster. I inspect my closest neighbors. To my right is what appears to be a young man, although his face is so bandaged I can't tell whether or not he's awake, or even if he is a he. Discerning the tufts of his hair moving inside his cloth cocoon, I am reassured he's still alive.

I look to my left. My heart hits my stomach. It's a young girl. She couldn't be more than eighteen or nineteen. Probably signed up for the marines as soon as she was eligible. Her assault gloves and helmet have been removed and lie on the hull beside her head. She has beautiful blue eyes and dark wavy hair that blows slightly in the wind. Looking down the length of her body, I find the reason for her admission. A sucking chest wound gurgles from her right side. A rasping sound sends a shudder through to my toes. She's having trouble breathing.

Her eyes study me quietly, with no sign of panic; she's just there. This was what could happen defending our ship. Her right hand splays out next to my arm. It's so pale.

Without thinking, I thread my fingers through hers, just holding them there. She tenuously grips back. Her eyes close, lips pulling slightly upwards. A tear crests over the side of her nose, making its way towards her other eye. I rub my hand off on my suit before using my thumb to brush it away.

I look back out into the swirling clouds. We sit there for what seems like an eternity. The medics haven't come back yet. They must have more pressing issues. I don't really blame them. Now that I have a purpose, I don't feel so thirsty anymore. A voice pulls me back from my thoughts.

"She's dead, lad."

Resurfacing from of my haze, I recognize the voice. A large shadow engulfs me. I look up into Olan's red face, staring at him uncomprehendingly.

Olan points his chin over to the girl. "The lass is gone, son."

I'm still holding her hand as I look over. I realize I haven't heard her pull for air in a while, and I know Olan's right. The bottom of my stomach falls out. Using my right hand to pull my left out of her cold fingers, I place her hand back on her chest.

Olan lowers his voice. "Did you know her?"

I shake my head. "You?"

Olan presses out his lower lip, shaking his head as well. "She was in the other battalion, I think," he says.

Thirst sets back in, nausea welling inside of me. I place a hand over my face, curling up.

Olan will not be dissuaded. "Well fancy seeing you here. I'm glad you're alive too."

I try my best to focus on something constant, collecting myself. "Sorry Olan, I just, don't feel very well right now," I say.

Olan snorts. "Don't feel very well? Lad, I've been shot."

Kneeling down, he puts his bloodied shoulder in my face. The gash in Olan's flesh does little to calm my writhing stomach.

He stands back up. "Some fool sniper thought he could end me with a bullet! Fancy that! He should know it takes more than one to take out old Olan," he says, thumbing at his injury. "The bastard just ended up giving away his position. We made short work of him."

My dehydration leaves me with less patience than usual. "Then what, pray tell, are you doing here?"

Olan shrugs. "My cad of an officer sent me back to make sure no arteries got nicked. Low and behold, I'm just fine. Wound's through and through, just flesh for the most part. Truth is, I think he just wanted a greater share of the glory."

I study Olan from my hunched position. Honor and glory. His bywords. The man's a walking time paradox. With his pistol clipped to his leg and his massive claymore strapped to his back, he would confuse most history books. The giant sword was crafted on the *Artemis* by Olan's father. He was a smith on the lower decks all his life. His magnum opus was designed to pay tribute to his Scottish roots. What better way to demonstrate your lineage in lost culture than smelting a five foot sword?

"Lucky for you," Olan starts up again. "I saw those medics lead you in here." He pulls out a gallon of water and some tape. "Also lucky for you, I know that these medics don't know their heads from their arses. So I helped myself to their stash."

My eyes widen. "My God, Olan. That's a capital offense!"

Olan shrugs. "It's also already been done," he says, tilting my head back and gripping my jaw. "I know you're supposed to get this in a bag, but we'll be doing it the old fashioned way I'm afraid."

A cascade of water rushes down my throat before I can protest. Coughing and sputtering is the only thing that gets Olan to relent long enough for me to catch a breath and not throw everything back up. Even with the little medical knowledge I have, I know this isn't the way to rehydrate someone.

Becoming frustrated with my attempts to resist, Olan plants

the half-empty gallon on the ground next to me. "Alright fine. If you're gonna fight me about it, you can just nurse it yourself. You'll be quite good at it if you drink your water anything like you drink your beer," he growls.

Leave it to a Scot to insult my drinking ability as I lie here dying from dehydration. "At least I have a soul," I cough.

I took a risk on that one. For a second, it looks like he's going to slap me. A smile cracks over my broken lips, which seems to defuse the situation. When in doubt, employ ginger jokes.

I cry out in pain as Olan grabs one of my hands, wrenching it over in front of him. "Give it here! I'll start working on your hands while you suckle from that, he says gesturing to the gallon.

The prospect of Olan repairing my hands is more worrisome than him drowning me, but I don't really have a choice.

Exhaling, I try my best to focus and relax. "Do you happen to have a bullet I can bite?" I ask.

Olan glares at me under his red hedge brows, unclipping his side arm. "I've got nine if you don't shut yer mouth. Now lay back," he says.

Obeying, I let fate take its course as Olan's sausage fingers press together, patching up what's left of my hands. Although not known for his dexterity, he actually does a serviceable job. I just wish my fingers would stop tingling from loss of circulation.

Satisfied with his medical venture, Olan pulls me up by my straps.

"What are you doing? Where are you taking me?" I ask, confused.

Olan breaks into a smile, gesturing with a platter sized hand towards the popping sounds to our left. "Back into battle of course!"

Fear wells up. I look away, trying my best not to let my hands fidget.

Olan shakes me. "Do you want this triage center to get overrun or not?"

I open my mouth to respond, but just glare at him instead. He always knows how to provoke me into doing something I don't want to do.

"Alright, let's go," I mutter, reaching down to grab my rifle.

He slaps my hand away. "You won't be needing that. Too slow and unwieldy." Before I can respond, he reaches over, plucking the saber from the dead girl's kit. He gives it to me to strap to my hip. "We'll be heading into close-quarters combat. All you'll be needing is that, and your trusty sidearm," he growls.

As Olan hauls me down the rows of wounded, I look back at the dead woman, silently thanking her for her sword. With a last glance at her glassy eyes and slack mouth, I promise her that it won't be dry by the time I'm done with it.

7

The water begins working its magic. My shriveled body starts coming back to human form, like a soaked sponge. With each step, my reliance on Olan diminishes. Eventually, I carry my own weight, using his shoulder only every once in a while to steady myself. The closer we get to the bow, the sterner the faces around us become. Making every effort to operate under my own power, I focus on burning away the mental clouds. For many of these men and women, I'm their superior officer, so I need to look the part.

Olan and I fall in line with his platoon. A steady stream of bloodied wounded are being carried back the other way. Even though we control well over half of the zeppelin's deck, this fight's far from over.

My muscles tense as we reach a wall of marines. Shouts, gunshots and the clang of metal on metal echo just over the other side.

Olan nudges me. "The containment wall. The ruckus is coming from the first platoon that's gone in. The second platoon's here to contain the fighting and make sure they don't break through our lines."

Wounded and dead marines emerge out of the holes morphing in the perimeter, supported by their more able-bodied comrades. Whatever's happening on the other side, I want no part of it. All of the kindness in Olan's eyes evaporates; it has no purpose in this function of his life.

"Since we're in reserve, we may be committed to this melee as well," he says.

That's when I hear her. Out of habit, I freeze, standing at

attention. A one-eyed fury charges the lieutenant who is leading our platoon, going nose to nose with him.

"Where the hell have you been?" growls none other than Captain Janna Dixon.

The lieutenant sputters out a response, but it does nothing to appease the Captain.

Dixon's eye sweeps the fresh platoon. "Doesn't matter! You're the flanking force now. Hit the other side of this fight from the through-way. Watch for choke points. These assholes are vicious, but they aren't stupid."

The lieutenant snaps a quick salute, relaying the orders to his sergeants even though everyone's already heard them loud and clear.

Dissatisfied with the pace of execution, Captain Dixon windmills her arm towards the front line. "Let's MOVE!"

"Cry Havoc!" everyone responds, breaking into a run.

We turn left at the perimeter towards the through-way. I appreciate their convenience on my own ship, but the through-ways that once provided easy passage to the different parts of the deck now seem cramped and claustrophobic. Their narrow routes make the perfect death trap. The clatter of our boots reverberates off of the steel walls, making a deafening sound. With all this noise, whoever's waiting for us at the other end must know we're coming.

The narrow passageway opens up into a large enclosure with crate sized generators dotting the floor. If it's anything like our ship, this place provides power for a significant portion of the living quarters below. This is a huge find. Without power, it'll be awfully hard for the pirates to fend off our siege. But how can it be so unguarded?

The screech of a hatch at the far side of the enclosure answers my question.

It's not.

A large machine gun punches its muzzle through, firing tracers across the open area. The marines in front of me are immediately cut down. Some dive behind the small generators, while others split to the sides in a panic.

The lieutenant spins to face us. "Take cover in the through-ways! Move to either si-"

A bullet pierces the skin of his throat.

A look of surprise hits his face as he clutches the side of his neck before collapsing to the ground. Fear strikes so fast, I actually stop moving, frozen by indecision. What do we do now? A bullet whizzes past my cheek, stirring me back into action. The generators out here aren't big enough to provide enough protection.

A strong arm grabs me by my collar, throwing me in the direction of the left through-way.

"On the hop, boy!" Olan shouts, picking up a wounded marine and throwing her over his shoulder. "You'll find no kindness here!"

My muscles engage as they're trained to do, just like a call for a downed plane. My legs kick in; all of my previous wounds no longer mattering. I lunge towards the through-way in a dead sprint. It's just large enough to house half of our platoon. At the rate we're being whittled down, that may be all who's left.

Covering the last ten meters, I slide into safety with a handful of marines who've already made it. Some sit in the corner covering their heads. A few have taken up combat positions, firing back at the machinegun nest.

Pock, pock!

Behind me, bullets strike a marine in the leg and chest as he runs to safety. His carbine clatters to the floor, his body sliding to a stop. Looking over him, I see Olan running towards our platoon as fast as his mass can move; speed never was his strength.

Snatching up the fallen marine's carbine, I stand over the other soldiers, providing fire cover. I've never used a carbine before, but its recoil's gratifying. Each shot makes me feel less helpless. Olan was right though; I never would have made it to the through-way lugging this around. Bullets begin ricocheting off of the paneling in front of us as the nest's line of fire skips up. The marine in front doubles over, lead finding its home in her chest.

The iron sites of my carbine explode as the weapon wrenches from my hands. A searing piece of metal cuts through my eyebrow. I drop the gun, clutching my face. My hands come away bloody, as a warmth trickles down past my jaw. Hunching back behind the wall, I blink my eyes repeatedly, making sure I can still see. My hands are still there, this nightmare is still there.

Olan barrels toward the entrance. He cries out, his body shaking as he clears the passageway. He slides in, one leg in front of him, dropping the poor woman to the deck. He swears to himself.

I duck around, trying pull him further into the alcove.

"Ah feck! Baz, they got me in the fecking arse! God above that stings," Olan grunts.

Pulling him in further, I reach down, tapping him lightly on the face. "Could have been worse!"

Olan reaches up to push me away. "Feck off!"

Satisfied with my friend's safety, I survey the killing field. Most of our platoon's made it either to this through-way or the one directly across from us. A shocking number of us lay prone in the middle of the open area. The nest rakes through the enclosure, shooting at anything that's still moving. It's sickening.

The dull thud of bullets echo as they find their targets. Wheeling around, I spot a marine just out of reach from us. He's still moving, smearing the deck with the blood leaking from under his sergeant's markings. We lock eyes.

"Get me out of here!" he yells.

I press a finger to my lips, motioning for him to stop moving. It doesn't seem to register. The sergeant continues writhing, attracting the nest's attention.

A young marine in front of me dives to his hands and knees, also trying to get his Sergeant to relax. "Matsumoto, you gotta stop moving!" he pleads.

The Sergeant snarls in a slight Japanese accent, "You try to stop moving when you've got hot lead pouring through you!"

The young marine pokes his head out from behind our barricade, just enough to try hooking the Sergeant with the muzzle of his carbine. His rifle explodes in his hands. The young marine ducks back into the enclosure, bullets beginning to rain around his Sergeant. Matsumoto curls into a protective ball.

I hear the wrenching of metal behind me. Turning around, I catch Olan pulling a water spigot off the wall. Shaking the bolts loose, Olan folds it with his bare hands as one would a balloon creature.

My mouth drops. "Olan, stop! You'll bleed out."

He waves me off. "The battle's not over yet!"

Content with his design, Olan uses his massive hand to push the young marine aside, and begins fishing for the Sergeant. Olan grins, succeeding in hooking one of the Sergeant's straps. Then, angling with the pipe, Olan begins reeling him in. Matsumoto wraps his arms around the deformed piece of metal, leaving a faint trail of blood behind him.

He's almost to safety. I reach out to grab him.

A stream of bullets tears the spigot in half, bringing the sergeant to a stop. Before I can do anything, Olan lunges out, grabbing Matsumoto by the strap. In one heave, he throws the marine over to us.

Olan's helmet rings loudly.

My heart stops. The world slows. The helmet spins off Olan's head as he falls over into our alcove. Tracers fly by lazily as I try recollecting myself. What they don't tell you about time is, once it slows down, it has to speed back up to repay the deficit. Faster than I can remember anyways. When I catch up, I'm hunched over Olan, pulling him all the way back into the alcove again with the help of three other marines.

I kneel over his face, searching for the entry wound. All I can find is a giant welt next to his temple. Not knowing what else to do, I yell his name, trying to shake back him to consciousness.

No response.

As I rearing up to slap him, his hands clap over his face. Growling, he twists over to his side.

"God bless it, that smarts," he mutters through his fingers.

Relief washes over me. Exhausted, I sit against our savior of a wall, looking up at the sky.

What do we do now?

I scan our little recess. We have one medic. He's already lined up the wounded and begun to prioritize their injuries, making marks on their faces as he goes. He's completely overwhelmed and thus, no use to me. Our highest ranking officer is Matsumoto, who's now lined up against the wall with the other wounded and not fit to command. Our lack of leadership weighs heavily on all of us; I glance around, sensing the other marines are also trying to hatch their own plans of escape.

Running a thumb over my Corporal's chevrons, I realize that, as the senior enlisted man, I'm in charge. It's up to me now. Two engineers who've been attached to our platoon catch my eye. Light flashes as they use their welding tools to cut through the supports of a nearby generator. I crawl my way over to where they've laid out their tools.

"What are you doing Specialist?" I inquire of the head engineer.

The Specialist turns off her torch and flips up her visor. "Trying to save our arses, if you wouldn't mind."

She has intelligent green eyes flecked with spots of hazel. You can tell that she's used them to take in a lot of information over many years.

"And how are you planning to do that?" I ask.

The Specialist pulls me by the shoulder, pointing to the killing field. "You see that?" she says. "Everyone who's not currently behind something solid, is quite dead right now." Her Irish lilt dances over the shots continuing to pour from the machinegun nest. She then turns me toward the now unhitched generator. "That's something quite solid, wouldn't you agree?"

Nodding, I finish the rest of her plan in my mind. I look at the burned supports of the unit. "I bet you need help turning that over, huh?"

The Specialist lets go of my shoulder, making a grandiose gesture towards the generator. "Would you kindly?"

I point to two marines, waving them over to our position. Thirsty for some sort of leadership, they vault over to the generator, allowing me to quickly explain the plan to them. We have to use the generator as a mobile shield until we get close enough to toss explosives into the machinegun nest. The major hitch is that we don't know if it'll stand up to continuous fire. I guess there's only one way to find out.

Before I get my men into place, I turn to the Specialist. "And who can I thank for masterminding this plan?"

The Specialist's eyes light up at the praise. It's not common for *Artemis*'s leaders to recognize the accomplishments of groups beyond their own wing. The Specialist takes my hand, pumping it quickly. It's obvious she's no stranger to physical labor.

"The name's Diz!" she shouts.

I give her a look.

"Dizzy McAlister, at your service, Corp." she clarifies.

"Sage Basmon!" I yell back.

Content with our introduction, Diz applies a thick layer of grease to the side of the generator we'll be pushing, motioning for us to tip it over. Together, we shove our shoulders into the unit until it yields, crashing to the ground. One of the engineers undoes his grenades from his belt, clenching them in his fists.

"I really hope this fuckin' works," he mutters to no one in particular.

Diz stuffs her mane of curly red hair back into her helmet before throwing her shoulder against the generator with the rest of us. We must be quite the sight, pushing an upturned generator toward an almost certain death.

As we round the corner, a hail of gunfire smashes into us from the other side. The oily residue under our feet makes it hard to grip the floor, but I can't imagine moving something this size without it. Beads of sweat drizzle down my face. Grunts of fear and desperation are the only things I can hear besides the constant hammering on the other side.

We're almost halfway across the killing field before the rest of the platoon realizes what we're doing. There's a pop of carbines as they begin laying down suppressing fire. The machinegun nest appears confused about which target is more dangerous, beginning to swing its arc of fire from side to side; a steady stream of death ricocheting wherever it points.

Hearing the fans on the other side of the generator getting pummeled into small bits leads me to believe the nest has chosen us. More worrying is the fact that the echoes reverberating from inside the destroyed generator are getting deeper. My anxiety spikes when I notice the deep gouges the upturned generator is carving into the floor; the oily layer of grease underneath it is wearing thin. We won't be hidden for long. A bullet punches through the unit, right next to my face.

Everyone pulls away from the generator, but without straying from its protective shadow.

"Back on it. There's no other way!" Diz snaps.

Just like that, we're all back to pushing. The proposition's a horrifying one: I'd much rather be able to see where the bullet that might fell me is coming from. We duck and weave, struggling to push as more stray bullets punch through our makeshift shield.

There's a small clang as one of the strays pierces the other engineer's welding fuel canister. His back ignites in a burst of flame. I don't know what's worse: hearing his screams as he unsuccessfully tries to pull off the pack, or the smell of his burning flesh. Both contribute to my own need to vomit, but I choke it down. I close my eyes, pushing the burning room away. There are no cinders anymore. My hands have been burnt for years. Focus.

"Keep pushing!" Diz shouts.

I have to give her credit; when she makes a plan, she sticks to it. I throw my shoulder back into the unit, heaving with the others. At least it's impossible for me to spontaneously catch fire.

The generator halts, scraping almost to a stop as we use up the last of its grease and our strength.

Diz will not to be stopped. "Just five more feet you cads! Then we're there!"

Five more feet is exactly what she gets before we screech to a standstill and curl up at the base of the generator. I raise my fatigued hand, signaling for each side of my fractured platoon to generate one last burst of suppressing fire. Two walls of bullets rush past. When the second whistles by, our soldiers take the opportunity to pop their heads out just enough to toss a volley of precious explosives into the machine gun nest in front of us. Most of the grenades find their mark, exploding with a satisfying reverberation. Blood arcs up the opposing wall of the nest, disclosing that at least one of the operators is down.

Before I realize what's happening, footsteps pound behind me. A berserk Olan rushes up, bounding over the generator with his claymore clutched in both hands. In the blink of an eye, he jumps the distance between us and the nest. Startled voices erupt from the bunker.

A shot rings out.

Olan ducks, and the bullet buries itself in the husk of the generator. He punches his fist into the hole, ripping out the offender. The pirate struggles as Olan slams him onto the ground, spitting him on the spot. Olan draws up his bloodied weapon against the wall, peering into the opening for more victims.

His thirst for blood is infectious; my fatigue melts away, supplanted by anger. I find myself on top of the generator with my saber out, roaring for the rest of the survivors to press forward. Somewhere in my mind, I know there's no way this recklessness can end well, but that thought's completely dominated by the prospect of blood.

Hitting the ground, I charge the side door of the bunker.

Without losing any momentum, I lower my shoulder and crash into the wooden door. I'm overzealous; the door falls inwards and I lose my footing, falling right on top of it. Hitting the ground, I brace for the blades and bullets bound to tear through me, but my enemies are just as surprised as I am.

Pressing the advantage, I lunge upward, skewering the operator standing next to me. He stumbles backwards, coughing up blood onto my hands. Something pops against the blade inside of him. I struggle to pull the sword out, knowing he's not the only one left in the room. Nobody ever taught me the physics of killing someone.

A concussed pirate staggers into the hallway. Abandoning my sword, I grab the pistol on my hip. In one smooth motion, I tear my sidearm from my leg, firing two rounds into her. She falls gaping-mouthed to the floor as the nest's door flings open behind me. A pirate covered in the same oversized mouth war paint dives out. It has the desired effect. I fight visceral panic, trying to drive more bullets into my sidearm. Apparently the operators only had the one machine gun to rely on, because he's almost on me, wielding just a knife.

Whirling, I level my gun, but he's too fast.

He tackles me full on. The knife slits through the air, but nothing else. He forces me backwards, using his momentum. I keep my balance, but drop my gun trying to get a hold of the knife's hilt. Hitting the wall, I angle myself so his bald head takes most of the impact. The collision stuns him. Grabbing hold of the hilt with both hands, I plant one of my boots on his back, twisting his arm upwards over his head until I can feel his shoulder muscles straining against the pressure.

He cries out as I dig my boot into his back, wrenching his arm even farther over his head. The knife drops from his hands as his yelling intensifies.

I don't care. I'm gonna finish this.

I grin, feeling his shoulder reach the absolute limit of its range. I throw my back into it, pulling even harder. I hear the cartilage and muscle tear. His arm flies over his head, no longer limited by tendons and tissue. I can barely hear his cries of pain. Blood pumps past my ears, engulfing my hearing. Laughter bubbles up from somewhere deep inside as I climb off of him, reveling in his writhing state.

It's not enough.

He turns his head towards me. I swing my right foot up, driving the steel toe into his face. Pleasure consumes me as I hear the crunch of cartilage and bone.

I raise my boot up to cave in the back of his head.

A force hits me in the chest, pinning me to the wall.

Confused, I grapple with my new assailant, but my blows are blocked and my arms shoved up against my chest, immobilizing me. I hear yelling. Slowly, I see the red curls. My vision begins focusing on the face. Diz's furious green eyes pierce through my confusion.

"We can use him!" she yells.

I stop struggling. My muscles twitch with exhaustion.

Diz shoves me further up the wall for increased emphasis. "Don't waste your energy trying to kill someone we can fucking capture! Information can be more valuable than gold."

I feel the fight drain out of me. Nodding my head, my rage is gradually replaced by embarrassment and nausea. Diz slowly lets me down "Use that energy to kill the ones that still have weapons. Savvy?"

Before I can manage another nod, I double over shaking. I pull in gasps of air, but can't catch my breath.

Diz turns around, surveying the carnage. "Well, you've made short work of this lot."

The doorway frames a young marine. The whites of his eyes dominate his face. It's probably his first fight. I give him a half-hearted thumbs-up, trying to disguise the fact that I'm a monster. I furtively look down at the face of the man with the overly large, painted mouth. His right cheekbone's caved in. A streak of red pours from his nose, and he's not moving.

Marines surge through the door. They step over the bodies I've created, making their way down the hall. Shots ring out. The clash of sabers reverberates back as they clear the rooms one by one. I try getting back on my feet.

It doesn't work.

My knees buckle as the very last of my adrenaline gives out. My back aches, and searing pain pierces its way back into my face. If I keep this up, I won't have a body left to fight with. Diz watches me as I try to collect myself. It's not working. Fighting the darkness pooling at the borders of my vision, I fight to stay conscious.

I bring a leaden arm up to wipe my nose. "Thanks for bringing me back Diz."

Silence materializes between us.

"Cry Havoc," she replies quietly.

8

The sun drowns below the clouds as night takes over. The gunshots cease. Our platoon did just what it was supposed to do: they broke through the line and took The Legion by surprise. The pirates didn't have much fight left after that. Isolated pockets continue to resist inside the ship as the marines painstakingly sweep every single cabin until the living quarters are ours. The only thing left is the cargo bay, and that team's already been dispatched.

The triage center's transformed into a full-scale field hospital. We take up a good quarter of the ship's deck. I'm somewhere between receiving care for myself, and providing it to the more gravely wounded soldiers. Everything aches. I can barely keep my eyelids open, and I take frequent gulps of water just for the cold stimulation.

My mind is numb. I've seen battles before, but never like this. It's always been through a window, or a door of a plane, amounting to little more than exciting flashes with toy soldier figures going at it. But never like this.

As I administer cold compresses to a wounded marine who's showing symptoms of a fever, I prick my ears for the sound of a popping flare. That one sound would bring me all of the joy in the world. I want my bunk. I want to find Cass and discover if this morning was just a dream. I want out of this hell.

I don't get my flare. Instead, I get an excited Private sprinting through the tent, shouting my name.

"Corporal Basmon!"

Barely able to keep my eyes open, I look up from my compresses. "What?"

The Private finds me, weaving his way through the wounded to get closer than hollering range.

Closing in, he snaps a quick salute. "Corporal Basmon, you're needed in the cargo hold for a Captain's Meeting." he says.

I thank him, furrowing my brow. "Captain's Meeting' is a bit of a misnomer. It isn't necessarily comprised of captains, but it does involve most of the leadership still left on a vessel, bringing them together to make a decision. What could they have possibly discovered that requires that kind of conference?

"What'd they find?" I ask.

The Private shrugs "Not sure myself," he replies. "They just found me, and sent me up as a runner. They said if you asked, that you'd need to come see it for yourself."

I bite my lip. I hate cryptic messages. The world would be a much simpler place if people didn't feel the need for grand gestures. Handing him my remaining compresses, I thank him again.

I shuffle out of the tent, the smell of blood slowly clearing from my nostrils. Or at least it's less noticeable out here. Many of the bodies have been stacked up or laid out based on their allegiance. The prisoners taken in battle are lined up facing the wall, their helmets and hats knocked off for good measure.

As I round the corner by the cargo hold bulkhead, I come upon a group of soldiers taking turns kicking a tightly bound prisoner as the senior officers look the other way.

I understand; it's been a long day. Each kick represents someone they knew. Frankly, if I weren't being summoned right now, I may have taken a few shots myself.

The dank stairwell leading to the cargo hold is reminiscent of my daily commute to the Cellar. Winding steps creep down into the darkness. But the smell's not familiar. I gag at the oppressive odor. I'd easily trade the acrid blood smell of the field hospital over whatever this is. Reaching the bottom, a horrific sight stops me where I stand. What appears to be almost two hundred shoddily clothed men and women stare back at me. They peer from behind bars, their distended stomachs suggesting that they haven't eaten in some time. I don't even have the courtesy to keep my mouth closed.

The Legion weren't just pirates . . . they were slavers.

"Corporal Basmon!"

My head snaps to the right to survey the cluster of uniforms gathered in the corner next to the makeshift brig. The faces of most of the officers remaining on the ship glow in the lamp light.

"I see you have the same penchant for tardiness concerning Captain's Meetings as you do for basic training," smirks Captain Dixon.

At least she remembers me.

Too tired to defend myself, I shuffle over to the group taking in the scene. A dead pirate lies just inside the prison. It looks like The Legion realized they were losing the fight, so they dispatched this unfortunate soul to cleanse the population below. Apparently he didn't realize how many of them there were. It appears that they overpowered him, taking his weapon, - among other things. A Sergeant fills me in on the standoff that occurred with the armed prisoner and the clearing team who discovered the captives.

Now, I bet he regrets giving his gun away.

The discussion begins out of earshot of the prison bars as one last Lieutenant joins us. The question is: What to do with the prisoners? One officer believes we should leave them on this ship because they're not our responsibility. This is met with disagreement. Another proposes we release them, as well as give them control of the captured zeppelin to make their way as they choose. As ideal as this proposal is, a Lieutenant points out that they don't have adequately trained personnel among them.

That's about when I pipe up, "Why can't we take them on board with us?"

This draws looks of surprise from some of the superior officers. I brush it off. If someone summons me for my opinion, I'm going to give it.

A sandy-haired Staff Sergeant cautions me. "Corporal, we don't have enough provisions to make it to Shipwreck if we take them on."

The utilitarian inside of me rises to the surface. "Is that using old math?"

The circle seems confused.

Deciding to press my luck, I continue. "All of you have been summoned here because you're the highest in command onboard this ship. " I take a second to try phrasing my thought as politely as possible. "In reality, we're the highest ranking officers still alive aboard this zeppelin. I wouldn't be here if we had our full complement."

A few of the officers' eyes narrow as they follow my reasoning.

I take a deep breath. "What I mean to say is, that for every officer who was killed, how many more marines also died who no longer require food?"

An old Captain with grey sideburns regards me coolly. "You savage the memory of those fallen soldiers."

"How?" I ask, keeping my voice level.

The grey Captain draws himself up to his full height. "Even if we do have food that no longer needs to be eaten by our dead troops, do you really intend us to assign some louts to live with the grieving families who have been left behind?"

I hadn't thought of that.

Licking my lips, I offer. "While I was still airborne, I saw the *Artemis* take several hits to the Living Quarters and other vital areas." I need to choose my words even more carefully for this. "The families who were living in those areas most likely did not survive. The death toll could easily be three figures. We could repair those quarters for our new guests quickly enough with all of the materials we've found aboard this ship."

There's an uproar.

"You unfeeling bastard!"

"You love strangers more than your own people?"

"Calculating slag!"

I let it run its course. Once they quiet down, the grey Captain steps up. "Corporal, you obviously know nothing of the pain of the families affected by the battle today."

Something inside snaps.

Wheeling around, I go nose to nose with the Captain. "Don't you fucking tell ME about the pain of families affected by combat!"

Caught off guard, the Captain takes a step back.

I cover the distance. "Have you ever had a shell burst open your whole life, right in front of you?" I growl. Holding up my hands, I splay my fingers so everyone can see the scars etched across them.

"Have you ever tried pushing off cinders hot enough to melt your flesh, while choking on the smell of your own hair burning?" I ask.

The Captain says nothing.

"I didn't think so!" I shout. Seething, I realize this outburst doesn't serve as a good representation of me within the leadership.

"The Corporal's right."

Captain Dixon's sure voice rises up over the group. Stepping to the center, her violet eye passes over the circle. "If we don't take these people in, what separates us from the rest of the barbarians trawling these airways?"

Her endorsement not only shocks me, but helps ground my senses again. I'd forgotten she was here.

"We must make every effort we can to assimilate this population with the *Artemis's* passengers," she continues. "There comes a time when we must make sacrifices for strangers, and this is one of those times."

A brunette Lieutenant begins protesting about the availability of food again.

Captain Dixon whirls around, fixing her with a glare. "We will ration our food if we have to. It's not like we haven't done it before."

She walks up to the Lieutenant, leaning in and cocking her head to the side. "And if there are those who haven't done it before, then it's about fucking time." Dixon's eyes narrow as she growls. "You could lose some weight anyways, Lieutenant."

Drawing herself back up, Captain Dixon turns around to face the rest of the circle. "Is it agreed?" she asks.

No one says a word.

The grey Captain raises his hand, stepping back into the circle. "If we were to take on the task of assimilating this population with our own, who would be in charge of that operation?" he asks.

I take a deep breath. The words stick in my throat.

"I . . . I will take charge of assimilating the new population."

The words tumble from my mouth before I can rationalize them.

The Captain nods before gesturing. "Then it is agreed."

The other officers also mutter, one by one, "It's agreed."

The pit in my stomach threatens to envelop everything else. After robotically contributing my own agreement, I turn to the two hundred or so hungry people behind me, gazing at them.. They're my flock now . . . for better or worse. I can't even keep my own quarters clean, and I volunteered for this?

Dixon sends word for the green flare to be fired. As the

runner sprints up the stairs, one of the officers warns the prisoners to stand back before she shoots off the lock. They shuffle backwards, watching her with hungry eyes as she shatters the lock with a few shots of her pistol. The door grinds open, but the prisoners make no movement.

Captain Dixon nudges me. "You're up kid."

I swallow hard, slowly making my way to the center of the cargo bay. The stench is unbearable. Large piles of refuse dot the deck. The bodies of those who expired are tucked away in the corners. These people have seen a lot.

A little girl stares at me with hollow eyes. I have to give them something to hold on to.

I clear my throat. "Hello. My name is Corporal Basmon of the USS *Artemis*."

No response.

Turning to the other side of the cargo bay, I continue. "From what I can tell, you've received horrible treatment at the hands of The Legion. I would like to extend *Artemis* citizenship to you for a chance at living a better life."

I look to Dixon for guidance, but find a stone wall. Wetting my lips, I push on. "If you choose to accept this citizenship, it will be my responsibility to find you appropriate quarters and rations. You may depart the ship once we've docked in the Northern Territory. You may make your life from there, or you may continue to stay on with us, if you so choose."

A silence reverberates off the dark walls of the cargo bay.

Smoothing down a ruffle on the arm of my uniform, I say softly, "Would you please follow the officers up those steps so we can get you some food and water? Please signal to us if you cannot walk, or if someone in your party cannot move under their own power."

The promise of sustenance stirs the prisoners from their positions. Slowly, one by one, they leave their spots, making their way towards the door.

Some prisoners begin signaling that they're having trouble moving. One such signal catches my eye. A glint of metal catches the faint light of the cargo bay as I make my way to the huddled group.

A young woman hunches over a noticeably pregnant prisoner. Standing over her is a severe looking man. He stands about six and a half feet tall, with a sharp, crooked nose reminiscent of the beak of an eagle. He also has the glare to match.

The only thing tearing my attention away from the intimidating force to the left of the pregnant prisoner is the woman tending to her. Her features appear washed out, as though she once was vibrant, but the ebb and flow of stress slowly ground her down. That's not to say she isn't striking, but she's hiding something underneath her haggard visage.

She's cut off the sleeves of her shirt to make cooling strips for the pregnant woman. Following her placement of the cloths, I see her most prominent feature extending from the fingers of her right hand up to the edge of her shoulder. At first it appears to be an elaborate tattoo, but I soon realize that it's three dimensional in nature. There appear to be small chunks of metal embedded in her skin.

When she moves to apply more cool strips of cloth to the pregnant woman's head, I can see that the foreign objects extend to the right side of her midsection as well. The light reflected by her metallic feature is the same color as her hair - a shocking blonde. What's even more intriguing is the way she holds herself. Almost as though she's being pushed off balance, but I can't figure out what she's fighting against.

I catch myself, realizing I'm staring. Glancing at the eagle man, I sense he's been keeping a watchful eye on me the entire time.

I clear my throat again. "Excuse me ma'am, is there any way I can be of assistance in moving this woman?"

The studded woman keeps her eyes on her work. "Yes. She needs a stretcher," she replies calmly.

Nodding, I can't help but take another look at the studded woman's arm. This feature's new. The wounds are fresh.

I try once more to get her attention. "I'll get that stretcher for you right away, ma'am. May I also get you a medic to take a look at your arm?"

Satisfied with her work, she raises her eyes to meet mine for the first time. They're an azure blue that remind me of melting ice. I catch my breath as her cold look washes over me.

She takes her unstudded hand, lightly caressing her damaged arm. "You can certainly try. However, given that the last doctor who observed them said their removal would result in my hemorrhaging to death, I'm inclined to leave them in for now."

That's my cue to leave. The glaring look from her stoic companion confirms this as well. Making my way back towards the mostly disbanded Captain's circle, I search for someone to find a stretcher. All of the runners have already been dispatched, leaving me with just my two hands.

That's fine. The thick stench down here is beginning to wear on me anyways.

A refreshing gush of air blows its way past me as I reach the bulkhead, beckoning towards the setting sun. It's bizarre. The deck I see now is so different from the one I knew only hours ago. Many of the dead are gone. Supplies and people now flow freely from ship to ship over the newly assembled gangplanks. It's a shame I missed the signal flare. It's always a cathartic moment, even if I've only ever seen it from the other side. Knowing you can finally go back home. Knowing you still have a home to go back to.

Not far from the gangplanks, I find two gurney boys taking a well-deserved rest from their efforts of the day. Greasing their palms with a few dollars each, I make sure they're in tow when I head back towards the cargo bay.

Ensuring the pregnant woman is properly taken care of, I thank the boys for their service. The studded woman gathers up what little worldly possessions she has, while her bodyguard fixes me in his sights. There's something about this woman I can't figure out. Walking up to her side, I introduce myself. The giant on her left flexes the muscles in his jaw.

Slowly, I extend my hand. "Thank you for helping that woman. My name's Corporal Sage Basmon."

She looks at my open palm. "I know, you already gave a speech introducing yourself. Remember?"

I blush, but don't retrieve my hand.

Seeing my determination she sighs, reluctantly taking it. "My name is Sabine."

Stealing a quick look at her guard, I reply, "It's a pleasure to meet you. We could use more people with your kind of heart on board."

Sabine gingerly removes her hand. "I'm sure you could."

She goes back to her packing. That's enough conversation for now.

Turning to her bodyguard, I extend my hand again. "Corporal Basmon."

I muster up the will to look him in the eye as my hand hovers in mid-air. No shake is forthcoming, so I let it fall to my side. "Alright."

As I turn away, the sound of gravel fills the air.

"Talking to me is a privilege."

Slowly, I turn back. "Well in that case, I'm glad I could earn it," I say with a hint of a grin.

Leaving his gaze, I catch the sides of his face twisting into a grimace. This man's not used to being toyed with. Regardless, I think I catch the beginnings of a smile on the side of Sabine's face as I walk by.

Making my way back out into the fresh air, I see the light of the day is nearly gone. Its last rays pour over the cloud bank in a way that would have made Michelangelo proud. It's the kind of sight that stops you where you're standing so you can breathe in, just because you know you still can. It's brief though. I get carried along with the tide of people making their way back over the gangplank.

I've always been impressed with the sturdiness of the gangplanks. You'd think something that's been inserted between two goliath airships would be more unstable. I suppose there's still the chance of a rogue gust blowing the two ships apart, killing all of us in the process, but there's still no better way to transfer people and supplies.

Grasping the railing of the fore plank, I scan the banisters to see if anyone I know is waiting for me. Most people have already reunited with their loved ones, so the crowd's begun thinning out enough to see individual faces.

No Cass. At least, nowhere that I can see. I was expecting too much. With the number of casualties I saw today, Cass will probably be elbow deep in organs for the next week. It doesn't exactly set the stage for a fairy-tale romance. So much for my tear-streaked, throw-myself-into-your-waiting-arms arrival. It would've been perfect with the sunset too.

C'est la vie.

Setting foot back on the Outer Rim, I do catch a few friendly faces, mostly acquaintances and friends of acquaintances; no one I really know that well. That doesn't stop us from flashing our index and middle fingers out in the shape of a 'V' to celebrate our victory. People see my uniform and grab my arm, shaking my hand. One elderly woman takes me by the face and delicately kisses my forehead before whispering something in Portuguese that I can't understand.

Making my way through the crowd, I spot my group of hunched ex-prisoners. They've all mostly collected just outside the Living Quarters bulkhead, waiting for some direction. Taking a deep breath, I remind myself how important it is to keep my promises. Drawing myself up to my full height, I try exhibiting power I know I don't have; these people need someone to rely on, and I'll be damned if I let them down.

I walk to the middle of the group. Some of them seem to recognize me. Feverish murmurs carry on the wind. I call out in the strongest voice I can. I tell them that I'm thankful for their ability to be calm. I inform them of what I am going to do and how I'm going to do it. I talk about how, initially, there may not be enough food for everyone, but how I'll find a way to make it work. I say how I might not be able to find housing for each family, but I'll find some place safe to put them. Their hollow eyes follow me as I pace nervously back and forth in between them, not quite sure whether I can be trusted. Even so, they know there's no alternative.

And there I leave them, to run to the housing supervisor, the quartermaster, the head doctor, and all of the other positions of power who hold the well-being of these people in their hands. Most are willing to assist me to the fullest extent. Many of them have faced similar challenges where one act of kindness saved them from a sure demise. Now they're willing to return the favor. For those who are less generous, I describe the children's bloated stomachs, the austere sunken eyes of their parents, the shriveled bodies we found. One by one, they all give in. . . at least to most of my requests.

By the time I find everyone a place to stay and enough food until morning, it's the dead of night. I wander the Outer Rim like a ghost. It's gotten to the point where I'm so exhausted I don't even feel drowsy, just . . . old. No one walks the deck except for the watchmen. Their dark coats glisten with the condensation of the fog that's begun to roll in. It's so thick, visibility's dropped to about hundred feet.

My brain functions on auto pilot. Winding my way up and down steps and walkways, I miraculously find myself at my cabin. I fumble with my keyring, trying every key except for the correct one. When I finally open the door, it swings wide to reveal two empty cots. I stop. The panic rises up just underneath my ribs.

I take slow, deliberate steps over to Olan's empty bunk and peer in.

"Hi Uncle Sage . . . " a sleepy shadow whispers to me.

A sigh of relief quells a fraction of my stress. "Hi little lady. Where's your Dad?"

Part of me doesn't want to hear the answer.

Aoife takes her small hands and rubs her eyes to better take part in the conversation. "He said he would come back later."

I bite my lip. "Weren't you scared today, hon?"

Aoife shakes her head, not unlike her father. "Nuh-uh, the neighbors always let me pet their dog when the sounds happen." She lowers her voice, whispering conspiratorially. "I don't think he likes the loud noises very much either."

I pause, not quite sure what to do next. Olan and I were separated after we stormed the bunker. I haven't seen him all day. The image of his body on one of the stretchers flashes in my mind, but I shake my head to eradicate it. Fighting the haze, I come up with a new plan.

"Hey Sweetheart, we're going to go find your Dad, ok?" I offer quietly.

Aoife's eyes light up, nodding enthusiastically. She holds out her hands and I take her in my arms. She's so light. Her mother's features eerily shine through in the moonlight. The only things she and her father have ever had in common are their hair and their attitudes. I'm holding the bravest five year-old I know.

As I carry her back out onto the deck, Aoife buries her head into my chest and curls up. Neither of us make a sound as I amble towards the Medical Ward, hoping that is a better bet than the Morgue. Looking out into the cloudy blackness, I just hope for this one gamble to be true.

The lights of the Medical Ward break through the darkness. I can already hear the moans of the wounded, and we haven't even opened the door yet. A quick look down at Aoife reveals she's fast asleep. I hope she stays that way. Upon opening the door, I see row after row of wounded bodies stretching to the starboard side of the ship. Walking down the corridor, I recognize some of their faces. I'm glad they've made it this far. From a distance, I glimpse one of the nurses. My heart leaps at the silhouette. It has to be Cass.

As we make our way towards her, I notice her arms are caked up to her elbows in other peoples' gore. She doesn't seem to notice as she continues applying bandages to the marine beside her. I draw up next to the wall on her right and just watch as I hold Aoife. Cass's hands are so delicate as they dance across the marine's body. Applying ointments here, ripping tape to secure gauze there. In that moment I let my guarded heart slip further than I should. How can someone with that much compassion be alone in the world the same as me?

She doesn't notice us until after she applies the very last bandage and straightens up to take a deep breath. Surprise runs across her face. She's compartmentalized her mind to address only the necessities of saving the sick, and I've caught her out of that element.

Her beautiful smile finds her face. "Hi Baz."

A warmth I've never quite felt before flushes over my frayed nerves. "Hi Cass."

She looks as if she wants to reach out and touch my shoulder to see if everything's still ok, but her blood-soaked hands and the small child in my arms present an insurmountable barrier.

Folding her ruby red hands behind her back, she leans over to address Aoife. "Hello little one," she whispers.

Aoife's eyes flutter open just long enough to respond. "Hello."

Cass turns back to me with questions in her eyes.

"Cass, please tell me Olan's here," I say breathlessly.

Cass's eyes don't spark any recognition. Worry scrapes through my insides.

She shakes her head slightly before answering. "I'd have to check our registry. We have hundreds of people here tonight."

I look over all of the other beds and can't find him.

"Cass you know he's a hard guy to miss." I plead.

There's the spark I'm looking for.

Cass's eyes dial up the giant's location. "You're right, it looks like he made it in after my shift started," she nods, motioning for me to follow her.

The three of us journey to the far side of the ward, reaching the less critical cases. Thankfully, they're also quieter. I glance down at Aoife; she seems entirely undisturbed by the cries of the men and women around her. This is the only world she's known. The sounds of death and destruction meld together to create some perverse lullaby. Shaking my head, I try thinking of less depressing things. How is she still such a sweet kid?

Cass's voice breaks through. "Here he his." she says flipping over a page. "Thank God, it looks like he's in a stable condition."

Looking up, I find a wrapped and bandaged Olan on his back in a cot. At the sight of all these bandages, I'm suddenly not sure bringing Aoife here was a good idea. A nurse working nearby seems to notice my struggle.

"They found him collapsed a few dozen feet back from the front line," she calls over to us. "Severe dehydration. Not to mention he'd been shot twice and had already lost a lot of blood."

I sigh. Oh Olan. Spending all his time making sure I recover, never once taking a drink of that precious water for himself. He was so caught up in the heat of battle he didn't even realize he was losing pint after pint of blood.

"Is it ok if I leave the child with him?" I ask.

The nurse nods furtively and goes back to her work.

At a second glance, I realize where I know her from. She's Janna Dixon's daughter, Fiona. Her quiet, calm demeanor is a striking difference from her mother's. I can't even imagine growing up in that household.

We approach Olan's cot. His eyes flutter open as he hears our footsteps. They flick down to Aoife, filling up with tears. He does nothing but hold out his arms. I don't know if injury or emotion prevents him from talking, but I kneel down and give him his daughter without a word.

"Daddy!" she cries out, finally recognizing him underneath all the gauze.

My throat clenches. It's embarrassing. I want to see be strong in front of Cass, but her eyes are glistening too.

Olan's voice breaks as he brings her close. "Hello Love."

Aoife's little giggle escapes as her father pulls her tight. "You look like a mummy," she observes.

Olan's smile carefully curls across his torn face. "That I do Love, that I do. I didn't mean to scare you."

Aoife looks up at her father. "You didn't, I just missed you a lot when you were gone," she says.

"I missed you too Love," Olan says, his voice carrying all the weight of the world.

He thanks me silently as his eyelids get heavier. I just smile back. Father and daughter eventually fall into a peaceful sleep together.

I turn away, taking this chance to wipe my eyes and run my hand through my hair. Looking up, I catch Cass watching me. She doesn't look away when our eyes meet.

She comes closer. "That was a really sweet thing you did."

"He's my cabin-mate, what else was I going to do?" I ask, looking at my feet.

She puts her hand under my chin, lifting my eyes back up to meet hers. "I know a lot of men who would've chosen sleep over her." She lets her head tilt to the side. "But not you."

I say nothing. Instead, I just smile, letting her appreciation sink in. She keeps her hand under my chin, pulling in close and planting a soft kiss on my lips. A warm sensation flows out to my fingertips. I let the feeling linger as she draws away.

"Come with me," she says, taking my hand in hers.

Exhaustion settles in as she leads me to the corner of the ward used for women giving birth. The cots are a cloudy white and ringed with special equipment. It's a quieter part of the ward and the pillow on the nearest cot calls to me. The sensation of Cass's lips on mine still lingers as she lies me down. I look up, quietly thanking her as she pushes back a lock of my hair.

She glances back at the rest of the ward. "I still have to finish my shift, but I promise you'll be safe here. Get some sleep Sage, you deserve it," she says. Her finger tips trail across my cheek as she leaves, assuredly casting some sort of spell. Peace spreads over me gently.

But it doesn't last long. I begin taking notice of the injuries of the day. They sting and throb. I adjust my body again and again, trying to find some position that doesn't feel as though I am lying on a drawer of knives. After an hour of rearranging myself, I'm almost certain I'll need a pain killer to even bear it anymore. Then I hear her. It's just a quiet tune, but it's loud enough to hold my attention. I don't recognize it, but its effect is immediate. Just as Aoife received her lullaby, it seems that I'm getting mine.

The tune gets louder as she makes her way towards me. A weight depresses the side of the bed behind me. Cass climbs in, wrapping her arms around my waist. She pulls me close. Her head only comes up to the back of my neck, but her body contours itself to mine.

Looking down, I see the blood still crusted underneath her nails as she holds me to her. It doesn't matter; some things are just worth the price. Her warm breath flows over the back of my neck at an even pace, inducing wave after wave of goose bumps. The warmth of her body quells whatever pain I have, until finally my eyelids can no longer stay open.

It looks like everyone has someone to cuddle with tonight.

9

Rays of light pierce my eyelids until I can't ignore them any longer. Turning over, I find not Cass, but a very composed Admiral Khan.

Startled, I draw back.

The Admiral greets me, ignoring my surprise. "Congratulations Mr. Basmon. I was unaware that you were expecting."

I wrack my brain for an answer, then I remember where I am.

"I assure you Admiral Khan, if I were, you'd be the first to know," I respond, kicking my legs out of the bed.

A smile appears underneath his salt-and-pepper goatee. "Well that is good to hear," he says. "If you had been, I would have felt very guilty about sending you into battle in such a condition."

His grey eyes follow me as I collect the sheets to remake the bed. "It has happened you know: pregnant women charging into battle. The kind of valor that stems from the protection of a mother's child, unborn or otherwise, cannot be replicated."

I say nothing, instead focusing on the enigma that is the fitted sheet.

The Admiral continues. "Speaking of valor, I heard you had a very eventful day yesterday."

I bring myself to look into his wintery eyes. "Well Admiral, if getting myself shot down and falling over a bunker door is considered eventful, then I'd say that your reports are correct."

The Admiral's face contorts with impatience. "What my reports told me, is that you had no less than two confirmed kills. In addition, you were allegedly the first soldier to storm a bunker that had already claimed the lives of a third of your platoon."

"Well, when you say it like that . . . " I falter.

The Admiral doesn't let me finish. He pulls a box out of his pocket, setting it in front of me.

I take it in my hands, glancing at him warily.

"Open it," he gestures. It's an order.

Flipping open the clasp, the box opens to reveal Sergeant's chevrons. I stare, unable to speak.

"Congratulations Sergeant Basmon, you are performing even better than I had hoped." the Admiral says with a smile large enough to draw up the corners of his goatee.

Performing . . . There's something about that word I don't like.

I take my eyes away from the chevrons and look up, meeting the Admiral's. "Mr. Khan, this makes no sense." I manage.

His iron will bristles underneath his words. "It makes perfect sense Sergeant. You're starting to gain a following. People are beginning to take notice of your actions. Everything you've done so far has been in the name of the *Artemis*. For the community that lives here. If people can see that acts of valor are rewarded, they will continue to band together and perform their own."

As long as I'm in the spotlight, Sanjar must maintain control.

I look down into the box again. "Thank you Admiral."

He waves away my thanks. "Quick, quick, put them on. If I stay here any longer, you'll be late for your Unveiling."

My head snaps to the analogue clock above the cots. 11:17. The Unveiling starts at noon. I have enough time to get myself cleaned up and into a new uniform. I snap the box shut, stumbling to my feet.

"I hope you have a good day Admiral," I offer.

He stands with me. "You as well Sergeant," he replies.

I make it to the threshold of the Birthing Ward, then stop. "Ah . . . Admiral. You didn't happen to see Flight Nurse Dawson on your way in, did you?" I ask, looking back.

The Admiral raises his eyebrows. "No, I did not. I can only assume that she is carrying out her regular duties, just as you should be."

Point taken. Thanking the Admiral again, I sprint through the ward back to the Living Quarters.

Somehow, I accomplish the impossible and show up to the Cellar in a freshly pressed uniform with four minutes to spare. Gold Squadron has pulled up landing equipment to form a circle at the center of the hangar. Members of the Red Swans glance over in disgust as they tend to their aircraft in the corner; I can't really blame them. While Gold Squadron gets drunk, they're charged with the defense of the *Artemis*. C'est la guerre. .

I quickly find my drop wing, or what's left of them anyways. Yeti stands awkwardly on the outside of the circle nursing his beer while Wilhelm tries engaging him in conversation. One other freckled woman with her arm in a sling stands next to them, gazing out over the docked craft.

Out of our wing of seven, Volley's-Two, Three, and Five were killed outright in the fighting. Our freckled friend Rita Samuels, aka Volley Seven, had her wing blown off over land. Luckily, she bailed out and a Helios was able to locate and retrieve her. I'll have to get the full story from Chet on that. Yeti was the only pilot other than our wing leader, Wilhelm Petrowski, who was able to bring back his plane intact. I can hear the Admiral tallying the losses now.

"It could have been worse," Wilhelm offers. "I've seen entire wings get decimated." He sips his drink, his eyes going somewhere else. "Everyone fought their hardest. Four out of seven ain't bad."

He swallows. "Right?" he asks no one in particular.

No one answers.

Yeti claps him on the shoulder. "You got us back Willy, and I'm grateful for it."

I look down at my drink. "I swear I'll be in my head enough to actually listen to your directions next time, Captain," I promise.

Before Wilhelm can respond, Rita asks, "We're allowed to view our planes now, correct?"

Wilhelm closes his mouth again before nodding. "That's correct. Please enjoy the drinks and food. It's a small token of our gratitude, but I do want to thank you for volunteering," he eyes Rita's arm, "and for your sacrifice."

With Volley-Five in need of replacing, all three of our planes are lined up side-by-side in the hangar; large maintenance tarps have been thrown over each one. My plane was the last of the *Artemis's* inventory. From what I can see of the fuselage's protruding snout, it looks like it too. As long as it flies and shoots, I'll make it work.

Rita splits off to inspect her replacement as well.

"What are we waiting for?" Yeti asks.

"Ah, is there some sort of ceremony or something?" I ask.

Yeti sweeps his arm around the gathering. Some of the younger, drunk pilots vomit out of the open hangar bay. "This is it!" he says cheerfully.

"Alright," I concede, "let's see what this thing looks like."

Grabbing the sides of my tarp, we both pull it down in one fluid motion. The light grey paint reveals an image on the fin of a sword slicing upwards, and the word *SABRE* stenciled on the base of the tail and engine. It's a little sparse, but enough of a base for me work with.

"Why'd they spell it the British way?" I ask.

"They probably saw you were a gringo and figured it would be a safe bet," Yeti retorts. "Either way, it looks awesome man!"

I nod, lips downturned. Can't argue with that.

"What an absolute shit emblem," The Voice says.

"Shut up," I growl.

"What?" Yeti asks.

"Nothing." I try to cover.

Arching an eyebrow my way, Yeti turns his attention to his plane. "Aw man, I can't even wait to see what they chose for me," Yeti says, rubbing his hands together excitedly.

Ducking under the tail of my Jackal, I grab hold of Ettero's tarp. Together we heave it off the fuselage.

An image greets us of a crudely drawn snowman covered in hair.

"What the fuck is this?" Ettero cries.

I clap a hand over my mouth, trying to stifle a laugh. "Take a look at the tail for a clue."

Ettero's eyes flit to the tail's base; he finds the letters *YETI* stenciled in yellow.

"It's like they didn't even try!" Yeti shouts.

I double over, my abs starting to hurt from the laughter.

"Ah, put a little paint to it and you'll be grand," Diz's voice says behind us.

"Miss McAlister," I say, straightening myself.

She walks under Yeti's fuselage, giving me a hug. "Good to see you lads."

"You as well," I say to Diz. "It'll be alright Yeti; we'll all pitch in with a can of paint and that decal will look properly ferocious."

Yeti tsks, shaking his head. "Hey Diz, are those some new duds?" he asks.

I realize she's wearing the same color as our deckhands, but a new designation glints on her left breast pocket.

"Crew Chief, huh?" I ask. "Did they finally accept that you were the one who came up with the idea of using the generator as a shield?"

Dizzy exhales. "Well, seems so. Then again, it just so happens there was a vacancy in the position."

"What happened to Harker?" I frown.

"Crew Chief Harker was organizing things here while we were down on the Legion zeppelin's deck. Apparently, one of the Legion fighters strafed into the bay and a ricochet caught old Hark. Didn't kill him outright, but he died of his wounds sometime last night."

I glance at her fiery red hair tied up in a braid. "Diz, the deck's a pretty dangerous place. You sure you're up for this?"

She shoots me a withering look. "Saved your ass didn't I?"

I nod, tilting my head. "True enough."

"Plus, I wager your man'll be on a proper warpath from here on out," Diz mentions.

"What are you talking about?" I ask.

Diz moves closer. "Word on the Bridge is that while we were fighting those Legion bastards, one of the Admiral's old war buddies got proper buggered: Cedric Vitortov."

"Vitortov? Like, Vitortov of Iluster Arsenal?"

Diz nods.

"Who killed him?" I ask.

"They don't know," Diz says. "The outfit came in the night and was gone before the morning. Took most of the armory with them."

I swallow. "You're right, that will raise hell. I'm pretty sure most of the guns we carry are Arsenal made."

"Were Arsenal made," Yeti offers.

I grimace, looking up. "What do you mean they 'took most of the armory with them'?"

"I mean, that's all I know. The main manufactory's almost all gone. Even stranger, it wasn't explosives. No score marks . . . just concrete crumpled like it was nothing."

Yeti leans in, "Vitortov's headquarters wasn't that far from here, was it?"

"Maybe two hundred miles south or so. Stationed in Split Rock. Doubt it'll be enough to make that Old Man turnaround though," Diz says quietly.

I shake my head. "Well. . . whatever path the Admiral chooses, here's to friends, both alive and dead. May we stay the former."

A clink of glasses is all that's needed to seal that conversation.

The day wears on. I opt to stop drinking, remembering I have about two hundred men, women, and children to look after. The last thing they need is a drunken caretaker. With our day cleared for celebration, I take the chance to tour the cabins where I've deposited my people.

Most of the groups are stable. Requests for more food is common. The brunt of the medical situations have either been resolved, or are being tended to. I make my way through the influx of marines on crutches. Some of them are making a quick recovery. I stop the ones who aren't, thanking them for their service. I'm hardly restoring their ability to walk, but it may help them try to rationalize the price.

The crowd thins as I take my normal shortcut. Eventually, the only sound that remains is that of my footfalls reverberating off the walls. It feels good to be alone after so much stimulation.

A door creaks open. Dark eyes peer out, checking for anyone else in earshot. Most citizens are out on the deck enjoying their right to a post-battle promenade.

A gravelly voice calls out from behind the shadow. "Sage Basmon! Your presence is requested. Be discreet."

I stop, staring at the shadow. "Apparently. Who are you?" I ask cautiously.

The shadow steps out from its spider hole. Rays of light stripe the stark face of Sabine's guardian.

Why? This isn't the location where I housed them. I'm also

not quite sure how they got access to the room. Curiosity and an alcohol-induced loss of inhibition spur me on anyway. Taking off my flight cap, I enter the small room.

The door slams shut, plunging me into complete blackness. I freeze. Before I make a move, a match strikes, and the crescent of Sabine's face illuminates behind it.

"Are you afraid of the darkness?" she asks.

If I'm honest with myself, there's a part of me that still is, to some extent. Sometimes I let my mind wander to hidden horrors, creeping behind a door or hiding in the shadows, but of course, I can't admit this, especially if I'm supposed to be a soldier.

"No," I answer, trying to keep my voice even.

Sabine looks at me inquisitively. "Well you should be," she responds.

Hairs prickle up the back of my neck.

"There are in fact, hidden horrors that lurk in dark corners. They are things that go 'bump' in the night. They may not be in your bedroom . . . yet. But give them enough time and freedom to do as they please, and they will find residence there soon enough," she says quietly.

I say nothing, keeping my eyes on her. Where's her manservant? The match flickers, nearly dead due to the high altitude. Pitch black lunges to reclaim the room.

"There are ways to keep the monsters at bay though," Sabine says, flicking her chilly grey eyes up to mine, "perhaps even banish them entirely."

"How?" I indulge her.

She smiles. I can tell she enjoys being able to pace the conversation. Sabine waves the match just enough to give the flame sufficient oxygen to flare up again.

"You find sources with more fire than you can muster on your own," she responds, lighting the corner lamp behind her. "You ally with them. Find a way to make them realize that this darkness must be repelled."

She relights the match with the flame she's just created, moving over to the other side of the room to light a second lamp.

Her platinum hair falls over her shoulder as the second lamp ignites. "You use that momentum from your first ally to make way for others."

She continues lighting each lamp until all corners of the room glow. "Pretty soon, what appeared like an impossible task seems almost manageable," she says.

She walks up to me until out noses nearly touch.

"And by then, the monsters have fewer places to hide," she states quietly.

I bite my lip. My eyes dart to her manservant, who's appeared with the lighting of the last lamp.

"What kind of monsters are we talking about here?" I probe.

A shock blond lock falls across her eyes as she shifts her head. "I'm willing to wager you've been wondering how I received my wounds?" She gestures to the metal embedded in her arm.

I shrug. "It's crossed my mind once or twice."

Pausing as if to debate whether or not to continue, Sabine makes a decision. Her eyes sharpen again. "Would you like to hear a story?" she asks.

I flinch as a wooden chair drags across the ground behind me. Her manservant's secured me a seat. His feral eyes bore into mine.

"Well, it doesn't look like I have much of a choice," I concede.

"Good," she responds, clearing throat. "What you have to understand about my people's history, the Tesarik Clan, is that we were a strong seafaring tribe. We were one of the few left capable of fielding a navy that wouldn't meet its fate on the ridges jutting from the First World, or any of the sunken cities beneath. The last of the Carriers. As natural sea captains and fishermen since the fall of the First World, we were eventually able to adapt to the new currents and topography. We flourished on the sea bed as the rest of the world fled to the skies."

I chafe at the comment. I don't like the inference that I was born here out of desperation.

Sabine brings her voice above a whisper, competing with the wind filtering through from the hall. "With our capital ship, we had access to alcoves and landmasses where planes and zeppelins could never dream of landing. We struck out on smaller skiffs, scavenging all of the seaborne nooks and crannies that airborne companies had never touched. One day, we made a discovery . . . and it changed everything."

She takes my silence as a cue to continue. "What we found, was an ore deposit the Tesariks had never seen before . . . Once treated, the material becomes as light as pumice, but stronger than steel."

"That sounds highly unlikely," I cut in.

"That's what our elders said at first," she counters. "What we came to find, was not only does the ore possess those qualities, but it's also magnetized towards other elements of metal. Its properties are similar to an exceptionally tough, naturally occurring Neodymium Iron Boron, but we coined the term 'Neo Magnetite' for the lay person."

I put up a hand, stopping her. "Wait, Magnetite is already a known metal. It doesn't possess any of those qualities, other than being slightly magnetic."

It's Sabine's turn to raise her eyebrows. "I didn't mark you for much of a scholar."

Ignoring the insult, I lean back into the conversation. "There's not much else to do as an orphan suspended at ten thousand feet."

She mulls this over. "Understood. That's precisely the reason why I made the distinction of 'Neo' Magnetite. It's the first time it's ever been recorded occurring naturally on Earth. Every other time it's existed, it was man-made in labs."

She gestures around the room. "As you well know, there are very few labs still in existence today. Our engineers postulated that the sheer force of the sea caused veins of this ore to churn up to the surface for the first time since the Drowning."

The grey pieces of metal embedded in her arm flicker up at me. She holds the arm at such an odd angle. The whole side of her body looks fatigued.

"That's all well and good, but how did that discovery change anything?" I ask.

Sabine's features pinch in thought. "That was only the beginning. If our tribe has a second love behind sailing, it's engineering. I took part in a large-scale project to research the creation of electromagnetic cores meant to power our ships using this newfound metal.

"You're an engineer?" I ask.

"Was," Sabine answers. A tinge of pain rises in her voice that

I haven't detected before.

Sabine's eyes are somewhere else. "Our leader grew very interested in this research, and took it on as his own."

"Were you able to get them to work?" I ask.

She takes a deep breath. "The smaller models were unsuccessful, initially. The real. . . breakthrough occurred when our leader was able to complete the first working core. He and his team super-sized the schematics and addressed the imbalances that were causing us to fail."

"So again, why is that life-changing?" I ask, sitting back.

Sabine's eyes flit back up to mine, "It's life-changing because this new core allows a magnetite structure to form around it however you wish to design it. With it, our leader sought to make something that would withstand the test of time."

A silence rests between us. There's more.

"So what'd he build?" I ask.

Her chin falls almost to her chest. "A fortress."

"And where exactly is this fortress located? I ask, picking at my teeth with a thumb.

She shakes her head. "I don't know."

I sit back up slowly, taking my hand away from my mouth. "What do you mean you don't know? I thought this thing was supposed to be a monument to your leader's power, or something," I say.

The skin around her cheekbones tightens. "I don't know where it is, because it flies."

"What?" I shake my head.

She stands up. "The Neo Magnetite is so light, that with enough power from the engines, the fortress can suspend itself in the air," she explains.

I lean back in my chair, massaging my temples. "So we have a rogue, impenetrable, flying fortress, cruising around who knows where?" My alcohol sheen burns away as I debate leaving the room and the delusional people in it. "What does this stuff even look like?" I ask.

Sabine holds her out embedded arm. "You're looking at it."

I take in the gruesome pock marks and healed-over magnetite protruding from her flesh. "And what's this, some sort of art project?" I goad.

I flinch as Sabine's manservant jolts up, knocking his chair to the ground.

Sabine turns around. "Calm down Raltz. We need him," Sabine whispers evenly.

Smoothing her shirt against her sides, she turns back to face me. "Our leader was once a great man. But when he lost his wife to a bandit raid, he buried himself in religious texts," she continues, placing a hand on the back of her neck. "Some of us were worried about his grief affecting his leadership. How he dealt with our armada. But we soon discovered his grief was the last thing we needed to fear. He renamed the fortress, *The Ark*." She swallows. "I feared his for stability, and his intentions, so I fled. Both Raltz and I fled."

She looks back at her large friend. "Raltz did his best to protect me, but as we escaped *The Ark*, an explosion sent shrapnel from the Neo Magnetite in all directions. Unfortunately, one of those directions was mine."

Sabine holds up her metallic arm to the lamplight, allowing it to glow with a new vigor.

As she lowers it, her eyes fix on mine. "In addition to its magnetic properties, Neodymium Magnetite's toughness makes it incredibly resistant to physical trauma."

My eyes widen, putting it all together. "It makes an excellent armor."

She nods. "That's correct. Our former leader now pilots one of the most formidable war machines ever created."

Images flash in my mind: pictures in the books I read as a child. Rupturing mushroom clouds flicker to the surface. Mass graves. Our ancestors used to level one another with the flick of a switch. No wonder this is the world we inherited.

"So how do you propose we stop this thing?" I ask.

The enigma returns to Sabine's eyes. "I'm still formulating a specific plan, but as of right now it appears that brute force is our best option," she says.

I lower my voice. "Brute force? You think brute force is the best way to tackle a structure that's built for warfare?"

She walks along the side of the table, running her finger across the top. "Yes, and it will be its downfall."

I sit back down. "So even if this man pilots this great war

machine, he hasn't used it yet, right?"

Sabine takes her finger from the table, tapping it back down decisively. "Incorrect. He has the blood of an entire village on his hands," she says, digging her nails into the wood. "At the very least."

"Did he just gun them down? What happened?" I ask.

"It was worse than that," Sabine replies. "He buried them in their own soil."

An odd answer. Thinking of all of the possible ways this could be accomplished, I ask the simple question, "How?"

Sabine's eyes flick up to Raltz. He gives her a slow nod before she continues. "Our former leader, Garon Tesarik, discovered a way to harness the power of the core he created. Before he led us, he was one of our top engineers, always tinkering with things. He was responsible for the hull integrity for a large portion of our fleet."

She draws up next to me. "Later on, as he became infatuated with *The Ark* and its capabilities, Garon's thirst for the naturally occurring Neodymium expanded beyond the vein we had discovered. It became obvious that the Core could be used to interact with the magnetite, manipulating its form. One of the other top engineers had a revolutionary idea. By shutting off all other auxiliary power outlets except those that kept the Ark airborne, one could concentrate the raw magnetic power of the Core in any direction they chose."

"So instead of just using the Core to pull exposed Neo Magnetite up to *The Ark*, it could be augmented to rip the stuff straight from the ground," I say, meeting her eyes.

Sabine's severe visage breaks ever so slightly. "You know, you really are smarter than you appear."

"Thanks," I answer curtly.

She tilts her head to the side. "Since you're keeping up so well, I'll give you another question to answer."

I pull myself forward, resting my elbows on my knees. "Shoot."

"Where are most precious metals located above sea level?" she asks thoughtfully.

I make the realization. "The mountains . . ."

"Correct," she says. "And where have most settlements been established Post-Drowning?"

The blood leaves my face. "The mountains."

Confident I understand, she returns to her stern manner.

"Correct."

Her eyes take her far away from this place. "We stopped above a small coastal village perched on top of a bluff. I thought we were there to trade with the locals. It turns out we wanted much more," she says.

Her eyes clear, turning back to me. "Before I knew what was happening, the Core pulsed. The ship quaked underneath my feet as all of the ship's power redirected toward this little town."

She falls silent.

"Garon got what he wanted. I witnessed the shards of Neo Magnetite explode up from the ground, upturning houses and cutting through villagers, - burying them in furrows of earth. Hearing the impact of it all hitting our bay sickened me. We were high, but not high enough to miss the screams echoing from the village. To this day, I haven't slept a night where those cries haven't haunted my dreams. The second the first shard hit, my bodyguard and I knew we could no longer be part of it. So we ran."

I look up. "Bodyguard? Why did you need a bodyguard?" I ask.

Sabine looks away. "Because I am Sabine Tesarik. I am our leader's daughter."

"Of course you are," I respond, running my hand through my hair. Storing this new discovery in my mind, I ask one last question. "So why's your father harvesting that material? What could he possibly want so badly that he would be willing to kill hundreds in the process?"

Sabine tucks a blonde lock behind her ear. "It's hard to tell, but before I escaped, my father splintered from the Tesarik armada and created a fleet of his own called the Cascade. He spoke to me of creating a weapon that could cut through the heavens. I wasn't sure what he meant at first. But, I think I understand it now. I'll tell you more once we know we can trust you."

Unease seeps into the room.

"That's a tough proposition considering how vague you're being," I say.

Sabine nods. "This is true. Allow me to leave you with this to consider: my father plans on washing the earth clean and starting again. Perhaps that thought, and his desire to cut open the sky, are connected."

My eyes widen. "The reports. The deaths. The attacks on the

Southern settlements. You're saying your father's behind all of them?" I ask.

Sabine places her hands behind her back. "Most of Raltz and my time since our escape has been spent being held in captivity by the Legion. There weren't many radio broadcasts or papers in that brig, but if I were to guess, my father has already begun his death-march up the coast."

Quiet falls on the three of us. The creaks and groans of the ship rise from the walls.

Sabine moves in front of me. "What I'm asking, Mr. Basmon, is, will you be my first lamp?"

A coolness balls in the pit of my stomach. I clench my teeth, glancing at the bright lights in each corner of the room. Their warmth laps against my skin even from there.

We lock eyes.

"Someone has to be the first, right?"

10

The wind whips against my overcoat, delivering an unseasonable chill. I fight to get a good grip on the cold rungs as I climb the look-out ladder. A large chunk of bread and a hard-bartered jar of jam are firmly wedged into my coat pocket. I hate this climb. It's unreasonably exposed and lacking in any safety measures. It was designed as an afterthought, although now it's the only way to reach the sniper's perch nestled just below the brim of the *Artemis's* balloon.

I hold on tightly as a particularly strong gust takes its turn trying to push me off, mulling over Sabine's words. Could any of it be true? Even if it is, why would she choose me to confide in?

As I crest the landing of the perch, I spot a figure hunched under a cloak with binoculars tight to their face. I bring my legs over the top of the ladder as the first drops of rain speckle my boots.

"Hello Baz."

The voice emerges matter-of-factly from under the cloak. She makes no attempt to move from her spot, keeping her binoculars trained out into the distance.

"Hello Stenia," I reply quietly.

She says nothing as I move towards the center of the small perch.

"How'd you know it was me?" I ask.

She adjusts a dial on the side of her binoculars with one hand, otherwise remaining perfectly still. "I could hear you. Your weight's off center. You could fix that if you didn't keep bringing me food," she says.

"I thought you were a fan of our exchanges?"

She says nothing for a few moments. "What are we trading today?" she asks.

The loaf of bread sheds a few crumbs as I hand it to her. She takes it without breaking her fixation on whatever point she's chosen today.

I clear my throat. "I was hoping I could have your company for a little bit."

She gives a curt nod.

I sit down. The rain drops get heavier, increasing in volume. Residual spray crawls into the covered haven. Tiny rivulets trace the floor, winding their way towards the ladder. Content with her vigil, Stenia takes the binoculars away from her face. Turning, she pushes herself up against the wall of the perch before proceeding to scan me. Her violet eyes sweep from my knit cap down to the toes of my boots, probing for the reason why I've come here again.

While she performs her diagnostic, my gaze wanders away from her eyes, resting instead on her right cheek. A purple crosshair sits there, just beneath her eye. About the size of a fingernail, it's accompanied by several others of varying sizes and colors. Together, they cascade down her face, continuing past the right side of her neck. The rest remain buried below her dark uniform, uncountable. I prefer it that way; it's best not to know how many.

Stenia was one of the kids who ran with my group when we were young. She was a member of our food-finding missions, a participant in our games, always there to be an ear when you needed it. Like any animal, children without supervision find that odds of survival increase in packs. As we grew older and more sophisticated, our packs sorted themselves out by the skills of each member. Thanks to shrapnel, errant bullets, disease, or any other form of Deus Ex Machina, we never had a shortage of new recruits.

Stenia was never short on survival skills. Not only that, she was my most constant companion in the ship's library. Even then, she was withdrawn, but she could see and hear things that others couldn't. Her heightened perception wasn't overlooked by the powers that be, and she was sponsored for Fleet Defense when she turned fifteen.

Her straw-colored hair, sharp violet eyes, and uncanny proficiency with a rifle stood out from among the ranks. As a result, she was chosen for special training. Becoming a sniper was natural for her; she was content to sit many long hours without having to talk to anyone, quietly listening, waiting for any sign of danger that might come hunting for us. The long, scoped bolt-action lying on the cotton sheet next to her hip ensures those dangers don't make it within a quarter mile of the ship.

My reasons for coming to see her now are two-fold. Both selfish.

First, when I heard we were destroying the pirate zeppelin instead of letting it float free, I wanted to make sure I got a good spot to see the fireworks. The Bridge was able to trace the ledger of the captured ship back to the British merchant vessel *The Cornelia Marie*. According to the Northern Expedition Trading Company, the *Marie* was taken several months ago, with all of the crew presumed dead or captured. It seems I inherited some of them among the band of refugees I volunteered to look after. *The Cornelia Marie* was deemed too dangerous to let float, lest another pirate group find it and refit it for plundering. In turn, our engineers rigged the *Marie's* ammunition to explode remotely. If I squint hard enough, I swear I can see a splotch of Diz's red hair hovering on the *Marie's* deck.

Second, I need someone with a level head and a tight mouth to discuss my encounter with Sabine. I need to know what to do with the information I've been given. With any luck, Stenia will hear me out the same as she did over a decade ago.

Stenia opens her mouth before I can open mine. "First of all, yes, you can watch the explosion from here."

I smile. Her perception's only become sharper with age.

Her violet eyes continue dissecting me. "Secondly, you've got something weighing on you that you'd like to discuss. Maybe that's what I heard when you were climbing up here?" she adds.

I keep my smile. "Right as always."

The smile fades as I look out into the steady rain. "Stenia, have you ever known something that could change the course of your life, but you were afraid to act on it because your brain's at odds with your gut?" I ask.

She also looks out, mulling over my words. "Baz, it's my daily duty to call in threats to this ship," she says. Her voice seems far away. "There are times I'll be on my tenth or eleventh hour, and I'll see something flit past in the clouds. Could be a bird, could be a trick of the eye. Chances are that it's nothing. That I'm just tired."

She brings her gaze back up to mine. "But figment of the imagination or not, it's best to call it in." Her voice takes a decisive tone. "Because the consequences can be serious if you don't."

It's my turn to keep my silence.

She takes the loaf, tearing off the heel. "So what have you got for me?" she asks once more.

The bread flips back into my waiting hands. I tear off a piece for myself.

"Well, most important, I've got arguably-fresh jam," I smile.

Stenia's eyebrows betray a degree of interest as she reaches her hand back out again.

I hand her the jar. "Forgot a knife though."

"No matter," she replies, sliding a blade out of her boot strap. She wipes it on her sleeve before tenderly cutting through the initial layer of gelatin, listening intently.

Taking this as my cue, I relay my odd encounter with Sabine.

Stenia keeps her silence, as she always does. No interjections impede my train of thought, no excited clips punctuate any of my sentences. She offers no words, not until she's entirely certain I've finished my story.

A full minute passes.

"I think she's telling the truth," Stenia says softly.

My eyes detach from the doomed zeppelin, landing back on her.

"What makes you so sure?".

Stenia balls her hand into a fist, placing it under her chin. "This Sabine. The way you've described her, she seems like a very strong person. She wouldn't ask for your help unless she truly needed it." Stenia pulls her cloak tightly around her shoulders, blocking the spray of the rain. "Asking for help doesn't seem to be something that she's used to doing."

I reflect on this a moment before admitting, "You know, you're right. She was very sure of herself. Either that, or she's an excellent con artist."

Stenia seems unmoved. "Well, one way or another, we'll find out," she says between swallows. "Until then, consider another lamp lit."

"You'd join a cause for someone you've never even met?" I ask.

Stenia leans back up against her wall, nestling into her cloak. "I, like you, have served the *Artemis* my entire life. Even as kids, this was our home. I'd give my life to defend this ship."

A pause settles.

"So would I," I whisper.

"But see, that's all we've ever done. Defend. We coast through the skies from port to port, hoping we don't get attacked. We've never gone on the offensive for as long as I can remember," she muses.

Her jaw clenches. "We live in fear. We never get to feel that rush of making the first move, knowing we've created that destiny for ourselves. We just sit and wait, hoping the trade's good at the next port."

I push back up against the wall. "Of course - we're Merchant Marines. We're not some national fighting force. Open war's too expensive these days anyways."

Stenia fixes me with her violet eyes. "That's not the point Baz. Since the world went to shit, people are craving a purpose greater than their hand-to-mouth existence. We've spent so long trying to get back to where we were, we've lost sight of our higher ideals."

"What do you mean?" I probe.

The air smells fresh and moist. "Baz, how frustrating is it that we're descendants of the first group of humans ever to start over from square one?" Stenia asks.

I ponder this. "I . . . I don't know. I guess I've never really thought about it like that."

"Well I have," she says. "You and I could've been sitting in some high-rise right now, sipping some tea. Maybe reading the newspaper in some climate-controlled corner of the world."

Storm clouds begin rumbling in the distance. Each flash illuminates her Scandinavian features.

"Instead, we're sitting up here in a sniper's roost 14,000 feet above the ocean, trying to wrap a piece of cloth around ourselves to keep out the rain," she says.

I use my finger to redirect a small rivulet that's seeking to threaten my relatively dry area. "Hey, that's taller than a high-rise, huh?" I offer.

She rolls her eyes before tearing off another piece of bread.

"Stenia, that's a pretty romantic version of the Old World," I say. "I mean, if anything the books say is true, those people had weapons that could annihilate the planet with the click of a button."

She considers this.

"At least we don't have to deal with that anymore," I sigh.

Stenia draws her eyes back up to mine. "Well if anything that your Sabine says is true, it seems that we may."

She picks up her binoculars again, continuing her scouting. "Moral of the story is that I would very much like to feel something again. Even if only for that reason . . . you have my rifle."

"*I like her*," The Voice says.

"You always did," I mutter under my breath.

Stenia keeps her binoculars trained. "But from the sound of it, my rifle and your plane aren't going to be enough to stop a warship that size. On top of that, it looks like there was a hit put out on us," she warns.

"What?" I ask.

"The whole *Cornelia Marie* business."

"I thought The Legion were a band of pirates," I say, pulling my blanket over the back of my neck.

Stenia lays her rifle over her knees, pulling the cotton cloth over it. "That's what they would like us to believe," she says. "I have it on good authority from my source on the Bridge that they were actually a mercenary outfit."

I take a deep breath, considering this development. "Who placed the hit? A government? Another privateer group?" I ask.

"They don't know. The interrogations are still ongoing. From what they've got so far, it looks like it came from an independent interest."

"Well they shouldn't last very long at this rate. They know no one's coming to save them."

Stenia raises an eyebrow. "So we hope. Mercs tend to be a lot more durable than your average pirate. The only info we've been able to pull so far is the first name of the man who brokered the deal."

"What was it?" I ask.

"Noah. That's the only name the surviving mercs heard in reference to their latest contract," she says.

Exhaling, I let my head fall back on the wall. Just what we need. As if there weren't enough going on already. I pull up my mental checklist: training, lunch, providing food for starving refugees, recruiting warriors to combat a possibly non-existent threat.

Sounds like a full day.

Focusing back on the *Cornelia Marie,* I see our last Helios depart from its deck. The way Diz explained it, we've rigged the *Cornelia Marie's* own munitions to explode from within. Apparently, the ship's magazine is too heavy to scavenge without the proper equipment, and it's only a matter of time before another privateer group smells blood and comes hunting. With any luck, the initial explosion will start a chain reaction, destroying the ship entirely. Either way, it should be a spectacular sight.

I take a deep breath, allowing myself enough separation from my troubles to enjoy the next fifteen minutes or so.

"Don't worry, I'll get on it . . . After the fireworks," I say.

The faintest wisp of a smile appears underneath the binoculars. Stenia turns her wrist over, peering at a little black watch. "Should be any second now."

The rain thunders on the makeshift roof. The perch shifts underneath us as the *Artemis's* engines groan to life once more. Considering the fully-rigged magazine, I realize I'm ok with putting a little more distance between us and the *Cornelia Marie* before the show begins.

A crack arcs across the sky. I snap my head up in time to catch the back half of the ship explode. A line of fire races to the bow before the middle of the ship ignites. The brilliance of it makes it appear as though the sun has pierced through the storm clouds, lighting up the world again. The explosion blasts out in a perfect orb, sending a shock wave ripping across my face, causing the *Artemis* itself to rock. All at once, there's nothing left but the hiss of super-heated shrapnel as the rain makes contact during its decent. One lone propeller spins a fiery trail towards earth as the ship's balloon flaps through the sky.

"Stenia?"

"What?" she asks, watching the wreckage fall to its final resting place.

"When all of this is over, for once, I'm going to build something."

∎∎

The rain hammers the panels of the Cellar as I apply a fresh coat of grey paint. Our flight training was cancelled today, but all pilots have been encouraged to partner with their flight technician to perform scheduled maintenance. Since my new Jackal's seen less action, Ja'el and I don't have to worry about undiscovered bullet holes or severed fuel lines as much as the other teams. Ja'el was overjoyed upon discovering that I not only survived the last battle, but also succeeded in receiving a call sign.

"Saber." Ja'el said, rolling the word around in his mouth.

It was nice to see him in a state that's not so severe.

"I like it," he deigned, "We must begin tattooing your Jackal immediately!"

It was my turn to smile. Together we set out to carry on the tattooing tradition long-held by pilots who have successfully received call signs. I've already toured the hangar in search of inspiration before beginning mine. Lionheart's Jackal sports a clawing feline on the tailfin with the lion's muzzle covering the entire nose cone. An intricate mane flows over the plane underneath the canopy.

I'm less of a fan of Stinger's plane, but I'm amazed at his artwork. Both of his wings are covered in an iridescent paint, with interspersed dots and slats mimicking the membrane of a wasp's wings. Beautiful, but I'd be afraid it would make me more of a target. Maybe he's willing to trade that for the extra flair it provides.

One particular style that caught my eye was Tombstone's design. Nestled in the painted grass underneath his canopy is a well-drawn grave marker. Inscribed on it are the names of the different aircraft he's shot down. At the time of my encounter, he was painting his sixth victim.

With all of those ideas in mind, both Ja'el and I have spent several hours on our own aircraft. Together, we've already completed a good portion of the art. A large gray scimitar slashes out of the tail fin. Beginning from the left-most part of my engine, a painted laceration cuts through the canopy, ending in a straight line on the right tailfin. I'm working on the detail of the peeling metal when I hear a familiar voice.

"Hello Mr. Saber."

I steady my balance, looking up from my work. Standing next to my engine, I see Cass dressed from head to toe in Artemis black and gold. It looks like she was finally able to land time off from the infirmary. There isn't much of that to be had these days.

She runs her hand across the side of the Jackal, careful not to touch any of the wet paint. "She looks beautiful," she breathes.

"I'm glad you like her,", I say, grinning back up at the design. "Hopefully it'll strike fear into everyone else."

Walking up close, she delicately slips her hand into mine. I give it a small squeeze, painting a few more strokes with the other. Although it's not uncommon for pilots to flirt or intermingle with other crew, it's still considered bad form.

"You didn't expect to see me here," she whispers.

"Not so soon," I whisper back.

I attempt to find calm, assuring myself that her time off must mean the infirmary's having a slow day. In that breath, I sense the brush strokes from Ja'el's side have slowed down. He's more skilled in mechanics than subterfuge.

"Don't worry," she says, "I've made sure the galley's aware of the refugee's needs and insured that they're getting enough of a stipend to stay fed."

That is comforting. The cooks have a tendency to trust the nurses more than any of us pilots, and for good reason too.

Her sea foam green eyes raise up to meet mine again. "Speaking of which, I'm going to make sure they followed through with today's delivery." She wraps her arms around my neck, pulling me in. "I just wanted to make sure that you were doing ok first."

I wrap her up. "Thanks," I whisper into her ear.

"It was a brave thing you did Sage. It could have ended much worse. I'll try to make sure the food redistribution doesn't draw too much ire from the Bridge. You know how the Admiral likes to make sure his troops get fed first," she says.

I nod curtly, watching her as she walks towards the exit of the Cellar without looking back.

As I turn back to apply more paint, Ja'el's toothy grin greets me from underneath the fuselage. Finding my eyes, he keeps his overly large smile and raises both his eyebrows into a question.

"Get back to work," I say, shaking my head.

Ja'el closes his lips over his teeth, but maintains his grin. He shrugs as moves back to his side. I guess neither of us are very subtle.

Dipping my paintbrush again, I realize this is the first time I've ever done art as a form of recreation. It's something entirely different than the world I know. I'm calmer than I can ever remember; actually sensing each one of my muscles releasing their tension.

Of course, my relaxation is due in large part to Sabine for stepping up into the role of main caretaker for our refugees. They relay any problems or needs to her, and I provide the authority to get most of what they need. It saves me a lot of time, instead of constantly going from cabin to cabin checking on all of them. Cass has also proven invaluable in getting the refugees what they need, including medical care. Some of her fellow nurses, including Captain Dixon's daughter Fiona, have taken up the cause as well. Thankfully, everyone's remaining tight lipped about it.

Most families with whom we've quartered refugees are understanding. In many cases, they've found themselves in similar situations in the past, and like our quartermasters, agreed to return the favor. The process hasn't been without issues or conflicts, but somehow we've found enough space and food to keep most of the castaways alive and stable until we reach Shipwreck.

Likewise, the refugees are grateful for the kindness they've received. Many do everything they can to reciprocate. The ship's adoption of these people has made many of the passengers realize that their own lives could, in fact, be worse.

Despite this, the closer we draw to Shipwreck, the more I can see that passengers are on edge. The rumors about whole cities being leveled are becoming more frequent. The spreading stories all have one thing in common: the sudden appearance of a large, dark ship that blots out the sun. Of course, no one who's told those stories has actually been a survivor themselves. Regardless, the descriptions match Sabine's narrative, and it's enough to get me talking with other pilots and marines.

What makes the reports even more odd is the indifference the warship and its fleet display towards their targets. Other than engaging and destroying the local militia, it seems that their only function is to harvest the material beneath the chosen cities, then simply fly away. There's no occupying force, no executions, no chasing or routing of pilots.

Many passengers dismiss the rumors altogether. In their minds, the house isn't on fire unless they can see the flames. After all, what could possibly be more important than protecting one's own wellbeing? Unlike our refugees, resources are too scarce to help the people they cannot see.

I strain to keep my arm steady while applying a darker edge to the peeled mosaic under my cockpit, hoping that perception is not true.

The days go by. More reports surface. Among the latest attacks is Winchester City. One of the dead is one of The *Artemis's* most prominent munitions dealers, Lemmy O'Phelan. First an export king-pin, next a gun manufacturer, and now a munitions mogul. What's the connection? None of the men were extorted for money. Though they all had enemies, none have stepped forward to take responsibility. Whatever the motivation, it has our supply lines in flux. The Admiral has to find new trade routes, and quickly. With the logistics issues that have been plaguing Kafi Exports since Amani Ibrhim's death, and without Vitortov's guns and O'Phelan's consistent flow of scarce ammunition, the existence of the *Artemis* itself is threatened. My talks with the platoon sergeants and wing leaders become more serious.

To take my mind off it, I wind my plane's tattoo across its fuselage, focusing on paint rather than global conflicts. I only fly it for training missions and scheduled maintenance, but out in the cockpit, I can view the world in a way I've never see it before. I volunteer for extra flight hours, even taking midnight patrol shifts. I watch the sun go down right after dinner; there's something about the way the sky bleeds red around a perfect orange semi-circle. I love looking up towards the top of my canopy and seeing the red/orange mixture thread its way into the darkness behind me.

It feels like home.

Otherwise, it's been quiet in our airspace since The Legion attacked. The peace feels like it's come at the perfect time. Between the warship rumors, recent losses, breaks in our supply lines, and fatigue from the journey, I don't think the crew could take another assault.

Then again, that's what I would've said right before the Legion hit us.

11

The sun's rays pierce into my little cave. They're not the only things hindering my ability to stay asleep.

"Oi, wake up lad!" Olan says, pushing me.

I growl something incoherent, hunching myself further into my covers.

Not to be discouraged, Olan applies more pressure. "Oi, on your feet man!"

In a last ditch effort, I curl up into a tight ball, lying motionless. My sleep-deprived mind sincerely believes this will make me appear dead, and therefore not worth the trouble.

The pushing stops.

I smile at my triumph. It worked . . . Sleep is mine.

Until the earth turns beneath me. The bed gives way, flipping me into the air. Hitting the side of the wall, I slide back down to my now-exploded linens, unfurled and defenseless.

"Dammit Olan!" I croak.

I should've chosen to room with a weaker man.

"Oh shush," Olan replies. "We've caught sight of Shipwreck and I know how much you miss seeing solid land."

This is news worth losing sleep for.

"Really?", I reply.

Aoife pops her head around the corner of our door, giggling. "We get to dock soon!" she shouts.

This will be one of the few times in her life her father has let her set foot off of the ship. Most ports we do business at aren't places for children, or really anyone for that matter. Aoife runs down the hallway, outfitted in her absolute best: a vibrant red dress that her mother made. She can hardly contain herself.

Olan gives me a tired look before going off to fetch her. As worried as Olan is, Aoife's energy is contagious. She can look at the smallest things in life and find a way to make them spectacular. Then again, port landings are special for the whole crew. Even though the harbors we land at are often depressed or dangerous, they still provide a chance for everyone to get off the ship and stretch their legs. It's a great luxury. . . if you can afford the expense of flight.

While the merchants haggle and accrue inventory, the rest of the crew can find various diversions portside. Renting out one of the side arms from the armory and striking out to explore the port and surrounding areas is usually enough adventure for me. Not exactly the safest route, but I haven't had a chance to know anything more than the ship for most of my life. Living vicariously through books and stories is enough for a while, but one day I just had pick up and go see it in person.

Now that the tides are receding again, people are reclaiming our ancestors' land plot by plot. It's arduous, backbreaking work consisting of clearing out the dense thickets of amphibious seaweed, avoiding hidden quicksand, and uncovering the nests of creatures who've adapted to the area. Ah, the joys of everyday life at clearing camps.

Most of the population tends to stay far away from the tree line, so the camps are often inhabited by either the most desperate, or the most intrepid. Usually both. Either way, they're a goldmine for intel due to a few contacts I've made over the years and the general culture of having loose lips. I'm usually a welcomed guest since I'm a crewman. They appreciate any news I can bring them about the rest of the world, and are usually more than happy to trade me dinner and some inside info in exchange for a story about one of my adventures. They also don't mind counting me as one more weapon if the camp comes under attack.

There's something exhilarating about stepping out to the very edge of a sea forest and just peering in. Every once in a while, it's possible to catch a glimpse of a pillar, or parts of a bridge from the Old World. Most buildings and structures from back then have been decimated by the sea, but sometimes their foundations still remain. There have even been reports of entire sections of cities being found intact, but I've never been lucky enough to stumble upon anything like that. That being said, I usually don't peer into the maw very long before a low growl from inside sends me running back to camp.

Pulling my coat up around my neck, I step out into the gusts. When I get to the banister, the squall lets up for a few moments before picking up again. Stenia leans over the barrier taking in the view below. She doesn't say anything as I come up to her side. Her hair's tied into a tight military braid that runs down her back.

"What's on your mind?" I ask quietly.

She doesn't take her eyes away from the fields below. "You know I don't like landing, Baz."

I make a play to try catching her eyes. "Brings back bad memories?"

She keeps them fixed below, nodding silently. So much for taking her mind off of it. I take the bait, staring down at the encroaching earth. It's uncanny. I'm so used to being fifteen thousand feet in the air that seeing individual details on the surface is disconcerting.

A sprawling patchwork threads underneath us, dotted with tiny obelisks next to each small hamlet. Upon closer inspection, the shiny pieces of metal become upturned anti-aircraft guns. Constructed by local merchants and manned by the local militia. Shipwreck's governor stumbled upon the brilliant idea that a person would go to great lengths to fight for him, if it was to literally defend their own home. Smart man.

Another presence joins us. Sabine approaches; she's wearing a blue cloth dress with her eyes cast towards the earth.

"Anything interesting?" she asks.

Stenia maintains her silence. I pick up the slack. "Just getting ourselves prepared to walk on land again."

Sabine looks up with a coy smile. "Is that usually a difficult task to accomplish?"

I lean out over the railing. "The first time I got off of the *Artemis*, my first visit was to a local bathhouse. Once I finally got in the shower, I made the mistake of closing my eyes." I say, slapping my hands together. "Immediately lost my balance and landed face first on the tiling."

Sabine exhales in what could be a laugh as she reaches up for her studded arm. Her discomfort is becoming palpable.

"What's wrong?" I ask.

Sabine shakes out her left hand, using her thumb to flatten out her palm. "It's nothing."

I give her a prodding glance.

She gives a little more. "I don't know, my stones are acting up. They hurt more than usual." She gingerly touches her studded arm again. "I haven't felt like this since right after Raltz and I escaped." She lets out an uncharacteristic sigh. "I'm not sure what it means."

"It probably means you've got the jitters."

Stenia's voice cuts through the air.

Sabine looks up. "Yes . . . perhaps."

Stenia's already pledged to assist us if and when the time comes to go after Garon, so I'm comfortable talking with Sabine around her. Although Sabine has her allegiance, Stenia's done nothing to foster a friendship between the two of them. Truth be told, I think Stenia only pledged herself because of our relationship; she doesn't seem to like Sabine as a person, as much as she likes Sabine as an idea.

The moment's interrupted by the giggle of a child.

"Uncle Sage! Have you seen it yet?" Aoife shouts, running through the crowd.

"Seen what hon?" I ask, picking her up.

She uses her new height advantage to scan the horizon. "The balloon!" she says, "Daddy says we'll know we're there once we can see the big balloon."

I shake my head. "Nope, haven't seen it yet. But I'll be sure to yell once I do."

Aoife nods, rocking back and forth with her whole body. Abandoning her search, she turns to Sabine. "You're pretty," she says, hiding into my arm.

Caught off guard, Sabine furrow's her brow. "Thank you. And what's your name my dear?"

"My name's Aoife," the child responds. "Are you a princess?" she asks, getting back down to business.

Sabine's jaw tightens before relaxing. "You know? I suppose I am. Are you?" she asks.

"No," Aoife says, "I don't think so anyways." Her eyes fall to Sabine's damaged arm. "How did you get hurt?" she asks.

Sabine looks down, placing a finger on a stone. "There was

an accident."

"And we don't ask strangers about their injuries. Remember?" Olan says, finally finding us.

"I was just curious," Aoife offers as I hand her over to her father.

"Well, be curious with different questions, Love," Olan states.

Sabine looks up. "It's ok. The child has an enquiring mind. That's the sign of a good father."

Olan nods his thanks before moving to bring Aoife back to our cabin for final preparations.

"I hope you feel better!" Aoife yells as she disappears into the crowd.

As smile twitches over Sabine's face as she leans over the railing. Raltz and Sabine stand to either side of us, creating natural barriers against the flow of traffic. To anyone else, we look like two lovers trying to control our palpable tension as we enjoy the scenery. It's a perfect guise; chances are we'll be left alone.

"How many do we have in a pinch?" she whispers quietly.

I keep my voice low. "We have 14 pilots pledged out of 33. None of the Red Swans have taken us up on our offer. They're the ones I'm most worried about. Nothing's keeping their mouths shut but gold. I also can't imagine Lieutenant Baltier buying into the idea of having his mercenary core diverted for a task that wasn't in their contract. Either way, they're excellent fighters and well equipped, so we have to try to get them to help, at the very least. Lastly, three platoon leaders out of eight believe they could rally their soldiers when the time comes."

Sabine nods silently. Although she's playing at being aloof, I can tell Stenia's also leaning in to hear our conversation.

Exhaling, I give any built-up stress a chance to dissipate. "It's hardly an army, but it'll have to do for now."

Sabine eyes are lost in strategy, as she mentally places the available pieces where they need to go.

"I appreciate your help. You know that, right?" she whispers.

I manage a stretched grin. "I do. But we have to realize this isn't going to stay a secret for very long." I glance around at the passengers surrounding us. "We're getting the word out to far too many people for there not be loose lips."

Sabine inclines her head. "I know. That's part of the tactic. However, once word does get out, the hope is that we've built a strong enough base of soldiers who already understand the situation."

I bite my lip, considering it.

The land rolls closer, and with it the telltale blimp of Shipwreck pops up over the horizon. The settlement got its name years ago from a downed merchant zeppelin. An accident occurred when the ship's magazine pierced several of the compartments of its balloon, and the rest of the settlement was built on the carcass of the once airborne vessel.

The survivors of the crash realized they were too far from any trade lanes or settlements to be saved before their supplies ran out, so they foraged for food. Once they knew foraging wouldn't be enough to sustain them in the long run, they scraped out a meager existence in the land. Over time, their crash site was discovered, and eventually it became a regular trade post along the Spine.

Shipwreck's once white balloon has acquired a green hue over the years, and its hull has been hollowed out and fashioned into a town hall of sorts. Despite its dilapidated appearance, Shipwreck has endured as an example of the power of the human spirit. If this is what the pinnacle of humanity looks like, then I'd hate to see the alternatives.

I say my goodbyes to Sabine and Stenia before making my way to the Cellar. I need to make sure my plane's properly secured before landing. Wouldn't want someone taking off with it for some extra scrap. As I enter the Cellar, Yeti catches up to me from his corner of the hangar. "Hey Baz, you still headed out to the Treeline with Cass?"

Ettero arrives as he always is: gregarious and eager. Luckily for me, he's also proven he's the kind of pilot who's willing to lay down his life to keep his wing safe.

Waving, I keep on walking. "Hey Yeti. That is in fact, the plan."

Yeti matches my gait as we cruise past the Red Swan section of the hangar. About a fourth of the Swans are making preparations to move their fighters out entirely. It's not uncommon for this to happen once we hit major ports. Landings tend to mark the end of many mercenary contracts. Maybe they've had enough of a pilot's life, maybe they're transferring to a more profitable ship, maybe they're just going to squirrel away everything they've made so far and carve out a new beginning. It must be nice to have options.

Yeti doesn't pay much attention to them. "Well hey. I just realized you and Cass probably want your space, huh?"

I rub the back of my head without realizing it. I don't want to keep Ettero out, but sometimes things are a little bit more peaceful without him.

"Aw Yeti, you know it's not like that. We'd love to have you come along with us."

I'm not a very good liar.

For having such a buoyant personality, Ettero's very keen on reading people. He claps a hand on my shoulder, stopping me.

"Baz, you don't have to worry about me, man. Hey, I hear the Treeline's got more than a couple places to hide if you don't want to be found, huh?" he prods.

I grin in spite of myself.

Ettero backs up, raising his hand like a gun. "Just make sure you don't get eaten by the wrong kind of predator," he winks, firing in my direction. "Keep safe!"

With that, he runs off back to his plane, leaving me to wonder how someone who's never had a formal education could be so well versed in double entendres.

The cranes move overhead, transferring the departing Swans toward the front hatch. Listening to the electrical hum from above, I secure my plane and perform some last minute detailing. Before leaving, I reach into the cockpit and pull out my sidearm. It won't be much in the face of what we might encounter out towards the Treeline, but Cass and I have to make it there first.

The animals aren't the indigenous species I'm worried about.

I step back out into the Outer Rim. Rooftops flit past, almost scraping the bottom of our ship. We're flying in low, but that's what has to be done to make it into Shipwreck's capital docking bay. Once it was found again, Shipwreck's port became the hub of all its economic activity. The rest of the city spirals out from there. Plumes of steam rise high above the balloon, and its dark streets below are packed with denizens. Unlike most other ports, the people of Shipwreck never tiled their roads, so transportation's a mess.

Zeppelins and planes of all shapes and sizes buzz by, turning their wings towards their respective destinations. As with most ports these days, the mix of nationalities is readily apparent. An Iranian flag hangs off the back of the merchant class zeppelin sliding behind us, while a Russian one billows behind a hulking destroyer in the distance. Although I'm sure they mean no harm, an airship that well-armed still makes me nervous.

On our approach to the docking bay, I pick up the hum of the giant magnets within the shipyard. Through plenty of trial and error, the shipwrights found the best way to "catch" a zeppelin was not to touch it at all. This discovery came about when the Swedes discovered they were able to control a zeppelin's approach speed using large, negatively charged magnets. As a result, most of the hulls these days are also charged negatively to ensure they don't collide with the trade docks.

Although I've seen it countless times, I still can't help being fascinated by how we come into port: men and women in blue caps and overalls scramble up and down the dock. The port magnets increase their hum, buzzing disconcertingly.

A large fresco of a wooden galleon beached on a cluster of rocks over an orange background decorates the docking tower. The emblem of Shipwreck watches over us. We're finally safe.

My grip tightens on the railing as the *Artemis's* momentum decreases. As we slide along the edge of the dock, the wardens shout their coordination and throw lassos onto the ship from either side. One lasso misses its target, landing ten feet away from me. Sprinting over to grab it, I try finding the docking rung where it belongs. Shouts come from below. The workers point excitedly about fifteen feet to my left. Following their directions, I see the rung. Just as I feel the lasso losing slack, I successfully slip it over the post.

Cheers rise up from below as the lasso tightens against the rung, helping slow us down to a manageable crawl. Mixed in with the sound of humming magnets, the clicks and pops of winches make their presence known. With most of the lassos secure, the ground crew finally brings us level with the dock.

Once the ramps are down, our entire crew bursts over the sides. Civilian or otherwise, people are just happy to be safely on solid ground again. The feeling's usually short lived, but getting a break from air travel is worth every dollar spent on diversions.

As I glance at the trucks making off with our former passengers and refugees, one person stands out from the rest. Cass sits on a post at the bottom of the gangplank, sporting a smile that I pledge to myself to make appear every day. A shawl covers her head, complete with sun glasses. She lifts her shades up as I make my way to her. The mid-morning sun glints off her green eyes as their sea foam color bubbles up. It's good to be back on the ground again.

Crossing the etched mud field to the post, I let her wrap me up in her arms. Planting a kiss on my top lip, Cass looks over my shoulder.

"Have you seen her up close since we left the Charleston Flats?" she asks.

Turning around, I take in a full view of the *Artemis* for the first time in weeks. Gashes have left huge scars across large sections of the ship. Plastic sheets cover the sizable holes punched through the hull, and burn marks appear like tattoos along the sides of port holes.

I let out a low whistle. "Well, at least the Admiral has some time to allow for the repairs."

Cass's eyes turn their focus back to me. "You think we're going to stay here a while?"

I survey the rest of the dock. "If you take into account the time the merchants need to move their cargo on and off the ship, plus the time it's going to take rooting the officers out of the local taverns, I'd say we've got ourselves at least a couple of days."

Cass's eyes widen. "Yeah?" she asks hopefully.

Betraying a smile, I remind her. "Plus there's the fact that we need to go on that adventure I've been promising you."

Cass lets out a laugh, kicking herself off of the post. Brushing the dirt from her cloth pants, she shakes her arms out. "Ok . . . I'm ready," she breathes.

We wind our way down the streets, making muddy, sucking tracks as we go. Once we are outside the docks, we make no motions to indicate we're connected in any way. As Cass is well aware, we don't want to give onlookers the idea that one of us might be worth ransoming.

Stalls choke the side streets like plaque as we blood cells try our best to push through. It's impossible not to get accosted by the overzealous vendors. Decaying chicken is shoved in my face repeatedly. Fine-spun rugs hang everywhere. One enterprising storekeeper is selling all shapes and sizes of teeth. Although most of them appear to originate from various, odd creatures, a particular string of familiar looking molars makes me feel very uneasy.

Steam billows from the manufactories lining the sidewalks. Industry has come to Shipwreck and its tendrils are taking hold stronger than anyone could have expected. From inside, metric ton hammers stamp out the latest casts of whatever modern marvel's being commissioned. There's something reassuring about that consistent hammering. It resembles a heartbeat, one that sounds permanent. Yet, of all the things we could create, we choose to manufacture guns and iron blades.

Bikes and motor vehicles splash to and from their destinations. The taste of oil's thick in the air. Cass and I dodge through traffic towards the barely visible forest in the distance. We spend the rest of the day making our way from the port to the very edge of the trading post before the sun finally gives out. As the lamplighters patrol the streets with their candles, we figure it's time to end our journey for the day.

The road to the clearing camps is not one to travel at night.

The outskirts of Shipwreck are less claustrophobic than its beating city center, and Cass and I are able find a homey enough inn that will suit our needs for the night. I'm glad we can finally step onto a solid stone entryway. It's obvious we're reaching the edge of town: each step we take begins to sink into the mud a little more deeply, dredging up small puddles of water.

A tiny bell chimes as Cass and I duck our heads into the vestibule. It's odd that such a little sound like that can evoke such a sense of home. That feeling is magnified by the flavors wafting through the air from the inn's kitchen. Some meat's being spiced, and I can hear the chef chopping what could be potatoes. My stomach growls audibly. Reading Cass, I can tell her body's responding the same way. We haven't eaten unpreserved rations in over a month. The sheer thought of fresh food is almost enough to sway us from our mission. The possibility of just using our dock leave here and spending our money on racks of lamb is enough to make me wipe the side of my lip; rogue saliva's making a break for it.

That would certainly be the easier task anyways. In my experience, clearing camps have always been a wealth of information. The seajacks and camp guards living and working there are often quite liberal in dispensing their knowledge, but they're a rough sort. It's the perfect place to get away from the watchful eyes of *Artemis* officers to find out the latest movements of our Cascade friends. And to find out if they even exist.

As I attempt to refocus on the mouth-watering food, which I know for a fact exists, a song breaks out in the dining area. Cass and I peer in. We're greeted by a gaggle of Germans who have annexed both the bar and the surrounding territory of chairs. One's equipped with a fiddle, and a young, brown-haired soldier appears to be leading the chorus. He belts out an age old drinking song, much to the chagrin of the Turks trying to study the Qur'an in the corner.

Cass's eyes light up as she leans into me. Something about song reinvigorates her. It's not uncommon for me to tease her about absent-mindedly singing a tune while she's tending to her patients; it's a way for her to cope with her surroundings. The songs she sings are always happy ones, both in tempo and lyric. She's created a partition her mind. In the moments she's suturing up a little boy's arm, or putting a blanket over the slacken face of a corpse, she can live inside those lyrics and have some peace, even if only for a little while.

As much as I've teased her in the past, I have to admit the Germans' rousing music lights a small flame inside me that seems content to burn for rest of the night if I let it.

"We should join in," I say, looking down at Cass.

She looks back up, smiling. "But I don't know any German."

I keep my grin, glancing back at the group. "It can't be that hard. Just raise your voice and mumble some guttural sounds," I joke. "We'll get the hang of it in no time."

Cass's playful punch catches me square in the chest before I get a chance to defend myself. Instead of pressing the attack, she pulls me out onto the floor and we join our Eastern compatriots. Delighted with our participation, the Germans pull us in as they would their own. While the empty beer glasses accumulate on side tables, they slowly transition to more mainstream songs so we can sing along too.

I hate dancing. The actual body movement isn't what's irksome, it's the judgment of everyone around you. That being said, all of our would-be judges are far too drunk and jovial to pass critique on anyone, much less me with my awkward, stilted movements.

The night rolls on in this fashion without incident. Well, almost without incident. Between the beers and merriment, one of the fresher faced soldiers makes a play for Cass. Encountering her laughter, he decides it's best to settle as song mates rather than soul mates. To tell the truth, I can hardly blame the kid: it takes some balls to approach a woman that way, especially when her guy's standing right next to her. Little bastard.

Long after the Turks clear out to find a quieter place to study, Cass and I break away from the crowd. We have a long journey tomorrow, and we need all the rest we can get tonight. After reserving one of the last available rooms, we hiccup and stumble up the stairs, singing half-remembered foreign anthems. Leftover music wafts its way up beside us.

Somehow we get to our room and startle fumbling with the keys. By the grace of greater powers, one of us is able to find the keyhole and apply enough pressure to make the door give way. Without a word, we tumble onto the bed. Through kisses and muffled laughter, I try to see if I can recollect a happier memory. Nothing comes to mind.

Cass rolls over on top of me, kicking the door shut with her foot. Using the momentum of her strike to kick off one of her shoes, she looks up, suddenly stiffening. Her immediate response is enough to make me panic. I reach down instinctively for my gun. She doesn't breathe; instead, her sea colored eyes fix on a point across the dark room.

"What is it Cass?" I whisper though clenched teeth.

Cass slowly pushes herself off of me and flicks on the light switch. "It's beautiful,", she says.

Carefully, I turn myself over to look at the intrusive object behind me. Hidden away in the corner is a squat, ugly, upright piano. The thick layer of dust on its key guard leads me to believe it hasn't been played in a very long time. Cass slowly makes her way over to the corner, softly laying a hand on its side. Her slight contact reveals a swath of darker wood underneath the dust coating that's taken up residence.

"Do you know how to play?" I ask, crawling to the nearest corner of the bed.

Cass carefully opens the key guard with a squeak. "I did once." she says. "It's been a very, very long time,"

She gingerly traces her finger across the contrasting ivory keys beneath. Musical instruments are a rarity; using precious wood to create instruments that don't directly contribute to one's survival is considered by most to be a waste of resources. I thought our run-in with the fiddler below would've been the extent of our melodic discovery for the night.

"How could they just leave this piano up here to waste away?" Cass whispers.

I perch my chin on my hand. "I suppose it's easier to manage it as a regular piece of furniture than it is to maintain it as a musical instrument."

Her eyes still haven't left the keys.

"Why don't you try it out?" I ask quietly.

"It's probably way out of tune," she says. "I bet half the keys don't even work anymore." Her response is quick, but tinged with the hope she's wrong.

Rolling on to my back, I stare at the ceiling. "Well, there's only one way to find out," I sigh.

There's a creak as she tentatively pulls out the seat. Exhaling, I close my eyes. One solitary "plink" comes from the corner.

"The resistance feels weird, but I think I can make it work," she says confidently.

"The resistance?" I mutter.

She silently fingers the keys, taking up her position. "Yeah, the resistance of the keys. If the friction of the keys isn't right as you strike them, it can be really hard to play."

I wipe my face, sniffing. "I'm hardly one to judge."

She doesn't need my permission. Instead, she revives the piano with an escalating melody. It's short and stilting at first, but she plays with the range of the instrument, building the notes into something beautiful.

It seems we're keeping with our German theme tonight, since I'm almost certain what she's playing is Bach. Or maybe he was Austrian? I can't remember. I can't name the song either. All I know is that it's breath-taking, even if the keys are slightly out of tune as the piano struggles against its age.

My body rises off of the bed, carried by the mountains and valleys generated by Cass's fingers. The day's stress seeps away. Old scars slowly fade into the background as I let myself float away from all of it. For once, I remember my mother's face in a rare moment when she was happy. Surely there's no therapy greater than this.

On the way back down, the quiet melody plays out its final note. I let myself open my eyes. The ceiling comes back into focus, but my limbs won't move from their relaxed state. Cass exhales, shaking herself out. It seems that she went on a journey too; probably much farther than I did.

The bench creaks as moves herself off of it. "You know, despite what you may think, it's actually to your advantage that we got interrupted by this old clunker," she says.

I look up towards my forehead, anticipating her face coming into view as she makes her way over to the bed. "Oh yeah? Why's that?" I ask.

Her body hums as she hovers over my face from the side of the bed.

Her lips lock with mine. She takes her time, before pulling away just enough to whisper, "Because Bach turns me on."

12

Wind floods past as the cockpit cuts through the air. There's a lot of them, but I know we can still win this. I gasp for air, trying to keep calm. The sun's so hot. . . too hot to be the end of Autumn.

Even as I look through the sights, I can feel her there; her cold silent stare bores into my exposed neck. Instinctively, I move to wipe the feeling away from the back of my head. I don't want to look back. I don't want to meet her gaze. I haven't seen her face since she died that day on the deck of the zeppelin. I'm afraid of what might happen if I look at her now.

The leather pulls as hands creep up the back of my seat. Hunching forward, I try to avoid the gripping fingers. I accidently press the controls in, sending the plane pitching forward violently. The engine's overpowered by wind speed as we rocket straight down.

I strain to correct the instruments, but the joystick bursts into flame. In a panic, I fight to get a hold of the burning stick to right the plane. The sheer heat of the fire burns deep scars into my hands. Ripping them away from the blaze, I place them over my face, hyperventilating. Deep disfiguring marks carve themselves into my fingers. The ground rushes up. I don't know what else to do but yell. There's nothing else. As the scream surges up from my lungs, icy hands grip over my mouth.

I jolt awake. Bolting upright, I shudder, fighting to control my breathing. My side of the bed is soaked through with sweat. On the other side of the mattress, Cass is curled up in the covers, fast asleep. By some miracle, my thrashing didn't wake her. I swallow, trying to get my bearings. My heart's beating too fast for me to lie back down. I feel sick just thinking about it.

I try clearing my eyes, but wiping them does nothing to bring clarity. The bleariness of sleep follows me out of bed as I rock to my feet. I look outside, but the only thing the window frames is darkness. I make my way over to the only other familiar object in the room. Near the window, the piano sits motionless, silently keeping watch.

I press my hand up against it. I have the odd feeling that it's tense as well. Peering outside once more, I notice the fringes of a sunrise peeling back the deep black of night. It's disorienting seeing buildings perched underneath the horizon, but I could get used to it. So stationary. But something about it is still unnerving. I glance back at Cass, trying to let my anxieties dissolve once again. The selfish part of me wants to wake her up and have her play another movement to settle me down. I'm sure she wouldn't mind if I did.

A loud burst catches my ear.

My heart stops. The hairs on my arm prick up, one by one. That can't be right; this is one of the most secure cities on the Eastern Coast. Pressing up against the glass, I strain my ears to pick up something else: anything. Silence pounds; the kind of pounding that happens only when you know something's not right.

Almost in unison with my heart beat, two flak bursts light up the sky.

What could possibly be out there? There haven't been any sightings in this area for weeks.

I make up my mind that whatever's happening, we can't be here anymore.

Turning on my heel, I lunge into the bed. "Cass! Cass, wake up right now!"

"Baz, what's wrong?" she says, shaking awake.

I pull close. "We need to go."

Cass throws her covers off despite every impulse to the contrary. "Baz, what's going on?"

I lick my lips before responding. "Cass, I think we're under attack. We need to get back to the *Artemis*. Right now."

Cass's eyes roll up, listening to the commotion outside. The explosions are becoming more pronounced. Someone screams through the side wall. Without a word, Cass launches off the bed, grabs her pack and throws on her pants. She doesn't even bother changing her shirt. I follow suit before we both sprint down the stairs.

Families shout to one another, their children crying at the

unexpectedness of the situation. The click of rifles echoes off the walls as our German compatriots charge down the stairwell clad in full gear. Whatever allegiances they have fade into the background as they take up position around the inn. They must know someone here.

Running past the commander of the small platoon, I place my hand on his shoulder, managing a small but sloppy, "Danke."

He takes one look at me, nodding as we run past. The grimace on his face tells me it wasn't his idea to be stationed at this post.

The bare components of daylight creep into the surreal world. Dark clouds slowly give way to piercing golden rays. The booms and cracks blow in from the southwest. I still haven't seen our attackers, but I have one goal in mind: reach the *Artemis* before it launches. If Cass and I don't make it on the manifest, it's not Admiral Khan's fault, it's ours. With a crew that size, each crew member has to take responsibility when going out on dock leave. The sheer thought of being stranded in Shipwreck is enough to churn my stomach. Last night was paradise because we still had money to burn. Once our cash runs out, our life expectancy slims considerably.

Cass darts in front of me, struggling to remember the landmarks pointing our way back to the shipyard. Luckily, the dock's such a prominent part of the landscape we can see it in the distance. It serves as a solid reference point, but we still need to navigate the streets on our own.

Panic rises with the distinct sound of engines reverberating close to the ground. My first instinct overpowers all others as I tackle Cass by the ankles. Her chest hits the ground as three dark blue and grey planes streak by. I cover my head from showering glass as a warehouse in front of us bursts apart. Timber and brick rain down. Whoever's attacking is indiscriminately strafing the city. Our section of town has no military installations that I know of.

Cass draws up her knees, inspecting herself. "I appreciate the save, but next time you take my legs out of from under me, can you at least give me a little warning?"

"I'm sorry, it was a split second decision . . . We have to keep going!" I say.

Cass seems to understand as she wipes off the splotches of blood forming on both her elbows. Biting my lip, I help pick her up. I didn't mean to hurt her, but grated elbows are better than a bullet through the back.

"Did you see the markings?" I yell into her ear.

She shakes her head, running next to me. "No, I just saw the shadows. Did you count three?"

I nod, re-adjusting my pack. "I think there are a lot more than that."

Explosions reverberate in the distance. It doesn't add up. This is a full scale attack.

Cass and I churn down the dirt road with the shipyard looming in the distance. It's almost a half day's travel to get to the docks, under even the best circumstances. This is hopeless. We won't make it back to the *Artemis* before it raises planks. But if we don't make it to the ship before takeoff, the life we know is gone.

The only impetus keeping us running is the fact that we at least have to try, no matter how improbable escape may be. To either side of us, groups of citizens hurry to underground shelters, putting as much distance between themselves and the lead being hurled their way. The shelters are relatively rare since the water table's so high. It's a recent development to even be able to build on this ground, much less under it. With a poor enough foundation, structures can still sink up to the second floor.

More enterprising civilians rush up to the rooftops, rifles in hand. I respect their bravery, but lament their tactics. They just want to protect their families, but their dark trappings make tempting targets against the stark bleach of the stone underneath them.

A rib-shaking burst detonates behind us. My fear wins out over the age-old advice that says never to look back. I should've listened. The combination of encroaching sunlight and creeping explosions reveals a floating abomination. A gray and blue beast powers toward us. It is, at the very least, twice the size of the largest dreadnaught class vessel I've ever seen.

It dominates the sky, without the assistance of a balloon. Instead, four twisting rotors hold the vessel aloft and plowing through the pale morning sky. Its size is matched only by its speed, and it's gaining. A row of oversized, swiveling cannons defend the top of the ship, defying all known physics. There's no way a vessel of that mass could possibly fly without a balloon, or five.

My blood runs cold. This is the ship Sabine warned us about. This is the bogeyman that's been trickling through the rumor mill.

Except it's not a rumor; it's a nightmare.

Then I witness the source of the burst that shook me in the first place. The front row of the fortress's cannons turns and fires, rocking the lumbering dreadnaught. A column of flame a quarter mile high ignites the district below us, shuddering the ground beneath our feet. The clamor of the ship's churning engines is rivaled only by the drone of its fighters as they blanket the sky. Cass and I keep close to the walls as plane after plane shoots over the rooftops.

Sprinting through a marketplace, I hear another distinctive engine as a lone plane rockets by. By chance, I catch the emblem on the tail of the fighter: a growling bear. I dredge up the memory of the Russian dreadnaught that flew over us as we entered the city. It's a match. The residents of Shipwreck, both permanent and temporary, are rising up. Closing my eyes, I can hear the groan of several different types of engines.

The Russians aren't the only ones going to war against our surprise foe.

I don't get much time to bask in our unity before Cass takes me by my collar and slams me to the ground. My head bounces off the pavement, shooting nausea up and down my body. My knees hit my chest as bullets dig into the road around us. A group of watermelons in the stall next to us explode as the rounds find their homes. Turning over to Cass, I move to pick myself up. I press a hand to my swollen eyebrow. It comes away bloody. I've popped open the wound created by the exploding sights on the *Cornelia Marie*.

My worried expression isn't lost on Cass.

"We'll get that patched up once we're safe, ok?" she says.

Her face hardens, noticing something in the fruit stand behind us. I follow her gaze, putting pressure on my head in a halfhearted attempt to stem the bleeding. My hand drops at the sight of the mangled leg protruding out of the corner of the stall. It snakes up to the half connected torso of a man wearing a white turban. His eyes plead, his fingers crawling almost independently toward us.

Cass's eyes well at the corners. "We can't help him," she says, "We need to go."

I stop, staring at her. This isn't the response I was expecting. "Cass . . . " I say.

She looks back up, her eyes no longer misty. "I said, let's go!" she yells.

The terseness in her voice is enough to get us running again. The pleading man is no longer our concern. We have to reach the *Artemis*. If we don't make it, we're stranded. If the *Ark* makes another pass, there's not going to be anything left to be stranded in.

Even as I ponder that thought, Cass's reaction is still enough to make me wonder where the kind nurse I fell in love with has gone. Maybe it's something about the city that's triggered it, but the contrast scares me.

My thoughts are cut short as pebbles and rocks begin shuddering and jumping beneath us. The sheer rumble of the warship's engines is enough to make the ground shake. I wheeze as exhaustion sets in. Running as far as we have with the weight of our packs is finally starting to take its toll.

The droning roars louder. Chancing a look back, I see the rotors of the warship slowly leveling themselves out. The ship begins losing speed. Maybe this is our chance. Maybe we'll make it out of this after all.

Through the haze of dueling aircraft, I see the hangar bay of the giant open from below. How could they possibly be launching more fighters than they have already? I slide to a halt as a blue light illuminates the guts of the ship from within.

They're not launching anything.

A shockwave shakes the dust off of the city's surface, blasting me from my feet. I try sucking in to regain the air that's been knocked out of me. Sprawling on my back, I search for Cass. She's getting back to her knees a few feet away from me. She didn't feel the shockwave coming.

The ground heaves, but not like before; it's coming from below this time. From deep below.

Dark silver chunks burst from beneath the city's crust. The grayish shards erupt from the ground, upending and destroying the houses and pipes above. As the shards make their way into the ribs of the warship, I scramble over to Cass. The whites of her eyes threaten to envelope the rest of her face as she struggles to get back to her feet.

"What is it doing?" she asks.

I grit my teeth, pulling her up the rest of the way. "Harvesting this place," I say.

We waste no more breath, devoting the rest of our energy to

sprinting through the crowded streets. Plumes of fire leak from scattered buildings. Families run into the roads to escape anything with a roof; they don't realize their underground havens won't save them if the threat's coming from below.

I push through a Vietnamese prefect on the road, trying to direct traffic as best he can. The officer hits the ground swearing. I should feel sorry, but the new opening makes just enough room for us to make it through the crowd.

Sirens permeate the air. A small brigade of firemen arrives ahead of us, their hoses snaking out from the bed of their truck to combat the blazes. Following a curl of flame licking up toward the sky, I see the dots overhead come into focus. The winged specks pour streams of light at one another, chewing through ammunition.

The firemen point to the sky, abandoning their truck in the middle of the road. An explosion erupts behind us, peppering the street with shards of hot metal. Cass and I duck into a covered doorway as a dark aircraft bears down.

The plane plummets, making no attempt to pull up. The nose bucks just enough to bring the craft level, but the maneuver's too late. One wing catches a rooftop, showering debris on the crowd below. The fighter pirouettes into the street, flipping over several times before finally crunching to a halt.

I ball my fist, punching the doorway we've taken cover in. The crash is blocking our exit. Cass knows it too.

I take a breath and realize the pilot might still be alive. If he's part of the local militia, maybe he can tell us where the nearest airstrip is so we can make our escape. Cass and I break from the doorway as flames begin shooting up from the plane's fuselage.

I tug on her sleeve. "I'm gonna try and save him! Maybe there's another strip where we can catch a ride."

Cass says nothing, considering if this is good use of our limited time.

"It's the least we can do if he got shot down protecting this place," I plead.

With her curt nod, I race out next to the abandoned fire truck. Its hoses dance in the absence of their handlers. One such hose swings its head, catching me across the face with a high-pressure blast. Half blinded, I try clearing my eyes while dodging through the artificial rain. Only able to see out of my left eye, I can make out a hand trying to pull itself from the cockpit. The fire creeps in on its prey as I fight to cover the distance before it can.

As I sprint the last few feet, a head frees itself from the crumpled prison. Reaching the fuselage, I glance at the tail fin. A circle frames a grey tidal wave as it rises up over a blue background. Breaking spray spits out over the top of the wave. They must be from a long-range caravan, because I've never seen that emblem before.

I slide to my knees, yelling at the trapped pilot. His head's down, focused on pulling his legs out from the mouse trap of his crumpled cockpit. He throws out a hand, still fighting with his feet. I grab hold of his arm and elbow, pulling him part way out from the fuselage. Only his knees remain trapped inside, but with another good pull I believe we can get them free.

He looks up to thank me, but he doesn't say a word. His eyes lock on my lapel. They flit up to my face, then back to the lapel. His pupils dilate, muttering something I can't hear.

My arms freeze in place.

Before I can react, he unclips his pistol, leveling it at my head. The trigger clicks. I catch his wrist, deflecting the barrel towards the sky. The bullet brushes my temple as it flits past. Ringing of the shot drills down my ear canal. The grim determined look on his face and the pull of his arm readjusting to finish the job is enough to wrench me out of shock. Swinging the gun away, I lower my elbow, slamming my full weight into the bridge of his nose. The impact stuns him. So I keep doing it, three more times.

The gun finally falls to the wet pavement as I feel him go limp. A thick dampness collects in the crook of my sleeve as I push off of the road. My would-be assassin's face bows inward, partially crushed. His temple bleeds, but he's starting to stir again.

I take the gun, flicking it to Cass as she catches up.

"Baz . . . Baz! Oh my God, are you ok?" she asks, immediately tearing open my jacket to check for wounds.

I barely notice her as I glare at the bleeding pilot. Dark red pools around us as his life slowly ebbs away. Cass snarls, pointing her new pistol at the semi-conscious man.

I put a hand on hers, carefully guiding the barrel down.

"Save the ammunition. At this rate we're probably going to need it," I say quietly.

I watch the flames creep onto the pilot's legs, delighting in their first course. That'll teach the fucker to draw a gun on me.

"Serves him right!" I growl.

Cass stares down at the man slowly being consumed by fire. "Why did he try to kill you?"

"He knew who I was," I say. "Or at least who I worked for. Give me a hand with this!" I yell.

My eyes skim around the alley, searching for anything we can use as a tool. They land on the soaked entry mat of a nearby hovel. Perfect.

We rush over to the mat, ripping it up from the walkway. Luckily, it's worn and in disrepair. The stakes pull right out of the ground.

Some of the nails still dangle from the sopping mat as we drag it over to the burning nose of the plane. Getting our body weight under the dripping mass, we throw it over the top. A nasty hiss rises up as it hits, fanning clouds of steam out from the sides. I glance at the tailfin again. The crashing wave bubbles, curling from the heat. I know this won't be the last time I see it.

"That mat's not going to stay cool for very long," I say, turning to Cass. She holsters her pistol as I grab her by the waist. "You're going up first!", I shout.

With me supporting her hips, she launches herself up onto the mat. She cries out as she makes contact with the mat, barely separated from glowing metal underneath. She balls up, protecting her arms from the heat. Her forearms blister as she turns onto her hip, reaching down to pull me up. My throat tightens as I smell the burning skin. My blackened hands flash in front of my eyes. The cinders push down, choking me.

I try pulling myself up.

"Come on!" Cass screams, shifting onto her other hip to relieve some of the heat.

I can't catch my breath. I can smell my mother burning.

Cass throws all of her weight into dragging me up.

My eyes well with tears. I can't tell if they're from smoke or regret. Why would I condemn a man to the fate I fear most?

Cass gets me up on the top of the nose.

The extreme heat grills away the water particles separating the open flames from our bodies. With her job done, Cass launches herself off the other side of the plane. Before following suit, I take one last look back. The flames crawl up over the pilot's face, dancing over his open mouth. Over the crackle of fire, I hear his rasping screams. They will haunt me until I die.

I am a monster.

I slide down over the side of the nose, hitting the ground. Laying there, I make no movement to get back up. Cass kneels in a pool of water, trying to submerge her forearms enough to give them some relief from the burns. The mat finally catches fire behind us. There is no way back.

At that moment, the telltale sound of super magnets pulses into our alcove as they reverse their charge.

Cass and I both raise our eyes, watching the bow of the Artemis glide out of the dockyard as it gains altitude.

Cass slumps forward into the puddle, breaking the surface with her forehead. She pulls her arms and legs in quietly. I let myself slide back onto my elbow and look up into the sky. The dots are still fighting. Larger bannered zeppelins have moved in, firing volleys at one another in the confusion. We're going be swallowed by this place.

"We need a new plan," I say to the wind.

My statement echoes off of the deserted alleyway, greeted only by the hiss and pop of the fire behind me. Cass nods into the water, slowly pulling herself up onto her haunches. She pushes back a sopping wisp of hair as she looks down the road, trying to plot our next move.

I wait for the deafening engine of a low flying plane to pass before I offer, "If we make it to the dockyard, we can still offer to crew for any remaining ships."

Cass extends her arm towards the port. "And what chance do we have of there being any ships left by the time we get there?"

I draw a breath in through my nose, weighing our options. "What chance do we have of surviving if we just sit here?" I ask.

Cass rubs her hands down her face before standing up. "You're right," she says.

I stumble a bit, struggling to get my legs under me. My balance is still off. It must be a result of hitting my head after Cass tackled me, compounded with the ringing in my ear from the gunshot. Nausea wells up and over me, forcing my hands to my knees.

I feel Cass's hand caress my shoulder. "Do you think you're still able to run?" she asks.

I'm slowly getting her back again. Whatever steel barrier she put up this morning is beginning to dissolve as we recognize the goal of escaping on the *Artemis* is an impossible one. The warmth of her touch is a quick-acting serum that flows through my shoulder and clears my head.

I blink a few times, straightening back up for good measure. "I'm ready to move," I say.

We grab our packs, shuffling towards the docking bays. They're still too far off in the distance. I'm glad to leave this place behind. No one else needs to know what I've done. As we pass intersection after intersection, I notice our surroundings becoming starker in their appearance. Apartments and markets give way to a barracks and training grounds. Shipwreck's orange emblem adorns each corner. The prow of the beached 17th century galleon points us to our destination. We've reached the military district.

Before I can work this discovery into our strategy, a door bursts open to our right.

Three men in orange striped uniforms clamber out into the street. The sheer surprise is enough for me to draw my weapon, leveling it at the group. Before I can think, all three draw their side arms on me. Out of the corner of my eye, Cass's steady hand clutches the dead pilot's pistol, ready to fire.

I lick my lips, trying bring my senses back. "Are you Shipwreck Militia?" I ask.

The three pilots glance at one another before the one in front speaks up. "432nd Minutemen. Who're you?"

I turn my arm patch towards them without lowering my gun. "Gold Squadron, U.S.S. *Artemis.*"

"What the fuck are you doing drawing a gun on us?" the dark-skinned man in the back barks.

Stunned, I lower my weapon. "I . . . I'm sorry. I got ambushed by the last downed pilot we met. He took a few shots at us before we were able to subdue him."

The wing leader clips his gun back in, closing the distance between us. "Did you catch the emblem he flew under?" he asks.

The tailfin flashes to mind. "Yeah, it was a wave. A grey

wave over a blue background,", I remember, crooking my arm. "Looked like it was cresting."

The wing leader's face contorts. "Those fuckers!"

"Who are they?" I ask.

The pilot in the back walks up, joining his wing leader alongside the other man. "Bastards call themselves The Cascade. We've been getting reports that they just pop up out of nowhere, take what they want, then vanish."

The wing leader's getting impatient. "The Tower also says they're shifting this way. They've been concentrating their forces on knocking out all our military installations. We're next on that list."

Everything clicks: the wave, the ship, the shards.

"Do you have planes?" I ask, grabbing the leader's shoulder.

The leader shrugs off my grip. "Yeah, do you think you can fly 'em?"

I nod.

Cass steps up. "Where are they being housed?"

The wing leader points down the road. "We've got a little ways to go, but our base is just past that steeple."

The third man steps forward. "Great, more pilots. Now let's go! I swear to God I can hear it. . . . "

We all stop, straining our ears.

Under all of the commotion above, a droning from the south creeps closer. It's enough to make the five of us kick up clods of dirt as we turn, sprinting down the road. There's no way we can out-run it. Cold sweat breaks out all over my body as I hear the ripping of earth from behind. The noise resembles the sound of a plow scraping over gravel, accompanied by intermittent eruptions. An orange striped warplane takes off in the distance, marking our destination. We're getting close!

Blue crawls over the cobblestones and siding of the buildings. I chance a look behind us and find myself staring straight into the bowels of Hell. Shards of grey metal rip from the ground, spiraling upwards into the hull of the dark ship. The front of its bow glides over us.

We aren't going to make it. This escape was doomed from the beginning.

Debris spits up from the earth. Pebbles bounce, fliting past us as we run. I use the last of my energy fighting to stay ahead of the oblivion. The pebbles give way to rocks, and then chunks of granite as buildings burst apart around us.

This is it.

I grab hold of Cass, pulling her to the ground.

"Make yourself small!" I yell over the deafening groan.

The blue light deepens around us. Cass is about to protest, but instead curls into a ball against me. The other pilots keep running. A shard bursts next to us, through the center of the barracks. I shield Cass's head as cement rains down. My back tenses, anticipating the jagged shrapnel from below.

Instead, my body jerks up towards the sky. Cass's arms flail, trying to protect her face as her body arches. A stone cuts her cheek as she abandons her defense, struggling with the clip of her belt. The metal! We're being pulled into the stomach of the ship by our steel belongings.

Cass flips herself over in midair, fighting against the magnetic current. I do the same. My bow broach rips loose from my throat, shooting towards the sky.

There's a snap.

Cass falls from her magnetic grip, hitting the ground.

I can't get my belt loose! I struggle with the clip, but my body weight is bearing down on it, keeping me suspended. I twist around, looking for other options.

Cass's pack rockets past me. That's the first step. Loosening my bag's straps, I sacrifice all of our food and supplies in a bid for extra time.

The belt buckle is the last restraint pulling me ever further from the ground, but my weight keeps the clasp firmly in place. Grasping around my hips, I search for a knife or something sharp. I find nothing. There's one last option. The end of my gun strains against the holster as I pull it out. I almost lose my grip fighting to bring it level with my body.

Kicking out my legs, I hook the barrel into the belt. I thrust my hips away, pulling the trigger as fast as I can. Three shots tear through the leather before slowing down and spiraling in an arc towards the ship above. One last thread remains, carrying me towards certain death. A final twist makes it give way.

With a snap, the clasp snakes through my belt loops. Breaking free, it launches towards the sky, its tail flapping excitedly.

The force of it spins me sideways, breaking my grip on the gun. It too whips skyward, finally free from my grasp. With nothing left to suspend me, the world rushes back up. Ten, twenty, thirty . . . forty feet.

The dull impact is the last thing I feel.

Greg

St

</

13

Suffocation drags me back into consciousness. I try pulling in air, but sand and dust are the only options. Dirt weighs down on me as the ground churns. Hands grab around my chest, heaving me upward. Grabbing fistfuls of clay, I struggle against the earth's attempt to consume me. Another shard bursts through the ground next to me, pulling up ancient loam that's never before seen the light of day. The resulting shower forces us back under the soil. Cass's muffled gasps spark my consciousness, burning away the haze. I punch through the top layer of the earth, finding her hand. We swim our way to the top.

Something explodes from below. My shin slams against rock, launching me from the ground. Kicking away, I hit the ground as the shard continues its spiraling path towards the dark ship.

The impact knocks the wind out of me as a newly formed rock garden drinks in the blood trickling from the gash in my arm.

I lie there, pummeled and bleeding.

The sound of vomiting is the only thing giving me the strength to turn over. Cass lies on her side, throwing up our rich dinner from the night before. Grains of sand pour from her nose and mouth along with pieces of partially digested chicken. With the majority of it purged, she lies there shaking as the mixture trickles from the side of her mouth. The sea foam in her eyes turns to a frothy white. I've never seen that before.

"Cass," I whisper, kneeling next to her.

She doesn't respond.

I pull out a handkerchief, dabbing the spittle from her face. Taking a free breath, I survey our surroundings. They look like nothing from before. We might as well be on the moon. Smoking ruins glow around us. A geyser erupts unchecked across the street. The distinct smell of raw sewage hangs in the air. It seems that the plumbing's been ripped up from below. My eyes eventually come to rest on one of the Shipwreck pilots who joined us. He's the only one. The others are nowhere to be found.

The pilot digs at the gravel and rock. Even with his dark skin, I can see the blood. He's torn off all of his finger nails digging through the wreckage with his bare hands. He doesn't seem to notice, muttering frantically to no one in particular.

A screech rises up from behind. I duck as a supply truck swerves around us. Grabbing her legs, I throw Cass out of the way as the truck rumbles past. Oil barrels bounce on its bed as it grinds to a stop next to the digging pilot.

The driver rolls down the window. "James! James, is that you?"

The pilot doesn't respond.

The trucker opens his door, stepping down the driver's side. "James!" he yells.

I say nothing. It's probably better not to be noticed at this point.

The trucker closes the space between James and himself. "C'mon man! We need to get to the extraction point. They just missed us, and that thing's turning around. We don't have time fo . . . "

Before the trucker can say any more, he's drowned out by the engines of a fighter overhead.

Rounds skip up the pavement behind me.

I throw myself over Cass, her body tightening up beneath me. A shatter of glass combines with the echoes of metal on metal as the windshield of the truck blows outward. The oil carrier must have made a pretty tempting target.

Cass vomits up another fistful of sand from underneath me. "We need to get a ride," she chokes out.

I brush back a strand of her hair. "Do you think you can walk?"

She fights to prop herself up on her arm. "I don't have a choice."

I help her get to her feet. She's pretty unsteady, but her

balance gets stronger with each step. Her face is a mask of dirt.

She blows a wave of sand from her nostril. "Ugh, I need a bath."

I manage the smallest of smiles before looking up to ask the driver for a ride. He won't be much help to us though. The large red hole oozing from his side tells me he won't be much help to anyone. His hat lies next to his body, crumpled forward with his face in the rubble. His eyes open and unblinking.

His friend James doesn't seem to notice. There doesn't appear to be any progress with his hole either as his hands scrape dully at the bottom.

"The truck's still running," Cass says evenly.

She's right. Other than a blown tire, some damage to the chassis, and a leaking oil barrel, the truck and its engine still sputter on. I nod, making my way past James. I try touching his shoulder to snap him out of his fixation, but he just bats my hand away.

His mumbles turn into shouts.

With his shouting growing louder, Cass pushes me towards the truck. "We don't have time for this," she says.

We leave James flinging dirt and screaming. The illogical part of me hopes he finds his friends, the more grounded one realizes we have more immediate issues to tackle. I pause as we reach the cab, fidgeting uncomfortably.

"What's wrong?" Cass asks, moving around to the passenger's side.

"I . . . ah, I um . . . never learned how to drive," I admit sheepishly.

Being born and raised in the sky doesn't provide very many opportunities to pilot vehicles that don't have wings.

"Do you think you can drive it?" I ask.

Cass nods, hobbling over to me. I help her up into the driver's seat. Closing the door, she leans out through the open window. Adjusting her mirror, she spits into her hand and wipes the smeared blood off of her face.

"Hey, we all have our talents. We're going to need yours a lot more if we can find a plane," she offers.

I let out an uncomfortable grunt. It was supposed to be one of agreement. My rib cage has already taken enough abuse for one day.

As I slam my door, Cass throws the clutch forward and stamps on the accelerator. I clear the windshield shards off my seat while dark, black smoke billows from the exhaust. The truck lurches forward, shifting the barrels in the back.

Straining my eyes, I pick out an orange windsock billowing in the distance.

"That's where we need to go!" I point.

Windsocks mean aircraft. Aircraft mean we can get home. If we can't find a fighter before the *Ark's* next pass, we won't survive a second burying. The dark trails of smoke rising from the hangar do little to kindle hope.

Cass nods in acknowledgement, throwing her weight into the oversized steering wheel.

As we barrel down what's left of the road, a triangle of glass embeds itself in the side of my index finger.

"Ah, fuck!" I growl in spite of myself.

Balancing my arm on the side panel of the door, I carefully pluck the glass out of my hand. Examining the bloodied piece, my focus shifts to the trucks side view mirror. The dark warship fills its reflection, pointed in our direction.

"Ah fuck . . ." I repeat. "Is this as fast as we can go?" I shout over the din.

"Yeah, I see it!" Cass responds.

Approaching the guard house, I concoct plausible stories to gain us access to the base, but as we draw closer, I realize there's no need. The whole building's engulfed in flame. As we pass the destroyed pillbox, the heat licks at our faces through the window. The rest of the airfield's all but abandoned.

There has to be something left, some way to get out. Looking at the row of hangars, I notice one with its roof is still intact.

"Cass! The fourth one on the left. There's gotta be something in there," I say.

Cass responds by wrenching the truck in the direction I'm pointing and gunning the engine. As we cross the runway, I get another clear view of *The Ark*. It's close enough now that I can see individual pieces of debris fly into its center. I try exhaling my heart back down from my throat as we roll up to the undamaged hangar's side door.

After helping Cass down from the cabin, we move to the

opening. She's stronger now, having coughed up most of the foreign bodies in her lungs. The door swings open at my push, revealing a large plane within. A quick look at the cockpit tells me it's a two-seater. The quick scan also reveals two pilots prepping the fighter for takeoff. A Haitian flag's shoddily painted on the side of the orange craft.

Pressing a finger to my lips, I motion to Cass to keep low. I notice a toolbox on the crate next us. Alongside it are a pistol and a map, anchored by a compass. These are militiamen who've answered the call to defend their homes. Despite all the destruction around them, they're still fighting on. But if we don't get on this plane, the *Artemis* leaves us behind, *The Ark* goes on killing, and we die here.

I hate myself for this.

Before Cass can say anything, I grab the pistol from the crate.

"Sage, no!" Cass's voice rouses the attention of the militiamen.

They twist towards the noise. The pilot on the ground reaches for his weapon, not realizing that I already have it. The one in the cockpit moves to draw his sidearm.

I fire a warning shot, burying a bullet in the paneling next to his shoulder.

Flinching, he fumbles with the weapon. The gun drops from his hands, clattering to the ground underneath the plane.

"Ne tirez pas! Ne tirez pas!"

I freeze. "Ah shit! What language was that?" I ask Cass.

Cass steps up behind me. "I . . . I think it's French."

My mind races. Why am I doing this? "Can you speak it?" I ask hurriedly.

Cass wrings her hands. "Ah . . . I . . . A little."

The pilot in the cockpit angrily yells something at the man on the ground.

"Shut up!" I shout, firing another round through the ceiling.

They both snap up straight, raising their hands over their heads. Panic starts settling in my chest. This isn't me.

I can't go back.

"Cass, please tell them to politely remove themselves from the plane and evacuate the area immediately."

Step by step, I walk slowly towards my captives. Cass relays my instructions, stopping and starting as she strings together the proper verbs and nouns.

They seem to understand as the pilot in the cockpit works his way down the ladder with one hand still raised over his head.

As I reach the base of the plane, the older pilot runs one of his hands through his short cropped Afro while saying something. The stress in his voice sounds as if he's pleading.

"Cass, what'd he say?" I ask.

Cass keeps me between the captives and herself, refusing to look them in the eye.

Her voice breaks a little as she translates. "I didn't catch the first part of it, but what I could make out was, 'Please don't shoot my son.'"

My throat tightens. I've jumped a father and son crew. They want nothing more than to save their home. The son eyes the gun a few feet away underneath the plane's fuselage. He's got to have enough sense to know I'll put a hole through him before he makes it two steps.

Please don't go for it. Please don't.

His father senses the situation too, taking one of his raised hands and placing it on the shoulder of his son. He whispers something in his son's ear, drawing him away from the plane while keeping his white eyes squarely on me.

There's a clatter as the compass falls off the crate behind us. The now unimpeded map rolls itself back up. Rumbling shakes from the center of the earth. The *Ark's* on its way.

"Tell them we have a truck outside and that they should use it to leave as fast as they can." The wrenching of the earth is audible now. "Tell them there's not much time!" I shout as Cass struggles through my message.

I gesture the gun towards the door "Go!"

This English they understand, as they turn their backs on us and run.

"Je suis desole . . . ," I yell as they reach the doorway.

'I'm sorry.' It's one of the only French phrases that I do know. I couldn't spell it if I tried. An old Creole neighbor said it to me when he heard my mother was murdered. It was the only thing he could think to say.

If our ex-captives hear my apology, they don't show it as they disappear out the doorway.

I lower the gun, spreading my fingers out. They're shaking. My whole body tremors now.

Cass is already up in the cockpit, prepping the cabin. I put the gun in my belt before slamming the door control and making my way up the ladder. She doesn't look at me as I push past to the controls. We'll deal with this later. One crisis at a time.

"Let's hope this thing has fuel!" I shout back to Cass.

She answers by strapping herself in and pulling back the pin of the machine gun mounted on the end the cockpit.

I close the rattling canopy as I hit the ignition. The controls are similar enough to our Jackals that it only takes a bit of searching to find the instruments I need.

"You're lucky he didn't think of pulling this thing on you," Cass says evenly, referring to the large mounted gun.

I lick my lips, trying to guide us out of the open hangar door. "We were out of its turning radius," I answer.

"You didn't know that!" Cass snaps back.

This isn't the time to pick a fight, but I feel the need to defend myself. "Well, I took a gamble!" I shout back.

"Apparently . . . " I barely hear her say.

My words catch in my throat as the *Ark* takes up the windshield. It's here.

The end of the runway bursts up into the stomach of the warship. Pavement and grass vomit from the earth. There's not enough room! We can't get enough speed to take off.

Cass catches her breath as she sees it too, but she's faster back on her feet than I am. "Put all of your power into it and veer right!" she shouts.

Ratcheting up the engine, I swing the nose northeast.

I flinch as one of *The Ark's* cannon's fires a shot. The shell streaks past. The hangar to our right explodes, sending half its roof sailing up over the row of buildings. It lands on an abandoned fuel truck next to the runway. Flames shoot out from underneath the wreckage, catching all of it on fire.

I get an idea. There's no way it'll work, but we have to try. It's either taking that miniscule chance, or facing the certainty of being crushed by staying our course. I decide to push our luck just one more time.

"Sage, what are you doing?" Cass asks as our landing gear

thunders off the runway. I hear her struggle to keep the mounted gun under control as we hit bump after bump on the unkempt green.

"Something really stupid," is the only thing I can think to say back. The torched roof bears down on us. I hold my breath.

We hit it hard. I realize I've done everything wrong. Our landing gear tears from its base, launching us into the air. The plan failed. I thought I could get us the lift we were missing. The engine doesn't stall though. We're going fast enough to level out the nose and keep us flying.

That's exactly it though. We're flying!

The *Ark* swoops past us, swallowing the rest of the airstrip. I search desperately for a truck racing from the facility with red barrels bouncing in its bed. I can't tell anything for sure.

Guilt pours in as I angle our fighter towards the battle in the sky. If there's someone alive from our crew, we'll find them there. If the *Artemis* is trying to escape, Admiral Khan will have assigned pilots to cover its withdrawal. We just need to get close enough to establish radio contact.

Cass yells back over the roar of the engine. "Don't shoot at anyone unless you can tell they have that wave emblem!"

I nod.

"It's going to be a complete shit show up here," she adds.

"Got it!" I offer, hoping to reestablish some normalcy.

Planes of all denominations streak at one another, determined to take down their targets while fighting to dodge their own pursuers. Zeppelins scatter in all directions, some faster than others. The Russian dreadnaught from the day before drones beneath us, concentrating its fire on the *Ark*. Squinting, I can make out the name scrawled across the balloon. *Perestroika*. That's a hell of a name for a ship. For all the talk, those Russians have balls, or, if not that, then some insane sense of duty.

Scanning the radio, I turn the dial to the open frequency, keeping my eyes fixed on the dreadnaught. A mixture of instructions, swearing, and screaming in a myriad of languages floods the cockpit. The cannons of the *Ark* gradually swivel to meet the guns of the *Perestroika*. The crew of the Russian vessel continues unperturbed, firing shell after shell into the side of the *Ark*. I try honing in on any English that might be hurled through the speakers, hoping to find one with an American accent. Or at the very least, a language I recognize.

Suddenly, I make out one word that slims down all of the options considerably. "Mate." Twitching my fingers back up to the radio, I try readjusting the frequency to our English friend who crackled through.

Cass's voice pulls at my concentration. "Baz, we've got one coming in hot! Five o'clock, way low!"

A pylon of tracers bursts up from below. They miss our tail by just a few feet, but it's a mistake that can be easily corrected.

Pulling the joystick up, I roll the big plane before the bogey below gets a chance to line us up again. Cass's hair blocks my rear view as it cascades down from her head, no longer bound by gravity. The tapping sound of her gun fills the cockpit as she fires behind us. The light of her muzzle-fire strobes against the end of the cabin.

"Let me know if they start lining us back up again!" I bellow over the engines.

I don't think she heard me. Instead, I go back to finding fellow Anglophones. I trust Cass. She'll let me know if we need to make evasive maneuvers.

"Well you took your bloody time about it!"

That's it! It may be an argument, but English as a spoken language never sounded so good.

"I did the best I could. These guns are shite. They haven't been sighted in months!"

I hear the telltale sound of an engine overpowered by terminal velocity as it falls to earth. A dark plane burns past me from above, its halo of shrapnel catching up as best it can. Twisting up, I glimpse two silver planes rejoining a formation. I don't recognize their emblems.

"Excuse me lads!" I roar into the radio, "Are you attached to the Shipwreck Militia?"

They both begin dipping back into the fray. "Who the devil are you and how did you find this frequency?" one Brit shouts back.

I keep my eyes on the firefight between the *Perestroika* and the *Ark*. The *Perestroika's* beginning to bruise as a veil debris showers down with each direct hit it trades. In contrast, the *Ark* doesn't appear locked in a life-or-death fight. It sheds the *Perestroika's* volleys as they glance off its angled armor.

"My name's Sergeant Basmon of the U.S.S. *Artemis.*"

Silence.

"Do you know it?" I ask.

The British pilot's voice clips in, "The *Artemis*? I thought you chaps were black and gold with a bow?"

"Yes, a bow with three arrows. Have you seen it?" I ask, holding my breath.

The British Airman laughs. "Ah yes, a medieval weapon . . . how American. You won't find many of your friends here I'm afraid. None who are alive anyways."

My stomach drops.

"I think I last saw the *Artemis* bugging out heading northwest from the city center," the other pilot offers.

I turn my head back. "You hear that Cass? The *Artemis* is still flying!"

She nods her head silently, keeping her vigil.

The Brit speaks up again. "Why? Are you looking to turn tail and run as well?"

I clench my jaw. We're not cowards, but that's exactly what we're doing.

I have the urge to explain that the *Artemis* is a merchant vessel not meant for offensive actions. That we have civilians on board. But even I can't deny Admiral Khan's armed the ship to the teeth with soldiers and planes. That most of the zeppelins in this fight are comprised of innocents.

But we're still fleeing.

"Thank you," I manage.

I hit the radio, changing the frequency. Sometimes it's best to run from debate as well.

An eruption rocks our fuselage from below.

I peer over the canopy just in time to be blinded by the *Perestroika*. The explosion sends a shock wave across the sky, illuminating all of the hidden ridges of the *Ark*. Each of its mounted cannons are swiveled to one side, concentrated on where the *Perestroika* used to be. I can't tell if the *Ark* got a lucky shot and hit the *Perestroika's* magazine, or if its sheer firepower was enough to destroy it entirely. Either way, we don't stand a chance. With gravity pulling the wreckage of the *Perestroika* to its final resting place, I turn the plane until the NW of my compass locks firmly in front.

Forcing the fighter into a dive, I try losing us in the

maelstrom below. It's starting to get a little thin up here. My stomach rises as the nose of the plane dips. I try not thinking about the nausea Cass is probably experiencing. She's feeling everything I feel, but backwards and without warning. The gun clanks against the aircraft's tail as Cass lets go of it, grabbing hold of the sides of the cabin.

Down we go. Twisting and turning past the other planes, while trying not to draw attention.

"You know . . . that's an awful way to treat a lady."

I open my mouth to answer The Voice, but the words catch in my throat as the image of a furry creature flits by our cockpit. There's only one pilot in the world who would ever represent himself with an Abominable Snowman.

"It's Yeti!" I yell.

Cass's head snaps in all directions trying to spot him. "Where?" she says.

I search too. We've lost him in the mix.

"Use the squadron frequency!" Cass shouts.

My hand fumbles with the radio, clicking it to the right spot. I hold my breath, listening intently. Nothing but white noise. That can't be right!

"Yeti. Yeti! Is that you?" I call out.

"Wha- Is that you Saber?" a breathless Airman Eterro replies back.

"You got it Yeti! Why's this a dead frequency?"

Yeti's panicked voice rises from the speaker. "Because it's a dead Wing!"

I was concerned about finding a pilot we knew, but I never thought it would be this bad.

My mouth dries as I try forming a sentence. "How.. . . . ? What do you mean?"

Yeti's fear and anger pour through the radio. "How do think man? Everyone in Grey Wing's either rotting in a manmade crater, or bugged-out."

All of the familiar faces flash through my mind. He can't be right.

"What about Sergeant Samuels?" I ask.

Samuels is Cass's roommate, and an excellent Wing Leader. She wouldn't have let her Wing break and run if it weren't a tactical maneuver.

"Samuels is dead," Yeti says.

Silence.

Yeti's voice picks up. "Shot her through her goddamn face. They hit her in the cockpit. The rest of the plane was untouched. Like it was a fucking sport or something."

I shake my head, clearing the image of Samuel's matted hair plastered against a blood-soaked canopy. Over the engine I barely hear Cass's faint sobs. She and Samuels had become good friends since Cass joined our crew. Our other fighters, Ritka, Al-Fakani, Dobson, Montobo, Zhou . . . all dead or missing.

"Incoming!"

Yeti twists away as droning engines bear down from above. The tracers rain in a disorienting pattern. My confusion compounds as a fighter with Iranian markings explodes, arcing up past the cockpit.

I peel the nose of our plane sideways.

"There he is! Eight o'clock high!" Cass shouts. Her voice breaks, forcing her to take another breath to finish her sentence, but she's recovering quickly.

Following her instructions, I catch a glimpse of the telltale gold on black. Yeti's plane dips and pirouettes as a Cascade fighter boxes him in with tracer fire. I'm not about to lose the last member of Grey Wing.

Propelling the large craft upwards, I lock my sites on the fighter. "Don't worry Yeti, I got him!" I yell "Just keep shaking your ass!"

I struggle to keep my grip on the sweat-greased joy stick. Reaching deep, I concentrate on my breathing until everything comes into a sharp focus. Blood pumps past my ears. Slowly but surely, the wings and crosshairs become one. I squeeze the trigger. Fire streams on either side of me as the cannons search for their target.

Debris explodes from the Cascade fighter.

I let myself breathe. Direct hit.

My relief sparks into panic. The Cascade pilot continues his course unperturbed, opening fire. I try swinging my crosshairs back up, but it's too late.

"Yeti, dive!" I yell.

It's all too late. The Cascade pilot riddles Yeti from wing to wing. Ettero cries out as glass shatters over the radio. A jet of flame pours from his right flap.

"Nooo!"

I'm not going to be responsible for another dead friend because I can't finish the job. Taking advantage of the Cascade pilot's attempts to finish Yeti, I swing the crosshairs up again. I blow out another breath, leading the fighter with just enough room.

Pulling the trigger, I watch my duel stream of bullets pour in front of the dark fighter as he moves to evade. The nose of the plane crumples, causing a secondary explosion that rocks my cockpit and sends Yeti fishtailing. There's no way regular steel could provide that kind of protection.

"Yeti! Yeti, can you hear me?" I yell through the static.

The sound of choking is the only answer.

"Find another way for him to signal!" Cass shouts from the back.

My mind scrambles. "Yeti, if you still have control of your fighter, shoot twice."

Two tracers pop from Yeti's stricken plane. I exhale, letting guarded relief trickle back in again.

The com crackles. "I've been wounded," Yeti coughs. "I need to get back to the *Artemis* . . . so they can patch me up." He struggles. "Will you . . . will you make sure I make it back Baz? I'm afraid . . . I'm afraid I'm gonna lose consciousness."

He's our only ticket back.

"Of course . . . ! Of course. You chart the way back. We can't do anymore here," I assure him.

Yeti's fighter slowly peels off from combat, plotting a course north. We follow suit.

"You got lazy, Kid. Your letting your friend die." The Voice grates.

My heart misses a pump. It's getting worse. She can't know it's getting worse.

Cass keeps hands on the trigger of the machine gun, scanning the sky, even as we pull away from the fighting. Watching the light of the explosions illuminate her face, I can't help but notice the new creases near her eyes that weren't there before.

I want to take her away from all of this. Go find someplace quiet. Find out what it means not having to live day-to-day. I don't know if we could though. We're grounded in all of this. We're where we belong, and she knows it. It's not like there's any other place we'd be safer anyways.

Another British signal raises on the com. I move to silence it. I don't have the strength to argue with the Brits again.

As my hand brushes the dial, the voice shouts, "Mayday! Mayday! Mayday! This is the H.M.S. *Churchill* requesting all available support!"

Light bubbles up from the soup below. Fire erupts from the deck of a nearby zeppelin, illuminating the word "Church." That must be our man.

"This is Captain Raemar Belvadeer of H.M.S. *Churchill*,"", the harried voice crackles, "We are under heavy attack. Unable to repel our pursuant! Requesting assistance immediately!"

I follow the trail of smoke until the looming form of the *Ark* bleeds into view.

"Sage, do you see it?" Cass shouts, pointing below.

The front of the *Ark* swings open from either side, revealing a cavernous hangar.

"Cass . . . Cass I think we need to stay away from this one," I murmur.

The *Ark's* forward cannon pounds one more shot across *The Churchill's* engines. The fire on its deck burns brighter as the *Churchill* loses speed. The *Ark* begins enveloping the British carrier like a shark swallowing its prey whole. Captain Belvadeer's pleas become more distorted as the *Ark's* bay swoops over the stricken vessel.

The Captain tries once more. "We are being boarded! I repeat, we are being boarded! Mayday! Mayday! Ma-".

The *Ark's* hangar doors slam shut.

Nothing but silence crackles through the radio.

I've never felt so small, so out-gunned. The engineering needed to create that image is so far beyond anything we have in the fleet, so far beyond anything we've ever known.

It's time to decide. What am I? A soldier? Or a coward.

"Cass, let's just get home," I say quietly. "Let's all just get home."

She says nothing back.

At least cowards live.

Squinting westward, I follow Yeti's plume of smoke. The sun bleaches the sky red as it slowly sinks beneath the clouds. In the next few hours, Yeti strays off course several times, gliding listlessly to the left or right. Each time, I yell into the speaker until his plane snaps back to its original heading. We have a lot more riding on him than just our friendship. If we lose him, we lose the *Artemis*.

But as darkness falls, the clouds give way to a familiar form. The *Artemis* glides through the sky, accompanied only by lapping trails of smoke. It didn't make it out of Shipwreck before Cascade fighters found it.

"Sage . . . " Yeti's voice is almost impossible to hear over the roar of the engine. "Can you hail the *Artemis*, man? I need to . . . "

My attention snaps to the comm. "Hey, hey, hey . . . Yeti - stay with me ok? We'll get clearance in no time," I assure him.

Only silence greets me on the other end, but Yeti keeps his course.

"Artemis Actual, are you there?" I ask, switching frequencies.

A young woman with a French accent crackles in. "This is Artemis Actual. What is your call sign pilot? Know we have cannons trained on you and your escort, and that we are fully prepared to fire."

Understandable, given the ship's limping state.

I try being clearer. "I . . . I think you've got it turned around Artemis Actual. This is Sergeant Saber of Gold Squadron. I've commandeered a Shipwreck fighter and have RN Dawson onboard. I'm currently escorting Airman Yeti and his Artemis bound Jackal. He's in desperate need of medical attention. Requesting permission to land."

The comm clips out as I hear Artemis Actual pull away from the microphone. That's odd. Our scouts should be able to see Yeti's in dire need. I glance at the nests, hoping to catch the glint of Stenia's scope with the last of the dying sunset.

Worried, I look back. "What do you think Cass?" I ask.

Her features tell me what I already know. "I think we should be ready to jet, if it comes to it," she says.

Exhaustion hangs on her words. The back-lit ports of the Living Quarters taunt us with their warmth. A nice, safe bed. So close . . .

The static makes way for a voice. "This is Artemis Actual. You are cleared for landing," she says.

My head bobs, fighting the urge to fall asleep right in the cockpit. We have one last task before that can happen. Why did it take her so long to clear us?

Cass's voice pipes up. "I'm worried about Yeti. You think he'll able to thread the needle?"

I look at his stricken plane. The fire's stopped, but his control's a lot stiffer than before. His hydraulics are on their last leg.

"He has to," I say.

I corral Yeti, helping him circle up behind The *Artemis*. The docking crew lowers all of the sky hooks from above, deploying every one they have. All we have to do is catch one each. We both decrease our speed, approaching the contact point.

We can do this.

"Pop it!" I yell to Yeti.

His bar jumps up from the front, framing the top of his cockpit. Struggling through the different instruments, I find my own roosting gear. I pull the lever, watching the docking bar fly up over my head. This fighter's much bigger than weight regulations allow for the sky hooks.

This might not work.

Slowing down behind Yeti, I try boxing him so he'll thread on the first try. Luckily, he's always been much better at it then I ever have. Even in his state of blood loss, his technique is solid. The hook clangs against his bar, snapping the Jackal up towards the hangar bay. Yeti cuts his engine; most likely losing consciousness directly afterwards. With one emergency taken care of, I turn my focus to saving Cass and myself.

Our docking mechanism doesn't provide very much clearance between the cockpit and the bar itself. This aircraft was obviously meant to land on the ground, with the air bar as an afterthought. With no functioning landing gear, the Roost is not an option.

The Cellar will have to do.

The iron hook hurtles at us. Cass shrinks down in her seat, abandoning her gun. One wrong twitch and I'll send the hook right though our canopy. I duck as the hook's shadow flits past my face.

The bar catches, bucking our cockpit up violently. The hook strains, pulling our plane towards the hangar.

Panicking, I reach over and cut the engine. The fighter shudders to a halt as the crane above hauls its prey up into its web. The plane swings forward and back with the wind, sending Cass gripping for the sides of the canopy. The lone cable holding us aloft

twists and turns against the weight.
    Somehow, it holds as we rise into the light.

14

I yawn, fighting back the exhaustion plaguing us. We've accomplished the impossible. We not only survived . . . we made it home. The flood lights of the hangar pour in through the cockpit like a downy, luminescent blanket. Breathing a sigh of relief, I let myself relax for the first time in hours.

I glance down at our odd orange craft. We must look awfully out of place. The size alone is going to cause logistical issues. I rock up in my seat. They're not going to have room to set us down!

"Cass, I just realized this plane can't clip its wings. They won't have any place to put us," I say.

"Sage, it looks like they're going to have plenty of room . . . ," she replies quietly.

Confused, I look over our left wing at the floor of the hangar bay. What was a tightly packed living area populated with pilots and planes alike, now houses a much sparser collection of both. I can't make sense of it.

"How are we missing so many?" I ask in disbelief.

Cass shakes her head. "I don't know."

Our crane finds a bald spot on the deck and begins lowering us. Before the hull even touches the hangar floor, Cass throws her legs over the side of the cockpit.

She turns her head, holding onto the fuselage. "I'm going to make sure Yeti's ok. Check us in, and find Sabine. We need to tell her about what we saw."

Before I can reply, she's already disappeared over the side. I let out sigh: the double edged sword of loving a woman who knows what she wants.

The crane sets the fighter down on the deck. It immediately lists to the side. The destroyed landing gear strains to bear the weight for a few moments, but crumples despite its best effort. Sliding back the cockpit, I fight gravity's attempt to pull me back over the other side of the plane. Climbing down over the crippled fuselage, I try finding the nearest face I know.

I find it with Lieutenant Baltier. The middle aged Australian seems equally intent to greet me. As commander of the local Red Swan's charter, he's a fierce fighter, and even more protective of his source of income: namely, Admiral Khan.

Two dock technicians rush over with a dolly table full of tools. I try getting their attention, but they pay me no mind as they start their work on my plane. Classic deckhand etiquette.

I hail the Australian. "Is that you Mr. Baltier? Good to see you Lieutenant!"

Baltier clenches his rifle in his left hand, closing the distance between us.

"Likewise," he says.

His fist catches me across the jaw before I even see his arm move. Pain explodes as white lights dance around my cornea. Stunned, I throw an arm out, spinning to the ground. My mind flits from scenario to scenario.

Why?

Seeing double, I look past Baltier's polished boot. A platoon of armed soldiers crosses the hangar towards us. This can't be right.

Instinctively, I struggle to pull my knees underneath me to get to my feet. The Lieutenant doesn't like this. His hand claps under my throat, slamming me flat on my back over the rolling workbench behind us. The tools pierce into my back.

The two crew members scatter as Baltier pulls up alongside the bench, tightening his pincer grip. The sinews of my throat strain against his clamped hand, fighting for air. Dark spots blot my sight. Kicking, I thrash against his superior positioning. I succeed only in knocking the rest of the displaced tools onto the hangar floor, making even more noise.

It's just enough of a commotion to pull Cass's attention away from Yeti's wounds. I hear her cry out as her footfalls pound towards us.

Baltier nods to the other guards. Their boots hit the ground, rushing to meet her.

Apparently they underestimate her as an easy takedown. Out of the corner of my eye, I see one of the armed men crash to the deck. Despite the initial strike, I hear the fight turn against her as other guards rush to assist. She may have been able to subdue one opponent, but she can't overcome all three.

Blood rushes past my ears as a dark circle creeps in around my vision, closing in quickly. Realizing he's about to choke me out, Baltier releases the pressure just enough to allow me a quick breath. I pull in a ragged cough, pushing the circle back into my periphery. I greedily suck in air while I still have the luxury.

Baltier leans down and asks me one question. "Are you Sergeant Sage Basmon, call sign 'Sabre'?" he asks with unblinking eyes.

I thought we knew of each other from serving the *Artemis* during previous voyages. Baltier's led our Red Swan charter for at least three years. Utterly confused, I look into my attacker's face. His fixed gaze tells me he already knows the answer. I consider my options. Since they already have Cass, those choices are considerably more limited. There's really not much I can do but tell the truth.

"Yes, I am," I wheeze.

Baltier let's go of my throat, straightening up over the bench.

"I thought so," he grins.

The butt of his rifle closes the dark circle for good.

Shadows swirl together and break apart. There's no rhythm to it. It's very distracting. The only constants are two yellow lines on either side of my conscious, dancing along the borders, back and forth, swaying to some unpredictable beat. I know that pattern from somewhere . . .

Peering through the mist, I try breathing. It works, but I barely get enough oxygen. My nose is clogged and useless. I lick my tongue over the tops of my teeth, making sure each one is accounted for. They're all there, but my lips are ragged from the impact of the rifle. The sides of my cheeks taste like blood.

I would've checked all of this with my hands, but they're wrenched behind my back, bound with twine. Whoever tied the knot pulled it far too tightly. My shoulders strain at the seams.

The dancing yellow lines to my right and left aren't a path through the astral plane after all. The golden striping of the uniformed marines flanking me bleeds into clear focus. The knit lines on the right are frayed, pulling at the rest of the fabric. Either the marine holding my right arm has seen action, or just got dealt a rough hand when his uniform was assigned.

The dull pain in my knees pulses as they drag me across the floor. I make no attempt to get up. I don't think they realize I'm conscious. Maybe I can play it to my advantage. The least I can do is make it difficult for them to carry me.

My eyes sliver open again as we approach two heavily armed guards flanking a blast door. It's armor plated. Is it meant to keep people out . . . or in? The guards' boots click as the door opens. Cool air whooshes past. The sound dampens. I take another chance by opening my eyes into slits.

Everything's back-lit with a green hazy glow. Tight lipped personnel shuttle from station to station. Holographic projections plot every course, divulging all types of information. Colors change on a flickering cross sectional layout of our engine room. Apparently whatever issue that arose has just been solved.

This is the Bridge.

I thought this kind of technology only existed before The Drowning. What else is the Admiral keeping from the rest of the crew? I've never been close to the Bridge before. Even the Bridge personnel tend not to mingle with the rest of the population. The few times they do, they never betray much about their jobs. For the safety of the *Artemis*, of course.

Throwing caution to the wind, I turn my head to take it all in. Guiding lights blink blue and red on either side of the plate glass windows that extend out to the ends of the giant oval cockpit. A deep darkness spreads out beyond them. The bend of the outside light betrays that the glass is incredibly thick. Direct hits were definitely considered when the Bridge was engineered.

"To my quarters please," Admiral Khan's voice says sedately over the intercom.

My captors shift their course, dragging me down a ramp towards another door. A sign with the embossed letters "Admiral's Quarters" glints over the doorway. As my knees bump over the entrance, a luxurious recording of classical music replaces the fading sound of machines whirring on the Bridge. The melody dances emphatically around the room, entirely unaware of the dire circumstances lying within. The door shuts behind me. The volume of the recording rises, no longer able to escape out into the corridor.

My knees meet some comfort as they make their way onto a plush carpet from some distant land. Probably the Turkish Coast. Knowing the Admiral, he didn't get this from a local marketplace. He probably flew over to the source and hand-selected the piece himself. Why spare any expense when you're King?

Equally lush looking couches flank a table where the Admiral's cherished Victrola is perched. The intercom isn't hooked to the box. We're the only ones who get to enjoy this show. Aside from the music, rich tapestries adorn the wall. They vary from stylized scenes of battle, to a nude woman who appears entirely disinterested in the fact that she's being captured in oil.

I hear the Admiral before I see him.

Thud. Thud . . . Thud.

"I'm sorry to see you here Sergeant Basmon," he says to the wall.

The Admiral bleeds into view, pulling his custom knives out of a cork target. I search the wall around it looking for punctures caused by missed throws. There aren't many.

"I am too," I say, allowing my consciousness to be known.

The knives click as the Admiral grinds them together in his hand. He turns away from the board and approaches me with deliberation.

"It's truly painful . . . this business," he says, haphazardly throwing the knives on his desk. The small lamp on his table shakes, sending the shadows on the Admiral's face dancing eerily.

"You know, I gave you every chance to succeed here. Set you up for success," he says.

His eyes hide beneath the darkness created by his prominent brows.

"Tried to guide you on a more profitable and fulfilling path." He gestures down to the cargo hold below. "Give you power. Give you respect . . . Things most men lack!" he says, spitting out the last sentence. Hurt oozes from the Admiral's voice. "And instead of using all of these privileges to better yourself and everyone else around you, you use it to try to grab even more power. Mine. The very source that granted yours."

The knot tightens in my chest. The pacts. He knows about them. Does he know who was involved?

"Admiral, I think we have a misunderstanding . . ."

Before I can say another word, the Admiral clasps his hand around my throat. Clutching his powerful fingers around my neck, his strength lifts me from my knees. I sputter, kicking out with my bound legs. He makes no movement other than looking me straight in the face. His grey eyes fix on mine with a hatred I've never seen before.

Spittle and disgust fly at me with every word. "I hear tell of my men, MY MEN, swearing oaths." His arm strains against my weight. "Swearing oaths to some upstart FUCK of an officer, who thinks he can lead this crew better than I can! Do you know what it's like to hold this ship together in its current state? Why would you jeopardize EVERYTHING, just for your own benefit?"

I try swallowing to get enough room to speak.

"It's not what you think Admiral . . ." I choke out.

The very sound of my voice infuriates him even more. He lets me know this by tightening his grip. Struggling, I fight for breath, my gulps of air getting shallower and shallower. My body pulls against the rope binding my arms behind me. Through all of this, I hear the creak of the door before it slams shut behind us.

The Admiral's eyes flit away from mine, taking in the new sight. He smiles and grabs my jaw, jerking my head towards the door. Through the blurriness of my suffocation, I see Cass struggling against her guards. She's bloodied, but not subdued. In contrast to me, it looks like she's been fighting the entire way up to the Bridge. Upon closer inspection, I see her captors are almost as bruised as she is. A small fire lights in my chest. I chose the right one.

The Admiral seems to regain some of his composure in the presence of a lady.

Once more the gallant general, he sweeps his arms open. "Nurse Dawson, what a pleasure it is to see you," he says.

Cass doesn't seem to hear the Admiral as she continues searching for different methods to get free of her bonds. Her captors set her down on the rich carpet in the middle of the congregation of chairs. As her knees hit, they crank her shoulders down so she'll kneel facing me. A pulse of stress beats up and down my arm.

What are our options?

The sturdier woman wrenching Cass's left arm clearly enjoys her opportunity to retaliate. She looks up at the Admiral with a grin. "Sir, are you sure we can't just beat her senseless?"

Admiral Khan walks between us. "No, I'm quite sure that I need her conscious for this," he replies.

He turns on his foot. "You know, it's quite unfortunate, really. You were both shining examples of what this fleet could be. Courageous, willing, capable. Everything I could want in a soldier." He stops, pondering for a moment. "But therein lies the issue. You both possessed a little too much ambition. You forget the reason either of you are employed . . . or even really alive at all, is because I deemed it so."

He wraps his fingers around the maple handle one of his knives, dragging it along his desk. "You see, the reason we still need Miss Dawson sentient, is because I require leverage to make Sergeant Basmon give me what I need," he says, twisting the dagger in his hand. "I need her able to make every facial expression fitting for the situations I present." His gray eyes flick up to mine. "I'm sure you will find it quite effective."

The Admiral's voice cools. "I want the names of each and every one of the turncoats you've recruited, Sergeant Basmon."

I barely hear him over the sound of my heart pounding. There's no plan, no course of action. One thought bubbles to the surface, and that's to stay silent. So I do.

The Admiral exhales slowly, irritated by the process taking longer than he'd hoped.

"Fine . . . we'll do it my way then," he says softly.

Before I can react, he grabs one of the guard's guns from its holster, leveling it at Cass's head. As strong as Cass is, the thought of death on this carpet starts becoming very real. She shakes under the barrel's glare. I surge up, but my guards' hands force me back down. Another gun clicks behind me. This isn't how I imagined we'd die.

The Admiral smiles, enjoying his position of power. Something gnaws at him though.

He lowers his weapon, clucking his tongue. "My goodness, of all the places you could set Miss Dawson down, you choose to do it on the heirloom Corinthian carpet?"

Flustered, he turns to one of the *Artemis* marines standing by. "If you would be so kind as to fetch some plastic sheets, it would be truly appreciated."

It takes a second for the command to sink in, but the marine finally snaps a salute. "Yessir!"

He disappears through the door as Admiral Khan ponders the other furniture in his execution chamber.

Khan strokes his chin. "Hmmm, that should provide sufficient protection.", he mutters, tallying the totals in his head. "The chairs don't need a veneer; their value is sentimental only."

The other soldiers in the room nod their approval, voicing it in various ways. No one has the courage to address the absurdity of the situation. Satisfied his most valuable assets will be preserved, the Admiral strolls back to me.

"Here is the arrangement Sergeant," he says, squatting so we're face to face. "Once that plastic is laid down . . . I'm pulling the trigger." He taps the barrel of the gun on my shoulder. "That is, unless I hear all of the names of everyone who has conspired against me." He pauses, scratching his temple. "Then maybe I'll consider providing her some sort of amnesty," he offers.

Anyone caught in this trap knows that's not a viable option. My knowledge of our loyal members is the only token keeping us alive.

Different paths play out in my head:

Bite captor's leg, grapple for his gun . . . With my hands tied behind my back, I get shot.

Wait for the plastic to get here, say nothing, and Cass gets shot.

Rush the Admiral, tackle him, yell at Cass to run, and we both get shot.

Keep the Admiral interested with conversation until I can come up with a better plan.

A plausible option.

"Let's talk, Admiral," I say.

Cass's head snaps up. "Noo-", her disapproval is cut short by the butt of a rifle. She's still conscious, but reeling. I try not to let her pain cloud my judgment.

Grimacing, I continue. "I believe I have an option that will result in neither of us having to be executed, and you not having a costly civil war on your hands."

The Admiral folds his hands behind his back, arching out his medallioned chest. "I'm certainly listening."

Readjusting my bruised knees, I try to see if a little less pain will help me keep my clarity. "The only reason these pacts were formed was purely in the event that the *Ark* turned out to be a real threat." I clear my throat before adding, "You know just as well as I do that, at the very least, half of the rumors circulating trade towns carry no weight. The *Ark* could have easily been one of these fallacies."

For the first time, I meet his eyes on my own terms. "The fact of the matter is, the *Ark* is very real. You saw for yourself what it did . . . what it can do."

The Admiral considers this, shifting his weight. "The *Ark* is only one ship. It will be taken down with time." He lets his gun drop to his side. "You cannot attack that many outposts without the international community taking notice. It will be destroyed soon, like every other pretender who tries to tip the scales in their favor," he muses.

I inch closer, careful not to draw the ire of my guards. "But that's just the thing Admiral. Everyone who's witnessed *The Ark* has chosen to run, if they can. Those who stay and fight get buried underneath their own earth."

I pause just long enough to give the Admiral a chance to retaliate, but he says nothing. I need him to believe he's still in control of the conversation.

Shifting the weight of my knees, I inch forward once more. "Every time the *Ark* strikes, it fractures already fragile trading communities. You, yourself referenced our own ship as being an example of one of these communities," I say.

The door creaks behind us, allowing footsteps to echo from the hallway. Never has the sound of dragging plastic caused so much fear.

I lurch forward. "Admiral! This isn't the best way."

He shoves me back. "Yes, I cite the fragility of our crew often!" Seething, he turns back to Cass as the guards lay down the plastic sheets. "You'll make excellent examples for those who would consider a similar treason."

Frantically, I look into Cass's eyes. They brim with tears, but there's no regret that I can see. She's trying to make a decision: whether to fight and fall to a hail of bullets, or to wait and fall victim to just one. From what I know of Cass, I know I need to find another way to stall the process, and hurry; she won't go quietly.

"Admiral listen!" I yell, jumping to my feet.

Catching both of my captors off guard, they rush to restrain me.

The Admiral ignores my plea. Instead, he supervises his guards as they pick up Cass and lay the sheet underneath her knees. I don't get another word out before my legs sweep from under me. As I hit the ground, a boot jams into the side of my head. A white void blots out my vision. I fight to stay conscious.

"Careful now!" the Admiral's voice interrupts. "I want to make sure he's awake to see this."

Battling the white lights, I keep my focus on the Admirals; all four of them, as they swirl around one another. All four raise their guns to the side of Cass's head. I take one last deep breath. They all become one.

"I know you don't think there's profit in keeping us alive, but I can assure you that you're wrong," I say with as much calm as I can muster. Begging hasn't worked; it's time to take a position of authority. A hard thing to do when you're literally under the heel of a boot.

"If Cass or I die, the insurgents on this ship have been trained to act on their orders." It's bullshit, but it's the last card I have. "You said yourself that you don't know who they are." I look up at the guards. "They could be here in this very room, waiting for you to pull the trigger."

Admiral Khan's finger takes up slack in the trigger guard.

Stay calm.

I fight to keep my voice steady. "The entire reason the insurgency was formed was to make sure we addressed the threat presented by the *Ark* if you didn't. If you address the threat, then there's no reason for us to mutiny."

Khan says nothing, but keeps the tension on the trigger. An odd euphoria blossoms in my chest as I flip my last card in hopes of a straight flush. We're all in.

"Admiral, I saw how many planes were missing in that hangar. Saw how many pilots didn't make the boat," I say quietly, licking my dry lips. "How many soldiers didn't make it back on board before you ran? How many of those who did are still loyal to you after seeing what they saw? The deck's been shuffled. So the real question is: which half is still on this ship?"

I've breached the Admiral's calculating territory now, but it's all I've got.

"That would be quite the gamble," I say slowly, "to have spent the last thirty years creating your dream, only to lose everything on one bet."

The Admiral exhales, his eyes narrowing. "What did you say the name of the leader of this outfit was?" he asks.

"I didn't," I reply. A pearl of sweat drips down the side of my face.

"What is it?" the Admiral asks.

"His name is Garon Tesarik," I say.

The Admiral's eyes widen for just a second. Maybe I imagined it.

"Do you know his na-?"

"And what color did you say the light from his ship was?" the Admiral asks, stepping over my question.

"Blue," I respond, confused.

We all wait in silence as he mulls over the new information, his face downturned.

I have one last blow to try to finish this. "The *Ark* collects a material called Neodymium Magnetite. It's never been found in an organic state before this, and it possesses the chemical properties to create super light armor plating," I state.

Cass picks her head up just enough to look down the barrel of the Admiral's gun.

Keep still Cass.

"If we take down that ship, the first right to scavenge will be ours," I say. Careful now. "Do you think you might be able to find a market for a material like that?" I ask.

Silence.

We all wait, frozen in time. Heartbeats race up and down my neck.

The Admiral clicks his pistol up in the air. "I knew there was a reason that I kept my eye on you," he smiles.

Cass doubles over, stifling a sob. She shakes her head,

collecting herself.

The Admiral walks over, gesturing for the guard to take his foot off my head. "If I let you both go, you must give me your word that there will be no insurrection," he says.

Adrenaline floods my veins. "In exchange, you'll give me your word that we'll work together to address the *Ark* threat," I say.

The Admiral pauses, grinding his teeth for a moment. His eyes snap up to my gruff captor. "Silva, cut Sergeant Basmon's bindings please."

Concealing my smirk, I watch Silva's face drop as he comprehends the Admiral's order. Eventually, his knife cuts through the ropes. Standing back up, I try rubbing the feeling back into my wrists.

The Admiral extends his hand. "If we're going to do this, it will be like any other business venture," he offers.

Taking my still numb hand, I force it into his as convincingly as possible.

"Done."

Somewhere nearby, the smell of Burley tobacco hangs heavily in the air.

15

The guards escort us out of the Bridge and down to the Outer Rim. I'm trying my best not to faint. The day has drained everything emotionally and physically, and the stress of near execution almost overpowers me, but I won't let myself appear drained in this company. An awkward hand-off occurs as Cass and I leave their sight. The Admiral gave us both side arms as a sign of sovereignty, and as a down payment for our agreement. The gun weighs heavily against my thigh. I didn't care to look at the make and model when they were turned over to us. Did I see a revolver casting? It looks like polished silver. If so, it appears the Admiral will spare no expense trying to repurchase the loyalty of his crew.

Once I'm confident no other guards are in the vicinity, I stop and wrap Cass up in my arms. She does nothing at first, but then slowly returns the embrace.

I pull her closer. "I . . . I'm sorry about all of this," I say.

She shushes me. "We worked together. We wouldn't have made it otherwise," she replies, brushing back her matted, oily hair. "There's going to be a time where we sit down and talk about all of this, but it's not going to be tonight."

She runs her hands through her hair until her fingers get caught. "I don't know about you, but I'm going to go see if we still have running water. I want to wash as much of this day off of me as I can," she says.

I nod. "As much as I'd like to join you, I'm gonna check on Olan. There are a lot of people missing and I want to make sure he's not one of them."

For just a split second, I see the hint of a coy smile on Cass's face. "Even if we didn't just survive an Armageddon and an execution, I wouldn't let you join me anyways. No offense, but I've spent about as much time with you as I'd ever want to today," she says, brushing past me.

I let myself smile too. "Seems fair to me."

The wind blows her thick locks over her shoulder as she disappears into the darkness. The chill seeps through my jacket as I turn towards the Living Quarters bulkhead. My head hangs, thinking about my cot. I'm sure I could even get a hold of an extra blanket and just burrow into it.

No.

Olan first, then rest.

My feet trip over each other as I approach my floor. The same ugly, molding, red carpeting glares back up at me, and the cold windy chill's still there. I pause. A dim light seeps up from the corner of the corridor, casting eerie shadows. Something's changed here; a cold blast of wind accosts me.

"Just turn around kid."

I ignore The Voice as the smell of a freshly lit cigarette wafts through the air. I'm not going to let it control my life.

Rounding the corner, I find the source of the draft: a thirty-foot hole blasted into the middle of our little neighborhood. Our cabin wasn't far from the source of the explosion. There's nothing left.

"Olan!"

I can't hold back the panic in my voice. "Olan!" I shout, running quickly.

Next to the hole, shapes move from side to side. A blow torch illuminates the workers as they attempt to patch the *Artemis's* hull. My hurried steps catch their attention.

A burly welder steps in my way, catching me. "Whoa, hey. Where d'ya think you're going?"

I can't catch up to my breath. "That's my apartment!" I shout.

The welder looks over his shoulder, slowly pushing me away. "I'm sorry sir, that *was* your apartment."

Reality sets in. Nausea creeps up from inside. I let the worker lead me to the corridor wall. I think he can tell my legs are about to give out. Everything I've ever owned was in that room: the last photo of my mother, model plane collections from when I was a kid, everything I held dear. They're all gone.

Aoife. Olan.

I grab the welder's shoulders. "Where are the other occupants of this block?"

The welder pushes me off as consternation overtakes his face. He scratches his stubbled chin. "There's a small collection of them by the scaffolding over there."

He points to the one solitary lamp in the area, under which I can make out a few hunched forms. Thanking him quietly, I begin hobbling toward the light, using my very last vestige of energy. Now there's no bed for me to hide from the world. There's nothing left.

Breaking into the small circle of light, I see the hunched forms are the displaced residents covered with blankets and other scraps of cloth to help keep the night's chill at bay. I step silently over the various prone bodies. The cold, damp floor of the *Artemis* becomes more appealing with every step. Perhaps I can find a blanket for myself.

No.

I need to focus. Aoife and Olan have to be here.

I search for the next few minutes, using the flickering bulb to identify each face. There are too few people here to account for everyone from the block. I can only hope the others have found shelter with their other family or with some kind strangers. Logic tells me this isn't the case, reinforced by the knowledge that I can't find either Olan or Aoife anywhere in the whole group.

I begin panicking, frantically searching each of the faces once again, even though I know I've already checked them. I recognize a couple pressed up against one another as our elderly neighbors. Very kind people. I frequently run into the husband when I leave for my early morning trainings. He's not especially chatty, but somehow always optimistic. I never did catch his name. After so much time, I was too embarrassed to ask.

I kneel down beside them; they're my only option. The Husband seems to realize this, as one of his wrinkled eyes flashes open. A washed-out blue searches me intently.

"It's good to see that you are alive Mr. Basmon," he says softly.

I falter, ashamed that I still don't know his name. "I'm glad to see that you and your wife are also ok, sir."

Sensing there's more to this conversation, the Husband tenderly disengages himself from his wife. He's careful not to wake her as he folds her arm back to her side. If I didn't know any better, her sleepy expression would have persuaded me that this plate-metal floor was every bit as comfortable as the down bed they lost. Just as long as her husband's arms were around her. For one moment, my heart warms, just a little.

The Husband puts the blanket back over his wife, running a hand through his white hair. He looks ghostly in this harsh light.

We stand in silence. I'm afraid to ask the question.

"Sir, have you seen my two cabinmates?" I ask.

He looks over at the hole in the side of the ship, pausing for a moment.

I feel the need to clarify. "One was a very large man. And his daughter Aoife. About five?"

He says nothing.

"She's a little girl. Red hair. You must at least know her by sight," I plead with him.

The Husband shifts his weight before sighing, "I know Aoife and Olan, Sage."

A lump forms in the back of my throat. "Oh good," I choke, "Then you must know where they are."

The Husband takes me by the shoulder, guiding me away from the light.

"They both made it back onto the ship,", he says. "Olan went to go help with the defense, and told Aoife to go hide under your bed. There wasn't any time for her to find a better spot further inside the ship." He takes a deep breath. "Then Olan ran to the Outer Rim to help coordinate the launch and fend off the attackers."

I need to get away. I don't want to talk any more.

The Husband's pale blue eyes brim as they look up at me. "When Olan came back after we had broken off from the battle . . . he found this hole. Just like we did. We had been hiding in the mess hall."

His face swims. I can't focus on it anymore.

He holds his voice steady. "We looked everywhere for her. The only remnant we found was up by one of the welders. A little piece of her red dress. That's all we have."

He takes something from his pocket, pressing it into my hand.

A burnt piece of fabric unfolds in my palm.

My body lands against the wall, coming to rest in the angle that meets the floor. Sobs wrack my body. It's the first time I've cried about anything since I can remember. All the tension that's been building up is released; the only thing I can think about is how to do it quietly so I don't wake up the neighbor's wife.

Her giggles, her contagious little smile, her genuine kindness; none of it was enough to stop that shell. No power moved to stop it from crashing into the side of the ship. Every time I think I've gotten a hold of myself, my anguish is renewed with unshed tears. I fucking hate this world. The cruelty always seemed as though it was no match in the face of that little girl, but now it's taken her too.

My own mortality, the thing always scratching the back of my mind, now looms in front of me. I have no way to defend against it. Death was something that happens to other people. I was supposed to be immune, but it's a blind, cold creature always lurking in the shadows, waiting for those who least expect it.

I can feel it now, watching me with its dark, hollowed-out eyes.

A warm blanket interrupts my spiraling thoughts.

The frail hands of the Wife slowly press the blanket over my shoulders. I must have awakened her. Either that, or she knew the departure of her Husband signaled that all was not well. No matter the reason; my heart jumps to my throat. I'm so glad she's here. I don't even know her name.

Her eyes hide underneath the shadow of her inconsistently dyed hair. Her husband turns his head turns to the side, placing a hand over his mouth. His eyes hide under the shadows as well.

The older woman kneels down, running her thumb over my cheek to brush the tears away.

"There, there child. Let's go find Olan, shall we?" she soothes.

That's what I am right now: a child. Having one of my pillars of strength knocked out from under me has caused me to regress twenty years. I nod slowly, letting her guide me away from the hole.

I smell it: I smell the burnt flesh. My sister's blood splashed across the wall. I couldn't help you Pela. My mother on the ground. I couldn't help you either Mom. The flames creep in to feast.

I look down at my scarred hands. The winding lines sear themselves back into my fingers. Panicking, I wrestle to wipe them away, wipe them off my hands. As though it were that easy.

The Wife pulls me closer. "Focus on me, child." She grabs one of my hands, slowly guiding it away from the other. "Focus on me."

Something about her soft, wrinkled hands breaks through. They're something I never had in my childhood. The Wife is consistent. The Wife is a selfless person; I didn't know many of those growing up.

As I step out into the gale that separates us from the infirmary, recovering enough common sense for my own protective instincts to function. The driving wind and rain lash out in sheets over the Outer Rim. I use what little bulk I have to shield us both. It's not much, but she seems to appreciate the gesture.

Reality sets in as we approach the infirmary door, and I break down again. How can I look Olan in the eye? How do I even say anything to him when he's just lost his child? The tears and rain drops mix. My sister's face won't stop melding with Aoife's. They would have been about the same age. Pinching the top of my nose, I focus on that pressure to keep the image away, but the more I fight it, the more I see the remains of Aoife lying right next to my mother. The flames creep in.

No.

I won't let myself get distracted. She's not my kid. Olan's the one who's lost everything. I need to make sure that I can be there for him. I can't be caught up in my own emotional minefield. I wipe away the tears I can, hoping the rain camouflages the ones I've missed.

As expected after every battle, the infirmary's bursting at the seams. Nurses flit from bed to bed like dissatisfied humming birds. Patients do the same, but at a much slower pace. The smell claws into my throat, gagging me; it is a terrible mixture of bodily fluids, stale odors, and human refuse.

The Wife accompanies me to the entrance before bidding farewell. Her job here is done, but mine has just begun. I swim through the mass of people. Some reach out to me, desperate for something to eat or drink. I grasp their hands as I walk by, but that's all that I do. Someone will be there to help them soon; hopefully. I'm on a mission.

It doesn't take me too long to find him through the haze. An enterprising nurse took the liberty of pushing two cots together to accommodate Olan's giant frame. He lies there, face up, his mountain of a stomach slowly rising and falling. The clamor surrounding him seems to have no effect.

Closing the distance, I notice his arms and legs are bound to the beds. Concern ripples its way through my stomach. Reaching Olan's bedside, I stare quietly into his face. It's twisted, tortured by dreams. Still, at this point it's probably better than being conscious.

"He's been sedated."

The nurse behind me catches me off guard.

From beneath his bulk, I hook a finger up on his binding. "It certainly appears that way. Why?"

Fiona steps up next to me. "He's a danger to himself. Even sleeping."

I pull up one of the covers that's been haphazardly thrown over his chest. "What happened?" I ask.

Fiona straightens her back, clutching her clipboard to her chest. "Apparently the maintenance crew tackled him in the Living Quarters. He tried to jump through one of the holes blasted in the ship's hull. In the tussle, he tried taking a welding torch to his throat. The workers were able to wrestle it back before he could finish the job. With tendencies like that, it's best he not have access to objects that could kill him, or others."

The putrid wound on his neck gapes up at me. Olan, what have you done?

"You know these bindings won't hold him," I say quietly.

Fiona pauses for a moment before answering. "Under different circumstances, I would have agreed with you. However, I was on the infirmary floor when they brought him in. This man has no more fight left in him. That, and we've pumped him with enough tranquilizers to sedate a rhino."

The sincere urge to hit this woman bubbles into my chest.

I clench my firsts, fighting to keep a polite veneer. "Thank you, you've done quite enough."

Sensing my frustration, Fiona keeps her silence, disappearing before I can look over to confirm she's gone. Not knowing what else to do, I slide down next to Olan's bed post.

I have no home.

Everything I've ever owned is gone. Exhaustion saps my ability to problem-solve. Right now, there's no better solution than just to surrender to the overwhelming powers that be. That's exactly what I do, resting the back of my head against the bed post before letting the darkness surge in.

The sensation of saliva dripping from my mouth is the first indication that I'm awake. Several hours have passed, evidenced by the first rays of sunlight forcing their way into the infirmary. It has a rejuvenating effect on most of the patients, a reassurance that they've made it through another night. I've slipped off of the bedpost and fallen onto my side. My elbow's sore and my right arm tingles with paralysis. Slowly, I try massaging out the pins and needles that have taken up residence there. Kneeling, I twist around to peer at Olan.

His hollow stare startles me. Where has my friend gone?

"Good morning Olan," My soft voice reverberates off the infirmary walls.

He says nothing. I can't tell if he's still drugged, or if his heart's so broken that he just can't put forth the effort to talk right now. Looking up over the side of the bed, I see most people are still asleep. Some nurses mill about taking care of patients, but I haven't moved enough to draw their attention.

I look back into my friend's blank eyes. A pair of surgical scissors lays on the next cot over, just beyond Olan's line of vision. Slowly and silently, I pull them out of their pouch and begin snipping my way through the bond on his right arm. This is no place for a grieving father. I quietly work from below the bed, cutting through each band.

Another patient's wheelchair sits next to her bed. The golden bow on the back of it designates it as property of the infirmary. I'll feel less guilty since it's not her personal chair. Sliding out from under the bed, I noiselessly pop open the chair.

Seeing my plan, Olan edges himself towards the side of the

bed. With his help, I slowly get him into the chair. With the new weight, the back of it begins flipping towards the floor. I throw my body under it to stop the momentum, straining against the sheer mass. I feel Olan struggling as well.

Rolling his weight forward, Olan wins his battle. The chair lands on the tiles a little too loudly, but we're still upright. After collecting his personal affects, I wheel Olan towards the door.

I tense as we approach the nurses. They must know something is out of place.

I take a deep breath, reminding myself not to do anything to draw attention to myself. I keep a languid but consistent stride towards the door.

I freeze.

Fiona's exhausted brown eyes peek out from the huddle of nurses.

Starting again, I keep moving towards the door. Maybe we can make it out before she can say anything.

Instead, she takes a deep breath and nods silently. Thank you Fiona.

As the chair's wheels clank over the door frame, we escape from the ward. Once we make it away from the nurses and bindings, I realize I have no idea what to do with a drugged, suicidal, 300-pound man.

Possible options rotate through my mind. We don't have a home. We could go to the Veranda. Aoife's favorite playground? No, that's not a good idea. We could find Cass. To have her march us right back to the Infirmary? Also not a good plan right now. The safest move I can think of is the Galley. Olan loves food, and they knocked him out for a very long time.

Breakfast it is.

That's how we spend the rest of the week. We find an abandoned double bunk in the forward barracks and make a small camp there. The rest of the mercenaries and career marines mostly ignore us, save the occasional offer to trade. They've seen odder scenarios come through their door. As long as it looks like I can hold a rifle and don't cause trouble, they could care less about our story.

Throughout all of this, Olan doesn't utter a word, even though I know the drugs must have worn off by now. He only takes in nutrition when he absolutely has to. Even then, I can see a struggle in his eyes as he makes the conscious decision to continue living. If he really wanted to off himself, he could've taken hold of the railing and thrown himself over the side of the ship. With his size and determination, none of us would have been able to stop him. Instead, he just sits silently.

With Cass's roommate killed in combat, and me with no place to stay, we make the decision to move in with one another. The cot wasn't quite made for two, but I try to make it work by wedging myself against the wall as much as possible. During the time that I'm not with him, Olan stays in the barracks. As a member of the boarding party, he has friends there who also can't afford separate housing. They help me watch over him as we decide what to do. The other marines don't object. Neither does he. He just stares into some place that none of us can see, a world where his family is still alive. A place where he has more purpose in life than the destruction of others.

That's where he's staring now, as we sit in the middle of the Veranda. I've run out of places to take him to try eliciting an emotional response. Any response. Here in the middle of the swirling tiles, I thought it might stimulate him, even though the promenade isn't what it once was. There are a lot more holes than usual. Only a few amateur artisans tinker with what few materials they can contribute to the shifting mosaic. Most of them must have been left behind in Shipwreck. Maybe they're still on board, but are unable to bring themselves to pick up a hammer and chisel in the aftermath of the attack. I could understand that.

"You just gonna carry that sad sack of shit around with you until he dies?" The Voice says.

"I swear to God, you need to shut the fuck up," I growl to the wind.

"Did they get the message?" Stenia asks, appearing from behind a sculpture.

I start, twisting around to face her.

"How many are there?" she asks, leaning against the steel obelisk.

"What?" I ask.

"How many voices?" she clarifies.

I swallow. I suppose it's always been there, but talking about it makes it real. "Just one. . . I think."

"How long?" she asks.

I focus on the deck, shaking my head. "I don't know."

Stenia draws herself up on the side of obelisk, pressing her back flat. "Having it there doesn't make you any less strong Sage. You don't have to hide it. You're under the kind of stress that would kill most people." Her violet eyes probe. "Everyone breaks. It's just a matter of how you put yourself back together."

I clench my jaw, nodding. "All the same, I'd still appreciate it if you'd keep it between us. I don't need the crew thinking they're following a mad man more than they already do," I say.

"Has my trust ever been an issue?" she asks.

"No," I say, grasping Olan's chair as the *Artemis* begins descending. "No, it hasn't."

Stenia's faces stiffens, glancing down the causeway.

Following her eyes, I find Raltz and Sabine moving down the Rim towards us.

"Something is wrong about that one," Stenia states.

"Why?" I ask.

"The way she moves; she's carrying more secrets than shards in her arm," Stenia says, pushing herself away from the sculpture.

"She's also provided us more secrets about the *Ark* than we can repay. Are you worried the ones she hasn't shared could hurt us?" I ask.

"I'm not certain yet," Stenia replies, "but I will know soon."

I nod. "In the meantime, I need you to keep your suspicions between you and me as well. One rumor about her, valid or not, could blow this whole house of cards over."

"Wouldn't dream of it," she says, keeping her eyes fixed on the two approaching figures.

More people emerge from the bulkheads, blocking Sabine and Raltz from view as they approach. The ocean sweeps out underneath the *Artemis* as it continues losing altitude.

"Are we landing?" Sabine asks, coming to our side.

"No," I say.

Sabine glances to the men and women around us. They carry objects of all sizes. Some have boxes, others hold one single thing: a boot without laces, an old hat. They continue flowing from the bulkheads.

"What are we doing then?" she asks.

I glance down at Olan. "Saying goodbye."

A few crew members arrive with crude wooden planks. They set several of them up both port and starboard of the veranda, equipping either side of them with one marine each. The crowd surges closer to the railing as the marines tie the boards to the banisters. An *Artemis* flag is tied down over the top of each, covering the wood in black and gold.

Nurses appear through the crowd, pushing three gurneys. The people make way as two gurneys reach the port side, the third turning toward the starboard rigging. All three carry bodies: two men and a woman, each of whom died this morning as a result of their wounds.

Perfect timing, I guess.

The two marines on either side step forward, helping the nurses remove the corpse from the stretcher and lie it on the wood. The marine on the right pulls the black flag over the man's face as the nurse whispers into his ear.

The marine nods before returning to his post. He looks over the crowd as he takes hold of the wooden slat. "For Mihkail Zatsayev!" he shouts.

Nodding, he turns to the second marine and upends the board. The body slides underneath the flag; the colored material chasing after the corpse as it slides. The body disappears over the railing into the surging ocean below.

The marine gestures to a woman in front of us. She steps up, placing a wrapped sack on the board before saying something to the first marine. The marine nods before once again turning up the wooden slat..

"For Adrianna Clemout," he says.

The board upends, sending the sack and its contents into the depths.

"For Unknown," the officer manning the second slat says.

The board turns, sliding the body of the female into the ocean. Perhaps she was unconscious when she was brought to the infirmary. Either way, no one was able to identify her. I don't want to die alone.

Sabine's face darkens as she glances down at Olan. "Sage. Where is Aoife?"

My throat tightens as I reach into my pocket. The material

crackles against my hand as I pull out the charred piece of red cloth, showing it to Sabine.

She puts a hand over her mouth. Raltz's eyes study it without response.

"This is your father's work," I say. "This is all that's left. There's nothing else."

Tears leak from either side of Sabine's eyes. "No," she whispers.

Raltz moves to grab Sabine's shoulder. "My lady, you shouldn't have to see this."

She slaps his hand away. "No!", she growls. "No. This is the only thing I should see right now. I need to know what he's doing." She wipes her face. "What it's causing," she chokes.

My own eyesight blurs as I turn back to the crowd. There's nothing for us to offer the sea as a memorial to her; everything's gone.

I glance down at my clenched hand.

Well . . . maybe not everything.

I hold my hand up, offering the red scrap to the winds. "For Aoife MacDonaugh."

As my fingers move to release it, I hear words carry away on the wind. I freeze, turning to Olan. This would be the first time anything's come out of his mouth in almost a week. I grab back the red material before it blows away. Clearing my throat, I try regaining some control.

"Olan . . .   Olan did you say something?"

For the first time in six days, his eyes flit up, focusing on me. His mouth moves, but I can't hear the words; the wind and the people around us drown out the sound.

"Sabine, I'm going to take him to a quiet place. I think I heard him say something," I say.

She nods. Her hand stays at her mouth as a new stream of tears spills over her reddened cheeks. "Whatever he needs," she says.

"Do you need help?" Stenia asks.

I shake my head. "I should be able to make it through ok."

"If you need anything, I'll be in my perch," Stenia says before disappearing into the crowd.

I turn Olan's chair away from the banister, maneuvering it through the masses. Most people are kind enough to make way, while others take some persuading. Slowly, the crowd clears and people become less numerous. The wind also dies down, blocked by the bow's armor plating. The bow was installed to implement a worst-case-scenario ramming action, but it also provides shelter from the elements for those who would promenade during peacetime.

I step on Olin's break and we squeak to a halt. I come around to face him. "There are a lot fewer people here. What was it that you were saying?" I ask.

His hand darts past me, grabbing my sidearm.

Panics shoots through me as I try grabbing it back. That's a mistake. Olan's other huge hand slams in from the side, catching mine. Using brute force, Olan forces my hand into the trigger guard before jamming the barrel into his temple.

"I said, I want you to shoot me!" he yells.

His voice is gravely and broken. My hands shake, resisting Olan's broad finger pressing mine against the trigger. I pull in a breath, trying to think of a way to stop him. He keeps pulling the firing mechanism. We're running out of slack. Gritting my teeth, I try using my other hand to peel back Olan's grip. Who am I kidding?

"Olan, please don't do this!" I plead.

His eyes well with tears. "Just do it," his voice breaks.

The trigger tension pulls to the firing point.

I have no other options. Pulling both our hands down, I bring the gun level so his face is right next to mine.

"So that's how you're gonna do it, huh?" I gasp. My throat tightens. "So you're gonna cut down the MacDonaugh family tree for the Cascade now? Just do their dirty work for them?"

His eyes widen slightly.

"Huh?" I yell.

There's a tremor in his grip. "Why throw it away? You're a nightmare of a weapon, and you know it," I say, returning his glare. "You love it." Doubt tinges the words leaving my lips, but I have to save him somehow. "You want a reason to live? How about revenge?" I ask.

I try slowing down my thoughts. Every word counts. "Right now, we're preparing a full-scale assault on the Cascade flag ship. We finally have the Admiral's blessing." I probe for cracks. "We're going after the *Ark* on our own terms, and I need you there with me. It's the only way any of us are going to come out of it alive . . . and you know it."

I can almost match his grip now.

"They gave you an insurmountable debt. Don't make me settle it for you all by myself," I growl.

A window cracks open as his grip weakens. It's not much, but it's there.

I wrench the gun from his hands, throwing it as far as I can towards the center of the ram. Clattering, it comes to a stop at the base of the wall. A few worried onlookers freeze, unsure of what to do. There aren't any other weapons within reach, and I'm faster than he is. He knows it too.

Looking up at him, I catch the slightest hint of the Olan I knew.

"If I go with you, you put me on the front line . . . you understand?" he says slowly.

I nod.

This isn't enough. "If I follow through with this, you need to let me go," he says firmly.

I let the tension ebb. "The second you step foot on that ship, you'll be free to do what you need to do," I promise.

Olan keeps his eyes fixed on mine. "If Sabine delivers us anything other than Garon's head, I'll pull out the roots of her family tree and rid the earth of everything it's ever touched. When I'm done, there'll be nothing but a sterile fucking promontory for her to kneel on and lament what she's lost."

I get up to retrieve my gun. Tremors twitch up and down my legs. What's left of Aoife's dress scratches at my thigh through my pocket. I take a few steps before turning back around.

"If she does anything less than that . . I'll help you."

16

Apparently it's monsoon season over the top of the Appalachian Spine, because heavy winds and rain have driven everyone inside for the last several days. I place my hand up against the thick pane of glass, watching the deluge spray behind it. A gray darkness sets the mood. Bridge officers move about their posts, transferring information from console to console, measuring everything from the radar to the status of the engines. The tension's so thick it's like walking through soup. Running my fingertips over the glass, I try gauging its thickness as well; I'm putting it at about three feet.

A Bridge officer pulls out a tray close enough for me to engage him. I clear my throat. "Can this glass take a direct hit from a shell?"

The Bridge officer grimaces as he continues his task. "No," he replies after some thought.

I take my hand away from the glass, wiping it against the other to remove the condensation. "Then why do we have our most vital organ protected by only a window pane?", I ask.

The officer pulls out the document he's been searching for. "Because the Admiral likes to be able to observe the skies from 280 degrees," he says. Before leaving, he stops, raising his face to me for the first time. "And it will stop just about everything else."

His footsteps fade away. Turning away from the glass, I look inward at a greater spectacle. The Bridge is a dark place, illuminated only by the holograms of the different systems bobbing up and down based on their operators' needs. A spider web of green splays itself over the center of the floor. Small red dots ping through the net. I suppose we've identified them as non-threats since the rest of the staff appears unconcerned about their presence.

Underneath the three dimensional display sits a long table with two dimensional maps hanging over the edges. A congregation of people has already gathered there, but our two guests of honor still haven't arrived. I can't blame them; it's pretty hard to step into the wolf's den when you know the alpha male's been on your scent.

Admiral Khan gave me his word, on pain of an uprising, that Sabine and Raltz would be treated with respect if they came to the Bridge. It's a big risk, but it's one we need to take. We can't launch an assault without their intel, and there is no assault without the crew of the *Artemis*. It's my wager that their brains are of much greater use in their heads than decorating the side of a wall. I glance once more at the clock, trying to subdue my rising stress.

They're not going to come.

Diz seems to sense my anxiety. She leaves the planning table, coming to my side. "Don't worry Lieutenant, they'll be here soon," she assures me.

Lieutenant.

For this meeting to take place, the Admiral had to ensure that my power was legitimate. By promoting me, Khan still holds control and keeps me in the fold. That, and he gets his war hero back. I can't imagine that my odd, accelerated track is lost on the rest of the crew. That being said, people are focusing on more pressing things than the career arc of one officer.

Lieutenants lead platoons, and that's exactly what the Admiral needs right now. Thus, as he always does, he deemed it so.

Both Cass and I received official recognition for performing "indispensable reconnaissance" during the fleet's full blown rout at Shipwreck. All we did was report the *Ark's* ability to focus its firepower on one target. That, and we provided our eye-witness account of the capture of the *Churchill*. The sound of the *Ark's* bay doors slamming shut and cutting all radio contact still haunts me. I shrug my shoulders instinctively, shaking off the memory.

The Bridge doors hiss open, revealing a small group. Everyone looks up at our new arrivals. A brace of seven pilots and marines surround a barely visible Sabine. They're armed, with rifles cocked to their shoulders as they sweep into the room.

Bridge personnel draw their weapons, taking cover behind their consoles.

I freeze. This is not what we need for internal relations right now.

"Thank you!" I shout "Thank you, but that won't be necessary."

Inserting myself between the two groups, I wave off the turncoat servicemen. One of them moves to confront me. Saving face, I close the distance to him.

"Lieutenant Basmon, are you certain we're safe here?" a thoroughly disguised Raltz questions.

I'm at a loss. "Raltz, are you trying to get yourself shot?" I hiss.

Raltz observes his surroundings. "None of our weapons contain live ammunition,", he replies at full volume.

Defeated, I gesture to the large rifle strapped to his back. "No, but you've still brought them into a restricted area. They really don't take very kindly to that," I say.

"If I had wanted them dead, I would have done it a long time ago."

Admiral Khan's voice echoes down the Bridge. He adopts a joking tone, but it's also a clear demonstration of the balance of power.

"Come, let's discuss our grand strategy shall we?" he offers.

The Admiral stretches out his hand, motioning for us to join him and the rest of his brain trust.

Raltz's eyes fix on Khan. He doesn't move.

I exhale. "Raltz, it's going to be fine. And if it isn't, you have my word that you can kill me later."

Raltz shakes his head slightly before taking off his bandana. "No."

I stop to ponder what he means. Am I having a breakthrough with Raltz?

He continues. "No, I won't have to wait. If this goes wrong, the first shot I fire will be through your left eye."

I put a hand on his shoulder as he gestures for the other militia guards to stand down. "Always the charmer."

Not today, I guess.

The guards lay down their weapons and file to the back wall. One by one, they leave Sabine to face the rest of us. Her arm and side are freshly bandaged. Bright scarlet splotches pool beneath her clothing. I can't tell if these are new wounds, or remnants of her escape from the *Ark*. Sabine, as always, appears entirely unfazed.

She raises her arms. "Let's begin, shall we?"

The circle forms around the table. We're an odd group, really, comprised of a mixture of Bridge staff, Admiral Khan's top advisors, pilots, engineers, gun crew, and a few high ranking marines.

Sabine and and her bodyguard take their positions across the table from the Admiral. Raltz places as much of himself between Sabine and the officers as possible. Sabine doesn't seem to take notice of any of the perceived threats.

Across the table, Captain Dixon stands at attention. Her focus stays with the Admiral, but exudes an air of impatience. Next to Captain Dixon stands Diz. The Crew Chief peeks under her red locks and winks at me. Her hair's streaked with engine grease, but no one else seems to notice.

Behind all the others stands Stenia. She's wearing a wool cap and full scarf. Odd choices, but I think she's just trying to be respectful of the older staff who don't look so fondly on tattoos. As always she says nothing, but sees everything.

Admiral Khan clears his throat. "Good evening!" he booms.

Everyone echoes his greeting; some more committed than others.

"Thank you very much for joining me in my home," the Admiral continues. "Hopefully you will find it just as comfortable as I do."

There is a small chortle from the gathering, but nothing gratuitous.

His gray eyes sweep the crowd. "We're all here tonight to decide how to best tackle what most people would consider the impossible." He gestures outwards. "But it's nothing that we do not do on a daily basis."

His eyes fix on me. "Many thanks to Lieutenant Basmon for bringing this opportunity to my attention. Lieutenant, could you please explain to the crew the plan you have assembled?"

I freeze. I didn't expect to be put on the spot so soon.

Taking a breath to steady myself, I respond, "All of you were present to witness the destructive power of the warship that has come to be known as 'The *Ark*'"

Tension rises in the room.

"If you remember, the *Ark* leveled the entire city of Shipwreck, destroying several zeppelins in the process. Its fleet downed countless pilots, despite being vastly outnumbered."

I look into the center light, trying to draw some power from it. Focus on the facts.

"In my search for more information about the vessel, I discovered that the ship and its fleet have raided no less than seventeen other trading posts, from the Louisiana Bogs straight up through the Appalachian Spine, ending here." I tap the northern most island in Appalachia. "This is where Shipwreck fell."

I place markers on the attacked areas and turn the map towards the Admiral.

Diz speaks up. "I've been studying tech from the downed Cascade fighter wrecks we recovered."

She pulls up two chunks of gray metal, setting them down on the map.

"Most of the fighters used by the Cascade aren't made from regular steel or aluminum," she continues. Diz looks up to Sabine, motioning her over. "Sabine, if I could."

Sabine nods, making her way to the Crew Chief.

Diz grunts, picking up the smaller chunk of metal and flipping it over onto its side. "If you'll observe, this was a piece taken from one of our downed Jackals. The pilot survived, but I also requested that the Helios crew take a piece from his wreckage if at all possible."

Diz sticks a finger through the quarter-sized hole in the piece of armored plating. "This was caused by a regular slug; tore right through it. Almost caused Archangel's early demise," She says, sweeping her green eyes back up to the group. "Moral of the story being that the Cascade are still using conventional weaponry."

"Where it gets interesting though," Diz says, picking up the larger chuck of grayish material and flipping it over with relative ease, "is looking at what the Cascade have for armor."

Diz smiles, taking the piece of broken fuselage and spinning it into her other hand. "It's super lightweight, pliable, . . . " Diz presses her fingers up under the armor, turning it towards the glare, "and very durable."

We all lean in, observing a small divot in the metal.

"Same slug, different result," Diz continues, twisting herself around slowly so all can see. "We literally have to shatter these lads if we want to take them down."

She turns to Sabine, "May I?"

Sabine nods as Diz rolls up her sleeve. The same grayish material flickers underneath.

Diz takes great care in pulling the sleeve up over Sabine's fresh bandages. "The metal found in the fighter's armor is a match with the shrapnel our advisor Sabine Tesarik took when she first fled the *Ark.*" She lays Sabine's arm on the table next to the armor. "It's a naturally occurring material that's a sister mineral to Neodymium Iron Boron. We don't know how the Cascade found it, we just know that they found a lot of it, and they're in a constant search for more."

Sabine holds her arm up for everyone to see. "When my father first began his crusade, he looked for areas that would be rich with this mineral. The easiest way the material can be harvested, is from within the mountains. The second is from the bottom of the sea. Since Garon is a man of efficiency, you can guess which option he's pursuing."

She peels one of her bandages back, revealing a bloodied fragment embedded deep in her arm. "Besides being lightweight and durable, the Neodymium exhibits strong magnetic properties. To best harvest the material, my father's reengineered the *Ark's* power-source to double as a super magnet. Since the magnetite already has a strong polar charge, the Core can be used to pull the material up from beneath the ground."

Her eyes scan the room. "We've already borne witness to such an event."

Some of the officers shift their weight uneasily.

Sabine runs her finger along the exposed edge of the rock in her arm. "It is largely a coincidence that the most mineral rich areas are located below established trading posts. It's only natural, since these are often areas of high elevation the sea has pushed up from below. That being said, my father is indifferent to all the lives within them. In a sense, it matches his end goal."

Sabine's eyes lose their focus, her voice coming from some place far away. "I began planning my escape when my father announced his intention to 'cut open the sky'. He had discovered how to use the emissions from the Core to break down pure ozone."

She presses her hand on the table. Some of the blood from

her wound trickles down the side of her arm, spotting the backlit table. Large red circles expand on the ceiling of the Bridge. Their tint is unsettling.

Sabine appears unaware of this, and presses on. "For those of you who are unaware; the lack of O3, also known as Ozone, greatly contributed to the initial stages of the Drowning."

Some officers nod their heads. Others appear bewildered.

Sabine looks up from the table. "My father aims to drown the world once more, so that the Chosen people can repopulate it in peace."

Scoffs of disbelief erupt from the gathering.

"How ridiculous is that?!" yells one particularly grey lieutenant.

A fist slams on the table, silencing everyone.

I follow the white light of the map on the table. Tracing along the path, I find the riled face of Captain Dixon.

"Were you not all at Shipwreck?" she shouts at the officers behind her. "What makes you believe that this theory isn't true?"

No one says a word to challenge her. If we play this right, we've just gained a powerful ally.

In the ensuing silence, Captain Dixon addresses Sabine more quietly this time. "I assume the Chosen people your father is referring to are the Cascade?"

"That's correct," Sabine nods.

Lieutenant Baltier speaks up. "So what are we gonna do about it?"

Hearing the bastard Australian's voice spurs me into action. I clear my throat. "We're going to hunt down the *Ark* and destroy it from the inside."

Laughter flows through the crowd. They think I'm joking.

Baltier waits for them to die down. "Yeah, alright. And how do you propose we do that?" he presses.

I've been waiting for a chance to pay Baltier back for his welcome the night Shipwreck was attacked. This might be just the time.

"While escaping Shipwreck, Nurse Cassandra Dawson and I witnessed the *Ark's* capture of the British carrier *Churchill*. The *Ark* enveloped it completely, within a concealed hangar bay. I hold my gaze before continuing. "If I were a betting man, I'd say the Cascade dismantled the carrier and repurposed the surviving crew."

A middle-aged veteran stops me. Her military braid falls over her shoulder as she leans across the table from the other side. "And what part of this story makes us believe we can challenge the *Ark's* capabilities?"

"What I propose is a trick that's been used for thousands of years with great success," I offer.

I motion to Diz. She bends down and presses a few buttons on the side panel of the table. Colored holograms glimmer to life above us. Three polygon ships appear, one after another, the first markedly larger than the next two.

"Who all has heard of the 'Trojan Horse'?" I ask.

A few hands snake into the air.

"Excellent . . . well, we're going to compound that tactic with a 'bait and switch' maneuver," I say.

I wait for interjections. None come. I gesture once more to Diz and she slowly turns another dial. The ships jump to life.

"We've already received support from the British vessel, the *Agincourt*. Although it's a smaller frigate, the souls onboard are determined to help rescue, or at the very least avenge, their lost brothers and sisters of the *Churchill,*" I explain.

The glow of the holograms cast an ethereal light on the crew around me.

"I've spoken with Crew Chief Diz McAlister, and she's confident that we'll be able to create dummy fires aboard the *Agincourt.*" As I say this, crude flames begin protruding from the *Agincourt's boxy* likeness depicted above us. "Crew Chief McAlister assures me that although there is a risk that we could lose control of the flames, we should be able to keep them contained, while still believable enough to catch the *Ark's* attention."

Making a circling motion with my finger, I indicate for Diz to increase the speed of the display. "Our gamble is that the *Ark* will move to capture the *Agincourt* in order to take one of our main ships out of play."

Diz jumps in. "What the Cascade won't be expecting is that we'll be keeping a close eye on the *Ark's* hangar doors."

The pixilated vessel above opens its front and begins pursuing the model *Agincourt*.

My eyes track the path of the *Ark* as it bears down on its

prey. "When the bait's taken, that's our cue to rapidly descend and enter the hangar bay instead."

There's a silence as a dark *Artemis* swoops down from above, entering the *Ark*. Even the computer animation of the maneuver is awkward; I can't imagine that demonstration instilled much confidence that we would be successful in real life.

A Major slams his hand down on the table. "With those tactics, it's going to be a hell of a short battle!"

The Admiral's baritone voice rises up from among his group of aides. "With these tactics we have a fighting chance, Major. May I remind you that this is my ship and my mission in the first place?"

His grey eyes sweep the crowd as he booms. "All of you were there for the battle at Shipwreck. We will not last long against the *Ark's* guns. Neither will our cohort. We must infiltrate the *Ark* and destroy it from the inside. That is our only recourse against its plate armor."

The Admiral gestures to Diz as she manipulates the display. The shapes pause before zooming into *The* Ark's hangar.

The Admiral points to the now docked *Artemis.* "The grand battle will take place in the *Ark's* hangar bay."

Triangles of different colors appear on either side of the screen, engaging one another.

The Admiral presses both his hands on the table, leaning over it to continue his narration. "The battle is mainly a distraction however. With this ruse, we can split their crew in two. One half will be dedicated to protecting the ship from external threats, and the other half will be dedicated to dealing with us. We want their manpower to be as divided as possible while our special teams do their work."

Diz turns the overhead display so the hangar bay's doors are the most prominent. "My engineers and I will use the initial shock to our advantage and make a beeline for the bay itself. I have a hunch that the second the *Artemis* docks inside, the Cascade will slam the doors on us."

I shiver at the thought.

Diz appears unfazed. "Assuming my hunch is correct, my team and a small escort will set remote explosives on their hinges."

A younger woman with several different colored tassels adorning her uniform interrupts. "If we're setting explosives, why don't we just fly in there, give 'em both broadsides, then fly back out? It'd be a hell of a lot easier, and save us a lot more men."

Unperturbed by the interjection, Diz turns to her. "I'd agree that would make this a tad bit easier. The only problem with that plan is the power of our own cannons. The shrapnel and heat created from the blasts would certainly kill quite a few Cascade, and maybe even cripple the *Ark*, but it would surely kill us all as well." Diz pauses before looking to the rest of the gathered officers. "That being said, I'm fairly certain none of us are flying this far north to catch our own flak."

The tasseled woman twists her mouth, considering other simpler options.

Assured that there will be no further interruptions, the Admiral picks up the conversation. "The second group to take advantage of the distraction will be our strike forces. Both Sabine and Raltz have volunteered to guide our teams down into the bowels of the *Ark* to where the Core is being housed."

Sabine motions for Diz to zoom in on the battle now in full pitch above us. "In order for our teams to be able to reach the Core, we have to break through the hangar's main entrance. The difficulty is that the gate is also the main throughway for the Cascade's boarding crew and any reinforcements they might receive."

The green triangles push the red ones back from the arch.

Sabine continues, "We will have to create an opening and fight to maintain control of it until our strike forces can make the rendezvous point. I also realize achieving this goal is highly unlikely, so we may just have to make a run for it under covering fire from the *Artemis* if our line folds."

Sabine's steel gaze meets the Admiral's. "Once we reach the archway, I can guide our strike groups down maintenance passageways that are not likely to be used by the brunt of the *Ark's* garrison. However, I cannot promise that our teams will not take casualties."

Sabine stops, straightening her shoulders as she addresses the rest of the officers. "In fact, it will be an arduous task that should only be undertaken by those who are truly willing to die for this cause."

My heart drops as the reality of the situation sets in. The collective stress of those around me escalates. Why did I lobby so hard for this?

Captain Dixon leans over table. "Admiral Khan, it would be my pleasure to lead the strike force."

The Admiral chuckles to himself. "Of course it would, Janna. As always, I appreciate your zeal, but I need your leadership on the deck, fighting the main battle."

Captain Dixon keeps a face of stone. "Understood Admiral. They won't know what hit 'em."

An older gentleman in charge of the gun decks steps forward. The soot on his face does little to tone down the rose color on his cheeks. "If my boys and girls are gonna be fightin' from the lower decks to beat back the Cascade, then who'll be leading the charge inta the heart of the beast?"

The Admiral's eyes flit to me. I break into a cold sweat before I can speak.

Admiral Khan gestures. "Lieutenant Basmon will be leading the charge into the Core with Lieutenant Baltier serving as his second."

The bile rises. I will vomit right here and now.

The Admiral continues, unaware of my flash sickness. "Both are good fighting men, and this assault is Lieutenant Basmon's brainchild in the first place. It would only be fitting."

I do everything in my power to keep from fainting. Controlled deep breaths are my last defense to prevent the blackness from surrounding me. All eyes come to rest on me. From across the table, Baltier chews on unspoken words. I try to say something, but nothing comes out.

Diz comes to my rescue. "I witnessed Lieutenant Basmon break through a bunker chokepoint on the *Cornelia Marie* almost singlehandedly. A fine choice Admiral."

She buys just enough time for me to clear the lump in my throat.

"And by 'almost single handedly', Crew Chief McAlister means 'with her help.' I'll have to improvise without her ingenuity at my side, but I'll find a way to get the job done." I finally speak up.

This seems to satisfy the crowd, many of whom discontinue their intense gaze. I hope they can't see my legs shaking from where they are. I thought I'd be watching this battle from the cockpit of a plane, far away from all of the gouging blades, flying bullets, explosions, and screams of the wounded and dying.

From behind me, Stenia takes my hand and slowly removes it from its clamped position on the side of the table. I shake off the pain as blood rushes back into my fingertips. A quick glace down reveals my fingers are bone white.

She places a hand on my back as the war games continue without us.

"Don't worry Sage. I'll keep things together here. You take care of what needs to happen on the inside, ok?" she whispers.

She's reassuring me, but I know her well enough to hear the worry in her voice.

A question is raised by one of the mechanics. "Even if we were to try executing this plan, how would we even go about finding the *Ark?* It must be at least a hundred miles away by now."

Sabine fields this one. "A valid question. I can answer it by giving you some information I discovered during the battle at Shipwreck."

She pulls up her sleeve, revealing her bloody, metal filled arm. "As you now know, when I first escaped the *Ark*, I was wounded by shrapnel from an explosion of Neodymium magnetite. We were unsuccessful in removing the foreign objects without risking a fatal hemorrhage," she says.

Sabine traces her fingers over the tangle of skin. "My body healed over many of the pieces, maintaining a firm hold on those that it cannot cover. If you remember, Neo magnetite is a highly magnetic material, which is how my father is able to mine it so efficiently. What I discovered, is that no matter where the Core is focused, it generates an auxiliary energy that attracts other metals. I didn't recognize the sensation at first, because I had never experienced it before. However, when the *Ark* was at its closest, the magnetite buried inside my arm nearly freed itself at the cost of my life."

The group's ghostly faces peer uncomfortably at Sabine's arm.

She seems unaware of their discomfort. "I will remain on the Bridge with Admiral Khan, using my body as a compass. If done correctly, I will not only point us in the right direction, but also sense how close our quarry is. This will save us time and resources, allowing us to keep our formation relatively tight."

She lets her sleeve slide over the bloody mess. "Once we

dock with the *Ark*, I will be infiltrating the Core alongside Lieutenant Basmon and Lieuntenant Baltier. Raltz Tesarik will continue to function as my bodyguard. Should I be incapacitated, he has as much inside knowledge of the *Ark* as I do, if not more. In either event, he will make a fine guide."

'Should I be incapacitated' . . .

The cold grips the inside of my stomach as the gravity of the plan sinks in.

The smell of blood pours back into my nostrils. A symphony of cries reverberates off the walls of the room. The girl's pleading eyes look up to me again. I try to shake her, but I can't get her face out of my head. I didn't even realize she was dead. I let her pass on alone. Her fingers creep up the side of my back.

Taking a deep breath, I force the darkness to clear again. With each breath, the pressure from the advancing hand diminishes, the last fingertip fading away as it grazes the back of my neck.

"Can't stand the thought of your own death? Some poor excuse for a leader." The Voice chides.

"Well, that caution is the same reason I'm here and you're not.", I say.

My frustration ebbs as I realize this is the first time I've ever seen members from all of the different crews in one place at the same time. The grizzled gun commanders sit right next to Diz and her engineers, formulating their own strategies. Small sections of the crew nurses press up against the side of the table, still speckled by the day's work. Countless marines and pilots stand behind them with Stenia and her sniper team.

Maybe there's something to be gained from this struggle after all.

17

The cold beer is a perfect pick-me-up after a day of performing maintenance. I momentarily sit on an ammo crate, watching Cass as she works. She's just as adept with a paint brush as she is with a suture. Her staccato brush marks cover the tail of my plane. A dusty-colored saber sits just over the back wings. Cass's legs dangle over the side as she tries finding its center. Best not to waste paint if you can help it.

"The color's wrong!" I shout.

I can't help chiding her about it. How hard is it to mess up grey?

She leans back, steadying herself over the wing. "Oh shut up Sage, we're out of your shade of graphite."

I let myself laugh. "Whatever you say, hon. If Yeti's going to try flying her, he better look damn good!"

I can't help but just watch her up there. Painting seems as natural to her as any other part of her life. It's one of the few times I've ever seen her fully relaxed. That alone is worth everything we're doing.

The tone of the comm system reverberates throughout the hangar. It's a full crew message. Those are rare, so it can only mean one thing. My heart sinks.

Admiral Khan's voice filters through the PA. "Attention all non-operational personnel. Please proceed to the Large Craft Hangar Bay. Again, please report to the Large Craft Hangar Bay. Attendance is mandatory."

I was hoping the Admiral was going to wait a few more days before doing this. It can't possibly go well.

Cass exhales, slowly lowering her brush back into the paint can.

She doesn't want to be a part of it either.

We make our way outside and join the throngs of civilians and soldiers coursing through the Outer Rim. Marines line the way, flanking each side of the Roost's bulkhead. They direct the flowing crowd towards its final destination. What's the Admiral thinking? He's going to scare passengers with these tactics.

Maybe that's the point.

Speculation swirls around us as we climb the steps. Cass holds my arm so we won't get separated in the current. We're pressed shoulder to shoulder as we enter the Roost's cavern. The last of the day's sunbeams bleach the *Artemis's* skeletal roof. The Roost's forward bay is open to let in fresh air. It feels good, almost dispelling the heat generated by the mass of people, and the stress created by the unknown.

Cass and I locate our crew mates in separate ranks within the military personnel. Captain Dixon patrols in front at full attention. When she sees me, she gestures me over with two upturned fingers. Breaking through the lines of crew, I see a small podium has been constructed to properly address everyone.

I get within earshot of the Captain. "You can't be serious. He wants me to talk?"

"I'm damn serious. You better make a show of it too," Dixon fires back.

A lurking panic crawls into my chest. I've been dwelling on it for days now. I've talked with the shadows about it. Heard what they've had to say. Taken their revisions into account. But I've never said any of it to an actual person, much less the entire population of the *Artemis.*

The chatter of a hundred different languages flows up from the crowd as I take my place on the podium. Luckily for me, English is the primary trade language, so I won't have to struggle to translate my thoughts.

Admiral Khan and several of his advisors are already seated. I can't shake the feeling that I'm walking to my own gallows. My boots thud against the hollow planks that have been erected in order to make today happen. Admiral Khan nods, gesturing to the seat next to him.

He says nothing as I sit down. My nails dig into the small rickety chair they've placed on stage. I look once more for any noose the Admiral may have tied for me. He doesn't need any rope; he's letting words do the hanging.

For the next fifteen minutes, we watch in silence as the rest of the ship files in. I'm not focused enough to feel the anxiety. I'm so lost inside myself preparing that I don't even attempt conversation with Khan, or notice the multitude of faces looking up at me.

Once the Admiral's satisfied his full crew is in attendance, he rocks out of his chair. Step by step, he paces to the microphone at the center of the podium. His action brings a hush over the crowd. For a moment, I imagine what having that kind of power would be like; being able to silence a thousand people by just making one movement.

"Welcome everyone," the Admiral's baritone echoes through the hangar.

If I look closely, I can see his Adam's apple bob. This is one of the first times he's ever seen all the souls on the ship in the same place at once. I'm as awestruck as he is.

"As we are all painfully aware, we were attacked two weeks ago today," the Admiral continues, folding his hands behind his back and drawing himself to his full height. "This was no ordinary attack. We were not even the intended target. We were simply an obstacle in the path of a lumbering monster. One that has no remorse, no thought of diplomacy, no mercy."

The Admiral's grey eyes sweep the crowd, taking them all in. "We watched as they tore out the beating heart of our trade. We watched as they turned on us, eager to fill themselves on our resources, our people. With a little luck and an overwhelming amount of bravery on the part of our pilots and crew, we were able to escape the impending death."

Several in the crowd shift uneasily. One pilot in particular stands stone still, leaning over a crutch. I realize it's Yeti. His recovery has come a long way in just two weeks.

I pick up the Admiral's words again as he continues, ". . . was averted, I'm here to introduce to you a man that can provide us with a new hope, someone who will help me guide us to greater security and profit."

He's giving me all the rope I need to hang myself.

"I present to you, Lieutenant 'Saber' Basmon."

I stand up, my heart pulsing in my ears. My legs pump

mechanically. I'm so off balance, I'm afraid I'll fall over. Walking to the center of the stage, Admiral Khan gestures grandiosely towards the microphone. The expression on his face displays not so much encouragement as victory, like a chess master about to force a checkmate.

I nod to him silently, closing the distance to the open microphone.

My mouth cracks open as butterflies flap around in my throat. It's hard to get anything out, but I know I need to start.

I take a deep breath "How many of you know who Artemis was?" I ask.

It's a question that hasn't been posed in a long time. Who cares about a ship's name sake? We've been sailing at time-and-half speed to get away from the fallout of Shipwreck, and ancient mythology is the last thing on most passengers' minds. A few murmurs spread through the crowd, but no one answers.

"She was the Greek goddess of Protection," I say, "She watched over the young women, the cattle, the crops in the fields. Everything that a person could hold dear, she was charged with protecting."

Silence.

"When Admiral Khan christened this ship during its first launch 32 years ago, the world was a lot worse than it is now, if you can believe it. People were still being hunted because of the color of their skin . . . their ethnicity. Because their neighbor thought they had more food." I fold my sweating hands behind my back. "The Admiral built a place where people wouldn't have to worry about any of that, where any nationality was welcomed, where they could feel protected."

It's bullshit. He did it for profit.

"How many of you have lost a loved one to shrapnel? To combat? To disease?" I ask. "Maybe they're still breathing, standing next to you, but you have no idea who they are. Stress and trauma transforming who they once were. They don't laugh like they used to, or maybe at all. Their eyes always somewhere else."

I lick my lips. Pela, Mom, Aoife.

"These are the symptoms of prey. Telltale signs of the hunted."

Discomfort flows around me.

"But there was another domain that Artemis ruled over. She was the goddess of the Hunt."

I look out over the thousand faces. "For so long, we've spent our time being protectors. For the last 30 years, we've braced our hands over our faces, as blow after blow poured in. We'd fend off our attackers and called it victory." I pause.

"Today, we chose our target!" I shout, "they don't chose us!"

A cry goes up.

"Today we become the hunters. It's our destiny to taste of first blood, rather than the blood of our own wounds!"

The goose bumps rise. "How many times has the *Artemis* succumbed to attacks by bandits or privateers? Never! Like many of you, I've lived my whole life on this ship, and it's never surrendered. Not once."

"We've been given a unique opportunity. We know the location of our enemy, and have received pledges of support from no less than four other zeppelins and their crews. For once, we will be on the offensive. For once, we will dictate the time and place we attack *them*. It will be on our terms."

I think of the crew scattered around the *Artemis* who had to remain at their designated stations to operate the ship. The sound of my voice pumps through the PA system; I hope they hear every word. "But I know everyone doesn't come from the same place as me. Some of you are new arrivals, or just traveling a short distance. I understand that. Some of you have been here since the beginning, but you follow a pacifist doctrine. I respect that."

A bead of sweat runs down the side of my face.

"I will only take the willing. If this isn't your fight, I don't want you here. We'll never make it unless everyone onboard truly believes in this mission. We can't hesitate, not even for a second. It's our turn to protect others, not just ourselves."

A roar rises from below.

Blood surges through my veins, running on pure electricity. I turn to the Admiral in an effort to relinquish the microphone so he can complete the hardest step. His checkmate smile widens. Instead of coming to take the stage, he subtly motions for me to continue.

He was never going to do the dirty work himself.

My anger conquers any remaining resistance in my mind. "We will attack the Cascade at their heart."

I lick my lips. I only have one shot to do this right. My eyes flick to the military personnel flanking either side of the crowd. One last breath urges me onward. "If you're not a hunter, you need to make that decision now."

Personnel step in, separating the crowd into two parts. "We will be resupplying at World's End. If you have family you would like to keep safe, or you yourself choose to turn in your arms, I would recommend that you disembark and schedule alternative transport from there." I say.

Angry growls meet the end of my last sentence.

"We will not be docking at New Boston as our manifest originally states." I lock eyes with the Admiral once more, confirming my next order. "Being given the option to serve during the assault on the *Ark* is considered ample repayment for any inconveniences you may encounter due to this executive decision."

A lump forms in my throat. The officers lay down thick red tape through the center of the Roost. Military personnel push back the struggling halves until they stand on either side of the forming line.

I fight to keep my composure. "Those of you standing to my right will remain on the *Artemis* and fight alongside its crew. Those of you to my left, you will be released from service and contract at World's End when we set down there. You will be given your dock passes immediately, if this is what you chose."

Swallowing down the lump, I manage to continue. "You will have until the red line is established to make this decision."

Some in the crowd don't even wait that long, ducking under the arms of the personnel and running over to the left side. To safety. Parents push their children and spouses over to the safe side of the line. Spouses pause to kiss one another before stepping over. Mothers and fathers choosing to stay, toe the line as their family moves farther away from them.

I watch the volunteers' thoughts churn in their minds; they know they'd be safer together. Something keeps them from following the others. These are the men and women we need to fight for us.

Fuck you Khan. Fuck you for the way you chose to do this.

I turn around, expecting to find him gloating over his victory, but that's not what I witness at all.

The Admiral watches as the community he built from scratch

splits in half. His snide grin is nowhere to be found. As much as the separation affects the families below, it's taking a much greater toll on him. This is everything he has. For once, I truly understand what we're gambling to win.

Looking back, the crowd continues surging as it sorts itself. I can't take my eyes off a particular young man. He can't be more than twenty. He cautiously toes the line from the left side. In front of him lies the story of a lifetime, if he lives to tell it. Behind him is a sure pass off the ship. That being said, World's End is exactly as its name implies: a bare mass of rock on the farthest tip of the North American continent. Ships still land there, but it's miles from the nearest major trade lane. Its climate is cold and unforgiving. I can't imagine there's much industry or choice in the way of honest employment. It is however, in the direct flight path between us and the *Ark*.

Watching the young man struggling with his decision, I force my feet over to the right side of the line laid out below the podium. No one in front will notice, but I will. I have to believe in it too. If I don't think we can do it, then I certainly can't expect everyone else to follow suit.

Despite my efforts, the left side of the Roost is heavily favored. Safety's an uncommon common luxury. Anytime risk can be minimized; most people will take the path of least resistance. We're looking for those who acknowledge that and choose to stay anyway. My bet is they're less likely to run when the time comes.

As the movements lessen, I recover enough to deliver the final instructions. "Those who have chosen to disembark, you will now receive your dock passes. Those who have chosen to fly with us and can hold a sword, you will be assigned to a battalion if you are not already. If you have flight experience, or believe you have the aptitude to fly in our ranks, voice it immediately so you may be assigned a squadron if you are not already."

I step back from the microphone, watching the yellow passes being distributed to those who won't help us; the sane ones. Officers patrol the ranks of those on the right, those who will, collecting their names so they can be sorted to where they're most needed.

The young man takes a step over to the right side and squares his shoulders.

What's done is done.

The next few days pass in a blur. Captain Dixon takes it upon herself to teach me proper sword play. She does so under the presupposition that if I were to fail in combat because I didn't know how to properly handle a sword, 'We would be the laughing stock of the Northern Hemisphere.' Always such a sweet woman.

Sleep's a precious luxury now. There's no malady; I just won't let myself do it. Every moment that passes where I'm not preparing for the assault feels like a moment wasted. My nerves begin to fray, holding their position against barrage after barrage of worry.

It's all I can do to keep the sword pommel up to block Dixon's blows. Each time steel clashes against steel, I breathe a "thank you" to whoever's listening that I still have both my hands. In truth, the Captain could have sliced either one of my arms clean off at least half a dozen times each at this point.

With each session, her frustration becomes increasingly apparent. She makes us practice with actual weapons at a higher pace than I feel comfortable. Dixon ignores my misgivings, telling me that it will teach me to respect the seriousness of the situation. I'm entirely aware of the consequences, but I could do without being reminded of them at every waking turn. This doesn't stop her from applying enough force to break the skin if she can sense I'm not paying attention.

Her latest reminder catches me between the thumb and forefinger.

Crying out, I nurse the blossoming cut, sucking on the ragged opening.

"Won't do you much good Lieutenant. Best to leave it alone and let the air do the healing for you," Captain Dixon growls.

She's losing her patience again. I feel the opening of the cut pull apart as I grip the pommel of the saber again. The feeling of open flesh expanding makes me so uncomfortable that, I unconsciously switch the sword to my other hand and start sucking on the wound again.

That's the last straw.

"Goddamit Lieutenant! Are you a fucking child? Do you realize that within the next few weeks I'm going to be a real Cascade grunt trying my damnedest to slit your throat?"

I pull my hand away from my mouth. "I know! I know! Can't you tell that's all I've been thinking about?" I yell.

The Captain grits her teeth, hitting the flat of her blade against my calf. "Yes!"

Recoiling, I instinctively put my sword back up between us.

She lowers hers, putting her face up to mine. "Try commanding a battalion. That's all I've thought about for the last nine years."

I sheath my saber. "Well now I'm the acting commander of a strike-group whose success is the keystone of the entire assault. Doesn't that count?"

The Captain's eye burns. "You get that sword back out immediately!" she growls.

Dixon's blade whistles down at my forehead. Adrenaline fueled by self-preservation is the only thing granting me the speed to react. I barely force the blade out of the hilt before it deflects the Captain's attack.

My back hits the floor. I twist around, scrambling back to my feet.

"Do you have any mercy at all?" I ask.

The Captain's mouth sets, watching me get back to my base. "No," she says quietly. Her eye flashes up to meet mine. "Because our enemies sure as hell won't."

Shaken, I try catching my breath. "Well, you had a first time commanding that many people. What do you suggest I do?" I ask.

"I suggest that you stop being such a pussy about it," she scolds.

Anger seeps back in, nullifying damaged muscle fibers.

"Just lead. You wouldn't be in this position if you couldn't do that," she spits out.

She doesn't realize the big picture.

"You've done it before Lieutenant Basmon. You can do it again," she says, gritting her teeth. "Now come at me, you fucking coward."

The adrenaline hits my heart. I rush at her, goosebumps bristling. I throw all my weight into slashes and parries, cutting wildly. It's what she wants, but I keep feeding into it.

Sprawling into a lunge, I know I've overextended. The fear in my gut collides with a physical component as the side of the

Captain's blade catches me in the stomach.

The impact knocks me skidding to my knees.

"Dead," Captain Dixon says dismissively, walking away with her sword on her shoulder.

A bead of sweat drips from my hair onto the floor. "I know, I know!" I shout, equally impatient. "It's all about balance."

The Captain twists around, approaching with her saber outstretched. "No Lieutenant, you don't know."

My feet fly back underneath me, preparing for another attack.

The Captain takes no notice. "It's about momentum, not balance. You could have the best balance in the whole world, but I bet I can still drive this sword through you."

I try rearranging myself, confused about how I should be positioned.

The Captain's eye fixes on me. "If you're perfectly balanced right now, that means you're a stationary target. What happens to stationary targets in battle?"

I let out an exasperated sigh. "They die."

Her eye widens. "Good! They die." She grips her blade, bringing it up. "Now you have to figure out how to flow through your enemies' attacks," she says, cutting her edge delicately through the air. "Most won't be trained like you and me. They'll be fighting for their lives. They'll act and react like it too."

My sweat chills at the thought of the melee.

Dixon pantomimes the maneuvers. "We either use our momentum to cut into a target, or let them use theirs to guide themselves onto our swords. What are we never doing?" she asks.

I bring my eyes up, meeting hers for the first time. "Standing still."

Her gaze softens just enough to make me believe I've made progress. "Good," she says. "Now get some rest."

The weight seeps back into my body again, no longer kept at bay by adrenal chemicals.

The hardness comes back into her eye. "Lieutenant?" she says.

I stop walking. "Yes Captain?" I ask, carefully turning around.

She sticks her point into the floor. "Never let anyone under your command ever know that you're worried."

I stay silent.

"And I mean never," she repeats.

My weight shifts backwards, absorbing her words.

"Not just on the battlefield either," she continues. "Most of the men and women under your command will be watching you wherever you go. They'll use you as a monitor for how frightened they should be feeling. For how certain you are of an order. For whether or not they're doing the right thing. You are always on stage."

The permanence of her advice sinks in.

"Do you understand me?" she asks firmly.

"Yes Captain," I exhale.

Just one more stage on which to be someone else's player.

18

Chill fogs the edges of our portholes as World's End slips into view. It truly is the edge of civilization. Black soot covers the smoky rooftops and dots the landscape as dark, frothy waves crash into the base of the mountain below. The sight of the grey foam curling back under the waves makes me shiver.

World's End is too far north to be the first accessible trading post between the American and the European Archipelagos, and not big enough to support any major trade that might find it by dumb luck. World's End exists through the sheer brute desire to survive.

As we coast over the town center, I glimpse the tops of blimps looming over the buildings below. The three allied zeppelins that have arrived before us take up nearly all of the port space in the small trading post. There will be barely enough room to fit both The *Artemis* and the Iranian merchant carrier *Sohrab*. The Persian vessel lumbers behind us, awaiting docking clearance.

I don't think the locals have ever seen a collection of zeppelins this size, or at least all at once. Most of the dock crew don't come out to help as we land, leaving us to do most of the work ourselves. The inhabitants of World's End seem unsure of our intentions as our crews exit the ship. That's fair, given our goal is to leave this place with every scrap of munitions and supplies we can find. With the due process of trading, of course.

The crisp, briny air is a welcome change as we disembark. A dense fog settles between the hovels of World's End, and appears to have no intention of leaving.

Summer's over.

Zipping up my jacket, I follow Sanjar and the rest of his

retinue down the gangplank. Families course around us like ants before a flood, carrying everything they have with no intention of coming back. Their colony has become a doomed place.

One little boy struggles after his family as one of the wheels of his luggage slips between the wooden slats of the gangplank. A cry of panic escapes as he tugs to get it free, fearing he'll be abandoned.

Pulling the handle on the side of the bag, I lift it up over his head. Straining, I rebalance the weight to keep it from pulling me over the side. The bag's heavy, even for me.

The small boy looks up with uncertain eyes, full of shame that he wasn't able to solve the problem on his own. I don't say anything, gesturing with my nose down the rest of the gangplank. It's enough to get him moving again. Shouldering the luggage, I peer through my breath at the crowd. We're the farthest north I've ever been.

Reaching the sunken bottom, I see that the family's gathered to the side of the plank. They must have realized they left one behind. As my shoes hit mud, I take the luggage off my shoulder, setting it down on the driest spot I can find. The boy rushes to grab the handle and redeem himself. The mother stops him, turning him around.

"What do we say?, she asks softly.

"Thank you," the boy mumbles without confidence.

I smile, pulling the brim of my cap towards him. My chest warms seeing them all together like that. It's a rare sight these days. They're not only all still alive, they even believe in manners. Together, those traits are almost an extinct.

"Lieutenant Basmon!"

Sanjar's voice cuts a swath through the crowd. The command group's drifted further into the human sea and I've begun lagging.

"Are you coming or not?" the Admiral questions. Before I can say anything, he turns back, disappearing into the crowd without receiving an answer.

Turning to the family, I lock them into my memory one last time. "Be right there Admiral," I say to myself.

When I feel that brokenness again, I'll conjure this family. Turning, I tramp my way through the mud.

The structures of World's End are much more basic than the trading ports where we spend most of our time. No steam rises from any of the buildings here. Even the architecture's mostly comprised of worn wood. As a whole, it looks like more of a fragile fishing town than a trading post. Large, knotted ropes stretch from rooftop to rooftop. Upon closer inspection, I can see freshly caught fish hanging from each line. Surprisingly, there's no rotten stench. The people of World's End know their business, and they execute it swiftly.

Most of the people in the streets appear to be residents. Carts full of fish and harpoons trundle through the mud. Vendors dot the landscape, trying their best to convince each passerby they need exactly what they're selling. Ocean spray thunders up from the cliffs below. The severity of the rock faces reinforces the feeling that this is the end of the known world.

The last of our small party disappears through an opening underneath the likeness of a large Nordic sea monster. Gilt letters under the monster's chest designate the longhouse as *The Longshoreman*. It's handmade pine stairs flex beneath my feet as I make my way up to the door.

The air's thick with flavored smoke as I take my seat amongst our crew. I count each ship. There should be five in total. The British carrier the *Agincourt* is fully represented with several of its sailors already sampling the beer of the *Longshoreman*. Each of their sleeves sports a single black arrow set against a dark red background.

The Japanese crew of the *Namazu* sits quietly in the meeting area, focused on the task at hand. A red whiskered fish jumps from the breast and backs of their white uniforms.

The French freighter, *Bastille* is represented by its crew intermingling with the other members of our little alliance. A small bronze cannon is fastened to the lapels of their otherwise blue-and-white-striped uniforms. As a burst of laughter rises from the *Agincourt's* congregation, the crew of the *Sohrab* files in the make shift command room. Most of their outfit is dressed in a solid olive green. A gray scimitar runs along the side of their flight caps and shoulders.

Sanjar rises, grasping one of the Iranians by the hand and shoulder. The bearded man must be the *Sorhab's* admiral. He doesn't look too enthusiastic about being here. If I remember correctly, Sanjar was born and raised in the Mesopotamian Flatlands. Knowing the Admiral, I'm sure he used that leverage to help broker the *Sohrab's* assistance.

With the exception of Sanjar, everyone takes their seats as

Lieutenant Baltier pulls the pub's doors shut.

The flickering chandeliers bathe Khan in an austere light. "Welcome brothers,", he says, looking around at the pilots and upper echelon collected around him.

I've given him the chance to finally be king.

Sanjar puffs his chest, booming. "Brothers are what we truly will be from this day out, if you choose to sail with us."

French, Japanese, and Farsi mix together as the translators from each envoy begin their work. I give another silent thanks for retaining English as the main trade language. It makes life so much easier.

"Becoming brothers means one thing for certain," the Admiral continues. "We must live in a state of total honesty. I owe that much to you at the very least. If you have any questions or concerns about our assault, we must address them now."

The Japanese commander speaks up. Her translator keeps pace with her as fast as she can. "Our Lady wonders to what capacity you require the *Namazu* and its crew?"

Sanjar listens carefully, nodding before he speaks. "The role of the *Namazu* and its crew will be the same as the roles of the *Bastille* and the *Sorhab*." Sanjar turns, addressing the other crews. "All three ships will garrison the brunt of their marines and available support crew on the deck of the *Artemis* for the remainder of the voyage."

The Japanese commander's face hardens hearing this. She brushes a graying wisp of hair behind her ear, narrowing her focus on the Admiral.

Sanjar regards the rest of the group. "Once we have engaged the *Ark*, our five ships will launch all fighters, spreading in five different directions. This will be our first defensive maneuver, drawing the *Ark's* main cannons away from a concentrated area."

Sanjar's gestures a leathery hand in my direction. "My crew witnessed the annihilation of the Russian dreadnaught *Perestroika* when all main cannons were allowed to focus on one target. I'm sure none of us are inclined to share that fate."

The French captain sits up, his translator equally incensed. "If we are to engage such a dangerous enemy, my men would wish to die on the deck of a French vessel rather than one of a foreign ship," the translator relays.

Sanjar runs his fingers down the bridge of his nose. "The

reason your troops will be garrisoned on the *Artemis* is because we will exchange places with the *Agincourt* and ambush the *Ark* from within. As I've laid out before, the only way that we can successfully destroy this ship is if we are able to divide its crew."

I scan the faces around us; all I find is grim uncertainty. The Admiral continues. "With such a massive vessel, we need to keep as many of their crew as we can focused on the remaining ships on the outside of the *Ark*. With this strategy, we gain a fighting chance from inside."

Sanjar stops, extending his hand out towards the French. *"Allez-vous battre à nos côtés?"* he says.

I let half a smile curl. The Admiral's forever on stage.

"Essentially he said, 'Will you still fight with us?'" I overhear the *Agincourt's* translator say.

The French captain gives a curt nod before sitting back into his seat. With his position reaffirmed, Sanjar turns to the rest of us.

"This assault team will be led by the *Artemis's* Lieutenant Basmon.", the Admiral says firmly.

The mention of my name shoots an impulse to my legs. I stand up from my chair. The heat of the lamps above play with my focus, obscuring the faces around me in deep shadows.

The Admiral raises his hand to me, before shifting it over. "And by Lieutenant Baltier, as Officer Basmon's second."

Baltier's glare is apparent as he rises from his seat, jaw clenched. He's not used to playing second fiddle. His years as a mercenary captain don't allow for excess humility.

The weight of five nations presses on me, gauging my strength. I won't back down.

"Once our alliance's troops garrison on the *Artemis,* your captains will assist me in hand selecting the men and women who will accompany us down to the Core", I say.

Slowly, my own words begin giving me strength. "Whoever we select must be fast and well versed in hand-to-hand combat. We're expecting to engage in very close quarters, and although we will be guided by our advisors, Sabine Tesarik and Raltz Kovac, we have no way of knowing what resistance we will encounter once we've broken through the initial boarding lines," I say.

If we break through the initial lines.

A small shiver crawls down my spine, but I try not to let

them see it.

The Iranian commander raises his hand and speaks. Even though it's in Farsi, I can still tell his tone is incredulous. From the look on the translator's face, she's trying to formulate a translation that's more polite than the one her commander's given her.

Raising her chin, she asks, "And what happens if we do not succeed in destroying this Core, or simply choose not to take the risk in destroying the *Ark* at all?"

Sabine stands, letting her cloak drop to her shoulders so her pale hair reflects the shivering lamplight. "What happens is that my father will be left unimpeded," she says. The focus of the audience shifts. "The reason I fled is because my father engineered a way to destroy an entire city in one day. You've all see it first hand, otherwise you would not be sitting here discussing reprisal. The reason I never came back is much more dire than that," she says, clenching her fists together.

A hush falls.

Sabine fights to keep her voice even. "My father discovered how to keep the Core's energy within, so he could power his warship. He discovered how to focus the Core's energy below, so he could harvest resources. Worst of all, I fear that my father has finally created a way to focus the Core's energy into the heavens above. If that's so, then we are truly facing disaster."

A British officer stands up. "Maybe I'm just a bit daft . . . but how exactly?" he asks.

Sabine's eyes flit up to meet his. "My father and I spent years together inventing things. His work bench used to be covered in schematics of things we could use to create a new power source," Sabine's says, her eyes softening with the memory.

"They spanned from growing food, to powering manufactories. There really was no limit," she says. "However, one night, a group of bandits attacked our fledgling fleet. Their hunger was fueled by the rumor that we had just seized a giant prize, worth a great deal in the right market. In reality, we had just scavenged the main components we needed to create our newest project. The pieces were valueless separately, but what we could make from them would change the world."

She leans against the table to help support herself. "In that attack, many of our tribe perished, including my mother." She pauses.

"In the months after my mother's death, I noticed my father's inventions straying further and further away from ways we could create. Instead, he focused increasingly on ways that he could destroy."

Her voice hardens. "Despite a lack of investors, my father did eventually create that invention. He deemed it the *Rozbalt*. The name essentially translates to 'The Unzipper' in our native Slovak."

"Why?, a Japanese officer asks in English.

Turning to address him, Sabine explains, "The *Rozbalt* was one of our most ambitious designs. Using power harnessed by a massive magnetic power core, my father created a way essentially to unzip the atmosphere. I use this word 'unzip' because the first "incision" in the ozone was already almost a millennium ago. The damage caused by uninhibited ultraviolet rays escaping through the ozone barrier would make tearing the rest of the ozone quite easy."

Sabine pauses, pulling out a map and rolling it out onto the table in front of her. "If you'll look, you will see that my father has systematically attacked each trading post in an almost direct swath up the Appalachian Spine. I fear that with this pattern, he is heading as far north as he can to put this weapon to use."

The Iranian commander stands up. "I still do not understand the significance of a weapon that can only be used on the sky," he asserts through his translator.

Sabine's slate eyes meet his. "The significance is that it will initiate a second Drowning."

As this is translated to the different parties, many of the officers and their cohorts shift apprehensively in their chairs.

"Why would someone do this? Such an action would doom us all," the Iranian officer asks.

Sabine acknowledges him. "For those of you familiar with Christianity and the Old God, you will not be surprised that my father's naming of his warship the *Ark* was not an accident. In the days before I took my leave, my father began cursing the world and its corruption. How easily that corruption killed those who were kind. It was his wish to wash it clean once more. I believe the catalyst for this line of reasoning was my mother's premature death."

The French officer speaks up; his translator is quick to do his job. "By doing this, he would destroy his own people as well. It makes no sense."

Sabine pulls her shawl over her shoulder. "Before we became airborne, the Cascade were almost exclusively dependent upon our seafaring ways, including fishing. We were one of the few tribes that possessed the ships and skills do this successfully. I believe this is his reasoning in that regard . . . although I do not believe that reason is taking much part in this."

The French officer responds once again. "I do not believe that he has this power. What you're stating is ridiculous. No one has this power", the translator states carefully.

Sabine doesn't have to say anything this time.

Sanjar stands once more. "I would not have believed that a ship could have the ability to level entire cities either, but we have all witnessed the terrible truth."

The faces of the surrounding alliance shift as the gravity of the situation begins sinking in. Sanjar furthers his agenda. "There is only one difference in the assault on this ship, and it is that we actually know our enemy this time. Not only that, we also know the stakes upon entering the battlefield." He pauses before asking, "I must ask you once more . . . Will you fly with us?"

With this, Sanjar unsheathes his sword and slams it on the table on the other side of his scabbard. The steel rings in a clear call to arms.

Barely a second passes before the scimitar of the Iranian captain hits the table on his opposite side, swearing an oath in Farsi. One after another, the Japanese crew and the French envoy follow suit.

Lastly, the *Agincourt* representative slips his cutlass out of his sheath and carefully places it to his right. Looking up from his sword, he offers, "We're with you mate. Let's torch these bastards."

19

The temperature drops as night falls. Fish oil lamps line the streets, but the brightest lights in the trading post are being thrown off by the *Artemis* as its crew works tirelessly to swap its goods. I'm sure the residents appreciate the business, but I doubt that the extra light and sound pollution are as welcome in this habitually silent hamlet.

I'm surprised to see Red Swan emblems mixed in with the five other nations as the *Artemis* deckhands rearrange the hangar bay. I thought they would all have left when Baltier gave them a chance. Perhaps the Australian was able to carve out some hazard pay for his pilots to retain some of them. Maybe they just care about the old girl more than I ever gave them credit for.

For our part, our small band of friends has taken shelter away from the rest of the crew. Huddled underneath blankets with our backs pressed against the outcropping of rocks, we watch as the waves thunder in. Despite the sheer power of the surges, there's something soothing about their rhythm.

"So how's everybody going to spend their last night earthbound?" I ask the ocean.

Yeti's bottle clinks against the cliff's overhang. "Well . . . I was planning on drinking a lot. I don't know about you,", he offers. He pulls his crutch close to him, eyeing the froth below.

The fact he survived his injuries at Shipwreck is a miracle. The fact he's not opting to stay in World's End is a tragedy. He somehow bribed the flight doctor to falsify a report stating that he was fit to fly. It's a lie of course. Truth is, we're so desperate for pilots we probably would've taken him anyway.

I watch as pain shoots across his face as he tries readjusting the thick blanket over his knees. At this rate, I don't know how he plans on pulling a joy stick in just few short days. When I asked him to sit out, he told me there were many names to avenge not to take advantage of this opportunity. I hope he finds his peace.

"Hmm, I was hoping I might be able to use some of it to spend time with you?" Cassandra offers. A warmth different from the influence of the beer flows through me. Cass doesn't usually expose her feelings in the open, but I love it when she does.

"I think that can be arranged," I smile. I glance down at the small shadow perched on the farthest rock on the cliff. "What about you Stenia?"

Stenia doesn't answer at first. As usual, she opens her mouth only when she is ready. "I'm not certain that I will sleep," she says as a wisp of blond hair blows out behind her flight cap. She continues her habit of seeing things we can't.

"It's very odd to me that this may be the last time that my feet touch the earth. Having spent so much time airborne, I'm curious about this place," she says, observing the oddly shaped rooftops and winding streets. "I believe I will trade my sleep tonight to see what else this place holds," she muses thoughtfully.

"I'm sure the Admiral would love to hear that his top scout's trading sleep to go sightseeing," I chuckle.

"I don't need much," Stenia says without turning her head.

Silence takes over once more. I think of those who aren't enjoying a beer with us on this chilly evening. Olan's locked away someplace quiet on the *Artemis*. He hasn't spoken much since we lost Aoife. In lieu of conversation, he devotes his time to the art of warfare. Practicing his sword forms and honing his aim at the practice range seem to be all that's left.

Spray vaults over the rocks as the ocean wind buffets from behind it. I brace against Cass as it blows over.

My shivering attracts a hand. It snakes under my blanket, feeling around the darkness until it finds mine. "Are you feeling ok, Sage?" Cass whispers.

I nod as a tear freezes on my cheek. "Yeah . . . Just cold." I'm thankful for the darkness.

She gives my hand a squeeze. "You know you're not the only one who's afraid, right?"

I shift my weight underneath the blanket. "I know. It's just . . . different this time." I exhale. "We know what's coming. And really, if we want to, we have the power to just walk away."

"Hah, we'll see how well that would go over", Yeti laughs. I hear the nerves in his voice.

The pressure of our destiny weighs on my chest. I need to put it in words or I won't sleep tonight "When I started all this . . . it seemed like the right thing to do. Of course you take up arms against those who do wrong, and of course you think that you're going to come out on the winning side." I massage Cass's hand with my thumb. "But now that I'm here . . . now that we're so close, I'm just not as sure."

Stenia's voice cuts through the dark. "When you think of Aoife, are you sure?" She stands up at the edge of the promontory. "What about the blood of all the innocents killed in all those trading posts?" Stenia bristles, taking a small rock and hurling it into the ocean.

"I prefer it this way," she breathes. "This way I can see the uniforms of those we're about to fight. I can study their tactics. I know their intentions." She twists to face us. "Every one of those fragments make them that much easier to kill . . . and it's exhilarating to have that advantage."

I nod slowly. Everything she says is true. The mention of Aoife's name lights a flame in my gut. I can feel it clearing away the uncertainty that's built up like rust.

"You're right Stenia," I say. "This is the course we set. We'll see it through to the end."

My train of thought's derailed by Cass's hand gliding up my thigh. My mind shifts gears from contemplating mortality to something much better. Glancing over, I see her eyes looking up at me.

"Hey Cass, are you getting a little chilly?" I whisper, squeezing her hand once more to cement the message. To my delight, I see her sea foam eyes light up in the darkness.

"You know, I could be persuaded that it's too cold to stay out here," she smiles.

I take my hand from hers, moving it up her knee. "May I persuade you then?"

Cass cocks her head. "You may."

With that, we both down the last of our beers. We wrap the

blanket around our shoulders as we try finding our feet on the rocks.

"I swear I'll find that someone eventually." Yeti yawns as we pick up our bottles. His hunched form gazes thoughtfully at Stenia.

"You knew that was a long shot from the beginning," Stenia says without turning around. "No pun intended."

As encouragement, I clap Yeti on the shoulder and give him a thumbs up. I nudge Cass, and she snaps her head up and nods in agreement. The downturned corners of Yeti's lips reveal a mask of strategy as we leave him to his work. Maybe he'll learn something from the waves below and figure out a way to wear Stenia down over time.

Wishful thinking.

Dawn breaks over the cliffs of World's End. I peer out at the shipyard from the docking bay. Trucks and cranes swivel, doing the last bit of refueling and rearming of the *Artemis* and its crew. It won't be long now before we cast off ties and chase our destinies. Everyone I know has already retreated deep within the bowels of the *Artemis* to go keep their minds on other things. No one wants to focus on the opportunity to stay behind and sit this one out. It's too easy to turn around and walk right off.

I've made the mistake of lingering too long, unable to make myself move farther than a few steps from the earth. I gaze at the small tufts of grass shooting up from the rocks dotting the landing zone. An impulse impels me to reach out and touch them, but I know it won't help any. I'll want to keep holding on until I just won't let go. I'd just stay here in this quiet little fishing village. Figure out how to fish. Maybe get lucky enough to be forgotten about.

I make no movement to go farther into the *Artemis* as this fantasy struggles to claw its way from my mind into reality. It doesn't last long though. The sound of familiar voices drowns it until it stops struggling.

Captain Dixon and her daughter Fiona round the corner of the docking bay. I'm surprised to see her in street clothing. Without her nurses uniform, I see Fiona as the young woman she is. Side by side, her features are just as angular as her mother's, but a little softer. Instead of raising her as a warrior princess, I think Janna's done her best to let Fiona live like a normal woman.

"Mom, I'm not letting you go up there alone. You really think I'm going to be better off in a place called "World's End" than with you and the *Artemis?*", Fiona asks. "You really think that I can't help you fight up there?"

I shrink back into the rest of the machinery in the docking bay. It's too late for me to leave without them knowing I was here, contemplating cowardice.

Captain Dixon shushes her daughter, wiping away the tears welling in Fiona's eyes. "Of course I know you can fight Hon, of course I do," Dixon says, wrapping her daughter up tightly. "But, I'm not sending you into battle when I know your gift is to heal others."

Even I can tell this is a tired excuse that holds less and less water each time it's employed.

Fiona stops, wiping her face with her sleeve. "Mom, you know that's not fair. If anything happens up there, I want to be there with you when it does. I don't want to have what happened to Dad, happen again with you," she says, pulling in a ragged breath. "I want to be there."

The mention of Fiona's father transforms Dixon's features from Mother back to Drill Sergeant.

"Fiona, we've talked about this. I'm not going to get to the age where I get taken by a heart attack. You're not going to sit there and spoon feed me soup while I keep asking you if you've ever met my daughter. It's just not going to happen." Janna straightens, making her daughter do the same. "How many times have I told you that when I die, it's going to be doing something useful? I'm not waiting to share the latest nursing home gossip."

"Mom, you're forty-six, you shouldn't be worrying about that," Fiona says indignantly.

Dixon starts, looking back towards the Living Quarters. "Jesus Kiddo, why don't you let the whole crew know?"

Some spittle shoots towards the deck as Fiona lets out an unexpected laugh.

Dixon gathers her daughter up in her arms again. "Hey, this kind of lifestyle puts a lot more years on your body than you think. Ok?"

Fiona swallows, staying quiet.

Janna rolls her daughter out of her arms, taking her by the shoulders. "Listen Fiona, I love you. You turned out pretty amazing, and I'm not going to let some Admiral's last hurrah ruin everything that you are."

Dixon slowly turns Fiona around towards the exit, keeping an arm over her shoulder. Janna leans over. "No matter what happens from here on out, always remember that you're a Dixon. You can overcome anything."

In spite of the tear rolling over her lips, I swear there's a hint of a smile on Fiona's face.

Captain Dixon takes a big breath. "Fiona, you know I love you so much, but it's time to go. So what are we going to do? We're going to set our shoulders, edge our chin up, and walk right down that gangplank into a new life."

She whispers into her daughter's ear. "Are you ready?"

I hold my breath as Fiona gives the slightest nod.

Dixon releases her daughter.

With her shoulders set and her chin up, Fiona Dixon strides out of the docking bay and down the gangplank without looking back. Once she's made it far enough, Janna Dixon hits the door release, closing the way for both of us. We stand there in red tinged darkness. In the quiet, she leans over the door controls.

"You know you're the reason that happened, right?", Captain Dixon asks the darkness.

I swallow hard. "Yes."

Dixon stands in silence once more with her arm up against the side of the wall. "She's tough, she's independent, and she doesn't need you,", she says, her voice as even as ever.

I nod in the dark.

"But, if something ends up happening to me . . . you need to promise that you will take care of that girl."

Silence sets in again.

"That'll be our trade, alright?"

I find my voice. "Alright."

Without saying another word, she takes her hand off of the controls and walks back into the interior of the ship. As her footsteps fade, I realize I'm once again alone in the darkness.

I let the echoes reverberate around me as I stand there, listening to the sounds of the ship preparing for takeoff. But it's not a sound so much as a smell that I notice: a pungent odor. One that I remember from childhood. It's been there over the last few months, but never as strong as it is now.

I freeze, finally placing it. It's not possible. The only person I know who smokes Burley Tobacco has been gone for a long time.

"Dad?"

I turn, finding a man in the midst of lighting a cigarette. He's dressed in a vintage version of one of our uniforms. The igniting cherry illuminates a tilted flight-cap sitting over bushy eyebrows. A full moustache covers a shrouded face. The milky blue eyes flit up to me. There's no mistaking him. What makes the whole situation even more unsettling is that he's not much older than I am.

"Good to see ya Killer."

The muscles wrapping around my jaw pull taught. "Don't call me that anymore."

My father coughs out some smoke, laughing. "Why? 'Cause it actually means something now?" he counters.

Blood froths up from the man's mouth. The pilot screams from the street. A woman hits the ground with a dull thud.

"No," I say, my palms starting to sweat. "Because you haven't called me that in twenty years."

My father nods absentmindedly. "Well, I've been gone a long time."

Anger bubbles beneath the surface. "You look like you've been doing pretty well for yourself. Being gone for that long."

My father squints. "What are you gettin' at Killer?" He takes a long pull on his cigarette, bringing the darkness back over his face.

"Would you prefer to remember me like this?"

The cherry burns brighter, revealing the fingers holding the cigarette as nothing but bone. Horror rises as the light creeps back up a moldy, waterlogged skeleton of a face. The mouth twists in a gruesome angle. A single, dark, worm arches up out of his eye socket, reaching out towards the shadows.

I throw my hands over my face. "No!" I shout, fighting to collect myself. ". . . No."

When I lower my hands, his face slides back into view. There's a smile on it. With flesh this time.

He lets out another smoky laugh. "I didn't think so."

Focusing hard on the full face in front of me, I struggle to banish the thought of his decomposing body. "What are you doing here?" I ask.

My father holds his cigarette like a candle, watching the smoke rise from the burning cherry at the top. "You've made a lot of decisions lately, Sage." He gives the cigarette a wag, sending the smoke curling. "And a lot of people are going to die in the next few days as a result."

"I already know that." I grate.

My father takes the cigarette, pointing the cherry at me. "See, I don't think you do though." His blue eyes pierce through the darkness. "They were looking for something to make them complete. You gave them a purpose." His sharp cheek bones keep bringing back the image of his skeleton. "That purpose just so happens to be a suicide mission."

He places a hand on his chest. "Everyone loves to be a martyr. Except when it actually comes time to die."

"Are you saying that we should just turn back now?" I say through my teeth.

He leans against the wall, taking another drag. "I'm not telling you to choose one way or another. I'm just trying to make you understand the full weight of your decision before you make it."

His skin looks so sallow.

He rocks himself forward. "It's so easy to charge forward with no thought for the future, only to deal with the consequences later. Anyone can do that. But only a real man understands the costs of his decisions before he makes them."

I roll my eyes. I'm so tired of being told what it's going to take to make me a 'real man.' I'm twenty-eight years old; it's a little late for that.

My father continues before I can stop him. "You put an idea into these people. Now you're responsible for them - no matter what happens."

His chiding demeanor cuts through, unimpeded. "They chose for themselves Dad. Every single one of them chose for themselves. No one's here who didn't walk over that line," I state.

My father brings himself to his full height. "You think drawing a line on a deck makes it fair? With all of their buddies watching them make that choice? How could you expect them to say 'no' in a circumstance like that?" He places his hands behind his head. "You phrased it in a way that they believed the world would end a second time if they didn't join you."

"It could . . . " I say, swallowing.

My father pushes his cap back. "You really believe that?"

Silence fills the room.

He nods. "That's what I thought." He shifts his weight, pointing a finger at me. "You know . . . it's funny. I always thought that your sister was gonna to be the fighter in the family."

Something akin to nostalgia fills his eyes. "You could see she had that fire, you know? Even at six, Pela had more balls than you." He pauses, his finger still frozen in midair. "You," he says, "you always had your head buried in whatever book you could get your hands on."

I throw my arms up. "What are you trying to get at?"

My father leans back up against the wall. "I know the real reason why you went along with this whole charade," he says.

I raise my eyebrows, waiting for an answer.

"Think about it," he motions, flicking his lighter open again to renew the dying cherry of his cigarette. "When do you feel most alive?"

Flying, Cass, tearing a piece of freshly baked bread in two, a vista sunset, the sound of that piano . . .

"No, no, no." My father waves his hands, the smoke trail of his Burly Tobacco cigarette curving wildly. "When do you really feel the most alive?

A different set of images flows in: the whiz of a bullet tickling my jaw, the feeling of bone snapping underneath my clenched fist, the recoil from that rifle, looking up as the smoke clears just in time to see that woman fall to her knees.

A cold sweat breaks out over my arms. I want to tell him he's wrong, but nothing comes out.

My father angles the burning cherry down towards me. "See. That's it," he says, his eyes dark voids. "You live to 'be shot at without result'. To watch the life drain from others."

I try objecting, but my mouth's so dry I can barely form words. He has to be wrong. I attempt again. "Geez Dad, you make me sound like some sort of psycho . . . " I manage.

He gives me a look of exasperation. "Well. You're talking to me, aren't you?"

I nod numbly. "Yeah . . . I guess you're right."

The corridor around us shudders. The magnets pulse outside,

reversing their charges and sending us away. Flickering hallway lights announce we're leaving ground.

My father turns his milky blue eyes from the lights to me. "I believe your crew needs you now, Lieutenant."

Taking a deep breath, I try focusing once more. I put my hand on the back of my head, turning away.

"So, whatever happened that day? Twenty years ago . . . ?" I ask.

Silence.

Stopping, I slowly turn back around. Once again, I'm alone in the darkness of the lower deck, the smell of Burley Tobacco wafting in the air.

20

The cold bursts over my face as I leave the bulk head. Snowflakes flit by as we power through the thin atmosphere. Pulling on my gloves, I push out into the current. The cutting wind probes for bare skin as I make sure my cap is snug. My leather armor secured, I allow myself to peer over the banister.

It's something to see, really. From the port side of the ship, the *Agincourt* plows ahead. The hulking *Namazu* follows in its wake, while the *Bastille* covers the left flank of our little armada. Somewhere behind me the *Sohrab* keeps a close watch on the right flank. If I squint, I can make out the dots of our multinational fleet flying from ship to ship, patrolling for anyone looking to give our convoy trouble.

As striking as it is, I'm worried about this tactic. There's probably a wire going out to the entire privateer network that a large shipment's headed due north. We hardly look like easy pickings, but in a pirate's mind, that means whatever we're hauling is worth more than what we've put in place to defend it.

Not a good image to create at a time like this.

Granted, if a pirate fleet successfully attacked us, they'd hardly walk away empty-handed. Captured crew aside, we're weighed down with as many munitions and supplies as Admiral Khan could purchase. It's not enough to fill our cargo hold, but the collection could still serve as a hell of a retirement plan for the right enterprising captain.

Ill-advised or not, our formation stirs something in my chest. It's not so much hope as a sensation of excitement. No matter what happens from here on out, we've successfully assembled captains and pilots from no less than five separate countries. Even if everything goes wrong, it's a feat that hasn't been accomplished in years.

Now, if only we could get the soldiers and pilots to mix as one fighting unit. Despite our common goal, each ship features disparate traditions and expectations. Having the ships' marines train together has already created tensions among the men and women. Sparring goes too far . . . or not far enough. I've been summoned to break up a few fights before they became something more, but it's not like anyone's been shot. Yet.

It's so frustrating. Each ship has specialties that could benefit the others tremendously. The *Namazu's* focus on disciplined swordplay far outclasses ours. The *Bastille's* marines are few, but battle-tested. The *Agincourt's* pilots have been attempting to instruct ours on the finer points of air combat, but none of the *Artemis* crew care to attend the seminars. The list goes on.

I keep telling myself that trust can't be built in a few days, but I'm worried about what will happen when it comes time to face the *Ark*. Will smoke and fire bind these people together . . . or break them apart?

There's only one way to find out.

Pulling my trench coat close, I march up the Outer Rim towards the bow. It's eerily quiet as my footsteps clank against the slick steel below. No vendors hawk their wares here; it's not worth the risk. Trying to sell to soldiers on a doomed ship? It's just not a good investment.

Two marines stand guard next to the door of the Cellar with their rifles on their shoulders, huddling against the wind. One cups his hand over his mouth, smoking a cigarette. The other stares into the cloud ocean, leaning her back against the bulkhead's arch. Neither says a thing to me.

As I descend into the Cellar, I see darkness eventually give way to a flickering light. The light wavers in and out of the doorway until I get close enough to hear the hiss of welding tools intermix with the thunder of ammo trolleys. Rounding the corner, I'm met again with a sight that inspires both pride and dread.

Deck hands pass underneath wings, racing from plane to plane throughout the hangar. Engineers of all different nationalities perch on cockpits and ladders, welding shut any outstanding damage or imperfections. We only get one chance to do this right. There are no do-overs.

Stepping over a fuel hose, I make my way into the flickering forest of tails and engines. Falling sparks reveal patches from all over. A British pilot patiently checks his tail flaps. An Iranian deck hand helps her pilot paint a flowing river running down the full length of a plane's tail. If it weren't an instrument of war, it would belong in a gallery.

At one point, I even see Yeti hauling a box of 50 caliber bullets on his good shoulder while resting the other one in a pale white sling. There's no way he'll be ready to fight by tomorrow, but I respect his willingness, regardless. Most pilots would've opted to stay in World's End where they at least might have a chance at starting life again. Not Yeti. He couldn't bear for us to fly off without him. Not when he could help even the body count. Even a few Red Swans and their Wraiths dot the hangar, their golden incentive long gone. Still they choose to fight with us.

Ducking underneath wings and stepping over paint cans and shell casings, I make my way to the Engineering deck.

Tucked into the side of the hangar near the crane tower; a hive of engineers buzzes with ideas and improvements. As I make my way onto the deck, the impact of rivet guns and electric screw drivers replaces the harsh symphony of welding tools. The engineers are even busier than the pilots, readying for tomorrow's attack.

A flash of red is all I need to point me in the right direction. Diz's hair is pulled back into a tight knot as she forces her greased hands into the center of a large metallic oval. Sweat drips down the side of her face. It's clear she's gotten about as much sleep the last few days as I have, which isn't much.

"Will they be ready for tomorrow?" I ask.

Diz doesn't look at me as she forces the rest of her arm up to her shoulder into the hole. "Not a good time lad," she gasps, peering up at me from under her freckled eyebrows. "These charges have to get set somehow."

Tensing, I notice the tables around me. Each oval sitting on the work benches around us possesses enough explosive power to blow a hole right through the *Artemis's* hull. That's their sole purpose.

Originally, they were created to be taken down to the Core to destroy it, but after a few trials, they were deemed too heavy to move all that way. Not to mention, a direct detonation of one of these smart bombs would be enough to destroy the Core entirely, most likely killing everyone on board in the process. Instead, smaller explosives have been substituted, with the goal of only knocking the Core out of sync. With the power source unsynced, it should give us just enough time to escape before it goes nova.

At least that's what I keep telling myself.

The only reason these bombs are considered "smart" is that their backing is one large magnet. Once activated, it locks itself onto whatever metallic surface it's placed against. The only way to access the charges placed inside is from a small hole drilled into the magnetic face. This way, it's almost impossible to deactivate the charges once they've been laid.

They're a trademark creation of Diz, birthed from the morbid reality that she and her team have a significant chance of not surviving the setting of the charges. Any enemy troops standing over their bodies at the time of detonation would disintegrate along with the *Ark's* hangar doors. A final "fuck you" from beyond the grave.

That's the worry, though. Once we're in, we know those doors are going to swing shut on us, just like they did with the *Churchill*. Diz has the delicate job of devising an explosion large enough to free us, but not so large that everyone in the hangar gets cooked alive. There are many people with whom I'd be more than willing to trade places, but Diz isn't one of them.

"You still happy you came with us?" I ask her, placing my hands on my hips.

"Oh, just beaming," she replies curtly. She winces as an audible click echoes out from the bomb.

I flinch.

She smiles, looking back up at me. "We'll . . . we're not dead. So we have that going for us."

The newly-set charge forces me to consider the wisdom of standing on a platform created for the sole purpose of manufacturing experimental bombs.

Satisfied, Diz removes her arm from the metal plating. "It's not like we can turn back anyways," she says.

I nod, stopping my feet from turning towards the opening in the tarp.

She wipes her soiled hands on an even dirtier cloth. "We don't have enough fuel."

Panic shoots through. "What?", I ask.

Diz throws the expended towel at the corner waste bin. She misses, but she's already too preoccupied with the next bomb to care. "Christ, Baz. I'm just taking the piss," she grins wearily.

Breathing a sigh of relief, I grin with her. Sarcasm is still alive and well here.

Diz threads her hand through the plating of the next subject. "Although, I suppose I wouldn't put it past the old bastard. Here's to hoping Sir Khan's planning to bring his gains back to the nearest port and make that profit you promised him."

I scratch the back of my head, remembering the pseudo lie of Neodymium being a precious metal. It's not that it's untrue . . . It has to be. The stuff comes from the unseen bowels of the earth. I just have no idea what it's worth.

Diz blows a strand of hair out of her face, the rest of it sticking to the sweat on her forehead. I can't tell if it's gathered there from concentration or nerves. Probably both.

"Because it's either that," she continues, "or we go out in his blaze of glory with him."

Diz shuts her eyes, gritting her teeth. My stomach clenches as I look into the darkness of the bomb's cavity.

Another click echoes out from its center.

Diz lets out a sigh. "Annnd . . . we're still here."

With that, I decide there are safer places to spend what could be my last day on Earth.

Snowflakes try sneaking in behind me as the bulkhead of the Bridge slams shut. The echo ripples through the hallway, into the darkness. The only light betraying the Bridge's location is a dim green glow that paints silhouettes across the wall. Stepping quietly into the control room, I admire the reflections of instruments dancing and pirouetting across the thick glass. I can barely see the snow outside, sticking to the windshield as the *Artemis* powers through the storm. Only the running lights of the *Namazu* and *Bastille* reveal that we're in a storm at all.

Only about half of the Bridge staff man the instruments, bustling from machine to machine as I pass by. The rest are either gone, asleep, or spending time with their families. There's only one more projected night before combat. Anxiety pushes a sickening fist into my stomach.

Standing out from among them is Sabine, poised on the floor at the forefront of the Bridge. A large tape compass sprawls around her. Her outstretched, peppered arm currently leads us somewhere between the crudely taped N, and the barely legible NE. Her eyes stay closed. I can't tell if it's out of exhaustion, or concentration. Again, I'm going to say both.

The Helmsman twists the tiller to align the ship's nose with Sabine's rigid arm. It's hardly sophisticated, but it's the only way we have to continue our pursuit of the *Ark*. I try stepping as quietly as I can as I approach the circle. It's late, and people don't want to be bothered.

As the sole of my shoe touches the makeshift compass, Sabine opens her mouth. "It's good that you're here Sage. I've been meaning to speak with you," she says, her eyes still closed.

Much like Stenia, she's identified something in the way I carry myself that's particular to me, just by listening to my dampened footsteps.

"Come closer," she says.

Moving to the center of the circle, my skin prickles at the magnetic pull. Although I'm a head taller then she is, I can still feel the power emanating from her, almost in waves. Gazing down past her finger tips, she reaches out into the darkness, pointing to where we'll meet our destiny. Whatever it is.

I can't help wishing that she would turn her arm, and the ship, around, back to where we came from. Away from all of the dangers crawling in the dawn, waiting for us to cross that threshold.

Sabine lowers her arm, opening her eyes into mine. The blast of their cold blue washes over me. They no longer remind me of melting ice. Instead, they're reminiscent of the blizzard outside, brooding and powerful.

"I've been meaning to thank you," she says.

"For what?" I ask.

"For helping to make all of this possible," she says. "Without you, we wouldn't have an army. Without you, we wouldn't be able to stop my father."

I'm at a loss for words. "We haven't done it yet," I say.

Sabine motions around the Bridge with her uninjured hand, gesturing to the running lights of the zeppelins flying in formation alongside us. "We united five separate nations under one cause. We raised an army from nothing. We're taking the action that has to occur in order to stop all of this." She pauses. "To me, that means everything. After seeing firsthand what my father's done, the people he's killed, children like Aoife . . . This is the only course."

Before I can process what's happening, Sabine threads her arms around my waist, pulling me close to her.

I stand there, frozen. I've never seen Sabine's make physical contact with anyone since the day we met.

She lays her shock blond head on my chest, pressing her studded arm into my side.

Slowly, I put my hands around her shoulders.

"You should get some sleep Sabine. You've been at this for hours," I say. "I think you might be getting a little delusional."

Sabine releases me. "I believe you are guilty of a similar crime, Lieutenant." She massages her studded wrist, looking back up at me. "You have to lead a much larger force than I do tomorrow. I know for a fact that you have not slept much either."

It's hard to sleep when you know that each passing hour creeps closer to the one that could be your last. I suppose it's always been that way, I've just never been so aware of it until now.

We stand in silence, watching the snow fall. A strong wind blows against the bow, rumbling soundlessly past us.

She shakes her head. "Sage, I –"

"Mr. Basmon – a word please."

The voice interrupts us from the side of the Bridge. Sanjar Khan leans out of his quarters, fixing his gaze on me.

Sabine stiffens, turning back around to continue her work.

"Go Lieutenant," she says, collecting herself. "I give you my word that I will be well enough rested to guide you tomorrow."

I open my mouth to protest, but her turned back says that whatever bizarre episode just occurred is over. Instead, I nod, making my way towards the Admiral's Quarters. Before I pass the line of the tape compass, I notice a set of grey points gleaming part way up a dark wall. Raltz's eyes cut through the darkness, continuing their vigil, watching my every move. I've never earned his trust. It's an impossible battle. And no longer my responsibility.

My footsteps echo off of the pale oak floorboards as I enter into the Admiral's office. The enveloping hum of the *Artemis* dampens to near silence as the door shuts behind me. My heart pounds as I make my way up the flight of steps to his desk. What could he want from me so late in the game?

"Good evening Mr. Basmon."

The Admiral's words are tired. Strain etches itself into his heavy eyes as he pours a glass of wine.

He takes a moment to look up, mid-pour. "Would you like some, Lieutenant?"

There's something warm about his offer; like he's finally ready to put the past behind him.

"No thank you sir," I respond. "Only water for me the night before a battle."

The Admiral lets out a half chuckle. "That's interesting. It's only wine for me the night before a battle."

The smile breaks across my lips before I can stop it. "Very reassuring," I say.

The Admiral's chair creaks as he leans back. "Well, when a man's about to gamble his entire fleet based on limited information and sketchy projections, he's entitled to a drink. Wouldn't you say Lieutenant?"

"I'd say that's fair enough," I offer, settling into the plush chair across from him.

The admiral sits back, regarding me for a moment. His grey eyes miss nothing, although there's something in them that I've never seen before. Maybe a hint of uncertainty? His hair has thinned since I've seen him last. There's much less pepper than salt now. Then again, maybe it's always been this way and I've just never had the perspective to realize it.

"Lieutenant Basmon, I'm sure you know that I didn't invite you into my quarters just to offer a drink." He pauses, as if to make one last decision. "I've brought you here, so I could give you this."

Demonstrating the agility he once commanded, Sanjar flicks a small black rectangle from inside his cufflink to his fingertips. Gingerly, he hands it to me across the table. It's no bigger than the palm of my hand. It doesn't weigh much either. Feeling grooves along its bottom, I flip it over to reveal a key pressed into the back of the plastic slat.

"What's this?", I ask.

"That," the Admiral says, leaning forward, "is something that I'm giving to you for safe keeping."

I furrow my brow, frustrated by his vagueness. "You can't give me any more information than that?"

The Admiral settles into his chair. "No. Because I'm hedging my bets on surviving this battle and retaining all the secrets that little rectangle has."

Sitting back, I inspect the object for more clues. A more in-depth search reveals nothing.

"So why give it to me then?" I ask.

The Admiral takes a large sip of wine before responding. "Because if I do die, I can rest well knowing that it's in good hands."

I turn the object over in my fingers. "And what's your plan if both of us get killed?" I probe.

The Admiral places his hand at the bottom of the stemmed glass, swirling it thoughtfully. "There isn't one. If both of us perish tomorrow, there is no one else who I would want to entrust with that key."

Now I'm totally confused. None of this makes any sense.

Aware of my bewilderment, the Admiral sets his glass down, getting up from his chair. "Lieutenant. As I'm sure you know, I have no living heirs. I have no wife. I have no brothers or sisters," he says placing a hand on the table and leaning into the light. "What I do have, is the crew that I've brought together. The families I've seen raised on this ship." He picks up his hand from the table, pointing at me. "You are a product of one of those families. I've watched you grow. I've watched you make decisions throughout your life. Not all of them good . . . In fact, many of them weren't. But, there was one common theme that ran through them all."

I sit, dumfounded. I had no idea the Admiral had any inkling of who I was before I joined his Air Corps.

His grey eyes bore into mine. "That common theme was your unwavering will to protect others." He scratches his mustache.

"That's not a natural occurrence in people. That's not normal. Nature's instinct is to take care of oneself and protect one's gains. To fight the world if you have to." He shakes his head. "But not you. I watched you get countless bloody noses and black eyes fighting to protect the other children from those who were stronger. You lost most of those fights. Beat unconscious in several of them. Yet, you put your body on the line for them each and every time."

Silently, I taste the blood in my mouth once more. Remember peering out through a clouded eye trying my best to see the pages. Stenia laughing at my side, begging me to read her another story. There's a knot in my memories; something that doesn't match up. Although we were on our own, we never truly went hungry. We certainly knew hunger, but there was never a time when I thought I'd die from it. Whenever things looked truly dire, we always came upon a cache of food left by a former passenger or some forgetful merchant. When worst came to worst, we were always able to pilfer enough from the Galley.

My eyes widen.

It was him.

He always made sure we never suffered. He never once revealed it, but he took care of us whenever we truly needed help.

I try to speak, but nothing comes out.

Sensing my epiphany, the Admiral sits back down. "Tomorrow is no different. Don't misjudge me; I still intend on becoming a very rich man from the remains of that ship. I still intend on killing Garon for laying waste to the families that looked to me for safety. I wouldn't have agreed to commit my forces without those incentives."

"It was you." The words manage to get out. "You were the one who took care of us."

The Admiral's face stiffens. "I don't know what you're talking about, Lieutenant."

I try collecting my words. It's like being in the middle of a chicken pen. "You were the one that took care of us when we were children."

Silence unfolds between us.

The Admiral breathes out slowly through his nostrils. "One thing I do know, is that it is very late on an eve we cannot afford to sacrifice sleep."

My clear cue to leave. Getting to my feet, I look the Admiral in the eyes. "Thank you very much sir."

Sanjar waves it away. "Nonsense, it's you who's doing me the favor. Keep it safe," he asserts.

"I will," I say, tilting my head forward.

Slipping the slat into my breast pocket, I turn on my heel. "Good night Admiral."

Admiral Khan grabs the neck of the half empty wine bottle as I go. "To you as well Mr. Basmon. Best of luck."

My footsteps carry me away as wine tinkles into the Admiral's glass once more.

It's late by the time I finally crawl into Cass's bed.

"I was wondering when you were going to make it back tonight," she whispers softly.

I pull her close. "Hmm, me too. There were a lot of things that needed taking care of before tomorrow."

Cass nods her head into the pillow, pressing her body up against mine. I can feel her heart beating through her back. Our hearts trade pulses for a few minutes. I don't want hers to stop beating. Ever. The thought that tomorrow might be the day that happens brings back all the stress I've been trying to keep locked outside her front door.

Shadows play throughout the room. Moonlight leaks through, illuminating the snowflakes passing by the window. There's a peace in the silence here. Except for the hum of the engines above, nothing else is awake to make a sound. I pull the covers over Cass's exposed shoulder so the chill rolling down from the window sill can't touch it.

"Are you afraid?" I ask.

"Yes," she responds, eyes open towards the white wall.

What answer was I expecting? Was I looking for her to tell me not to be afraid? That everything's going to be alright? I'm the one who set this course; I need to be the one to lead them through it. Not the other way around.

"I am too," I whisper, stroking a lock back over her ear.

Cass exhales, turning back over to me. Her sea foam eyes shine in the moonlight.

"Official preparations begin at 0600 tomorrow morning

right?" she asks.

I nod, thinking of all of the munitions that need to be distributed, people mustered, and equipment checked. Goosebumps raise on my arms. We've raised an army from nothing.

"And what time is it now?" Cass asks, a plan in her eyes.

I scratch the stubble that needs to come off before the fight tomorrow. "I'd say a little after 2300."

Cass looks over her shoulder thoughtfully. "If that's true, then we currently have a little under seven hours budgeted for what could be the last night of our lives."

She props herself up on her arm. "How strategic would it be to allocate, at the very least, one of those hours for stress relieving activities separate from rest?"

I run my hand over her taut stomach, resting it on her hip. "You know, for what could be the last night of our lives... I'm sure we could swing it."

For the next little while, I have something else to think about besides my own mortality.

21

As is the case with all best nights, dawn comes too early. Its tendrils pierce their way into our room, burning away any semblance of fantasy we may have created in the last few hours. We're soldiers, and today's the day we prove it once again.

We did end up going over our budgeted time, but I don't think either of us would've traded that fleeting but tangible feeling of being alive for the extra ounce of clear headedness we might have gained with proper sleep.

Our arms wind their way through the shifting maze of our respective uniforms. I watch the curvature of her body as she slips on her suit. I fight the urge to grab her by the waist and jump back into bed. My eyes rest on her fingernails as they zip up her boots. They're clean now. Perfectly white. I don't know why, but I stop midway through pulling on a wool sock, pondering this. The undersides of the nails of the Cass I always knew were always caked in others' blood. A thin red lining always clung to each tip, no matter how hard she scrubbed them.

She puts on her gloves, breaking the spell. Collecting myself, I try focusing on the duties that lie before me. I wonder if that's what she wanted?

Thankfully, the thundering footfalls outside our door pull my mind back to where it needs to be: the here and now. Preparation will decide what's to come, not what has been.

Fully dressed, Cass and I press ourselves into the alcove of her doorway as she locks her cabin. Fully equipped marines bustle from side to side, bearing weapons, ammunition, and gallons of water. The lighter equipped, nimbler pilots dart between the munitions-totting men and women, rushing to get to their hangars.

Very few civilians remain on the *Artemis*. Those who chose to stay are no doubt staking out the safest areas of the ship in an attempt to weather the approaching storm. What I don't think they realize is that we're ramming straight into the eye of it.

"So are you going to stop by the infirmary before we board, or is this the last time I'm ever going to see you?" Cass asks.

My heart sinks. I know she's trying to be humorous, but the joke cuts closer to home than she anticipated.

I put my hands on her hips, looking into her upturned eyes. "I promise that no matter what happens, I will be there before we jump off."

I pause. "But just in case."

I kiss her, pressing her up against the doorway. Grabbing the siding of the arch, I pull her in so she knows I mean it.

She looks back up, breathless.

My mouth says it before I can think it through. "I love you. You know that, right?"

She hooks a hand into one of my front pockets. "Well, if I didn't know it before, I certainly do now." Her smile satisfies any unanswered questions still in my mind.

I let myself grin back. "Do you think it'll be enough to hold you over until I can get down to see you off properly?"

She pushes away. "Believe it or not Sage, I'm a pretty independent young lady. We'll have to wait and see."

My heart turns over as the connection between our fingers breaks. I will see her again. I know it.

Before I can say anything else, she turns, running toward the small-craft hangar to check the stocks of our Medevac team.

There's nothing left to do now but face reality. Slipping my headset on, I test the frequencies. All of my crews should be patched in. Running to the Veranda, I click into Sabine's frequency.

"Sabine, how close are we?" I say into the mike.

There's a silence before she clicks back. "We're right on top of them Sage. They should be coming into physical sight within the hour."

Panic shoots its way up and down my body. I thought we had more time.

Lost for words, I ask, "How's the arm holding up?"

Sabine pauses. "It's quite painful. I know it will be much worse once we are inside the *Ark,* so I am currently binding it with a mixture of gauze and tape."

I push my way past an Iranian soldier and a Japanese marine who are comparing equipment.

"Sage?" Sabine's voice betrays more worry than I'm used to. "The *Ark* appears to have slowed its pace considerably. From what I can tell, it's almost at a standstill. We don't have much time."

I press the comm against my ear. "We'll take it step-by-step Sabine. We'll stop it in time," I assure her.

It's a complete lie. If the *Ark's* already prepping to fire the *Rozbalt,* there won't be enough time for us to blow the Core before permanent damage is already done. My lungs fill with fresh air, and a little more perspective. We have to prepare for the worst and hope for the best.

I check the hammer of my revolver. Its freshly oiled components click purposefully. It's also black. Hand painted from muzzle to stock, the revolver camouflages itself nicely with the rest of my uniform. The Admiral will probably throw me over the side of the ship when he finds out I've tarnished his gift. That being said, I'd rather meet my end falling to earth than in the crosshairs of a sniper. Waving around chrome silver weapons isn't a sound battle strategy.

The Veranda has been transformed a veritable parade ground. Gone are the aspiring artisans, replaced instead by blocks of colored uniforms and drab weaponry. Sergeants and lieutenants, young and old, yell at their respective blocks. Some preach encouragement, others know only discipline. A myriad of different languages ricochet off of one another in the frosty air.

I walk past the solid colors before reaching the more mixed ranks; newly formed militias who have stitched themselves together to make a fighting force. They're not professional soldiers or mercenaries. They're just disgruntled civilians who found themselves a weapon and finally have something to shoot at. Inexperience aside, their volume helps the Veranda appear less bare. At the very end, I reach the strike teams. Baltier stands at the ready in front of his hand-picked team. His Red Swan badge gleams in the pale daylight.

The differences between our teams can be seen with the naked eye. Baltier favors force and brutality above all else. Of the five ships and the few former civilians dotting the formation, Baltier has picked the strongest, most aggressive looking men and women he could find.

One of Baltier's recruits stands at the corner of his formation brushing up against my strike group. Her hair's tied in thick braids with a dark cloth cap pulled down over her head so it almost covers her eyes. Her hand rests on the pommel of her saber, backed by a muscular forearm to power it. A blue artillery piece glints across her left breast. She must have been either a dockhand or a farmer before she joined the *Bastille's* crew.

To her left is one of my men. He's short, with unruly black hair, a dark complexion, and a slight build. A gray scimitar arches its way down the shoulder of his olive green uniform. His dark eyes are the reason I chose him. How I chose most of them, really.

They reflect a terrible pain. He's lost someone because of all of this. He's eager to settle the score, no matter what it costs. Why train a person to hate the enemy when they can already come ingrained?

He may not be the super-soldier Baltier was searching for to fill his ranks, but he'll never break and run. His love for his lost one will keep him rooted to the spot until it's over, one way or another.

That's my gamble anyways.

"Equipment check!" My voice reverberates off the all-but-forgotten sculptures littering this place.

Aoife's laughter echoes back.

I pushing the thought away, rattling off the list of items each of my soldiers will need to make it through the day. Pacing to the end of the row, a movement catches my eye. Someone else walks through the ranks three rows in.

Opening my mouth to shout, the odor of Burley tobacco hits my nostrils. A hand with a cigarette mirrors my actions, the cherry burning behind the backs of my men. My father's tired blue eyes scan each recruit as he walks past.

"Does this one even have enough muscle to hold up a rifle?" my father says, pointing behind an older woman with a tight military braid.

A grimace crawls its way across my face as I come to a halt. "Absolutely," I say firmly.

The woman with the braid looks up, surprised. "Sir?" she asks.

I realize I'm staring at her.

Quickly, I turn on my foot. "At ease Specialist Mercella," I command.

Walking quickly in the opposite direction, I avoid eye contact with my father. Reaching the end of the line again, he's already burrowed two rows in, inspecting the face of a younger man in full Artemis black and gold.

"What about this one?" my father asks. "I doubt this kid's even been in a fight before." His eyes come to rest on me before probing. "You really think you're gonna to take him to the center of that ship and get the job done?"

I grit my teeth, spinning to the center. "Yes!" I yell.

My recruits' eyes come to rest on me, bewildered by my behavior. They can hear me. They can hear everything. I reel my senses back in.

"Yes," I say again, pressing my flight cap back to the center of my head. "This is exactly the group I envisioned. This team is composed of the toughest men and women aboard all five ships." I pause, leaning into the face of the Iranian standing next to the *Bastille* Hildegard.

"We've been brought together to exact revenge with a smile on our face. Do you think we can do that?"

From deep within the Iranian's eyes, a spark ignites. A cheer rises up from the ranks.

"We came together to claw to the very heart of that machine and make it play its final beat. Can we do that?" I ask.

The faces of my soldiers change, contorting into the very people I saw when I first recruited them. Another yell goes up.

Tapping my finger against my chest, I call out once more, "I have one last question for you. If it comes to you laying down your own life for the ones you love, will you do it willingly and without regret?"

A thunderous roar answers. I feel the power of it swirl the clouds behind me. I search for my father in the crowd to fix him with a look. He's nowhere to be found. I can't smell the tobacco any more.

Breathless, I say, almost to myself, "Then you have nothing to be afraid of."

As the words leave my lips, a deafening burst illuminates my shadow against the deck.

Everyone hits the ground, shrapnel and debris ricocheting off the platform. Pressing my head and shoulder up from the steel paneling, I try collecting myself. The cries of the wounded raise up around me.

"Everyone to their positions!" I shout through a dry throat.

Baltier's already on his feet, picking up his men, throwing them in the general direction of their positions. They've found us. It was supposed to be our ambush, but they've made the first strike again. There are no other options anymore. The rest of the plan has to work.

My men begin picking themselves up, dodging to their designated posts. Some lay motionless, while others writhe in growing red pools. Medics and officers stumble into action as I pull myself up against the banister of the Outer Rim. I run my hand over myself, only finding a small laceration on my calf. Making doubly sure, I grab my crotch. Everything's still there.

I got lucky.

The clouds begin to clear, revealing the hulking warship bearing down on our formation. Dark trails appear as the *Ark's* mounted cannons fire the rest of their barrage. The railing rises up, obscuring my view as the *Artemis* banks, beginning evasive maneuvers. On the starboard side, the *Namazu* and the *Bastille* break formation. Fighters already pour from both as airbursts choke the sky.

Pulling myself up over the railing, I see a large cloud of glinting particles dive from the *Ark*. The cloud arches up, swarming in our direction.

It's begun.

There's no time to say goodbye. I press two fingers against my com. "Yeti! You there?"

Silence.

A voice echoes back. "Baz? What do you need man?" The engines in the background threaten to drown out his voice.

I turn away from the approaching fighters. "Are you launching right now?"

There's less of a pause this time. "We're being fished into place right now, what's going on?" he asks.

I hunch behind the railing. "I just wanted to make sure you're careful out there. Let's try and get back after this in one pi-"

Yeti interrupts. "I've got some of the best pilots in the world dropping with me, man. Your time's better spent praying to protect your own sorry ass."

I manage a laugh as the hint of mirth rolls back the tension, just a little.

Yeti's voice crackles through again. "Hey, I'll cut you a deal. You survive the blockade run and the reactor explosion, and I'll make sure that me and the rest of the Goldies are in one piece when you get back. Alright?"

I grin again in spite of myself. "Ok, I'll take that deal." I can hear the pneumatic arm angling Yeti's fighter down into drop position.

"Good luck, man," he says quietly.

I stare at the white wall of the Living Quarters in front of me. "Good luck."

The line goes silent.

We truly will die here.

I duck as the first wave of enemy fighters blasts over. Displaced air from bullets ruffles my clothing, sending me scuttling underneath the railing. Fragments spark off the bulkheads and paneling. Covering my head, I pull my legs in as close as I can under the shadows. I'm tempted to stay this way until, out of the corner of my eye, I see men and women emerge from the Cellar. They struggle, pulling up the heavy, prototype bombs Diz and her team created.

The shadow of a fighter flits by, unleashing another shower of lead on the Outer Rim. Instead of flinging themselves away from the explosives, several of the crew pile on top of the bombs to prevent them from detonating prematurely.

My jaw slackens. If a group of engineers has the courage to shield a bomb from the raining bullets, then I can find the drive to lead the force I handpicked. I wrench my sword from its sheath, standing up so my torso clears the railing. Taking a deep breath, I flush out the cowardice.

As I steady myself, a hand catches my arm. I turn to find Stenia poised, gripping her rifle out to her side. Her violet eyes no longer the passive, wise ones I've always known; they harbor an intense flare, becoming something else entirely.

She squeezes my arm. "Get the job done quickly, ok? I can't hold them off forever."

I nod, lost for words.

Her purple eyes study mine. "I can only watch over you until you reach the main gate, then you'll be on your own."

I take in the battle around us, trying to catch my breath.

"Come back to me. Understand?" she probes.

I finally find my words. "I'll move as fast as I can," I say, taking a few more breaths to ground myself. "I guess nothing's really changed in all this time, huh?"

The slightest smile twitches on her face. "I guess not."

Before I can say another word, Stenia leaps to the nearest ladder, surging towards her perch. My own guardian angel . . . with a 4x scope.

Something nags at my concentration. Something about the *Ark's* position. Its stance appears entirely indifferent to the formation of five different zeppelins working to destroy it. It seems to have only one focus...

Us.

Cold realization floods through me.

Down the line, Raltz stands protectively over Sabine while she checks her weapons. They'll be the last to enter the fray once we hit the *Ark's* deck. The last thing we need is one of our guides catching a bullet their first step off the *Artemis*.

But that's it. That's why the *Ark's* shifting its course.

"Baltier!" I shout.

He looks up over his huddle of soldiers.

I point to the black mass. "They're coming for Sabine!" I shout over the engines.

Baltier grimaces, clutching his rifle to his chest. "There's no way! How could they know she's on board?" he asks.

The face of my would-be assassin in Shipwreck flashes to mind. The look in his eyes when he saw who was rescuing him. He knew me, or at least my face. Perhaps from a mug shot, maybe from a photograph in a dossier. However he knew it, he also knew I was worth a lot to the Cascade dead.

"They have plants," I whisper.

The faces of Bridge personnel, deck hands and engineers, all flash by. Passengers. Any one of them could be on the Cascade payroll. With the ship's manifest changing so often, it wouldn't be very hard to sneak them aboard. If their goal was to kill Sabine, they would have done it already. Which means . . .

They've come to take her back.

"They'll be ready for us! They've turned the tables on our ambush!" I yell, gaping wide-eyed as the *Agincourt* engages ahead of us.

I run down the line of men and women along the railing shouting, "They'll be prepared. Be ready!"

Clicks and pops of magazines being pushed into place punctuate my words.

"Wait for my signal. Keep your heads down!" I yell.

I grip the railing, keeping my eyes fixed on the *Agincourt* as it attempts to trade fire with the *Ark*. There's no contest. The *Ark's* cannons tear through the carrier as it turns to evade its attack. The British zeppelin spouts fire on both the starboard hull and bow, struggling to turn about. There's no longer a need for decoy flames; the real ones make a more convincing show than we ever could.

Small dots onboard the *Agincourt* rush towards the blaze as smoke and lead rake back and forth over each hull. Some of the *Agincourt* crew aboard the *Artemis* cry out as they watch their stricken craft move to limp away from the fight. I can't imagine what it's like, losing your home like that. Just having to sit and watch it burn. If our plan continues going this poorly, I won't have to imagine for much longer.

Multicolored waves of aircraft crash into the blue and gray onslaught. Arcs of fire and a stream of explosions ignite the middle of the sky. It's hard to tell who's who. For the first time, I'm relieved I wasn't commissioned as a pilot for this fight.

Behind the maelstrom of fighters, the Ark hasn't changed course. Instead, it's closing the distance to the Agincourt at an alarming rate. It doesn't appear to be slowing down.

I duck at the movement of impact as the *Ark* crashes through the *Agincourt's* balloon and hull.

Columns of flame explode outwards, sending propellers spinning off in all directions. The *Agincourt* crumples in on itself, its back broken.

Cries rise from our ranks. Sounds of panic, sworn oaths, and sobs echo up and down the line. I put my hand on the shoulder of a

British marine who's doubled over next to me.

"We'll get them back for it! I fucking swear to you we'll get them back for it." I yell. "Stick with me, and I swear to god we'll kill them all!"

A hand presses on my shoulder. I turn to see my father's smiling eyes. "Damn good message son!" he says, leaning in.

Bile collects in my throat. I release the grieving soldier, shaking myself free of my father's grasp. I need to make sure my words are my own.

The *Ark's* dark hull punches through the flames of the *Agincourt* unscathed.

We were never supposed to win this.

I push the desperation from my thoughts. It won't help me now.

Wiping the sweat off my face, I make my way back down the line. "Prepare your weapons! They'll be on us any second now!"

A Japanese soldier raises her head above the bunch. "I thought the plan was for us to board them?"

I stop, looking her in the eyes. "Not anymore."

Cold finality strikes as I glance above the railing. The *Ark's* bay doors swing open, revealing a cavernous hangar. Our helmsman realizes what she needs to do. The *Artemis* lurches, changing its course into the gullet of the *Ark*.

I flinch as the *Namazu* fires a volley into the side of the warship. The smoke clears. The only sign of contact are a few gray scratches etched into the side of the plating. The *Ark's* armor is living up to its reputation.

Once we get in, we need to move fast. The remaining ships won't last long against the *Ark's* firepower. Its dark cannons swivel away from us, fixing themselves on *The Namazu*. They're their problem now.

All turrets, save one. Flame engulfs the cannon, sending a shell rocketing at our bow. A deafening sonic boom bursts over us as it narrowly misses the *Artemis*. Several soldiers lose their balance as the air ripples.

Maybe they haven't come to take Sabine after all.

The deck darkens as the *Artemis* plunges headfirst into the maw of the black fortress. The nipping winds of the tundra below us are replaced by the cool of the cavernous hangar bay. Dumbfounded, I take a moment to look up at the sheer size of the ceiling above. I almost forget to be afraid as I consider the sheer amount of work that went into making this monstrosity.

My wonder is cut short by the sound of the *Artemis's* stern engines colliding with the *Ark's* hangar doors. Metal and fire rain down from the back of the balloon as the *Artemis* loses its last three rows of propellers. The ship sags, the rest of the engines straining to pick up the slack.

As I look over at the soldiers lining the railing, I find Sabine's platinum blonde hair. She's in visible pain being this close to the *Ark* and its core, but her expression's more determined than ever.

A thousand rifles snap out to either side of the *Artemis* as our marines search for suitable targets. I glance down at my hand, shaking off the layers of paint that have collected in my palm. I've been wringing the banister again. The disparity between the railing's colors suggests I've spent at least the last few minutes twisting away at it. Old habits die hard, I guess.

We shudder to a halt, reaching the end of the bay. Emitting a dull thud, the bow of the *Artemis* scrapes to rest on the deck. As the echoes fade, silence sweeps over the cavern. Whispers bounce back and forth. Our engineers press their hands on the explosives, ready to move at the first glimpse of my signal.

I jolt as the hangar bay doors slam shut, silencing all of the radio traffic from the outside world.

We are alone.

Holding my breath, I peer over the railing at the darkness below. There could be anything down there. There could be nothing. Uncertainty churns my stomach as the whistle around my neck hangs like a ten pound weight. Of all of the responsibilities I have, this one is the most important.

In the pitch black, I glance at the forms to my left and right. The most prominent one searches for a canister in their back pocket. I reach back, immediately finding mine. I've envisioned this moment so many times, and now it's finally here. It's all I can do not to vomit in front of my team.

Pulling out the cylinder, I follow a succession of nods from the team leaders. In near unison, we unlatch our canisters, pitching them into the darkness.

To my horror, several of the soldiers in front launch over the deck onto the hangar below. The words, "No! Wait for the whistle!", stick somewhere in my throat. They're completely worthless, because it's already too late. I grab at the sleeve of the *Artemis* marine jumping beside me, but he too disappears into the blackness below.

I don't get to shout before the thunder of machine guns erupts from the opposite side of the hangar. The overhead lights flash on in full. There's nowhere to hide. Bullets pound the side of our hull. I throw my head and shoulders under the lip of our metal railing. I can do nothing but listen to the cries of men and women as they're picked off from below, one by one. The smoke canisters haven't ignited yet. There's no cover. There was no signal. Why would they jump?

"Because you whipped them into a zealous fury." My father answers. He's taken the place of the soldier who's now splayed on the deck below. His hands rest on the banister with his chin pressed against them. "Nice work son," he says, glancing over at me.

Swallowing back panic, I press the whistle to my lips. I rest my head against the banister, waiting for the telltale pop.

It comes.

They all do. Different colors of smoke stream out of the canisters, bathing the entire hangar in a sinister, opaque rainbow.

Olan reaches over another soldier, locking eyes with me. "It's time lad."

Nodding, I get a full grip on the banister inhaling a lungful of air. It all goes out in one blow. The shriek of my whistle's immediately followed by Baltier and the other officers.

"Over! Over! Over!"

"Let's go!"

"On me!"

The ringing in my ears drowns out the gun fire as I hurl myself over the banister onto the deck below. The fall's farther than I thought. My stomach drops as weightlessness envelopes me. I hit the ground hard, rolling to try taking some of the momentum away from my legs.

The wind slams out of my lungs. I fight for breath as our marines pour over the side of the *Artemis*. One swoops down, pulling me up. Oxygen rattles back into me as I draw my sword, plunging into the gunfire. There's only one way to go.

Bullets whistle back and forth, cutting swirling paths through the thick smoke. Men and women on both sides of me fall to the deck, crying out as lead finds its home. Over the sound of the fire, another howl rises up on the other side of the smoke.

"Get ready!" I yell, turning back to my team.

My group raises up their weapons, tensing as we hurdle over the bay equipment scattered around the deck. Bounding over an ammunition rack, I hear the cry from the other side become fuller.

The first forms punch through the multicolored haze. My mind slows like some queasy nightmare. All sound shuts off. The only thing I can hear is my own breath. I suck it in, holding it. Picking the nearest Cascade soldier, I pull my saber to my shoulder, blade pointed downwards.

We lock eyes. She brings her sword up over her head to split mine open. I'm faster than that. I dive into her as she slashes downwards. My point sinks deep into her chest somewhere between the heart and sternum. It's not where I was aiming, but it works just as well. Using my extra weight, I drive her to the ground.

Her sword crashes past my shoulder.

My back tenses at my horrible positioning, preparing for the blades to plunge in. She coughs a palette of red before going limp. I have no time to regain my balance before two combatants crash into one another next to me. Pulling on the saber, I fight to retrieve it from her body. A familiar problem at the worst time. Panic rises as I twist my sword, trying to free it from the wound.

The two men locked in combat lose their balance, toppling over me as I struggle with the hilt. An elbow from one of them catches me in the mouth, their frenetic movements pinning me to the dead woman. The pressure of their weight breaks the seal of the wound. I twist, using the opportunity to pull my sword out.

The Artemis marine launches off me, only to be knocked down on top of us. Sparing no time, the Cascade soldier drives with his cutlass. My only instinct is to throw my trapped torso away from the point. It only moves a few inches, but that's all it takes.

Metal meets metal. The sword punches through the back of the stunned marine, vibrating off the cool deck. The man pinning me lets out a final breath before slackening. His full weight bears down now.

Seeing his blow wasn't enough to kill both of us, the Cascade soldier pulls his sword out, moving to drive it down again to finish the job. I try raising my saber to counter the blow, but it's not enough. My stomach tightens, bracing for the puncture.

A crack rings out.

My attacker's face explodes. The high powered round doesn't even slow as it hits. The sword clatters from his hands. Headless, he slumps to the side of our pile of bodies. The sound of swords scraping against one another rise back up around me. In turn, the cries of the wounded try matching it. I draw in a breath, resting my sweat-drenched head against the deck. Despite the surrounding chaos, I can't help but collect myself as I roll the fallen Artemis soldier off me.

From the corner of my eye, a scope glints in the distance. I know its location well. Stenia sits in her perch, as she always does, watching over us. Still my guardian angel. I can't rely on her though; she may be good, but she's not God. That being said, her power to smite the unrighteous is probably on par.

All sound rushes back in. Unengaged soldiers press forward with me, running though the melee. The colors meld, mixing together the uniforms with the dark malaise of hanging smoke. A blue clad assailant darts out from the fighting, tackling the young solder beside me. He cries out as the haggard woman jumps on top of him, pinning him to the ground. Turning, I realize I've heard that voice before. It's Cliff!

Confusion etches across his face, as he looks up at his would be killer.

"Patricia?" he breathes out.

Patricia doesn't seem to hear him. She picks up her weapon, slashing downward with it. One of his hands catches her arm, the other gripping the sword along its blade. It bites into the flesh. Blood runs down between his hand and the edge, dripping onto the deck.

"Patricia, stop!" he cries out again, fighting to readjust his position. "Patricia, it's me! Cliff!"

Patricia shows no signs of slowing down. Using Cliff's wounded hand to her advantage, she drives the point further toward his chest.

The desperation in his voice makes my hands move before my mind catches up. I cover the distance between us in a breath, cutting upwards along her straining neck in one swift motion. The pressure lets loose, spraying blood over the deck. Patricia's head tips to the side as the rest of her body slides off of Cliff's stomach. The Corporal stares blankly at where Patricia was, her blood trickling down the side of his face.

I crouch down as bullets whiz by, trying to shake him back to his senses. I should apologize for killing his friend, but my mind's in no place to do that right now.

Grasping both sides of his lapels, I pull him to his feet. "Cliff, we need to go!"

I press his sword back into his shaking hand, dragging him along behind me to the gates defenses. He begins running under his own power.

"I trained with her in the Royal Air Force. . . " he says, exhaustion seeping into every word.

My eyes dart from soldier to soldier, identifying potential threats. "Same crew?" I ask mechanically.

He draws up behind me. "No, I was assigned to the *Zulu* before I did my time, eventually booking passage on the *Artemis*. She was assigned to *The Churchill*."

A shiver makes its way down my spine, the name ringing in my consciousness. The response is a memory. The echo of the *Ark's* hangar doors slamming shut, silencing the pleas of the *Churchill's* comms officer. A lot of speculation has gone into what happened to the *Churchill* and its crew. Most preferred not to talk about it. It was just an uncomfortable subject.

The smoke around us begins to clear. Although it leaves us in the open, its departure also reveals the rest of the hangar bay. Parts of a stripped zeppelin hull and its scattered innards dot the hold around us like the carcass of a beetle in a busy ant hill. My sweat cools.

It's all connected.

I look at the blue uniforms fighting and killing in the open, comparing them to the more elaborate grey and blue camouflaged uniforms dug in behind the defenses of the hangar gate.

We're fighting the crew of the *Churchill*.

22

Horror pulls its black tendrils taut as we press closer to the defenses. We haven't even touched the Cascade troops yet; we're just fighting our own.

Brainwashing? Defection? Bribery? These must have been part of the side experiments Sabine was talking about. I don't get to think very long about the 'how' before a hand grenade clicks over the barricade, coming to rest next to the arm of a fallen woman.

Acting before thinking, I kick the grenade away. It doesn't sail very far before it explodes, showering the deck with shrapnel. Bright light pierces my eyes before the shockwave throws me to the ground. Trying to regain my sight, I fight to blink away the white splotches covering my vision. They clear enough to reveal a ghostly form above me.

A sword whistles downwards.

A hand grips mine tightly to the pommel of my saber, thrusting it out. Out of the corner of my eye, my father lies beside, me gripping the hilt with both hands. The counter-maneuver forces the Churchill crew member back with twice my normal strength.

I flick my revolver out of its holster, firing once. The man's head snaps back. His arms flail, falling out of sight.

I look back at my father. He eyes me incredulously, growling, "Now get your ass up!"

Strength returns to my legs as he grabs me by the scruff of the neck, throwing me upwards. Clambering to my feet, I wince at the errant bullet skipping past my knee. As I regain my balance, a hand grasps my shoulder, forcing me onwards.

The face above belongs to Cliff. "Looks like I get to be your escort again," he grins, "The smoke's starting to clear; we need to get to the barricade now!"

I let him drag me over my own legs as we dash through the battlefield, tailed by our remaining team. Details of the hangar sharpen as the manmade fog dissipates. Without it, there's no shield between us and the hail from above. The machine gunner at the forefront of the barricade knows this too. I hear a bandolier of rounds dragging into position.

I release myself from the Corporal's grip. "Cover! Now!" I shout to the remainders around us.

Pickings are slim. All that lies between us and the barricade are overturned munitions carts and fallen bodies. Unfortunately for Cliff and me, no carts have been deposited anywhere near us.

The front of the gate thunders, sending sparks ricocheting around us. The rain of death is as dazzling as it is disorienting. Sliding to the ground, we immediately cover ourselves with the nearest bodies we can find.

The gore's sickening, but not nearly as terrible as the screams of those caught in the crossfire above. It's so loud, I can't put a string of thoughts together. Not knowing what else to do, I just shut my eyes, huddling close to the body on top of me.

I have no idea who it is or who they fought for. I only know that they provide some sort of camouflage. I flinch as a wetness hits the side of my mouth. Looking up, I see a string of bloody spittle leaking from the lips of the dead man above me. Retching, I spit out across the cold floor, burrowing my head closer to the paneling. Flashes of light intensify around me. The gunner's closing in.

Curling up, I hear a second gun join the fray, then a third, but they aren't coming from the direction of the barricade. Peeking out from under my corpse cover, I see two of our Helios launching from the *Artemis*. There's just barely enough room for them to hover, but it's all they need. The gunships strafe over the battlefield, weaving from side to side to avoid incoming fire. In doing so, their rotors blow the last of the smoke away.

Pushing the dead man's head to the side releases more posthumous drooling. It's a small fee to allow a clear view of the top of the barricade.

Cascade soldiers run from end to end, pointing to the gunships above. The machine gunner pirouettes out of sight as the

Helios's fire tears through the rampart. A camouflaged arm drapes itself over the side of the wall, its owner missing a lung.

This is our chance.

Throwing the body off me, I rise out of hiding. "Breach it!" I yell.

I'm relieved when a large enough group rises from behind the carnage to follow me. With the Helios's distraction and the smoke gone, this is our only chance to break through the barricade.

We've barely collected ourselves before a sharp whoosh of air erupts from the parapet above. A trail of smoke follows the red jet of a rocket streaking up from the wall. It arcs over the battlefield before burying itself behind the head of a Helios's door gunner. The explosion lights up the hangar, blasting apart the tail and the right rotor of the Helios.

The flaming gunship careens in our direction.

"Watch out! Get out of its path!" I yell, switching course and motioning others to the side.

The spinning Helios hits the deck, igniting the streak of fuel leaking from its side. Dark, choking smoke billows from the aircraft. Our group shifts direction, running towards the flames. Heat scrapes against my skin as I close in on the wreck.

I look back to tally who's made it this far. Blood seeps from the side of Baltier's head, but his long, determined gait is easy to pick out from the mass of soldiers pressing forward. Even further back, I spot Sabine's shock blonde hair rushing alongside a heavily armored Raltz.

Screeches pour out of the cabin of the downed Helios.

Another rocket sails high overhead. It misses the remaining gunship, exploding instead against the roof of the hangar. Debris rains down from above as a deck light shatters to the left of my foot. Wrapping my arm over my face, I get as close as I can to the hull of the burning gunship. I wave on the troops passing me, signaling them to continue their assault.

A charred arm bursts through the wreckage. I fight back bile as the woman's screams become clearer. My eyes dry as I pull closer to the flames. Another arm reaches out of the fire as I hear her rasping breath.

"I'm here!" I shout. "I'll get you out of there!"

She doesn't answer as I grab onto both of her arms and pull.

It's a mistake. It's all a mistake. As I tug, I feel the blistered skin give way from the rest of the bone as both of her arms scrunch forward. The scream that follows will haunt me for the rest of my life.

Horrified, I let go of her, falling backwards onto the deck. Bile rises up as my throat closes. My efforts were enough to free her head and shoulder from the wreckage, but it's too late. Thatches of hair sizzle, as her scalp blisters. She makes no more sound.

Tears evaporate as they well up against the heat. I make no effort to get away from the flames threatening to engulf me as the smell of burning skin permeates the wreckage. Shutting my eyes, I try wishing it all away.

It doesn't work.

As I open them, I see a dark form sitting in the middle of the flames. My father's haggard eyes peer out from underneath his flight cap. Forms run past us. Some fall, unmoving. Others are pulled away from the fight. Most charge on. Without me.

"This was your choice, you know," he says, lighting a cigarette against the sheer heat of the fire. The smell of Burley tobacco pushes away the stench of burning flesh. It's just as nauseating.

"I don't understand how you could have thought that this was gonna go any other way," he says, flipping his lit cigarette in between his pale fingers. The exhaustion in his voice rivals my own as he looks down at the dead crew member.

He points to the burning woman. "You owe her something better than that," He says, blowing a lung full of tobacco smoke into the rest of the haze pouring from the fire. He leans against the white hot frame of the Helios before fixing his eyes on something over my shoulder.

Following his gaze, I find Cliff running over to my side. He pulls on my numb shoulders, trying to get me to my feet. Dead weight, I barely move as I stare at him, confused. Soundless words pour from of his mouth.

It all comes rushing back.

"Lieutenant!" he yells over the gunfire. "We've got an opening. We have to go now!"

The sound of hundreds of people's efforts rise up into one indistinguishable cacophony. With his assistance, I get to my feet before running through the flames blocking out the other side. The wall of fire gives way to the barricade right in front of us. A quick scan reveals our marines have fought their way through the gate and begun rolling back the Cascade on both sides. If they can't keep them back for the time it takes us to locate the Core, both strike teams will die.

Another rocket launches from the side wings of the barricade. The warhead misfires. Changing course, it skitters past, exploding at the feet of several Persian marines. I don't look back. I can't at this point.

Racing up the steps, we find the rest of our teams mustering at the base of the gate. Our numbers have almost been halved. We knew this would happen.

Sabine's voice rises above the fighting. "We have to slip into the engineering pathways now! The enemy will be reinforced at any moment and we must be gone before they come!"

Running up to the group, I point to Raltz. "You're with me! We need to make it through those tunnels as fast as possible," I yell.

Raltz nods, gesturing back to Sabine. "Please stay back with Lieutenant Baltier my lady," he says, rechecking the magazine of his rifle. "If we encounter resistance, I don't want you anywhere near it."

Flexing her jaw, Sabine runs further back in the echelon as we enter the main bulkhead, leaving the rest of the battlefield behind. The sounds of the fighting outside and the echoes of the melee within meld into a disconcerting symphony. As we stick to the shadows, Cascade soldiers ferry back and forth in the hallways ahead. There's enough confusion that as long as no shots are fired, we'll blend in with the rest of the dark corridors.

Raltz crouches behind a wall panel. I gesture for the rest of the group to stay low as I move up behind him. He lays his head against the panel with his eyes closed.

"What are we waiting for?" I whisper.

He holds up a hand and shakes his head, his eyes still firmly shut. There we wait, 20 seconds, 30 seconds, 40 seconds. Just as my stress rises to a breaking point, Raltz's eyes snap open.

I clutch the stock of my gun.

The panel opens from inside and a Cascade technician steps out. Before either one of us realize what's happening, Raltz snaps the technician's head back and jams his knife deep up into the man's neck.

Shocked, I freeze as Raltz tries handing off the dying man to me. I drop him on the floor as he convulses erratically. Without a sound, Raltz throws himself into the hidden door before it shuts again. His face betrays no emotion as he holds the door open for the rest of us. *Bastille* and *Namazu* marines drag the bleeding man away as the rest of the group courses into the cramped tunnel.

The sounds of battle become muffled. With each outside impact, month-old dust jumps from the wiring and walls. I flinch with each explosion, imagining the thousand-pound shells colliding with the side of the *Ark*. I don't care how strong the magnetite plating of the *Ark* is, eventually one of those shells is going to find a weak spot and we'll be the first to know.

An austere lighting shines from the bulbs swinging overhead as the corridor begins expanding just enough to breathe. My claustrophobia is offset by the tramping boots above us. No one said that it would be easy sneaking through the tunnels – just that it would be easier than forcing our way through everyone else.

Other passageways fly by us as we run. Raltz says nothing, his eyes flitting from entry way to entry way as his memory pieces back together a puzzle once assembled long ago. Over the course of the maze, we encounter a few unfortunate technicians and one marine guard. They're all taken before they can make a sound.

Raltz harbors no love for his former countrymen.

Other than them, there is no one else in these tunnels. They've all been committed to fighting in the hangar or manning the various guns on the *Ark's* exterior. Raltz mumbles to himself as he moves from tunnel to tunnel, using any trick he can to guide us in the right direction. His tricks appear to run out as we approach a four-way intersection. At this point, we have to be close.

Raltz's jaw tightens. He slams his fist into the wall. "We're so close! We're almost there. Why can't I remember it?" he growls. Heaving, he pulls himself upright as the two strike teams pile up behind us. "Saber, I need you to check the western tunnel. I'll take the north."

He points to another soldier under Strike One. "And you Vitala, you take the east. We don't have time to check each one separately. We need to go until we find the blue light." Raltz fans his hand out against the wall. "You'll see it pouring out from the end of the tunnel. If you find it, do nothing except return back to the divide."

My skin crawls at the mention of the blue light, enveloping everything it destroys. Unstoppable.

Corporal Vitala nods her head before gesturing for three other marines to follow her as she disappears down the eastern tunnel. Another two check their gear and step up to me, but I turn them away.

"No. Thank you, but I'll move faster alone," I say.

It's not true. I just don't want another person dying under my command doing a job that I could have done myself.

I disappear into the darkness before they have a chance to protest. The impacts from above become more frequent, the hits getting heavier. Dust shakes from the rafters as vibrations rattle throughout the tunnel. Either we're winning the battle outside, or the force of the *Ark's* cannons is slowly tearing the ship apart from the inside.

It's the first time I've been alone all day. Breathing heavily to myself, I realize I'm not frightened. The silence and darkness give me a chance to focus, to clear everything out. There aren't any blank staring faces here. No unmoving lips, no trails of blood. Yet.

I push forward, rounding a corner. What I see stops me in the soles of my boots. A man stands there with his head bowed over a cigarette. Light blossoms around his face and the surrounding walls as he lights it, releasing a few puffs. Even in the darkness I can make out the uniform.

He turns his head to the side. My father's profile cuts into the dim light as he fixes his eyes on me. Decayed teeth splay out across his grin as he sees who I am. He says nothing. The cherry lights up his faces as he moves his hand backwards. There's something in his eyes that I've never seen before.

Murder.

Time jumps as I realize what's happening. The gun comes out, its barrel angling towards at me as I watch it. There's no sound but the blood pounding in my ears.

A shot reverberates down the tunnel.

I stand there shaking. My revolver rattles in my right hand, a trail of smoke curling out from the barrel. The world rushes back. My sweat binds my uniform to my shoulders as my eyes blink, trying to take everything in. My father lies there, curled over, his gun fallen behind him somewhere. The shot echoes up and down the corridor, snapping me into action.

"No . . . No . . . " I murmur, rushing over to him. The metal teeth of the walkway bite into my knees as I kneel against them. Placing a hand on the shoulder of his body, I hesitate to turn him over.

"I . . . I didn't mean to," I choke out. My throat closes up as I press a hand against his shoulder, "Dad . . . I didn't mean to."

My vision blurs. I can't hold back the tears any longer. I've got nothing left. It's all gone. My muscles work one by one, independent of one another, and independent of my will. They contract enough to counter my father's weight. I turn him over slowly.

The first thing my eyes find is the Cascade emblem on the side of his chest. I stop, unsure of what I'm seeing. The texture and color of his uniform has completely changed. Holding my breath, I look up to his face. I find a bearded man staring up into nothingness; one of his eyes at least. The other is mashed into the back of his skull with the rest of his eyebrow and top part of his cheekbone where the round hit. A cigarette burns out halfway between the grate and the man's hand. My mouth hangs open as I try processing it all.

What's happening?

The tramping of boots grounds me enough to turn around.

"Lieutenant! You hit?"

The two volunteers catch up with me. The other surveys the scene. "We heard a shot. The rest of the Strike One and Strike Two are headed this way."

Against the impacts from above, I hear another pounding; footfalls of men and women coming our way. Sabine and Baltier round the corner with the rest of the two teams as I turn over.

"We called back Vitala and Raltz, but I'm not sure how far they've made it down their respective tunnels," Sabine says breathlessly.

She's trying to stay strong, but I can tell that being this close to the Core is taking a serious toll. The blood soaked bandages visible around her arm have only darkened in color since we've made it to the tunnels. The closer we get, the more the Core's magnetism threatens to pull her apart.

A gruff voice erupts from the back of the echelon. "I'm right here!"

The teams make way for Raltz as he pushes to the front. His eyes widen as he reaches me and the body.

"I think it was a perimeter guard," I offer, desperate to hide my confusion.

Raltz waves this off, his eyes projecting a laser focus. "Look up ahead," he says.

Following his hand, I see the faint outlines of the aqua light we've been seeking. My skin crawls at the thought of staring up into the throat of the *Ark*. Now we're here.

Pressing against the floor, I try picking myself back up. My muscles strain but don't complete the push. My body's frozen next to the small pile of debris next to my hand. Pausing, I look up into the darkness.

A support beam plummets through the black.

The world spins as I tuck and roll to the side. The beam buries itself upright in the floor as I hear one last shell hit the side of the *Ark*. The last straw breaks.

Men and women scatter as shrapnel and chunks of metal rain from the hole above. Whatever's been protecting us from our own ships can no longer repel the barrage. Raltz reaches in, pulling me out from underneath the downpour. He drags me to safety, ignoring the deafening sound of the collapse. Smoke clogs the entire tunnel. If the internal garrison didn't know we were here before, I'm willing to bet they do now.

Coughing, Raltz sets me down. "Sabine!" he shouts.

I'm not used to hearing panic in his voice. He doesn't look back before sprinting to the pile of twisted metal choking the tunnel. He begins prying away the debris with his gloved hands, shouting her name. Raltz is a strong man, but I already know there won't be anything he can do to remove the rest of the support beams blocking our path back. Sabine, Baltier, and most of the forward strike team have disappeared underneath the cave in.

I prop myself up on my elbow, dumbfounded. "Cliff!"

There's coughing to my left. "I'm right here, Lieutenant!"

The slightest bit of reassurance seeps back into my chest. Covering my mouth with the fibers of my sleeve, I try to protect my lungs from the raw, dust filled air. "How many of us are left?" I ask.

There's a silence as Cliff double checks his count. "Twelve

sir. Including you and me."

Twelve. We started with two full platoons, and now we've been whittled down to twelve.

I fight the urge to lay my head back down and close my eyes. "Do we still have the engineers?" I ask.

I hear a piece of scrap metal screeching across the ground as Cliff rights himself. "Brigadette!"

Silence.

Cliff fills his lungs again. "Giacomo!"

Nothing.

I get to my feet as my thoughts swarm like hornets, considering the remaining options. "I'm here!" a woman shouts out in front of us, "I've still got the explosives."

The hornets give way to one single plan. "Alright," I say with as much confidence as I can muster, "everyone on your feet!"

Forms around me rise as I make my way over to Raltz and his frenzied work.

The clank of objects falling to either side of him echoes up and down the tunnel. Shivering, I think of the pilot in Shipwreck burrowing into the soil until his fingernails tore off, trapped in his mind, trying to find his friends.

I move up behind Raltz as he muscles his way into the wall of debris. The shelling above renews, sending new pieces falling from overhead. The rumbling above warns me of much larger debris to come.

"Raltz!" I shout.

He continues burrowing.

"Raltz!" I yell with more force.

It has no effect.

Calmly, I place a hand on his shoulder. He tenses as I make contact, but stops trying to tear the wall apart. "Raltz," I lean in, "you know this is only wasting time." I try not to think of the severity of what's happened. I made a promise.

He says nothing as he stands up straight.

"There's only one way to go now," I say, trying to keep my voice steady, "and that's towards the light." I hear the shifting of metal behind me as the eyes of our survivors come to rest on us. "You and Sabine have brought us this far." There's no other way to say it. "We can't stop now, after everything it's cost us."

My throat swells, silently saying goodbye to Sabine. Even to Baltier. I can't give Raltz any more encouragement without betraying that I want to stay here too. Without a sound, Raltz turns his body away. Tears line his eyes, but he makes no movement to hide or wipe them away. His bloodshot, blurry pupils fix on me.

"Let's destroy this place," he growls. Pushing me aside, he picks up his gun.

The rest of us fall in line behind him as he marches forward. The blue light ahead thickens as we approach the curve of the tunnel. There's a pain in my chest as my heart fights the anxieties stacking against it.

We turn the corner.

What we see stops everyone where they stand. In front of us lies a giant capsule at the end of the tunnel. A large platform in front of the Core amplifies its unsettling vibrations as it pumps out the power needed to make this dark place fly.

I don't know why it happens, but it does. Before I can make them stop, my legs are carrying me to the Core as fast as I can go. I'm sprinting towards it so I can't run away. We're so close.

The footfalls of my team behind me do their best to keep up. Lights and doorways flash past as we burst onto the brightly lit platform. Wind rushes past, currents pushing air in from both the open bottom and top of the ship. They surge up around the sides of the giant suspended Core, keeping it cool. It's almost enough to distract me from the nagging question in the back of my mind.

The question that asks: "Why is this platform so well lit?"

The answer comes in the form of a grenade, thrown from somewhere behind the bright lights flanking us on either side of the platform. Sound clips away as it bounces to my feet. Silence reverberates as I turn on my heel to warn the others. As I pivot, more grenades rain down from above into what's left of our party. Noise forces its way up from my lungs, through my throat, almost making it past my lips before the grenade at my feet explodes.

23

I taste the blood before I hear the ringing in my ears. A fault line forces its way down the center of my head. I can't tell if it's a physical incision, or just the concussion. I try pulling in a breath; it doesn't work so well. I give my lungs just the bare minimum needed to keep me conscious. I open my eyes.

The beige metal plate panels to the side of my head don't have scorch marks on them, not ones from explosives anyway. Fighting the urge, I look down at the rest of my body. I still have legs. I still have everything, except the ability to hear and reason. The blue light given off by the Core pierces into my eyes, all but blinding me to shapes moving in front of it.

A form rises up from the shadows below. A man walks slowly and calmly towards me, flanked by heavily-armed Cascade soldiers. I recognize him, but I've never seen him before.

His lips move soundlessly as his face comes into focus. I realize I've seen the angles of his eyes and cheekbones before. His shock of trimmed platinum blond hair drives stakes through any other doubts.

It's Sabine's father Garon. He's come to devour his prey.

He draws closer. My hearing begins pushing back the ringing just enough to pick up the muffled sounds around me. Groans escape as the rest of my party comes to.

I've killed them all.

The chaos of noise diminishes just enough for me to hear Garon lament to one of his officers, "Personally, I would have much preferred a method where they could have retained all of their senses."

Garon walks up to our disoriented group, stopping short. His dark brown eyes glide over us. Their color gives an unsettling illusion that he has no pupils.

He raises his hands and starts clapping. "Haha, that was very good!" He points his finger into the air "Very valiant!" He pauses, pressing his face close to those scattered on the ground "Was it just as you imagined it?" he asks.

No one says a thing. I feel my team's eyes fall on me, searching for some direction. Scanning the ramparts on either side of us, I glimpse armed men and women in position behind the lights. If any of us were to make a move, it wouldn't even be a fight. Garon knows this as he strides through the group. The edge of the platform beckons. If we don't want to die by gunfire, there is another way.

The dark leather boots find their way to my side before stopping. Garon crouches down, his face no more than a foot away from mine. "Now you," he smiles, pointing at my chest, "I've been waiting a very long time to meet you."

My revolver lies no more than a few feet away from where we talk. I calculate the probability of grabbing it and hitting my target before we all get slaughtered. The odds aren't enough to take the risk. That, and I'm afraid of what happens when all this ends.

"Why?" I ask, raising my head.

Garon gets back to his feet and begins walking back towards the Core. "Because. You're an interesting one," he says, turning on his heel. The light of the Core nearly envelopes him from behind. "None of us would be here if it weren't for you," he smiles, raising both hands. "Yet, here we are."

He snarls, screaming, "I can't believe you thought you could counter an agent of God!"

I flinch. His outburst comes from nowhere. Testing my ability to move, I press my hand against the floor and prop myself up. "Do you really believe you were sent by God?" I ask.

Garon exhales slowly, letting his shoulders roll down. "No," he smiles, his composure once again intact. "In fact, I'm not all that religious." He puts his hand on the holster of his gun. "But it is truly amazing what motivates people," he says, shifting his weight. "Large groups are the easiest. Just find a common thread . . . and pull it."

I lean forward, gritting my teeth. "You're a fake."

Garon puts up a gloved hand, waving me off. "Ohhhh, shut up," he replies, looking at me incredulously. "I didn't do anything that you didn't do with your own men, Lieutenant Basmon." He spits my name out as he finishes his sentence. It sounds like a name he's read time and time again.

There was a traitor among us.

Garon's dark eyes bore into mine. "You talked of assaulting this ship as if it would provide some unity; as if it would make them heroes." He smiles. "From what I've witnessed, it's just made most of them corpses."

I want to tell him he's wrong, but the pit inside my stomach opens. It's all true.

"I want to thank you, by the way," he says. "It saves me the time of washing them all away myself."

The hypocrisy is enough for me find my voice. "Why are you doing this?" I ask, "Destroying cities? Trying to flood the world again? What for, if you don't believe you're a messenger?"

Garon scratches the bridge of his pale nose. "Because I wanted to see if I could," he says.

His nonchalant tone chills my blood.

"See . . . that's the thing about great men like you and me, Lieutenant Basmon." Garon points back and forth between us. "That last challenge we overcome is never enough." He smiles. "We're never 'satisfied' by our accomplishments. That's what makes us exceptional." He gestures to the surrounding group. "That's what makes people believe in us. Because we have ambition."

He raises his hands to the ceiling as the impact of another shell rocks the chamber. "I created all of this," he taps his temple, "from my mind. None of this existed before I insisted that it should exist." He throws his arms out to the walls. "Your intriguing alliance of nations never existed before you willed it to exist."

The flames of the *Agincourt* cut through my mind.

He laughs, putting his thumb across his mouth. "Though I must admit, watching our two brainchildren throttle each other to the death has been quite entertaining."

Garon cocks his head. "You don't even realize why you're here . . . do you?"

"What are you talking about?" I grate.

"Why did the Grand Old Admiral pledge his forces and

round up all of his old war buddies to help him?" Garon says. "Well, the ones who are still alive anyways."

"Because it was the right thing to do," I say.

"Ha! Ha-ha, the right thing. My goodness, they did a fantastic job choosing you," he laughs. Garon gestures to the core behind him. "Because they wanted to cover up their dirty little secret. They wanted to wipe it all away like it never happened."

One of our engineers shifts her weight. Garon snaps up his pistol in her direction.

I throw my hand in front of the barrel, pushing down towards her with the other. "Wait! Everybody wait," I caution.

Garon keeps the gun trained on her. "How do you think a nomadic seafaring nation gained enough capital to fund both an engine prototype and a refinery system?" he asks.

I shake my head, indulging him. "A deep-sea trawling industry."

"Wrong!" Garon answers. "That's how we sustain ourselves. The answer you're looking for is 'investors'."

It all clicks.

"To be fair, they thought they were investing in a new power source that could change the planet. O'Phelan, Ibrahim, Vitortov, Khan. They were all in it for the same thing. They weren't wrong, I suppose."

I cover my head, trying to catch my breath.

"It didn't last though," Garon says pursing his lips. "Eventually they figured it out. You don't get that rich without having an eye for detail. It didn't matter, in the end. I had spent the last 30 years keeping a fleet patched together with driftwood. Finishing what I had started with the money they couldn't retrieve was a simple task. Sure, they tried to get it back. Sent assassins, mercenaries, your average gun-for-hire; anyone they could to try shutting us down. They all failed. Killed several of my men and attacked my daughter, but they never got me. Although, I should thank one of my would-be saboteurs. One of the raid survivors returned to his employers and reported that I was dead."

Garon finally clicks the gun up. "God, the balls on that one. They eventually figured it out, but it gave me enough time to finish what you see around you now."

Reeling, I look up. "What do you mean 'they chose me?'" I

ask.

"Because you're a fucking Sea Scout," he says. "Eager to please and not too gifted in foresight. I already knew where the other three traitors were. You would think O'Phelan and Vitortov would have been tough targets, being the gun-runners they were, but they were just cowards in the end. That left your goddamn Admiral. The tough part about killing a zep captain is, he's always mobile."

Garon circles his finger. "So I figured, why chase him, when he could come to me?"

I lower my head, pressing my eyes shut. I've killed all of these people.

Garon turns his back, looking directly into the Core. "Here's the unfortunate thing for you Mr. Basmon – it's come time for me to declare 'Checkmate'. You know what the most beautiful part about this is? That you all have front-row seats to experience it with me. Welcome to the next phase of human evolution."

He snaps his head to the side. "Do it!"

My body jerks forward, all of the metal in my uniform pulling me towards the Core. My squad struggles against the pull as they slide across the floor. The air floods out of the chamber as the Core throws off a blinding light.

A sonic boom hits, threatening to tear my eardrums.

We blast back as the blue light explodes upward, surging violently from the base of the Core. Everything we've worked so hard for is gone. The pylon of energy focuses into the sky, punching a perfect swirling circle through the clouds. The last strands of Garon's hair fall back into place as he turns towards us once again.

"It has begun," he whispers. "We've made it this far . . . and there's no assurance that it will work. But by God, it is EXILHARATING!" His excitement echoes throughout the chamber.

"Now, down to business," Garon says. "Sabine! Where are you, my dear?"

Silence.

One of Garon's officers approaches him from the side. "She's not here sir. We've checked all of the captured."

Garon's eyes take on an even greater intensity. "What do you mean 'she's not here?'" His nostrils flare. "That's not part of the plan."

Shuddering, the debris falls in my mind, crushing our teams. Garon won't respond well when he hears what's happened to his daughter.

The female officer is quick to counter her leader's souring mood. "We were able to identify Commander Raltz, however."

Some of the fire disappears from Garon's eyes as a new task arises. "Bring him here," he growls.

Two guards grab the arms of the hulking mass at the edge of our circle, dragging Raltz in front of Garon. Raltz raises his head. A cut runs from the corner of his mouth all the way to his ear. He's been beaten severely, but his eyes don't betray any sign of defeat. I watch them judging the distance between him and Garon, then the distance between him and the edge of the platform. Neither length is very far.

I close my eyes, praying Raltz doesn't make a move that will get us all shot. We can work our way out of this; I know we can.

Garon watches with glee as Raltz devises a strategy. "Always the soldier, Raltz. Looks like I've trained you well," he says, running a finger along the top of his pistol. "Now tell me . . . where is my daughter?"

Raltz's face hardens. "She's gone Garon," he manages, bringing his eyes up to meet her father's. There's more pain in them than hatred. "A shell collapsed one of our tunnels, taking her with it," he says.

The din of the Core pumping its energy upwards is the only thing breaking the silence. Its light casts a full shadow on Garon's face. I can't read his expression from here. He makes no movement.

Garon exhales slowly, clucking his tongue. "I should have done this a long time ago."

Raltz barely lets out a shout before Garon pulls the trigger. The gun's retort drowns out most of Raltz's yell, snapping his head back. The guards let go of his arms, dropping him; even they seem surprised.

I hold my breath, digging my nails into the plating below. They're executing us. This is it. Eyeing the distance between Garon and the ledge, I try working out a scenario where we all don't die. All Garon has to do is give the signal, and it'll be open season on the rest of us.

The Chieftain sighs. "Tsk, I was expecting something far

more courageous from the great Commander Raltz. How disappointing . . .”

Shifting his weight, he kicks the expended shell casing off the ledge and towards the Core. It dips slightly before shooting into the Core’s center.

“I suppose it was my fault,” Garon continues. “I didn’t give him very much warning, did I? How was I supposed to get a good reaction from him if he didn’t even know to play his part?”

The cavern shakes as more shells hammer the *Ark’s* outer plating. Praying for some sort of deus ex machina, I glance at the celling, willing it to fall in. Just one more time; just enough to shuffle the deck and give us one last chance.

“What about you all?” Garon questions, looking to the rest of us. “I bet you’ve got some pretty expressive folks among you.” His footsteps echo as he walks to Cliff’s feet. “What about you sir, what’s your name?”

Cliff keeps his eyes forward. “Corporal Clifford James,” he responds.

From eight feet away, I can hear his breath quicken.

I coil my muscles. I’m not losing one of mine.

Garon leans in. “Well Clifford, I just wanted to let you know that I’m going to kill you today.”

Cliff’s head snaps up as he raises his hands. “Wait! Not like-”

‘This’ hits Cliff’s lips the same time as the bullet leaves the chamber of Garon’s gun. Tearing through Cliff’s outstretched hand, lead buries into his chest. The despair in the Corporal’s voice echoes around the chamber.

Garon stands with his eyes closed.

After everything, this is how my bodyguard dies; not by saving my life, but by being executed at the hands of a tyrant. Regret claws through my innards. It was so fast, I didn’t even react. The timeline for our escape jumps. We need to do this now.

Garon finally opens his eyes. “Now that . . .   That was just tasty. Mmmhhmmm. You don’t get to hear a cry like that very often.” He waves the gun at the rest of the surviving group. “You all should really count yourselves as lucky. Because that was rare.”

All of my bravado sinks to the bottom of stomach as Garon’s boots scrape their way towards me. Framed by the Core’s blue light, his face is as featureless as Death itself. There’s no reasoning with this zealot.

"Now you," he says, pointing the gun downwards. "It's your death that I'm looking forward to the most." His clenches his jaw. "You've made things INCREDIBLY difficult for me."

I say nothing.

He swallows, choking back a sob. "You've cost me my daughter," he motions over to Raltz's folded corpse, "one of my best commanders," he pauses, wiping a tear away "and the respect of my men."

He sniffs, looking around at his guards. "Although, crying really should be allowed for such great occasions," he laughs, his composure not quite intact.

His guards cautiously join him. Garon waves off the laughter with his free hand. "Mr. Basmon, I must say, despite the unpleasantries, it's been a true treat watching this experiment unfold with you." His hollow eyes take me in. "But unfortunately for you, I'll have your old geezer of an Admiral in hand soon, and every game must have its end . . . no matter how much fun it might be.", he says solemnly.

Garon's face becomes grim as he lowers the barrel level with my forehead. "This is checkmate, my friend."

I close my eyes.

Something happens when your body braces with every fiber it has. Your focus narrows to a fine point. Smells seep directly into your brain. Everything around you rings with perfect clarity. Instead of a shot, a voice shatters it all.

"No! Wait."

The knot in my throat releases. Stars circle as oxygen flows back into my lungs. Concentrating on the doorway, I try identifying the familiar voice.

Sabine makes her way through what's left of our huddled group. Garon's face freezes in shock, taking in his daughter for the first time in months.

My head falls to my chest. So this is how it all came to be.

Garon's hand moves to his mouth as she closes the distance. "You're alive?" he asks, his eyes flicking to her bloodied side.

"Why did you downplay your wounds?" he says, reaching out to touch her bandaged arm. "It was supposed to be merely cosmetic damage."

Sabine's cool eyes flash right past me, surveying the scene. They rest on Raltz's corpse for just a moment, but I may have imagined it. She then turns them on her father. Standing side by side, it's so easy to see their resemblance.

"Even the best laid plans go awry," Sabine answers, glancing at the shaking ceiling overhead, "You should know that by now Father."

It starts somewhere in the middle of my chest; it's just a spark, but it's enough to ignite the rest of what's inside.

Baltier - Samuels - Cliff. All dead because of this woman.

Raltz. Betrayed. All of his loyalty meant nothing in the end.

Aoife. She should never have been a part of this.

I slam my fist against the cold floor panel. The sound reverberates throughout the chamber as invincibility seeps back into my veins.

Garon and Sabine turn their heads as I place both feet under my knees, standing for the first time. I hear the sound of every gun in the chamber snap up. Feel their iron sights on me. I don't care anymore.

Garon eyes me quizzically. "And what, may I ask, do you believe you're doing Mr. Basmon?"

"She was just a girl!" I yell. "Just a girl waiting for her father to get home."

They both stare blankly at me, confused.

My head spins. My sister's face swaps with Aoife, back and forth.

"That's all she wanted," I growl. "That, and making sure you had a smile on your face every time she saw you."

The smell of smoke and burnt flesh choke me. The scars burn across my hands.

"You wouldn't know who she was." I bring myself to look directly both of them. A wisp of a burnt red dress floats by behind their heads. "But you . . . ", I say to Sabine. "You came to her funeral like you had no idea you were part of it. Like you didn't fucking kill her!"

Sabine's eyes hold their ice, unwavering.

"That little girl did more for the world in six years than you'll ever do in a lifetime," I spit out, trying to keep myself from shaking. The sickness pushes its way in.

Garon furrows his brow, raising his pistol at my head once

more. "Huh. Let's prove that hypothesis, shall we?"

I tense every muscle in my body, getting ready to lunge.

Sabine uses her free hand to pull her father's arm down towards her. "No, Father," she says.

She's fighting against the pull of the Core. Being so close could probably kill her at this distance. Blood has soaked through her bandages entirely. Her body strains against the metal inside that wants nothing more than to release itself back to the blue obelisk.

Sabine sweeps back, taking the pistol from her father's hand. "Let me," she says, bringing the gun level with my eyes.

I faced fire and hell to fight for this woman; to fight for all of us.

Raising my chin, I meet her cool stare. "So this is how you want it to end?" I ask.

Her father looks over at her proudly as she places her bandaged hand on his back. "Of course it is Mr. Basmon," he says, his smile widening. "She's a smart girl. She always knows how to put the finishing touch on our projects."

Silence pounds, her eyes locking with mine.

"So true father. As always, I'm doing this because . . . " she whispers.

The ice melts from her eyes. "I love you."

A click echoes.

It's not the hammer of a gun, but the release of a pin. Garon eyes sweep down, turning to the origin of the sound. I barely glimpse the grenade behind Garon's back before Sabine tackles him off of the platform. Her platinum hair whirls outward. She twists behind her father's back, firing her pistol as she clutches the grenade to his chest.

The guards to our left dive, her bullets finding their marks; the other half is too shocked to react. Her father's protests go unnoticed as Sabine hugs him close. Their upward arc completes.

The grenade and their bodies explode against the wall of the Core. They disappear into blinding light, replaced by a puncture in the Core. A blue beam bursts outwards in the perfect shape of the hole. Two guards above disintegrate in the beam's path as it cuts another guard in half.

Taking advantage of the confusion, I lunge for my revolver. The soldiers on the opposite platform spin, pirouetting to an orchestra of bullets. Before I understand what's making them fall, I fire two shots into the man and woman who helped execute Raltz. It's the least I can do. Crumpling forward, the man doesn't even put his hands out to break his fall as his head smashes into the floor. The woman slumps, clutching her stomach. Pain etches across her face as she searches for the source The muzzle kicks as I fire one more round into her, just to be sure.

The sound rushes back. Most of the gunfire echoes from the doorway. Marines post behind either side, strafing the platform. Some of our group lay motionless on the floor, claimed by the chaos engulfing the chamber. Others scrape for their weapons, rushing towards the corridor.

The blue beam of the Core chews through the paneling of the ramparts above. The giant pillar of light flickers. The Core pulsates as it turns, rupturing from the inside. Scrambling, I push off the floor as the tiling below gives way.

Lunging up, my feet power under me once more. We've just set in motion the destruction of the heart of the *Ark*. Without its power, this whole place comes down. Ricochets flit off the floor around me as the survivors trade fire. Holding my breath, I make it the last few steps through the doorway, into the corridor. About ten or so of our crew wait for me there, including a familiar face.

Baltier presses himself against the arc of the doorway, directing fire. I barely make out his words as he gestures for me to take the surviving crew back out to the *Artemis*.

Scrunching my shoulders down, I wave the group back into the tunnels. Without the Core's consistent support, the magnetite strains against its own weight. The walls shift, sparring with the remaining power.

We come to our first intersection. There's no way I could remember the route even if our lives didn't depend on it. There's little hope now.

I stop, my eyes darting from opening to opening. "Uh . . . "

Footsteps thunder behind me. Baltier's a blur, blasting past us into the tunnel on the right.

"This way!" he shouts.

I struggle to catch up with him.

He looks back. "Sabine told me another route we could make it back," he yells.

I skid to a halt. "We're not listening to her!"

Baliter grimaces, but doesn't stop running. "For fuck's sake Baz, follow me! How do you think we got to you in the first place?"

Perplexed, I move again, trailing behind the rest of the survivors who've passed me.

None of this makes sense. Sabine set us up, then killed her own father? What changed?

"Why'd she let Raltz die?" I yell ahead.

"She didn't!" Baltier echos back. "We got there right as Garon shot Corporal James."

Cliff's young, unblinking eyes stare up at me in the darkness.

"It took everything she had to pull it together and put on the show," Baltier says, fighting to catch his breath. "I don't care what you think - she's a goddamn hero!"

"Why don't we wait to call her that after we get out of here first!" I shout back up the echelon.

Baltier doesn't get a chance to respond before a cry goes up. Metal splinters as our section of the hallway caves in. Sticking close the opposite wall, we keep our heads down, squeezing through the opening.

24

Twisting and winding through the labyrinth, we find our way back to the surface. A chill prickles my skin. We've made it to the upper hallways. They're entirely empty.

"I don't like this," I whisper. "Where is everybody?"

An eruption ripples down the stairwell.

"I think we have our answer," Baltier muses.

Pressing myself up to the gate above, my lungs tighten as I catch sight of the *Artemis*. The balloon's checkered with blown compartments. It'll never fly, not in the shape it's in. This doesn't stop Baltier though.

Standing in the middle of the gate, he unclips his flare gun before leveling it at the the *Ark's* ribcage ceiling. A green flame explodes. It arches across the hangar, illuminating the maelstrom below. The middle of the deck is chaos. Flashes of muzzle fire, coupled with the glint of sabers, indicate the *Artemis* is overrun. We can't hold them.

Baltier clips his flare gun back onto his belt and takes his rifle off his shoulder. He looks back over at me, clearing its chamber.

I let myself breathe out. "No one said this would be easy, right?"

"Not a one," he says, nodding curtly.

Pressing new bullets into my revolver, I look back to the fifteen or so survivors still with us. "You ready to make history?" I ask.

One young woman looks back at me. "Already have Lieutenant," she says, tapping the point of her sword on the floor.

I manage a smile. "Well, let's go do it again."

We creep over the ramparts. Although most of the Cascade are rushing the ship, we don't need to draw any more attention to ourselves than we already have. The flare seems to have caused more confusion rather than giving away our position.

The sound of straining hydraulics escapes from the top of the *Artemis*. The giant engines begin turning over to face the front of the ship. If we don't sprint, the *Artemis* will leave without us.

I'm not being left behind again.

Most of the attackers are too engrossed in the fighting to notice us slip past them. Darting from cover to cover, we make it to the *Artemis's* hull. A rope ladder hangs over the side of the exterior as it shudders to life. Baltier and I take either the side of the ladder, directing our survivors up while scanning for encroaching Cascade marines.

A shot rings out.

One of our escaping soldiers drops off the ladder. She hits the deck, struggling for breath. Everyone dives, finding fallen pieces of wreckage. Our black uniforms on the *Artemis's* grey hull paint easy targets. We need another distraction.

A rocket launches less than thirty feet away.

"Cover!" Baltier shouts.

The impact rocks the hull, tearing a truck-sized hole into the plating. I clap my hands over my ears, but ringing is the only thing I hear. The smoke clears, revealing half a bedroom set spilling out over the side of the open wound. I calculate the distance we need to jump to make it up there. Every scenario tells me it's still too high.

From behind my overturned cart, I spot the rocket team pinning us down. One of the Cascade soldiers picks up another warhead, moving to load it into the launcher. Before he can, a high-powered round finds his right eye. The warhead drops from his hands, landing on its trigger pin. The barricade harboring the rocket team ignites, throwing smoke and debris high into the air.

"This is our chance!" I yell to the rest.

I follow the path of the mystery bullet to Stenia's crow's nest. Always the protector. She's probably low on ammunition by now. We'll have to make every shot count. With her intervention, half of the team is able to scamper up the ladder before more Cascade soldiers take an interest in us.

The flank presses in on the remaining survivors. The number

dwindles due to rescue or death. Baltier, two servicemen, and I are the only ones still left. With Stenia's help, we're able to evacuate the remaining two marines and get Baltier halfway up the ladder.

I start my ascent, bracing for the bullets destined to tear through the back of my ribs. Instead, a whoosh of air rises up behind me. The red of a rocket flits past the corner of my eye, arcing upwards. I shout out, but I know it won't do anything.

The rocket collides with Stenia's crow's nest, blowing it in half.

"No!" I cry through gritted teeth.

I've lost too many. There are too many dead from all of this.

I struggle to pull myself up and over the edge of the *Artemis's* deck as the burning remains of Stenia's perch crash onto the hangar bay. An arm grabs onto my back, hauling me the rest of the way as the firing renews above me. Swinging my legs up onto the deck, I come face to face with Captain Dixon.

"You need to get the fuck up," she growls, "you're not the only one who's lost somebody today."

Her salutation's a quick-acting serum. Banishing the thought of surrender, I force myself to my feet. I barely get my balance before the *Ark's* hangar bay ignites, sending shockwaves rippling across the ship. The explosion sends the bay doors swinging off their hinges, disappearing into the abyss below.

The engineers are out of time; they're blowing the doors now.

A pale light fills the hangar for what seems like the first time. Closing my eyes, I try adjusting to the sudden change. The cacophony of a hundred harried voices fills the comm in my ear. With the path cleared, the *Artemis* begins moving beneath me. We're escaping this place.

Intense heat rises from the stern. Opening my eyes again, I see fingers of flame curling up from the tail of the *Artemis*. We were too close to the hangar doors when they blew. If we can't divide our forces to combat the flames and fight off the Cascade boarding parties, the ship will be engulfed before we make it out of the blast radius.

"Fire on the aft!"

"Where's the CO2?"

"Our fire suppression system is shot! We got nothing."

"Where are the engineers??"

"Flush auxiliary systems. I don't care if you're filling buckets from the tap. Get to that fire now!"

I reach up, switching off my comm. There's too much going on.

Crew members rush to fight the flames as a marine leans over the railing, pointing into the melee below. "The engineers are cut off! They're not going to make it back!" he shouts.

Following his hand, I see the Cascade folding in on our ranks, blocking the passage of the fleeing grease-monkeys. Without our engineers, the *Artemis* has little chance of surviving, especially as damaged as she is.

Captain Dixon grips the banister, staring into the surge below. Looking back up, our eyes catch one another's.

"You're going to take care of her, right?" she asks, thumbing the pommel of her saber.

Dixon's words sink in. "Janna, there's got to be a better way," I say.

Her jaw tightens. "Not one we can work out in time. You and I both know that. You and I both know it takes a lot longer to train an engineer than a grunt," she says.

I flinch, crouching low as another shot buries itself in the siding. "Janna, you can't look at it like that," I plead.

She pushes another clip into her side arm before looking back up, "There's no other way to think about it. You take care of her, or I'll find you. You understand?"

I swallow, pressing myself against the railing. "Understood Captain." I say.

Before I can get in another word, Janna stands up among the crossfire. "Aries Vanguard! It's about time we proved our name again, wouldn't you say?" she asks.

"Sir, yes sir!" the black brigade surrounding us responds without pause.

Despite their agreement, the looks on some of the men and women's faces mirror another sentiment entirely.

Dixon grits her teeth, setting one foot on the railing. "That's not enough you sorry sons of bitches! I feel like I didn't get in enough killing in today," she says, glancing around wildly, "Let's get our bang for our buck, shall we?"

Cheers erupts into the creeping sunlight. Down below, faces

begin turning up at us, away from the trapped engineers.

Captain Dixon grabs the banister, turning to me with a face as hard as concrete.

"Find her," she whispers.

The impulse to grab her shoots through my arm, but it never makes it to my hand. Some destinies are meant to be fulfilled.

"Cry Havoc . . . 'Til the fucking last!" she roars, throwing herself over the railing into the fighting below.

"Cry Havoc!"

The rest of the black clad marines echo her cry, rushing after their mistress. Hitting the deck below, the group drives a wedge between the Cascade and our stranded servicemen.

I lose sight of Captain Dixon in the melee. Using the diversion to their advantage, the marines caught in the retreat burst through the gauntlet. As they scramble over the side of the deck, I see the separated engineer party. Many have abandoned their equipment, breaking into a run to catch the departing ship. Reaching down to grab one of the stricken soldiers, I notice movement.

The wreckage of Stenia's perch shifts, pieces of broken metal falling to the side. It can't be. I pull the woman up over the lip of the hull before rushing to the pile of debris. Grabbing onto the largest sheet of metal, I wrench it aside. The heat of it sears my fingers. Swearing, I pull them away.

I wave out my hand. Nothing they haven't felt before. Holding my fingers into my stomach, I angle my foot to get leverage. With the sole of my boot providing a little more protection from the heat, I kick away the large swath of sheet metal. A pair of violet eyes peeks out from below.

"Stenia!"

She curls inward, her body bent unnaturally.

"Stenia! Can you move?" I ask.

"I can't hear you Baz," she chokes.

"What?"

"I can't hear what you're saying," she says again.

I take another look, noticing the hair to the side of her face is singed. Burns run from her cheekbone, back behind her flight cap. Her right ear melts into the side of her head.

I recoil. "Stenia, turn this way." I point past her damaged ear. "I'm going to get you out of here!"

"Duck," she whispers.

"What?" I ask.

The glimpse of a shadow is the only answer I need. I hit the ground, her knife breezing just past my shoulder blade.

The Cascade soldier claws at the dagger in his forehead before crumpling onto the deck.

"Here I was thinking this was the first time I get to save you," I say.

"You still can," she responds, blood dripping from the side of her mouth.

I need help getting her to safety. That help's getting harder to find as the Cascade take advantage of the rank's collapse, rushing to board as well. Stenia shuts her eyes as a bullet sparks the fallen railing next to her head. Another whizzes past my nose.

Ducking, I turn at the source. One of Garon's men hastily loads a rifle before snapping it up to my chest.

Instead of a shot, I hear a roar. A sword glints as a large man explodes out of the bulkhead behind us, catching the Cascade soldier as it arcs downward.

The rifle splinters, slumping the soldier over the broken stock. The cry rises up again as Olan turns to face another blue soldier scrambling over the side. The man raises his sword to engage, but Olan rends him in half between the pelvis and stomach, sending the man's torso falling over the railing of the ship. Olan pushes forward, grabbing hold of the belt loop of his victim's legs. Twisting, he hurls them after their owner.

"You can feckin' keep those too, while you're at it!" he screams into the throng below. Without pause, he whirls at me. There's no recognition. His bloodshot eyes tell me words won't do a thing.

I draw my saber, bracing against his attack. It comes like a freight train. The claymore hits my blade at the apex, shattering it. Unhindered, the longsword slams into the deck. Out of options, I stomp on his blade and grab his lapels. Rearing back, our heads collide.

White and black obscure my vision, but I can see him shake his head.

"Olan!" I shout, slapping him in the face. "Olan, fucking listen to me!"

I ignore the blood trickling past my eye, focusing instead on the clarity returning to his.

"Olan, I need your help. Stenia's going to die unless you do something about it."

Olan grunts, shaking his head again. "Where . . . Where is she?" he manages.

Grabbing him by the shoulder, I guide him to her. She shifts to meet him, her left leg twisted at an impossible angle.

"Good timing," she coughs. "That was my last knife."

"Olan, I need you to carry her," I say "Be careful; she's got a least one broken rib, her left leg has a compound fracture, and she can't hear out of her right ear."

He nods, coming back to himself.

"I need you to find a way for both of you to get off of this ship!" I shout. "I saw the engines. If we take any more abuse, we're not going to last long!"

Olan kneels down, gingerly plucking Stenia from the wreckage.

"I'll hold them off for as long I can," I say, glancing at the encroaching flames.

"Khan hasn't given the AS, has he?" Olan asks, shaken.

"No, not yet," I say, "but it's only a matter of time. We're losing control. With these flames, I don't want either of you on here if the magazine goes."

"I'll see if we can prep a life boat, but I'm not leaving until the Admiral gives the call," Olan asserts.

"Fine! Just make sure you're ready," I relent.

"You're not coming?" He asks.

I recoil as another bullet slams into the ship's siding. "I'll be there soon!" I shout. "I need to find Cass first."

He nods once more before bundling Stenia away, past the fire and the fighting.

Artemis and Cascade men alike cling to the rigging below as the *Artemis* gains altitude. The hangar shudders. The source reveals itself as the middle of the deck explodes, a blue ray of light punching through. Shreds of super-heated metal fall to the deck, leftovers of the beam chewing through the ceiling above. The sides of the cavern buckle in, collapsing as the *Ark's* Core spirals out of control.

The hangar sweeps out of view, revealing the tundra 9,000

feet below. A crosswind tears up the rigging from beneath, shedding some of its human weight.

I catch my breath against the chill. That's right, we're out in the open again. Flipping my comm back on, I search through the signals.

"Cass!" I shout into the frequency. "Cass, where are you?"

Static responds.

I throw my weight into helping another engineer clear the banister. "Cass, answer me."

The winter sun begins taking on a dark red hue as I cycle the frequencies. She has to have made it through. "Cass!" I shout into the receiver.

"Sage!" a voice answers back.

A spark of hope threatens to ignite. "Cass, where are you?" I ask.

There's a fit of coughing. "In the Cellar! The Infirmary took a direct hit. We evacuated the surviving staff and patients to the hangar, but it's not any safer in here anymore." Shouting cuts through the frequency. "The smoke's getting thicker. I can already see some of the returning pilots are wounded." Cass's wracking cough disrupts her again. "I'm going to try to help them." She pauses. "Sage . . . it's only getting worse in here. I'm going to do my best to help, but if anything ha-"

"No!" I cut her off. "We've come way too far for that. I'm gonna find you!"

"I – " The frequency cuts off.

I try hailing her a few more times. I can't get through.

I sprint down the Outer Rim as smoke billows out of several of the portholes on the ship's side. In addition to the crew's drinking water, the *Artemis* has reserve water tanks for deck fires, but there's only so much we can do up here. The logistics of fire suppression is one of the many complications of living at this altitude.

I pay no attention to the different uniforms fighting in my path. Skirting the edges of the skirmishes, I don't draw attention to myself either. A cloudy haze greets me at the bulkhead of the Cellar. Staring down into the mess alone is enough to make my eyes water. Overriding logic, I force myself into the heat below. Clenching my fists, I fight to keep the scars along my hands from crawling at the thought of fire.

Some things are more pressing than your worst fears.

With the Cellar's high ceilings and open hangar, I can actually see through the smoke once I reach the bottom of the steps. Flames are gaining ground on both sides of deck, despite the crew's staunch efforts to combat them. Bounding over snaking hoses and deepening puddles, flashes of the Helios crash stab into my mind.

I shake them off.

Personnel of all nationalities shout to one another over the din, but they're blocked out by burning wood and choking smoke. I'm in my room again. My throat closes against the death around me. More smog scratches at it, forcing its way in. Panic flares. I close my eyes, trying to find a place that's anywhere other than here.

It comes in the form of a voice.

"Sage!"

I open my eyes. A silhouette plays starkly against the white background of the open hangar. Cass kneels over a sitting man, wrapping his abdomen in cloth. The unconscious pilot's propped up by the large parachute strapped to his back. The smoke seems a little thinner; the haze delivering less of a sting.

Rushing to her side, I can't help but focus on the unnerving "waterfall" forming next to us. The air pressure's pushing the smoke down and out, making it difficult to see the edge of the opening. Cringing, I kneel down next to her.

"Sage, I told you not to come. The *Artemis* is falling apart and there's nothing more you can do down here."

My skin crawls as a flame lashes out towards us. Sweat rolls down over my lips. "The *Artemis* has seen way worse than this," I lie. "If she's can make it through those scrapes; she can weather this for sure."

There's no way she believes me; she's too smart for that. That's why I chose her. She continues tying a tourniquet, unfazed.

"The Admiral will never give up the *Artemis*. She's his baby."

The chime of the PA system interrupts me.

There's a click before a record scratches onto the speakers.

A song from a happier time plays: "*I don't want to set the world on fire...*"

I share a worried look with Cass.

"*I just want to start,*"

The hanger plunges into a dark rose red as sirens rise up to compete with the blaring music.

"A flame in your heart."

Khan's initiating a full evacuation.

I reach out to grab Cass's arm, but a shell from the *Ark* makes its move before I can. We barely hear the whistle before it ignites a hole in the side of the Cellar, collapsing one of the loading cranes.

The Jackal attached to it plummets, sending two weeks' worth of welding and rivets to meet their match on the hangar's edge. Sparks bloom as the Jackal tears in half before pitching into the abyss.

Sparing no time, Cass hurriedly ties a double knot on the man's last dressing before kicking him over the edge of the hangar bay. As his feet disappear over the side, Cass pulls the top of the rip cord on his back. The canopy shoots outward, the man's head barely clearing the plating below.

"In my heart I have but one desire…"

I tackle Cass out of the path of the crane as it crashes down over the hangar bay, blocking our exit.

"And that one is you,"

I study her face as she curls against me. "Why?"

"We wouldn't have been able to carry him. You know that," she says, looking up beneath me.

The lyrics croon back in. *"No other will do."*

I say goodbye to every memory I've ever known and take her hand.

"I've lost all ambition for worldly acclaim…"

We cut through the smoke with the rest of the pilots as flames lunge in.

"I just want to be the one you love."

Off to the right, Ja'el fights the blaze with several other deckhands. I shout to him as we run past, catching his attention. Sweat pours down his dark face as it fills with recognition.

"Ja'el you need to get out of here before everyone cooks!" I yell.

Ja'el eyes the exit before turning back to me. "Not this time sir. You must take Miss Dawson and flee this ship. The fire is encroaching on the forward magazine. That cannot happen. We will save many more lives if I remain here with my section."

I search his eyes for any sign of indecision. There's none.

Ja'el grabs my arm. "You must go now Mr. Basmon. Every second I argue with you, the fire finds another foothold." He looks down to Cass. "Goodbye now Miss Dawson."

Cass's eyes widen. "Ja'el, no!"

I wrap my arms around her waist, picking her up.

"We're not leaving him!" she screams, kicking out against my hold.

I run with her just far enough to get space between us. I wouldn't have been able to hold onto her any further than that anyways. She tears away from my hold, but keeps our course out of the Cellar under her own power. Glancing back at Ja'el, I see him turn around and rejoin the fight.

The song bleeds back into my consciousness as we hit the stairwell. "*And with your admission, that you feel the same.. . . . "*

Cass rounds the stairs. The parachute still on her back from the infirmary evacuation bounces with each step. We need to find another.

Turning the last corner before the bulkhead, a speaker squawks the eerily mismatched song. "*I'll have reached the goal that I've been drea-"*

The music cuts out.

An impact ripples through the *Artemis*, lurching the stairwell sideways. The shockwave sends me into railing, nearly knocking me unconscious. My head pounds, trying to recollect itself. Cass lands on my chest, breaking her fall with my body.

Her hand grasps mine as she looks wide-eyed at the bow. "Sage, you need to get up. Sage, look." Her voice breaks as she points towards the front of the ship.

I try focusing on where her finger points. It doesn't take much concentration to see the spitting flames billowing from the *Artemis's* Bridge. The *Ark* looms behind it, shells still blasting from its cannons. From its middle, a blue beam pierces upwards, puncturing through the stratosphere and beyond.

The powers of self-preservation work every trick to get me to stand back up, but somehow I find the will to ignore every single one of them. This is the end of the dream. These are the decisions we make.

"Baz, get the fuck up!"

My morbid thoughts disperse like rats in a beam of light as Cass powers through, pulling me to my feet. Control floods back into me; we don't need to die like this.

Cass elbows her way through the crewmen running up and down the Outer Rim as flames shoot through the interior cabins.

"We need to find you a chute too, just in case things get worse," she yells back.

The nakedness of gravity weighs down on me as she mentions it. Her undaunted optimism shines through with the suggestion that we're not already headed planet-side.

A fireball falls from the Roost, plummeting toward us. Narrowly missing the Outer Rim, I make out the faint outline of a zeppelin hunter as it falls to earth. Separate from the plane, a flaming body follows close after it. Shuddering, I hear the unhindered engine of a second zeppelin hunter hurtling from the upper hanger. Dropping past us, I can see the cockpit's filled like a hastily packed suitcase. With the Cellar in flux below us, the Roost is the only place our life boats will still be functional.

"Cass!" I shout out ahead, "we need to get to the Roost! Olan and the rest are up there."

"Where'd you think we were going?" she shouts back, keeping her stride.

Despite everything we know coming down around us, she's still always one step ahead.

The world changes in pitch, rumbling in my chest. My ears strain against the low bass as the flickering blue pillar of light blasting from the top of the *Ark* catches my eye. Slowing down, I grab onto the railing, watching the beam struggle to fire upwards.

Once.

Twice.

Three times.

Then nothing.

Silence permeates the sky. I hear the whizzing of collective energy rising up from inside the beast. Blue tendrils pierce through the *Ark's* hull, listing the fortress to the side. Cass stops, turning in front of the Living Quarters' bulkhead to face the source of the building screech; it reaches an earsplitting pitch before ceasing entirely. *Artemis* crewmembers watch along the Outer Rim breathlessly. The blue beams punching from the *Ark's* hull disappear. I let myself breathe.

Then the sky tears itself in half.

25

An azure wave of energy erupts from the *Ark's* center, splitting it diagonally. The lower portion meteors into the ground below, throwing up snow and debris a mile high. The top half of the ship explodes outward into countless pieces. Unhindered, the circular shockwave lashes out into the rest of the world, carving a line into the earth straight towards us. I brace against the railing as the shockwave narrowly misses our burning bow.

But the sonic boom doesn't.

The sound-burst rocks the *Artemis*, sending the fire raging within the bulkheads blasting outwards. Time slows as the impact hits. The side of Cass's face illuminates as she turns to look back at me. A white hot blast surges up from the Living Quarters, knocking aside the solid metal bulkhead. The explosion throws Cass into the railing before forcing her up over it.

Stunned, I stare numbly at the empty space she used to be.

There's only one choice.

I barely feel the arch of my boot connect with the railing as I sail over the side into the void below. The cold air rushes up to greet me. Plummeting head first, blood pumps past my ears faster than I can think. Cass falls below me, outlined by the white world in front of us. Her arms and legs splay out.

Please just be unconscious.

A form blocks the sun to my right. Glancing over, I see a uniformed man hurtling upside down beside me. My father appears unfazed by his rapid descent; his eyes staying trained on me. I keep my focus on Cass as he falls at the same speed. I flinch as a burning engine crashes past.

He opens his mouth. "Sage. Whatever happens with all this," he gestures around to the falling debris, "I just want to let you know that I'm proud of you."

I fold my arms in, increasing speed. Ice crystals form on my cheeks as I rocket towards the woman I love.

He stays at my side. A smile creases his eyes. "I can't say you're the smartest," he lets out a raspy laugh, "but damn, you've got some guts."

Swallowing back the lump in my throat, I keep my eyes fixed on Cass. My father floats out of my peripheral vision as I close the distance above her. A spatter of blood flies up, hitting the bridge of my nose. The splatter spreads, nearly blinding me. Reaching out, I wrap my arms around her stomach as we crash together. Somersaulting, I strain against the centrifugal force. Her parachute moves to buck me off. Momentum tears at me, but I've already locked my grip around her straps.

She makes no movement.

The ground fills my view. I whisper into her ear, "I'm sorry . . . but we have to try."

Slipping the chute off her back, I slide it onto my shoulders. Clipping it closed, I stare hard at the ground rushing up to engulf us.

Holding her close, I whisper once more, "It was worth it."

The chute erupts from the pack as I pull the chord. My muscles knot as I squeeze Cass to my chest in our downward spiral. Warmth spreads over the tops of my arms as the chute catches the wind.

Cass wrenches from my grip as gravity tears her away from me. I pull her back, readjusting my hold. We're still going too fast. The chute was only meant for one person. Individual trees launch up from below. There's nothing else left to do. I throw my legs under her, closing my eyes one last time. I hold breath as the horizon disappears behind oblivion.

Impact.

I open my eyes.

Nothing but darkness stares back. My breaths come in, ragged and uneven. No breath I take gives me enough oxygen. Is my back broken? I slowly turn my neck to the side, testing it. My head moves, but nothing other than the blackness greets my sight. Moaning, I angle my head back down to my stomach.

I forget to breathe.

Figures rise in front of me. Faceless. Shrouded in white.

Panic surges as I draw in less and less air. The white figures crane their blotchy heads, creeping closer. I pull my legs up to my chest, unable to muster the strength for any other kind of escape.

A white outline, smaller than the rest, presses its way to the front of the figures. Approaching me, it reaches out. I hold my breath as the white appendage extends from the figure. It lands on my chest. On contact, there's a warmth, an almost electric vibration. It pulses through my body.

The pulse calms my panic. As more oxygen flows in, the figure in front of me sharpens. A wreath of hair defines from the rest of the apparition's face. Small shoulders connect to neck. Features of the form begin etching themselves on its face, starting from the nose.

"Pela?"

My sister's kind, green eyes do their best to puncture through the pale shroud around them. Her hand stays pressed to my chest. The touch is light, but power surges behind it. Another hand holds my sister's shoulder. Following the arm, I find my mother's face smiling down at me. She too, had green eyes. Darker though, and fuller, with more capacity to love than any of us had. And that's what I feel now. My heart begins beating in time with the pulse surging through the wedge of figures in front of me. It's a slower beat. The panic's gone. The worry's no longer relevant.

Another hand rests on my mother's shoulder. Further along the line, I find the creased face of my grandfather. I only ever saw him twice, but his signature fedora sits atop his head as he peers over his glasses. That much I remember. Behind him, another line of figures one person wider slowly shifts with oddly familiar features. I recognize them, but I've never met them before. Of that I'm sure.

The triangle of specters spreads back into a dizzying horizon. Looking into the distance, I start losing my calm. I quickly turn back to my sister's face. Focusing on it, I start settling myself once more. Her eyes never leave mine.

A flash forces me to blink. When I open my eyes again, a young woman stands in front of me. Her hair's long. Her freckles gone. Her eyes have become darker, like my mother's. She's beautiful.

Before I can say anything, the six year old Pela flashes back. She slowly shakes her head. Ripples arch outward with each turn of her face.

Are we underwater?

Pela points up. As her finger reaches its apex, light catches it from above. Following the finger, I find a hole filled with an encompassing glow.

I hold my breath.

So this is it then? This is what it means to die?

I flinch as the pungent odor of Burley tobacco hits my nostrils. When I glance back up into the light, a uniformed arm punches through, dispelling the golden halo around it. Clouds on a blue background float behind.

My father pushes his head out over the edge, staring down at me. "It's not quite time for that yet, son. Don't be in such a rush," he says, extending his arm as far as he can into the ether below. "C'mon now. We've got work to do."

I look back down into my sister's eyes, searching for some sort of permission. Meeting once more, her smiling face nods back at me.

I need to go.

Pulling against the ripples, I plant a kiss on two figures before turning my hand to the figures in front of me. Starting from my sister, then my mother, all the way down the line, each defined face draws a smile. Mirroring them, I reach up for my father's hand. He clasps it, pulling me up. Countless eyes follow my assent as I turn my own towards the circle sky. My father disappears behind the rim of the disc as my face breaks the plane.

The clouded sky fills my vision, becoming three dimensional.

In turn, my lungs fill with water.

Panic reignites. Coughing the fluid upwards out of my mouth, I desperately draw air into my lungs. Some of the ejected slop splashes up, sitting in the crevice of my eye. I draw in ragged breaths, making no move to wipe it away as I focus on my breathing.

"Good . . . morning."

I catch my breath, feeling the weight on my chest.

"I thought I was alone out here," the voice says.

I follow the myriad of lines protruding from my back up into the tree above.

It's a tree; a real tree. Our black and gold chute, still fully deployed, drapes over the top of its canopy. The colors of it cut a stark contrast to the white of the snow around us. A shiver forces its way through my body. I try craning my neck down. The outline of Cass's face peers up, spurring me to try pressing myself further upright. After an unsuccessful first attempt, I'm able to wedge my elbow under my body, using it as a base to hold the rest of my torso up.

What greets me makes me wish I had stayed on my back; my femur breaks the skin at a terrifying angle. I fight the waves of nausea crashing against my senses. A dark circle lassos around my vision. I push the edges back, but just barely. The bone prods through the skin not far from Cass's head. Around us sits a halo of blood in the shallow water below; it's impossible to tell whose.

I try my best to keep my hands from shaking. Cass's pale seafoam eyes study mine as they see what she can't. She can't know; I won't let her know. I close my mouth, focusing back on those gorgeous eyes. Taking my free hand, I press it along the side of her pale face, blocking the view of my shattered leg.

"Hey there, beautiful," I say, smiling at her. It's all I can do not to break down.

"I was so scared," she whispers, "I thought I was all alone."

I pull her head and shoulders close to me, holding her tight. "No. Never. I'm here," I say, rocking us back and forth. "I'm here."

She closes her ocean eyes, pushing tears out the sides of both, nodding.

We sit there for a while, rocking.

Staring out into the distance, I push back a curl of her dark hair. "How do you do it?" I ask.

Her eyes open again. "Do what?" she asks softly.

I press back another strand. "You just fell fourteen thousand feet and your hair would still make a model jealous," I say.

She closes her eyes again, leaking one more tear down her cheek. She shudders, managing what could have been a laugh in another life. I try smiling as I lean over her, massaging her temple.

Silence creeps back in.

"You know . . . ", she starts, "It's kind of beautiful . . if you don't let yourself think about it."

"What?" I say, looking down.

Her eyes open once more, staring far past me, up into the sky. Following her gaze, I find the fixation. Above us, the *Artemis* falls toward earth, fully engulfed in flame. The giant hull spouts vibrant reds, oranges, and pinks, trading places with one another.

Everything I know is crashing to the ground while everything I want leaks away through my arms.

"Do you think any of our friends made it out alive?" she wonders.

I stroke the side of her face. "We made it out, didn't we?"

I glance around us. Made it out to where?

She nods into my chest.

I pull her closer, the cold beginning to seep in. Even shock has its limits.

"Hey Sage?" she whispers.

"Yeah?" I say, fighting to bring a smile to my face.

Her beautiful eyes stare up at me, ignoring the armageddon above. "Thanks for keeping me warm."

Cradling her head close to mine, I measure out a breath to keep my voice steady, "Always."

There's no sound now but the water lapping lightly against our thighs. A light wind blows the strands of her brunette locks back over her face. The hair brushes a dilated iris. The rolling seafoam waves have ceased their cycle. Silence stares back, surrounding me. There is no audience to stay strong for anymore.

I pull her to my chest, letting everything else go. When you're sitting on the edge of the earth, no one else can see you cry. My wracking sobs echo off the snow drifts, releasing up into the endless horizon. No one will find us here. I raise my eyes to the sky. The darting planes above us have no interest in our fate, only self-preservation.

Self-preservation.

That's all that's really left at this point. With tears beginning to freeze to the side of my face, I try taking inventory of what I've been marooned with. A string of mucus stretches from my nose to the lapel of my jacket. I try wiping it away while I think. I have the chute from the *Artemis*, if I can untangle if from the branches above, but with my leg, that will be a near impossible task. I have the bag from the parachute. I have all of the clothes on my person. I have the body of the woman I love. I hold my breath . . . The woman I loved.

There's nothing here that would allow me to survive the night.

And then I feel it. Pressing against my thigh. Barely distinguishable from the numbness of the surrounding water. Reaching down, I unclip my revolver from my leg. I pop open the chamber.

One solidary bullet stares back up at me.

Pressed in and ready to fire.

I must have more. There's got to be more. I rifle through all of my pockets. There's not even lint.

Fumbling with my breast pocket, I find the Admiral's black token. It still betrays nothing about its nature. Gritting my teeth in frustration, I use every muscle fiber not to throw the black rectangle into the depths of the pool around us. Stuffing it back into my pocket, I feel a shell roll into place. Digging with my thumb and forefinger, I pull it from its hiding spot. A revolver round glints back at me, but it's waterlogged and too bent to fire.

I have one round.

My eyes rise back up to the sky.

One round is all I need.

I put the revolver back down. A cold wind blows against my face. The bloodied water hugs my knees, lapping around Cass's cheeks as it flees from the gust. Watching the tundra around me, I'm suddenly aware of the complete silence. I no longer hear the planes overhead. Crystals sparkle in the distance as the last of the sunlight hits the snow. Under other circumstances, this would have been a beautiful place, a calm place. One of my greatest fears, when I had the luxury of abstract phobias, was the fear of being alone, of being left behind. Devoid of people. I glance down at Cass.

Well . . . at least I don't have to die alone.

Closing my eyes, I inhale slowly. The fresh air comes in. Days of summer flash onto the back of my eyes, afternoons spent chasing friends. When I looked over the railing into the abyss below, I recall musing about how I was going to make my way. I remember seeing Fall for the first time. While we were docked at a port towards the top of the Appalachian Spine, an actual tree was shedding leaves of all different colors. I knew there were only so many, but as I watched, it seemed like an infinite number of them fell from it that morning. It wasn't so different from the tree we're sitting under right now. At least I'll be laid to rest next to a relic of the Old World. Maybe I'll get to see it.

I pick the revolver back up. It's much heavier than I remember. I let the weight of it roll the barrel sideways, finding the grip. The muzzle grazes my head as I wrap my finger around the trigger. Maybe you were right Olan; maybe I shouldn't have stopped you.

I clench my teeth, pulling the tension on the trigger.

A low growl nearly stops my heart for me.

My eyes snap open, finding a pair of yellow ones. A large marsh lion crouches twenty feet away from the end of Cass's boots. His beige and white coloring betrays him against the pool of water, but otherwise he blends perfectly with the tundra around us. His eyes aren't fixed on me though. His tongue glides back and forth over his bottom incisors, panting. The cat's face is sopping wet and the rest of his fur clings to his body. Despite the coiled muscles underneath his skin, it looks like he hasn't eaten in a while. His golden eyes bore into Cass's body as she lies against my rising chest.

He wants a meal.

"You're not getting her," I say.

The words reverberate off the landscape as I lower the revolver from my head. The lion closes its mouth, a string of spittle slipping out of side of its lip. It arches its head, sniffing the air.

"This one was supposed to be for me,", I spit out, clutching Cass close.

Using the last of my strength, I raise the revolver, drawing it level with the marsh lion's head. It crouches lower, pulling its lips back. Its teeth push forward as its muscles coil tightly.

Blinking back tears, I keep the gun trained on his head. He's really no different than me: broken, hungry, and transformed by terrible circumstance.

"One day, we'll all be as rare as you," I say, "but you're not getting her."

The marsh lion sways his hind legs side to side. His white tipped tail flicks at the air, preparing to spring. I look down the barrel into his golden eyes. We're out of time.

I pull the slack on the trigger.

Water explodes around the crouched animal.

I flinch, firing my shot wide. Panicked, the mountain lion runs from one side to another, chased by fire raining from above.

Flicking his tail once more, he cuts into woods behind us, water erupting behind him. The rounds snap off tree limbs, following him into the forest, finding their muted homes in the dirt below.

The pool of water begins pushing out from the center. Small waves get larger as they lap against my chest. I look up, finding the source. A red and black Helios glides down from above, blocking the sun. I start shaking as a tear escapes, rolling the rest of the way down my cheek. Reaching down, I do my best to keep Cass's head above the water. The Helios pushes the rest of the waves to the side, coming to hover above what's left of the pond. A young man fully clad in a winter uniform jumps out from the gunner's seat.

He can't be older than his mid-twenties, with blue eyes and brown hair. It's a little long for Air Corps standards, but gunners and auxiliary crew can usually get away with it.

"Excuse me sir! Excuse me! We've got you now. You're gonna to be ok!" he yells above the engines.

I fight to focus on his face. It's eerie; he's shorter, and his eyes are a different color, but it feels as though I'm staring at a younger version of myself.

He reaches out a gloved hand. "We won't be needing that any more, right?"

Confused, I look at the sagging barrel of the revolver still pointing in his direction. Slowly I shake my head, struggling to push myself up to press it into his hand. I can't move that far. Comprehension washes over his face, taking in the dark red bubbling around us.

"Doc!" he yells back into the cabin, "Doc, we need your help out here!"

"I'm a little busy right now!" a voice answers back.

It's familiar. Worry scores into the face of the young man.

"Doc, there's two of them. If we don't bump priorities, they won't make it!" he yells.

A face emerges from the cabin's shade. Chet's weathered features are immediately recognizable, but his trademark smile is nowhere to be found.

"My God . . . Sage is that you?"

Chet's face drops even more. "It's Sage!" he yells into the cockpit.

Chet jumps down from the struts as the side panel door

opens. A flight cap barely hides a thatch of brunette hair as Katz looks out. Closing my eyes, I begin losing consciousness, leaning back into the water. I hear a gasp from the cockpit. The cold has a good grip now. I let my guard down.

The young gunner reaches out, catching my shoulder before I submerge. "No, no, no. Wait a second."

His arm sweeps under my shoulder, pulling me up from the abyss. I keep my hold on Cass as Katz's feet splash through the water to us.

"Baz . . . " she says quietly, covering her mouth when she sees Cass.

Her worried eyes flash up to Chet.

I see her mouth. "Is she . . . "

I know the answer to that question, but I can't say it.

Cass is still clutched tightly to my chest as the gunner tries securing me.

"I'm not letting go," I say firmly.

The gunner leans down. "You don't have to," he assures me.

I fight to keep my throat from closing as I look up to him. "Please don't make me let go of her."

His concerned blue eyes meet mine. He reaches down to my hand, helping me wrap it around her even tighter. "I wouldn't do that," he says. "Keep her close, ok?"

Ripples spread out across the pond. Katz leans down, hooking her hand underneath my other arm. The ripples seem to go on forever, separating what's actually sky and what's an impostor. They span out from Cass and me as we're dragged to the ship. An explosion materializes out in the distance ahead of us. It seems so natural now.

"Hey! We need to get moving," another voice chimes in. "They're not the only wounded, and we're a big fuckin' bullseye down here!"

The voice originates from the cockpit. Frustrated with our sluggish progress, the pilot fidgets over the controls. Sasha would've never done that. She was tough on her crew, but she always treated the recovered like the people they were. That treatment was sometimes the only thing keeping them together.

"The patients are almost secured," Chet answers back as we reach the struts.

Squatting down, Chet looks me in the eye quietly. I stare back at him without saying a word.

"Sage, could I please see Miss Dawson?" he asks gently.

My throat tightens, my eyes welling up at her name. Staying silent, I nod as best I can.

Chet leans down, carefully taking Cass from my arms. Red droplets collect at Chet's elbow, dripping as he cradles her delicately. She looks so small in comparison to him.

As Chet climbs into the cabin with her, the gunner turns to me. "We're gonna have to get you up there with that leg. Are you ready?" he asks.

I nod. Both he and Katz support me from below as I climb in.

Pain immediately shoots through my body now that the water's no longer there to support my mangled leg. A grunt of pain escapes as I hit the floor. The smell of vomit and blood rise to greet me as sand flares out across the floor next to my nostril. Five other recovered litter the cabin. Three lie prone, and one is propped up against the cabin window. The last pilot sits in her chair, watching us with hollow eyes. Water drips from her stringy, auburn hair. She makes no attempt to move.

The gunner and Katz pick me up by the shoulder straps, easing me into the back next to Cassandra. Lying on the floor of the cabin, my body tries shutting down. I fight to clear my vision. I can't go yet.

Pressing a hand on my shoulder, Katz leans down. "You're safe with us now, Baz. You don't have to worry anymore," she whispers.

She stands up, moving back to the cockpit as Chet puts on his stethoscope and turns Cass over. I already know he won't find a heartbeat, but I don't have the strength to say it.

Katz's door slams and the gunner settles back into his seat as the engines rev from above. My vision becomes a tunnel as I turn my head to look at Cass. All I can see is the dark of her ear. A brunette shock of hair covers the top of it, but not enough to shut me out completely.

My neck muscles strain as I lean over. "I'm sorry," I whisper.

Then the blackness takes me.

26

White bleeds in. The sound of an unseen medical device compressing is the only clue that I haven't made it to the other side yet. I try blinking the whiteness away, but it's structural rather than physiological. A stark overhead light bathes the room in an uncomfortable glow. I let my chest rise and fall a few times, just to appreciate the fact that it still can.

"You know . . . We find ourselves in the medical bay far too often."

The gruff, familiar voice almost brings a smile to my lips. Turning my head, I see the red, grizzled face of Olan. He looks tired. Blood's still spattered across his uniform and the smell of his sweat permeates the room. The fight's over, otherwise he'd still be out there.

I close my eyes, focusing on my breathing. "I'm so glad you're alive," I manage. "You have no idea."

He raises his eyebrows, turning his head to window. "Me too."

Yeti, Ja'el, Diz, Baltier. Where are they?

Olan stops me as I open my mouth. "You and I have already seen enough hell today. There needn't be any reason to go adding to the list by talking about it," he says.

I suck in another breath instead. One of the perks of having a friend like Olan is always knowing where the other stands.

I don't want to talk about our dead friends. I don't want to think about the blood, the smell. There will be a time for that, but it's not right now.

I don't want to think about how I failed Cass.

"Where are we?" I ask.

Stick with the facts. Never speculate on what could have been.

Olan clears his throat. "We're on the frigate *Namazu*."

I rest my head back on the pillow.

"The Japanese made it," Olan continues, "and so did the Irani."

"The Persians?" I ask.

Olan huffs. "Whatever. The *Sorhab's* crew's so mixed you probably couldn't pick 'em out in a pub in Glasgow." He scratches at his beard. "The *Bastille's* still burning in the snow, the *Agincourt* was rammed in half at the start of the fight and . . ", he pauses, taking in a deep breath, "The *Artemis is* scattered over the drifts below us."

"So it did fall," I say without emotion.

It's just a new piece of information. That's all it needs to be at this moment. Out of the corner of my eye, a shaggy tuft of red bobs silently.

"We don't need to talk about that right now," he states again.

The deep dark of the night sky mirrors the mood in the room. I've been unconscious for several hours.

"I do, however," Olan mentions, "have to talk with you about this."

I raise my head as he leans over holding a blinking object. A small dark shape lies in Olan's palm. The keepsake the Admiral gave me before the assault! My hand gropes over my breast pocket, only to find the device missing.

Olan waggles the blinking rectangle. "I had to convince the nurses that you hadn't armed yourself with some sort of booby-trapped grenade,", he says, his exhausted eyes meeting mine. "Took a big risk believing that wasn't the situation so they could operate on you."

The tightness curls in my left leg. A cast cements it in place as the residual pain throbs from within. The incisions are fresh.

"So . . . ", Olan leans in looking around the facility before asking, "What is it?"

The green overlay pings once more against the black casing.

It all comes together.

"That's exactly what it is," I whisper.

It wasn't pulsing green before I fell unconscious, which

means it wasn't pulsing before the *Artemis* hit ground.

Olan creases his eyebrows. "Well, what is it?"

Something akin to adrenaline fills me, struggling to roll back the pain.

"Help me up," I say, trying to push myself from the bed.

"Where are you going? It's three in the morning," Olan asks.

Paying him no mind, I continue trying to right myself. "It doesn't matter. We need to find it right away . . . Before someone else does," I say to the pillow.

Olan leans back in. "Find what?" he growls.

I dodge the question, asking one of my own. It doesn't feel good, but the Admiral entrusted this task to me alone. "Can you pull together a crew large enough to man a Helios? We need to go now," I urge.

Olan fixes me with a glare.

"Is he awake?" a voice from outside asks.

Before Olan can answer, a bloodied Yeti leans through the door.

"Oh my God! He's awake. Now we just need Sleeping Beauty to do the same down the hall," Yeti says, hugging me too hard.

I cry out in pain, but two words force me to ask a question instead of preserve my recovery. "Sleeping Beauty?" I ask, tinged with hope.

Yeti sighs. "Ah . . . I'm sorry man. Listen to my dumb mouth going off like that. Stenia! Stenia made it out thanks to this guy," he says, gesturing to Olan.

Olan nods slowly. "We wouldn't have made it out if you hadn't pulled me back to earth . . . again. Thank you for giving us that chance Sage."

"She's still unconscious, but the docs say she's out of critical condition for now,", Yeti says. He kneels to my side, taking my hand. "Sage, I'm so sorry about Cass. She was an amazing woman."

Olan clears his throat. "And we don't have to discuss her passing right now. I would tell the lad to heal mind and body first, but it just so happens that Baz won't rest until he finds himself a pilot."

Yeti's eyes turn between us. "Yeah? Where we going?" he asks.

I finally succeed in sitting upright. "Can you two trust me on this?" I ask.

Olan's blue, angry eyes study mine. "You do realize, that if you leave that bed, God's liable to take you up to his kingdom just from the exertion alone?"

I light my own fire from within.

"If I can do this one last thing . . . I'll let him."

The wind rifles through my hair as I watch the sun rise from the open door. After a few hours, we were able to assemble a skeleton crew to sneak out a Helios for an unapproved mission. Looking into the cockpit, I see the red reflection of Diz's hair from the co-pilot's seat. We found her while searching for folks who, instead of sleeping, were willing to entertain the wishes of a red-headed giant, an animated Mexican, and a cripple.

The market was very sparse.

With Diz's help and with the proper persuasion, we were eventually able to recruit friends of friends to join us. Extra rations of cigarettes were our currency of choice. Another reason I don't smoke: extra bargaining power. Luckily for us, Helios crews are still running search missions to retrieve stricken crew from the area.

We can't stay much longer. With this many Zeppelin wrecks, and whatever treasures the hulking carcass of the *Ark* holds, bandits and pirates will be coming to take their share soon. We can't be here when that happens.

The green blip draws my eyes back down to the device in my hand. The pulse moves further and stronger down the sides of the slate now. It's working just the way I thought it would. We're moving in the right direction. A shiver runs down my spine and through my hands. I can't tell if it's from the cold or the anticipation. As always, probably both.

The crest of the sun bleeds a beautiful red.

Smoke billows up from below, countering the winter wind with fumes and flames still burning from the wreckage. The once proud *Artemis* is now a forgotten jigsaw puzzle, spread across the face of the white world underneath us. We're not interested in most of these pieces. We need the Bridge, hopefully intact. It would certainly make our job much easier. If I'm right, it will be hidden somewhere there. The image of the shell hitting the Admiral's Quarters flashes to mind.

Maybe we'll find Sanjar too...

As we crest a hill, a sea of shattered glass rises to meet us. The two halves of the Bridge remain intact, but the glass plating of the cockpit must have ruptured when the *Artemis* hit ground. I shudder, thinking of the doomed crew still trapped inside on impact.

I tug my comm to the side of my mouth. "Set it down here, please."

"You got it," Yeti yawns back, wiping sleep from his eyes.

Olan clutches his rifle to his chest, lurching as the Helios begins its descent. He never liked traveling in small ships.

When our feet touch the ground, it's a surreal sight. Pylons of oblong plate glass litter the field, dotted with the dark uniforms of flung bodies. Yeti stays with the ship, along with two other guards. As I hobble along with one hand on the crutch supporting me, and the other on the flashing device, the rest of my crew takes the time to retrieve dog tags from the prone forms.

There's a job to do. Formalities can come later. The pinging from my slate becomes more rapid, increasing in strength as we approach the bottom half of the forward Bridge.

"We're almost there!" I shout, careful not to alert anyone other than my handpicked group.

Arriving at the side of the dented hull, I zero in on the source. Abandoning my crutch, I drag my leg over to the side of the ship. Following the lights, I push aside the glass and snow, kneeling down to a nearly buried section. A perfect green circle blossoms out from the center of the tablet.

The hackles on my neck raise. "It's here!" I wave.

Diz steps over the tinkling wreckage to where I kneel. Donning her welding gear, she lights her torch.

"Are you sure?, she asks, doubtful of the position.

"It's right here," I say, pointing into the hull and crossing my fingers in the shape of an 'x'. "Can you get it?" I ask.

Diz gives me a rare smile. "You bet your sweet arse."

Flipping down her mask, she begins cutting through the hull. A shower of sparks rains out from her torch as it sears against the metal, motivating the rest of our small crew to give her space. Only Olan perches nearby, keeping a close eye on our surroundings as Diz makes her incisions. The extra illumination will make us vulnerable to any surviving remnants.

Time passes. The rest of the recruited crew takes to searching the bodies deposited in the landscape around us. I'd warn them not to wander too far, but I'm too fixated on Diz's progress to care.

Finally, the torch makes it all the way through. With a gentle push, a sizable chunk of the hull falls to the ground, immediately melting the snow around it. I hold my breath against the fumes as I reach into the hole. My fingers search around the blackness, but find nothing. My pulse spikes. It has to be here. There's no other way. I stand on my toes, careful not to touch the glowing edges of the freshly cut steel framing my arm.

I graze a heavy object.

Exhaling, I get as strong a hold as I can on the case, dragging it from the inside the Bridge's hull.

The black case crashes to the ground, sending up a shower of glass laden snow.

Diz's wide eyes dart over the case. "That's the *Artemis's* black box . . . Isn't it?" she asks.

Nodding slowly, I move my hands along its side. "It's the whole story of everybody who lived and died on it. So people can know what happened here," I say.

Olan keeps his eyes on the horizon. "Do you really think we did it?" he says, blowing out a thick cloud of breath. "Saved the world?" he clarifies, turning in our direction. "I mean, we took down the *Ark* and all. But every one of us saw that beam shoot from its top." Olan eyes me. "Baz, you were in the middle of it for fuck sake. You of all people know it wasn't firing for a short ticker."

The dull thud of a bullet burrowing into Raltz echos in my ear. I shake my head, trying rid myself of it. "I know. It's what I chose to believe."

Diz sits down on the newly shorn chunk of metal. "Well, I suppose there's only one way to find out," she says. "Worse comes to worse, if there is another Drowning . . . at least we'll be ready for it, right?"

I run my hand along the edge of the crate. My pulse pounds as I find what I've been looking for. The recess of a small, concealed keyhole presses up against the point of my finger.

"Only time will tell," I say, popping the Admiral's key from his tablet. "That's about all we can do." I insert the key into the hole, listening to it click as I turn it. Taking a deep breath, I use both hands on either side of the lid to open it.

The lid gives way.

What greets my eyes leaves me dumbfounded.

The actual size of the black box isn't even close to the dimensions of the dark crate protecting it. The rest of the space is taken up by band after band of hundred dollar bills. There are so many, so tightly packed. I can't even comprehend the amount of currency set out in front of me.

The Admiral hid his wealth here. He knew this fight would be his last, so he prepared accordingly. But his wealth isn't the only thing he placed alongside the black box. Laying on top of the sea of bills is one single picture.

I pick it up, taking in its sepia coloring. Two men stand next to one another, an arm across each shoulder, smiling at the lens. The Admiral's grinning face looks up at me, thirty years younger, full of possibility. The man next to him startles me. My father, in his old flight suit, grins back as well.

They were friends from the beginning. When the *Artemis* was just a concept. When the Admiral was just starting out, and my father had just begun flying. Holding my breath, I turn the picture over. Two words are scrawled against a fingerprinted white.

Start again.

Exhaling, I let myself rock back onto the ground. I look up at Diz. She's not paying attention. Instead, she's looking at the sunrise with Olan in foreground. Olan continues scanning the outlying woods. Neither of them realize what I've discovered. My hand drops back into the case with the picture still clutched inside.

"Well Baz, seeing as how we found it . . . what do we do now?" Olan asks without looking back.

I glance back down at the picture before taking in the horizon; all of it. With the money here, it should be enough. It should be just enough. There's a lot of work to be done, but the horizon beckons more than it ever has before.

"We start again."

ABOUT THE AUTHOR

Born in San Diego and raised near Boston, Greg Stravinski now lives in Madison, WI where he works for a hospital system. When not writing, he likes to try out for the local plays, attempt standup comedy, and camp and cook with his girlfriend.

Author's Note:

Word-of-mouth is crucial for any author to help tell his or her story. If you enjoyed this book, please consider leaving a review on Amazon. Even if it's just a sentence or two. It would make all the difference in the world, and be very much appreciated:

amazon.com/Eyes-Turned-Skyward-Gregory-Stravinski-ebook/dp/B01DON5V6W

Either way, thank you very much for reading!

-Greg Stravinski

Printed in Poland
by Amazon Fulfillment
Poland Sp. z o.o., Wrocław

56173165R00181